ANGIE SLOWED HER BREATH AS MUCH AS SHE WAS ABLE, LISTENED TO THE MAN BARGAINING WITH THE DEMON.

She picked up a few more details, enough to know the man was close to making his deal. They were haggling, setting terms. But something felt off. Something she couldn't put her finger on.

Something in the way the demon was bargaining.

Hard to tell for sure with her ears stuffed with tissue. Maybe she just wasn't hearing the conversation well.

Sebastian leaned back and against her ear said, "I'm going in. Stay here until I've gotten between the man and the demon. Can you take care of the man?"

She nodded.

He brushed his lips against her cheek, a gentle kiss that left her startled and breathless.

Then he was gone, sliding out from behind the SUV, walking straight toward the demon.

Bone Lantern Witch

Spiderweb Witch

Storm Shadow
Witch

Darkling Mist
Witch

Apocalypse Witch

SPIDERWEB WITCH

A DEMON WITCH NOVEL

KAT SIMONS

SPIDERWEB WITCH
Copyright © 2022 by Katrina Tipton
All rights reserved.

Published 2022 by T&D Publishing
Cover design: © 2025 T&D Publishing
Interior book design © 2025 T&D Publishing
ISBN-13: 978-1-944600-54-9 (Trade Paperback Edition)
ISBN-13: 978-1-944600-55-6 (Large Print Edition)
ISBN-13: 978-1-967786-04-6 (Hardback Edition)

This book is licensed for your personal enjoyment only. All rights reserved. No part of this book may be reproduced, scanned, or distributed in any print or electronic form without written permission from the author, excepting brief quotes used in the context of a review.

This is a work of fiction. All of the characters, places, organizations, and events portrayed are either products of the author's imagination or are used fictitiously. Any resemblance to actual persons, living or dead, business establishments, events, or locales is entirely coincidental.

First printing T&D Publishing edition: September 2022
Second printing: December 2025
For information, contact T&D Publishing: https://tanddpublishing.com

Spiderweb Witch

For my husband, who has my back.
And my sons, who keep me on my toes.

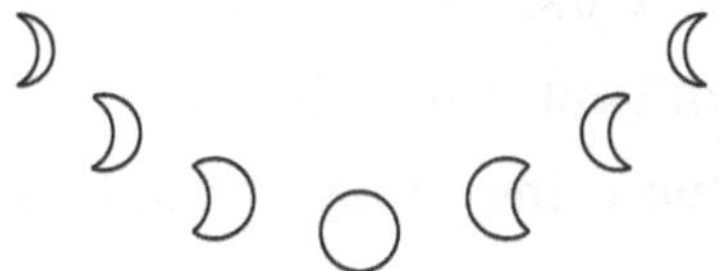

angela Jordan stared up at the stars racing by overhead, smiling faintly at the pinpoints of light and the tapestry of swirling, colorized gases. The only problem with living in New York City was that she had to come here to the planetarium to see the stars. Or drive out into the country. But she'd sold her car two years ago, after finding her current apartment and realizing parking would be impossible. She lived near enough to work, and New York public transport made having a car mostly unnecessary.

But she did miss seeing the stars in person.

The planetarium show raced from the Big Bang through the large structural pattern of the universe, whizzing past galaxies in a dizzying fashion that made her happy. The vastness of the universe was good for settling her soul, reminding her of her own insignificance.

"Thought I'd find you here," a voice murmured near her ear.

She sighed, but didn't look away from the show overhead. She did hunch farther into her cushioned seat, though, trying to avoid the inevitable.

But of course, she couldn't.

"Whenever you were worried about something, I'd catch you watching the stars," Sebastian said, sounding nostalgic, his English accent faint in his whisper.

She'd given up being annoyed that he knew her so well. After two years of loving him, and two years of trying not to love him, this was just where they were at, like it or not. He knew her. She knew him.

And that didn't solve any of their problems.

"I told you I needed time to think."

"It's been almost three weeks," Sebastian said. "And they're expecting you."

"I've said on multiple occasions that I don't give a fuck what they're expecting." She whispered, so as not to disturb the others in the show, but she'd picked a seat near the back of the circular room, up against a wall, with very few people sitting near her. The center was a better seat, getting the full effect of the universe overhead and around you as the show played out on the domed ceiling. But she liked to experience it on her own without the ohs and ahs of people sitting right next to her.

Sebastian leaned closer. "We've talked about this."

In the darkness, with her gaze focused resolutely on the ceiling, she was unfortunately, uncomfortably, aware of his heat so near, and that deliciously clean soap smell of his. She was half convinced he used whatever soap he used on purpose because he knew it did things to her, muddied her thinking when it came to him.

She still refused to look at him when she said, "And I haven't decided if your plan is a disaster waiting to happen or not."

"It's the only way, Ang," he whispered. "They won't leave you alone. And they're dangerous."

She snarled. So much for the show calming her mood. So much for perspective and feeling insignificant. She might be insignificant to the universe, but apparently, to the demon hunters' council or whatever the hell they were, she was important enough to *lock up* if she didn't agree to become a demon hunter.

Lock up! As if they had the right. She had been in a low level state of rage over that since Sebastian had told her. And the only reason she hadn't cursed the lot of them, forgoing her own edict about not using curses, was because she understood consequences and wasn't prepared to pay the consequences of that curse.

It was a close thing, though.

She was a witch. A *witch*. Not a demon hunter. She didn't belong in their world, despite attempting to be there so she could be with Sebastian. She'd given them two years of her life, working with Sebastian. And it had almost killed her. More than once. Getting dragged into a demon realm and almost trapped there had been her last straw. The one that had finally driven her to try and escape the demon hunters' world, even if that meant giving up Sebastian.

Things hadn't exactly gone as planned the first six months… But eventually, Sebastian had been true to his word and left her alone, and she'd had a year and a half of peace. No demons. No demon realm breaches. No demon hunters.

A year and a half to learn she'd been absolutely right to leave the demon fights behind. She was a witch. It was her calling. Magic was her realm. Where she belonged. Where she intended to stay.

If she could just get the hunters to leave her alone.

She wanted to rage against it all, but taking out her anger on Sebastian wasn't fair. He had tried to give her space. Tried to let her go. This council of his, whatever they were—whoever they thought they were—hadn't let him. She couldn't entirely blame him for being in this mess.

Being completely honest, she couldn't blame him at all. The skill, the curse, the rare talent she had to thin the barrier between demon realms and this one, was something she'd had her whole life. Not something any of them could help. Not his fault she had this ability.

Still, a petty part of herself she wasn't proud of wanted to blame him, to take out her anger on him, on someone she knew could take it. Because the anger was going to consume her. And that was a dangerous, dangerous thing.

"You're screwing up my attempt to keep my curses to bad language," she muttered.

"I know. And I'm sorry." He hovered his hand over hers

where it rested on the chair's plastic armrest, not quite touching her.

She sighed again, turned her hand up, and let him settle his palm against hers, twinning her fingers with his. She took a beat before the contact to make sure her control over one of her other skills was firmly in place—she was a touch psychic, an ability she'd been mastering control over since she was a child, because otherwise living in this world would have driven her insane a long time ago. She rarely got flashes of past and current events, sometimes future events, on accident when she touched things or people now. She mostly only got those images and flashes when she opened herself to them for her work.

But with Sebastian, when she was feeling this much emotional upheaval, she needed to be a little more careful. She didn't need to accidentally read him, to learn things he maybe wasn't ready for her to know, and have that added to their already complicated situation.

His large hand wrapped around hers warmly, reminding her of different times, different planetarium shows, when being in the dark with him under the stars had been all she wanted from life.

They sat in silence for the rest of the show, holding hands, staring up at as the panorama of universal awe played out overhead. And eventually, Angie found that moment of peace in her own insignificance again. The joy in knowing she was just a little speck in something so unfathomably huge.

As the show ended and the light slowly came back up, the

presenter gave a few parting words while people shuffled around, letting their eyes readjust to the dimmer light before facing the ordinary bright lights outside the domed room. She kept her gaze up for a few more minutes, staring at the blue ceiling, not really seeing it as she clenched Sebastian's hand. She didn't want to let go. Didn't want to move from this spot and have to face the decision she had to make.

A decision she'd been avoiding for weeks.

She'd been stalling. Stalling with the excuse that she was thinking. But she'd already made her decision. Made it the minute Sebastian suggested a solution.

She just wasn't happy about the choice she was about to make.

As everyone got to their feet and the door leading out of the planetarium opened, she finally let go of Sebastian's hand to stand. She dropped the strap of her oversized bag over her head so it crossed her chest, and carried her jacket out over her arm.

The autumn chill had grown over the last few days, giving more hints of winter to come. She loved winter in New York. A lot of her colleagues at Dana's Cauldron—the eclectic pagan store in the Village where she did psychic readings—who'd lived in the city longer than she had hated winters here. But she liked the changing seasons, and the snow when it happened. Even if the pretty white part of the snow only lasted a day or so and the piles of gross dirty slush seemed to last for weeks. She still liked the snow. She liked the cold.

Probably because it didn't remind her of most demon realms.

Sebastian put his hand against her lower back as they moved along the curved row of seats toward the aisle that led out of the planetarium. She tried not to react, but she still let out a soft sound. Something about his hand on her back like this, when he was guiding her around some obstacle or through a door, reminded her so sharply of their early time together it left her a little breathless.

He hadn't done this often since he'd come back into her life…what, a little over three weeks ago? Less than a month anyway. Had it really only been that long? Having him around felt so shockingly normal. Like he'd been there the whole time over these last two years.

And yet, a part of her, still thought of his presence as an intrusion.

But when his hand was on her back this way, and they were close enough she could feel his warmth seeping through her skin, the time they'd been apart shrunk to nothing and she was six years younger and they were meeting for the first time. Those early moments when she was just starting to fall…

When she still thought they could be together without life forcing so many consequences on them.

When she thought she could still be with him without having to become a full part of the demon hunter world.

A dream she'd finally, after all this time, let go.

CHAPTER TWO

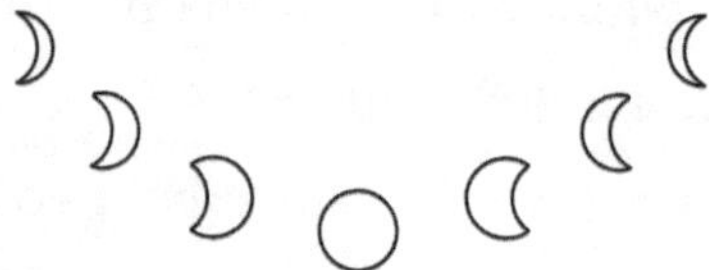

They stepped outside the planetarium's dim light into the bright sunshine pouring in through the massive, three story windows forming two full walls of the Rose Center at the American Museum of Natural History. The exit took them on a spiraling walk around the Center's central sphere—a sphere that was the planetarium but also represented various things for size comparisons made throughout the displays. Here the sphere represented the known universe compared to our local group of galaxies, there the supercluster compared to the size of the Milky Way. There the sun compared to the planets. Near the far end a cell compared to a virus and proton compared to an electron.

The entire central part of the upper floors for the Center were designed to awe visitors with size comparisons, and it worked every time for Angie.

But she took less notice this time. She usually loved

following the timeline along the spiral ramp leading from the planetarium show down to the exit on the second floor, too. Today, she barely looked at it.

She did take some comfort in having Sebastian's hand on her back as they walked with the crowds down the ramp, and when they reached the end of the ramp, they broke off from the others to exit for the main part of the museum.

"Tea?" she asked him.

He pulled a small, rectangular packet from his jacket pocket. "Yes."

She grinned despite her bad mood. He was a tea snob and really didn't like what passed for tea at most places in the US. She'd told him for ages to carry his own with him. After all these years, the fact that he'd finally remembered to do so amazed her.

"Good," she said. "Now I won't have to listen to you gripe."

His chuckled tickled her spine, and she found herself leaning back into his touch a little more.

They exited the Rose Center into the main part of the museum, then took the wide marble stairs down to the Food Court. As it was well past two in the afternoon on a weekday, when kids were in school, the Food Court was half empty, giving them plenty of tables to choose from. She bought herself a cup of tea—she didn't mind the ordinary bags the Museum carried—and an oversized chocolate chip cookie. Because she was going to need a cookie for this conversation.

They chose a table near the front of the Food Court but far in the corner so there was no one close to them. If he needed to, Sebastian could will their conversation to be private. A demon hunter's will was an awesome thing to behold, the thing that made them hunters and, if stronger than a demon's will, the thing that kept them alive.

But it was easier if they managed a private conversation without him having to exert will to keep it that way.

Not that any of the few scattered people at the round tables throughout this section of the dining area even gave them a second look. She half wondered if Sebastian was showing the world a harmless image. He could do that too, make himself look ordinary, unremarkable, easy not to notice. That was a very useful skill all hunters developed.

The first hunter she'd met, Sebastian's mentor, was probably the most ordinary looking human Angie had ever seen. Nothing about Aidan stood out in a crowd, and if you didn't look too closely into her eyes, and spot that flash of red in the depths of the brown, you'd never guess Aidan was anything but an ordinary woman. Even then, most people wrote that hint of red off to a trick of the light.

That red was a side-effect of being a hunter, of dealing with the demon world and demons for so many years. The hunters absorbed a tiny bit of the essence of demons over their many years in the fight. A sign of a connection to the demon world that could be hard to hide. If someone knew what to look for. Fortunately, most humans missed that hint of the otherworldly. And hunters moved through the world unnoticed.

Angie had never really been sure if Aidan projected that air of ordinariness or not. The older hunter inhabited the look so well, it was impossible to tell if that was just how she looked or if she manipulated those around her to see someone harmless. Sebastian was another story all together. He was anything but ordinary.

Just a little taller than her six foot height, wide shoulders, trim, sexy build, and a face to make angel's weep. He'd gone from clean shaven to a goatee in the two years since they'd been together, which she found sexier than she'd have thought. Maybe just on him. His dark brown skin showed no signs of his age. He could have been mid-twenties or mid-fifties—he was actually forty-three. He kept his dark hair cut short and tight to his head. And his dark brown eyes were so captivating she couldn't meet his gaze for long without getting lost.

That had been the way from the beginning. Looking into his eyes had always sucked her in, made her lose track of time and place. Make her want things that were… complicated.

The flash of red was there too. He'd been a hunter for long enough the signs were unmistakable if she paid attention. But sometimes… Well, often, she missed that reminder that she shouldn't be with him, that she wasn't supposed to be a part of his world. Too often, she forgot what he was and just saw the man she'd loved for years.

But she couldn't be in his world. She was a witch. Not a demon hunter.

Which was the crux of not only their personal problems. It was the thorny and irritating issue they had to deal with now thanks to his fucking demon hunter council.

Something she'd only learned existed recently. That the hunters had any sort of governing body, for a group that mostly acted independently and on their own instincts, struck her as absurd. But maybe she should have realized. Even the exceedingly independent world of witches had elders in most disciplines. Sometimes covens organized. All to help set…if not rules, then standards of practice that kept everyone safe.

Not that witches always paid attention to their elders or covens or standard setters. Like cats, most witches preferred their own council.

She was no exception. She'd assumed the hunters had a similar sort of autonomy and independence. It had always seemed that way to her. Apparently, she'd been wrong.

"They're…pushing to have you brought in," Sebastian said. "They won't wait on your…" He folded his lips in and she knew he didn't want to use the words that had actually been used by any of the council members. "They're growing impatient," he finished.

"Tough. I'm not theirs to summon." She raised a hand when he opened his mouth. "I realize they don't like that either. But that doesn't change things. They want me to join them, they will wait on my decision. And if they think they can…" She swallowed hard but her voice still came out a guttural snarl when she said, "If they think they can lock me up, they are sorely mistaken." She might not have a hunter's will, but her command of magic was no small thing.

"They've been warned." His mouth twitched but she couldn't tell if that was from amusement or some other emotion.

At one time, she'd been able to read him so easily.

She wrapped her hands around her paper tea cup and sighed. "I don't want to bring the council down," she said quietly. "I don't actually care about them at all. Hunters do good in the world. If the council helps that happen, I'm fine with them. I just need them to leave me alone. I'm not going to loose an apocalypse of demons onto the earth."

At least not anymore. She was, mostly, very careful about that unique skill. And until Sebastian had come back into her life last month, she'd managed to avoid breaching the realms accidentally for a very long time. Yes, she was a little out of practice because she hadn't had to be *in* practice much over the last year and a half. But that only emphasized her point. If she wasn't around demon hunters, she avoided all things to do with demons, and that included being around the wrong kinds of trees and risking disaster.

Her conscious felt the need to remind her she'd recently gotten caught twice on accident. And a demon had nearly forced her to open a realm breach when it took over her body.

But the only reason she'd been in a position for a demon to take over her body was because the demon hunters had insisted on pulling her back into their work. They were perpetuating their own problem this way, not ending it.

And making this her problem too, which was enraging.

She tightened her grip on the cup but it wasn't very hot anymore so the soothing effects of the heat weren't enough to calm her spikes of anger. She took a sip and grimaced a little.

Sebastian raised a brow and her expression, then took a long, slow sip of his own tea and let out a long sigh.

She rolled her eyes, and tried hard not to laugh. Smug bastard.

"It's getting cool," she said defensively. But she did envy him his better tasting tea just then. She picked at her cookie and didn't meet his gaze when she said, "Much as I hate all this, in my bones, and much as I don't want to bring down this council of yours… I—reluctantly—acknowledge that I need to at least humor them until I can prove they're misguided in their attempts to make me a hunter." She felt the faint crackling of her magic just under her skin, and she did meet Sebastian's gaze then. "And that they are very very mistaken in thinking they can lock me up."

He nodded, not flinching away from her gaze. "If you can succeed where Aidan and I haven't, I'll be impressed."

"Prepared to be impressed, then," she said.

Which made him smile. And that made her melt a little.

She shoved some of the too-sweet cookie into her mouth and dropped her gaze to the table again.

"What next?" she said after a moment.

"We still need to go to that meeting. The one they expected you to show up for weeks ago."

She rolled her eyes.

"And that attitude will irritate the hell out of them, so definitely do more eye-rolling while we're there."

She didn't choke on her cookie, but it was a close thing.

"I'd come prepared with some shielding spells. They'll test you. They'll test your will."

"My will is more than sufficient for magic. It is not a

demon hunter's will. If I prove that, will they leave me alone?"

She wasn't sure *how* she'd prove that. Short of letting them exert their will on her and having to give in to that will —which grated against every nerve and instinct in her body —she wasn't sure how to prove that her will wasn't enough to carry her through demon fights. Her *magic* was useful in those fights. Her skills as a witch. But…

But she was terrified of demons. That affected her in the fights. That influenced her will. Weakened it. If she had only her will to rely on, she'd die in a demon fight. She knew it.

Fortunately for her, she had her magic, and her instincts as a *witch* that had kept her alive to this point. Even then, her panic had nearly gotten the best of her a few times.

Like when she'd been trapped in a demon world. When Sebastian had had to reach in and pull her out, using his will to hold open a portal between realms that he couldn't even see.

And even more recently, when a demon had invaded her body, taken her over, almost used her ability to open portals between the realms to release a hoard onto this world. Sebastian had had to use his own will to prop her up then, too. To give her something to hold on to and bring her back to herself so she could force the demon out.

Without *his* will to help her, she'd have been dead. Or worse.

She was well aware of her inability to do the job the council wanted her to do. The fact that they still wanted her to do the job without the proper skills, wanted to put her in a position to get killed…

She stopped short and straightened in her seat. Cookie forgotten.

"They want me to die," she murmured.

Sebastian's gaze narrowed.

She stared at him hard. "They know I don't have the will to be a real hunter. Your council wants me to fail."

Failure as a hunter didn't mean having to quit because you couldn't do the job. Hunters, for the most part, didn't retire. Or quit. Or walk away from the job. When a hunter couldn't cut it…

They died.

"They want me to fail. They want me dead."

CHAPTER THREE

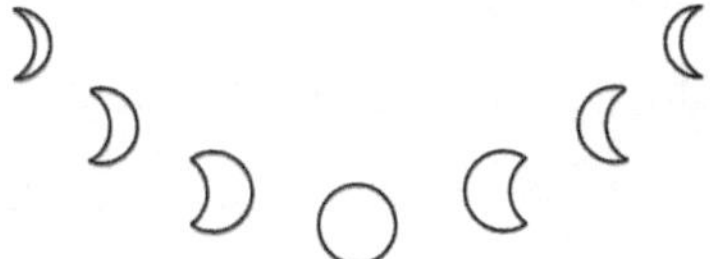

$\mathcal{A}$ngie's heartbeat thumped loudly, painfully against her ribs, and her breath came out in shallow flutters. She was going to hyperventilate if she wasn't careful. But her epiphany left her dizzy, spinning with a kind of panic that was strangely out of place in the quiet museum Food Court.

Why hadn't she realized this sooner? Why hadn't she seen this before?

"They don't want me to really be a demon hunter. They want me to be a *failed* demon hunter."

According to Sebastian, the council wanted her "brought into the fold" because she was too dangerous to be outside their purview. She could open passages between this realm and demon realms. An extraordinarily dangerous skill, and something counter to everything the hunters fought for—to keep the bloody demons out of this realm.

She was all for them succeeding in that, too. She didn't *want* to loose demons on this realm on accident. She'd spent her entire life working to avoid that.

If she'd been a different kind of person, with a different kind of calling, maybe things would be different. But from the hunters' perspective, she was a disaster waiting to happen.

And always would be.

Hell, she couldn't even really blame them for wanting to have some measure of reassurance that she wouldn't turn rogue and create a demon apocalypse. From their perspective, given the objectives of their entire lives, she was a threat.

But to plot for her death…

Not just lock her up. Get her killed.

She carefully, with a great deal of controlled concentration, wiped the cookie crumbs off her fingers with a paper napkin. Her hands shook slightly. She flexed her fists a few times to stave off the panic.

If the demon hunters wanted her dead, she wasn't sure what to do to stop them. She needed a better plan than their current one. At least, she needed more of a plan. Because she wasn't going to stand by and let them kill her any more than she intended on letting them lock her up.

Maybe Sebastian was right. Maybe they'd be forced to break the council itself. To bring the whole thing down.

But then what? Where did that leave the world and the demon hunters?

"This changes things," she said.

"Not really," he said, quietly.

She looked up sharply and met his gaze. He didn't flinch away. "You knew? You knew that's what they were ultimately hoping for?"

"I'm not sure they realize it's what they're hoping for," he said. "At least not all of them. I think a couple actually think you should be a demon hunter, that you belong as one of us. But there are one or two. Influential individuals. One in particular. They are…pragmatic to an extreme."

"They know I'd make a sucky hunter and are hoping I'll die on the job and take the problem of *me* out of the equation."

He shrugged. "Possibly. They don't consult me. Obviously."

"They sent you to spy on me."

He winced, but didn't deny the charge since it was true.

Early on, before she and Sebastian became…more, Sebastian had been charged with "keeping an eye on her" by this council. Watching her to ensure she didn't unleash an apocalypse. They might have even hoped she'd forgo magic in favor of becoming a hunter back then. The will to fight demons had never been an abundant trait in humans, and it was a rarer and rarer skill as the years progressed. There were only so many hunters in the world. Discovering new ones was not common these days, from what both Sebastian and Aidan had told her. Which meant the council wanting her to be a hunter made a lot of sense.

Back then. Before they knew for sure she didn't have the will for the job.

Now, they had to know she wasn't suited for it. Sebastian would have told them. They'd worked together for almost two years, her having his back in demon fights. In those years, it was abundantly clear that she wouldn't have been able to win those fights on her own. Certainly not without her own magic to help her. She had never been the hunter. Just the backup. And the one who could open a portal if needed, so Sebastian could force the demons back out of this realm.

Still expecting her to become a hunter meant they knew she wouldn't succeed.

If they couldn't control her, then they would arrange for her to be killed. No technical blood on their hands. Just her failure. Problem solved.

"This is different," Sebastian said. "Now is different."

"Yeah it is. Now is them trying to kill me, not recruit me."

He let out a sigh. "Which is why I think the only way to protect you is to destroy them first."

"And then what? Where does the leave the rest of the hunters?"

"The demon hunters will continue to hunt," Sebastian said, his voice low. "It's what we do. Who we are. Even without the council. They aren't a historically necessary body."

"They aren't?"

"They've existed for…five hundred years maybe. Maybe a little longer. But there have been demon hunters among humans since the beginning of the human species."

She hadn't known any of that. Finding out just how much

she *didn't* know about his world, despite having thought she knew a lot, was…disorienting.

"Five hundred years is a long time," she said. "Long enough for most hunters to be used to having an overarching council. It will disrupt their work. Throw them off their game. And that risks letting demons in."

"Or it will free them to just do their work," he said. But he shrugged, as if this wasn't an important question, or a significant point. "The council helps with…logistics. Hiding some of the more dangerous demon relics we find, ensuring our historical records are kept, providing safe havens for hunters if and when we need them, medical support if that's necessary. It's only recently that the council has started… overstepping themselves. Acting like a governing body and not a group just for support. And I'm not the only hunter chaffing at that change."

"How recent?"

"The last twenty years. When a few new members joined the council."

"That hunter I met after the bone lantern…incident." Too soon to talk about that out loud.

"No. She's been on the council for years. But she doesn't object to the idea of them taking more of a governing role. She finds the hunters unregulated ways dangerous in the modern world."

"Dangerous?"

"Too many external factors to navigate—legal, governmental, technological. The internet with all its attendant issues hasn't help matters."

"She thinks the hunters should be regulated so they can hide from the mundane world better? I'm not entirely sure that makes sense."

But the issue of the mundane world finding out just how *not* mundane life really was was an issue for all of the preternatural community. Different groups handled it in different ways. Some ignored the problem and didn't care if mundane humans discovered the otherworldly elements among them. But most made attempts to keep the stranger things in life secret. There were enough issues with humans summoning demons as is. If the entire planet discovered the possibility, there wouldn't be enough hunters to stop the demons from getting free.

Especially since hunters were becoming rarer. Fewer humans with the will for the job were showing up, and the fewer hunters there were, the more chance of a disaster.

But none of that was her problem, because she was a witch. Her community had its own issues.

She understood Sebastian's chaffing against a ruling body, though. She didn't even belong to a coven. She was a solitary witch. With teachers and mentors and other witches in her life, yes. But she regulated herself. And abided by the "harm no other" edict as much as possible. It was an impossible edict to follow perfectly. But she tried. Especially with her magic.

"Sense or not, the council has been slowly...overstepping the original intentions for their group, and it's complicating things. Stopping them isn't just a matter of stopping their threat to you." His fingers flexed around his paper tea cup. "But it is the only reason I'm involved."

She wanted desperately to reach out and take his hand in hers. She kept her hands clenched around her own tea cup instead. It was nearly cold now, and starting to taste bitter. Or maybe that was just her mood.

She let out a breath, and was about to ask more questions, but Sebastian sat up straighter in his seat and frowned.

"What's wrong?" She searched the half empty Food Court for a problem, part of her expecting to see the hunter from the council walk in to complicate their already complicated conversation. But she couldn't see what had caught Sebastian's attention. She looked back at him in time to see the red deep inside his brown eyes flare just a little. Easily excused as a trick of the overhead florescent lights if she didn't know better.

He stood, taking his mostly empty cup with him and she scrambled to follow, snatching up the remains of her cookie —which had really been too sugary—her cold tea, and her jacket and purse. She dumped the cookie and tea into the trash, behind Sebastian's tossed cup, and followed him out of the Food Court into the museum's basement lobby. He was staring across the marble-floored space, to the stairs leading up to the subway platform that connected with the building.

She wanted to ask what was wrong again, but a little pain in her gut warned her she already knew. He only ever got that look, turned this focused, over one thing.

A demon was about to escape the hold of its summoner.

Sebastian was being called to the hunt.

CHAPTER FOUR

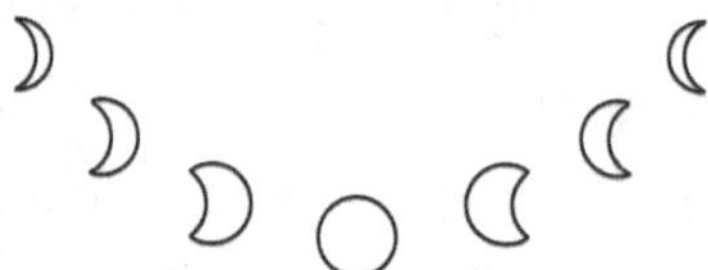

ngie very nearly let Sebastian go into this hunt on his own. She wasn't a hunter and had no business following him. That was the whole problem. The reason she'd left him to begin with. The reason she'd argued against his plan to even pretend to go along with the council's attempts to make her a hunter.

The problem was she couldn't just let him go fight a demon without going with him to have his back. He didn't technically need her to be there. He was an excellent hunter. The issue was all hers, and her inability to let him run into danger without trying to help.

That, her own stubborn refusal to stay out of the hunt when Sebastian was involved, was the reason she'd moved to New York and tried to end their relationship. She couldn't stay out of the demon world if the man she loved was a part of it, not while still being with him. She couldn't.

And the demon world was going to get her killed.

Didn't matter. She followed him out of the museum and up the marble stairs to the subway platform anyway, not asking questions. Waiting for him to explain when he could.

They were on the B train heading downtown before he leaned in close to her ear and murmured, "You should get off at Times Square and head home."

"No," she said just as quietly.

He let out a loud breath through his nose but didn't argue further. Not with so many people nearby. Keeping their conversation private now would be a waste of will he was going to need soon.

He did say, "I thought this wasn't what you wanted."

"It's not. Still going with you."

"They'll…assume you've decided to join them."

"I have."

He blinked and looked hard at her.

"We'll talk more later. After. Focus on this now."

He nodded and faced forward, but she caught his frown from the corner of her eye.

They got off the B train at Broadway-Lafayette Street station and came above ground in Soho. The area was a mix of boutiques and apartment buildings and of course the ubiquitous coffee shops. A few big chain stores as well, but the expensive kind. They were on Houston, one of the bigger roads through the area, so the traffic was loud and heavy as the evening gridlock geared up. The area smelled like the traffic too, all hot cars and gas and warm tarmac, but with just a hint of sweetness from the spiced nuts vendor right outside the subway entrance.

The cold air cooled Angie's cheeks after the too-warm underground ride, letting her release some of the tension that had built over the trip. The sun was low on the horizon now, but it was still bright enough to be called daytime.

Which made it an unusual time for Sebastian to get called to a demon fight. Especially so spontaneously without any buildup. Usually, demon hunters were called to a place for an impending fight with more time to spare.

But the way Sebastian moved down the street, so focused and intense people scrambled to get out of his way, assured her the fight was imminent.

Who the hell summoned a demon in the middle of the afternoon?

There were power times during the day, month, and year for magic work. And demon summoning was magic adjacent —the summoner didn't have to have magic or be a magic wielder in any way. In fact, most of them didn't have actual magic. But they used ceremonies that often drew on religious and magical context. And while the idea that midnight was a special time was maybe a little exaggerated, it was typically considered "the best time" to summon demons.

Nighttime wasn't actually required, though. A determined person could summon a demon at any time during the day. There was no real difference between midnight and noon. Just more people moving around who might notice. And more potential distractions from outside the ceremony. A distracted human trying to control a demon was an extremely dangerous situation. Demons took advantage of distraction. And the summoners could more easily end up dead.

She'd always assumed that was why the books coached potential demon summoners to perform their ceremonies at night. The less to distract the person from controlling the demon, the less likely they were to lose control. It was a pragmatic dictate rather than anything to do with the time having more power.

So if someone was summoning a demon at four thirty in the afternoon, they were either ignorant of the timing dictate, in a hurry to get whatever it was they wanted from the demon, or so confident of their control, they didn't care about distractions.

Every single one of those possibilities were extremely dangerous.

Not particularly reassuring.

"Definitely something happening immediately?" she asked, just to make sure she hadn't misread the situation.

"Yup," he said without looking at her. His focus was on the road ahead. He turned abruptly down a side street, this one narrower and with less traffic, the street itself still retaining its cobblestone charm from a bygone era. That charm was significantly offset by the giant blue construction dumpster taking up most of one side of the sidewalk, and the scaffolding encompassing the building above the dumpster.

Sebastian kept them on the side of the street opposite the construction, stopping finally in front of a red brick building next to a graffiti covered garage door. The heavy metal door covering the garage lifted at that exact moment and an SUV that looked too big to drive around the city rolled slowly out. Without a word, Sebastian ducked inside the garage. Angie hurried behind him, holding her big bag at her hip so it didn't bounce around as they jogged forward.

"Good timing," she murmured as the door closed behind them.

He didn't comment.

So, maybe not *just* good timing.

The garage was dim, the motion sensor lights flickering a little and then going off as she and Sebastian stood to one side of the rolling metal door, taking in their surroundings. Cars stacked two deep on either side of the central aisle meant there was probably a garage attendant around here somewhere, someone to rearrange the cars to get the ones blocked in the back row out when their owners needed them.

"That attendant?" she whispered.

Sebastian looked around but still didn't say anything.

She fell silent again, but she strained to hear any sounds. All she heard was a little clink clink clink of a cooling engine and a noisy fan to one side circulating the air. Someone had just dropped off a car before they'd arrived, if that cooling engine was any indication, and since someone had just left, there had to be someone in here who'd been moving the cars.

A faint scraping sound caught both hers and Sebastian's attention at the same time. They turned toward the noise and edged silently forward.

Angie started murmuring a spell under her breath, keeping her words almost silent and her hands low as she made the necessary finger gestures that accompanied the spell.

She couldn't hold a lot of half-set spells at once. She'd practiced in the years she'd worked with Sebastian and in the time since coming to New York, but she'd never been able to hold more than two at once in that state of almost ready but not finalized.

The problem with magic, at least her kind of witchcraft, was that it took time to recite a spell and set it. The time required for a few spells could be quite short, only taking her maybe thirty seconds, but others could take a full minute or more. Complicated spells took even longer.

In a fight with a demon, a minute, even thirty seconds, was a very very long time.

This particular spell would give her more time if she needed it. A distraction that would give her precious moments to set a protection circle. From inside the circle, she could do more spell casting. But it was that initial instant, the time she needed to set a circle, that usually created the complications.

And sometimes, the protective circle itself complicated things. She couldn't move around as much. She couldn't keep Sebastian protected from inside a circle while he had to fight the demon. Most magic cast inside the circle would stay inside the barrier's confines until she broke the circle. That was the point under normal circumstances.

Still, having the option—and time—to build up a protective circle if they needed one was always good.

Over the years, she'd found her distraction spells were useful all on their own, too.

A sound deeper inside the garage. Near the back where it was still dark, and they couldn't see. Like a stone tumbling across the concrete floor. Hitting something softer with a thud. Then a murmured voice.

Sebastian headed that direction, his movements silent. She followed, still holding her oversized bag in one hand so it wouldn't swing and bounce and make noise. Her attention divided between the spell she was holding and moving as quietly as she could, she almost missed the tell-tale flash of red up ahead. That distinctive and eerie glow in the surrounding darkness.

A man's quiet voice said, "Thanks for waiting. I'll get caught if I don't get their cars when they call." His accent was distinctly Eastern European, maybe Russian. Hard to tell as he spoke so quietly.

"You wouldn't have to worry about that if you listened to me," a deeper voice said.

The sound of that second voice grated against Angie's ears, worse than fingernails on chalkboard or across paper. This didn't just give her the chills and set her teeth on edge. This made her feel like her brain was being poked with an electrical current and her ears were on fire.

That wasn't good.

She'd had to listen to many demons over the years. Demons talked. A lot. Trying to manipulate and tempt the ones who summoned them. They made big promises and big threats and hoped the humans they were dealing with didn't notice the catches and loopholes built into the bargains they designed. Most humans didn't, and that was the problem. Missing the loopholes often meant a death sentence for the summoner and a freed demon turned loose on this realm.

Unless a demon hunter got there first.

This was the first time even listening to a demon speak had made her head hurt in quite this way. Like ants had invaded her skull and were biting as they walked across her brain. And that was from one sentence, one rather typical sentence even. What would happen to her poor brain if that thing ahead talked more?

She wanted to ask what type of demon that was. They weren't close enough to see it yet so she wasn't sure. But Sebastian would know. He probably had some instinctive idea what they'd face even before they'd entered the garage. But she also didn't want to give away the fact that they were here. And if they could hear the human and demon talking, the human and the demon would hear her and Sebastian if they spoke.

Still, the idea of hearing the demon's voice against made her physically ill. She lifted her bag and quietly as she could dug around in the depths, careful not to make clinking sounds as she shifted the bags contents until she found a small packet of tissue. She pulled out a couple of tissues without removing the packet from her bag, then let the bag down to her hip and stuffed the tissues into each ear. It wasn't much, but it did deaden the sounds around her. And when the demon spoke again, the ants crawling through her brain were fewer and less intent on biting.

"I can only help you as much as you'll allow me," the demon said.

"I only need one thing. I don't want the other stuff you're offering."

"You'd have more money. You wouldn't have to work this job, for these people."

"I like my job. And most people in the building are nice. I just need the one thing."

"Wealth would help you there, too. Ensure you could always protect your daughter."

"If she dies, what use is wealth. No. I just need her healed. That's all. Just… Just whatever it takes to heal her."

Ah hell. Angie *hated* these kinds of situations. When a parent was so desperate to save a child, they resorted to demons. It was horrible horrible horrible on so many levels. She'd rather deal with a greedy human summoning demons for the power and wealth. The ones who were desperate to save the life of a loved one, so desperate they resorted to making a bargain with a demon, grabbed at her empathy and made everything else so much more difficult. The demon had to be vanquished and the bargain couldn't be maintained. And the human usually resented being "rescued" from the demon in a way that was hard to begrudge.

This kind of thing hadn't happened a lot in the time she'd worked with Sebastian, but it had happened more than once. It was one of the things she'd been more than happy to leave behind when she'd tried to extricate herself from the demon world. These situations hurt so so much. Almost as much as this demon's voice.

She did have to wonder how the human man was able to listen to the demon without curling up in pain. A less horrifyingly heartbreaking question, so she focused on it and not whatever ailment the man's daughter had that had pushed him into demon summoning.

Sebastian dropped behind a large black SUV, hiding from whatever was ahead. She followed suit, wordlessly. She'd walked into enough fights with him before that they didn't have to discuss much. She did notice that the usual fear that tightened her gut and made her a walking nerve wasn't as overwhelming. She was too worried about the human summoner. Too upset by the deal he was trying to make. Too focused on holding her distraction spell at the almost done point.

She was still afraid. She would never *not* be afraid of demons. But that fear wasn't dominant this time.

Which was strange enough she filed the realization away for later examination, even as she rubbed her fingers over the dime-sized pentagram-inside-a-circle charm hanging from her white beaded bracelet.

Sebastian looked around the front bumper of the large car and studied the situation. Angie couldn't see much now. Sebastian must have willed the motion sensor lights to remain off because they hadn't triggered them as they'd walked toward the back of the dark garage. The only light was the red glow ahead. No overhead lights where the demon was either. That seemed strange. But maybe the man had disabled them.

They were near the back wall. She could tell that much in

the dark. So the man must have a spot big enough there for the circle, even though everything Angie had seen of the long garage was a lot of cars stacked tightly together and not an awful lot of maneuvering space.

She waited, slowed her breath as much as she was able, listened to the man bargaining with the demon. She picked up a few more details, enough to know the man was close to making his deal. They were haggling, setting terms. But something felt off. Something she couldn't put her finger on.

Something in the way the demon was bargaining.

Hard to tell for sure with her ears stuffed with tissue. Maybe she just wasn't hearing the conversation well.

Sebastian leaned back and against her ear said, "I'm going in. Stay here until I've gotten between the man and the demon. Can you take care of the man?"

She nodded.

He brushed his lips against her cheek, a gentle kiss that left her startled and breathless.

Then he was gone, sliding out from behind the SUV, walking straight toward the demon.

CHAPTER FIVE

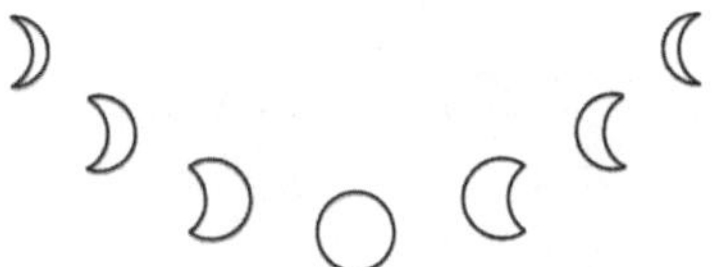

    ngie knelt behind the SUV and watched Sebastian approach the human man and demon. Her first sight of the demon left her heartbeat hammering. Too many demons over the years. She couldn't believe she was purposefully putting herself in the way of more.

This particular demon was one of the mid-level power demons. Not a weak one—though even the weak ones were dangerous and deadly to humans. They were only weak in relation to other demons. The mid-level ones were more clever, though. Sneakier with their powers, their ability to manipulate as dangerous as their strength.

It wasn't a very tall demon, standing only a little over the head of the man. Its upper body was vaguely human shaped, with bright red skin but not the lava, glowing, or fire skins. A more human looking skin, just in a bright red color no human had. It had thick horns coming from the back of its skull and down its back before curving up at the ends like the tips of long braids. Its lower half was covered in a thick brown fur and its feet were two-toed hooves. Its eyes glowed demon red, and its four arms ended in hands tipped with sharp, black claws on each of six fingers.

The species name escaped her. She'd have to look it up. But this wasn't a demon she'd dealt with before. She would have remembered the effect of its voice if she had. Even through the tissue stuffed in her ears, its voice made her brain hurt.

Watching Sebastian walk up to it without any obvious protection didn't help her brain even a little bit.

The human man was relatively innocuous looking. Medium height and build, gray hair shaved close to his head. The only light in this part of the garage came from a small storm lamp set up at the edge of the chalk circle containing the demon, light she hadn't seen from her vantage earlier. The area inside the circle glowed faintly red, but the demon itself didn't glow, and there was no fire anywhere that Angie could see.

She realized abruptly what a good thing that was at the back of a garage full of cars and the possibility of at least some leaked oil. The space where the circle was drawn was open enough, with only one row of cars on each side, not the two deep of the rest of the garage. Even with the extra space, though, a fire demon or one that required a containment circle made of fire would have been disastrous.

Had the man done this on purpose, chosen a demon that wasn't directly associated with flames? Or had this been a fortuitous accident? Humans didn't always—or even mostly —choose the type of demon they summoned. They found a ceremony or spell somewhere, they used it, and they got the kind of demon they got. Many summoners didn't have any idea there were so many species of demons even.

A deadly bit of ignorance, that.

But whether by accident or design, this particular demon summoner had gotten one that wouldn't immediately light all the combustion engines on fire. And that was a relief.

Neither the demon nor the man seemed to notice Sebastian approaching, which gave her a moment longer to study the set up the man had used. His containment circle was etched into the gray concrete floor in simple white chalk. Not the strongest of substances, too easy to smudge by a careless footstep and leave a hole the demon could get through. She was always a little amazed at how many people *only* used chalk without reinforcing the chalk with something more, like salt or stones.

But she supposed ordinary humans who didn't have a lot of experience with magic might not realize they needed another layer if that information wasn't in whatever book or text they'd come across with the ceremony. Some summoners even made a ceremony up on their own, smashing together bits and pieces from different religious practices and their vague idea of magical practices. Those were usually the worst ones for hunters to counter and reverse, the ones without a structure, just spaghetti thrown at a wall until something worked and a demon arrived.

Beyond the chalk circle, there wasn't much more

paraphernalia involved here, though. No candles—thankfully!—no extra drawn symbols, no books of power or documents that she could see. Just a plane white chalk circle on the gray concrete, the man, and the demon.

And Sebastian.

Who finally allowed the others to see him when he was within two feet of the circle.

The man let out a sudden curse and threw himself against a car, clattering against the hood. The demon hissed and snarled at Sebastian, stomping one of its hoofed feet against the concrete in a scraping noise that was almost as painful on Angie's ears as its voice.

Angie used their focus on Sebastian to hurry forward. She stepped up next to the man, who was still half sprawled on the hood of someone's car, staring at Sebastian. He startled again when he noticed her.

"Who are you? What are you doing here?" Then he sort of melted against the hood. "I'm fired, aren't I?"

"We don't live or work here," Angie said. "We're here to help."

"What?" The man's gaze jumped between the demon, Sebastian, and her. "Help?"

"Your demon here was about to escape, mate," Sebastian said, his English accent heavy in his voice as his will seeped into it.

"No. No," the man protested, although he didn't lift himself from the hood. His own Russian accent got a little stronger as he said, "She said the circle was secure."

She? "Someone helped you summon the demon for this

deal?" Angie asked quietly. She had no idea why she was being quiet. The demon could hear them just fine and there was no one else in the garage. She supposed she didn't want to attract anyone who happened in. Having to keep another person safe from a demon would complicate things.

"Yes. I… I wouldn't have thought of it, if she hadn't…"

"Enough!" the demon roared. "You interfere with our negotiation, hunter. Be gone."

Even Angie, from a distance and safely outside the containment circle, felt the push of the demon's will. And the sound of its voice through the tissues in her ears made her eyes water.

Shit. That wasn't good.

The man winced, which brought her attention to him.

"Why did you wince?"

"Its voice," the man muttered. "Why does it sound like that now?"

"It didn't before?" Interesting that he hadn't heard the painful quality earlier. Maybe a little scary? The demon had control over that ability—at least when talking directly to someone.

Sebastian let out a long, deep sigh. "You will not enter this realm," he said, his voice dropping even deeper, rumbling out in a sound that almost echoed in the tight garage space. "You are not welcome in this realm."

"You cannot command me, hunter," the demon said. "You did not summon me."

"You will not enter this realm," Sebastian continued.

And now Angie felt his will in his voice. She was glad

not to be the focus of all that will. Just a peripheral contact was enough to make the fine hairs on her arms lift.

"Wait," the man said, lurching toward Sebastian.

Angie caught him around the shoulders, holding him back easier than she'd anticipated. She wasn't exactly fragile and weak-muscled after growing up with two rambunctious brothers, but she wasn't physically a fighter either. She was a little surprised the man couldn't—or didn't try to—pull away from her.

"You have to stop him," the man said, looking up at her with wide, pleading eyes. "The demon is my only hope. She said so."

"Who? Hope for what?"

"The woman… I can't tell you her name. She swore me not to."

That didn't sound good. "She summoned the demon for you, so you could make a bargain with it. What bargain?" She'd heard enough to know already, but she wanted to hear from him.

"My daughter. She's sick. She needs help. She's so young. Doctors aren't helping. She needs help."

Angie squashed down her empathy. She'd feel this pain later, when she had time. "Demons can't help you," she murmured. "No matter what this woman said. There's always a catch, a consequence. A price to pay. And its never what you think it will be."

"I would sell my soul for my daughter," the man said confidently. "I am not afraid."

"I understand. But that's not what you think it is, selling

your soul. And it still wouldn't help your daughter in the long run."

Humans understood so little about the actual price they paid when they made a deal with a demon. They assumed their soul was that ephemeral thing that wouldn't experience pain. Or if they thought it would face pain, it wasn't the pain they knew in this life, and so they didn't actually consider the torture. If they were of certain religious beliefs, they thought of eternal damnation, and those humans feared the consequences, the eternity of being cut off from their concept of a god.

But none of them *understood* what the demon would do to them. They didn't understand their "soul" to a demon included their physical body. With all its ability to feel pain and fear. They didn't *get* what a demon would actually do to them if it fulfilled their bargains.

"Be gone, beast," Sebastian said, his voice thick like a physical thing in the narrow space.

The demon snarled and tried to take a step closer to the edge of the circle. This close, Angie got a better look at the chalk.

And realized abruptly, there was a small smudge in the line. The circle wasn't sealed completely. There was a weak point.

A place the demon could get out.

"The circle's already weak," Angie said, no longer trying to keep her voice low, terror making her heartbeat pound hard.

Sebastian didn't take his gaze off the demon, but she saw the way his shoulders tightened, just a little.

They'd barely arrived in time. The containment circle had never been secure. The person who'd helped this man summon the demon had meant for it to break and the beast to escape.

She pulled the man farther back against the car behind them, still holding him around the shoulders. He flattened against her, as if eager to put more distance between himself and the demon. His breath caught and he started muttering something in Russian. She didn't speak Russian, so she had no idea what he was saying, but the rhythm reminded her of a prayer.

"Be gone, beast," Sebastian said again, his will even stronger in his voice now.

The beast snarled. Its hoof touched the part of the circle where the white chalk was smudged.

And Angie triggered her distraction spell.

CHAPTER SIX

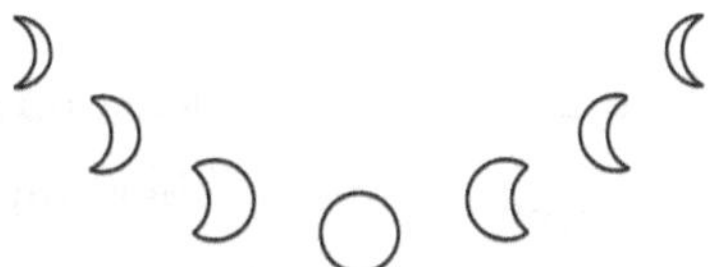

$\mathcal{D}$istraction spells were always a strange thing when contained within a small space. This particular one was no exception, because the overall darkness at the very back part of the long, narrow garage made the sparkling lights and fireworks more pronounced.

The flapping butterflies the size of the demon's head, the jumps of light sprites like leaping dolphins in front of the demon's face, the whiz and zoom of multicolored fish-like sparkles. All of it filled the turnaround area against the back wall, making the area a giddy whirlwind of chaos.

The chaos didn't faze Sebastian at all. He'd seen her distraction spells before. But both the demon—whose hooved foot had just touched the place in the confinement circle where the circle was weak—and the human man who'd been bargaining with the demon startled and jumped and flinched away from the light show.

The demon took a step back from the edge of the circle to swat at some of the glowing florescent illusions dancing around his head. Angie let out a small breath. On her next breath, she murmured the spell for a protection circle and mentally drew the line around herself and the man she still held firmly by the shoulders. He was staring up at the run of fireworks against the low roof and didn't seem to notice she was speaking.

When she said the final word and connected the ends of the circle, a blue light flared in her mind's eye as the protective barrier came up. It was a small circle, encompassing her, the man, and the car at their backs because the car was in the way otherwise.

As if he sensed that she and the man were now inside some protection, Sebastian stepped closer to the chalk line, to the place where it had been smudged and the containment barrier had been weakened.

"Be gone, beast," he intoned again, the waves of his will reaching out like a hand to push the demon backward a step.

The demon roared, a sound that bounced around the garage walls like a bowling ball looking for a target.

Her circle kept her and the man from the worst of that sound, but her ears still hurt.

"I will have my promised reward!" the demon screeched.

"You will return from whence you came," Sebastian said. He raised his hands and made a circle in the air in front of him, then drew an X in the circle and punched a finger into the center of the X.

The demon screeched again, taking another step back.

"Be gone, beast," Sebastian said again. He repeated the gesture.

This time when he poked the center of the invisible X drawn in the air, the demon scrunched backward as if something from behind was pulling it through a space too small for it.

"No!" the demon wailed.

The man flinched and half turned away from the demon to cover his ears. Angie wanted to cover her own, but she didn't want to let go of the man in case he tried to run away and broke her circle. She'd created something to keep dangerous demons out, not something to keep terrified humans in. Those were different spells, the circles did different things, and she wasn't as good at combining those two types of circles as she'd like. She needed a lot more practice and training. Right now, with the ability to do one or the other, she'd chosen safety from demon as the priority. She could physically keep the man from running away.

Except that she really didn't have to. He was still leaning heavily into her as if he could barely keep himself upright. And, she realized suddenly, there were tears streaming down his cheeks.

That tugged at her heart, but they had other worries that had to take precedence.

The demon wailed again as Sebastian made the invisible circle and X shape again. Before he could poke the X, the demon lunged forward, reaching with clawed fingers toward Sebastian, dragging itself closer to that weak space in the containment barrier even as some force from behind tried to drag it back.

Sebastian didn't balk even a little. He stood as if the demon's efforts were no more worrying than a fly diving in front of his face. He poked the center of his air drawing. Held the demon's gaze.

"Be gone beast," he said, more quietly but with so much power in the tone even the human man with Angie gasped.

The demon's face contorted into a twisted scowl of fury. It dropped to its knees and scraped at the floor with all four hands, its claws leaving deep gouges in the cement, dragging itself closer to the weakness in the chalk circle.

But the force pulling it backward was stronger.

The demon's fur-covered legs and hooved feet seemed to squash together, twisted and distorted, pulled longer and stretched, disappearing into the empty air. Then its body followed, more twisting and distortion and shrinking and stretching. All of it looked painful and reminded Angie of the spaghettification that was supposed to happen to a body going down into a black hole.

The demon was forced into a shape smaller than it had been, narrower, longer, and as it fought the drag of whatever pulled on it, it screamed. The sound so piercing Angie's knees actually trembled, despite the protection of her circle.

"Be gone, beast," Sebastian said again, this time so quietly she almost didn't hear him over the demon's ear-piercing protests.

The lower, stretched part of the demon's body disappeared, dragged through a hole Angie couldn't see, then its torso, and finally the still protesting head, stretched into something obscene and almost too horrible to look at. The final parts of the demon to disappear were its hands as it continued reaching toward Sebastian.

Then it winked out of this realm, dragged back into its own, an echo of its final protest the only thing to remain.

When the echo of the demon's voice died down, when there was no sign of it remaining, Sebastian broke open the containment circle with a sweep of his foot, smudging the chalk line into wide streaks until the metaphysical space where a demon realm met this realm no longer existed.

Breaking the circle when the demon was no longer in it, meant the demon couldn't sneak back into that little bit of space that was its realm in this world. Breaking the circle when the demon was still in it, freed the demon into this realm.

The latter was something the hunters tried at all costs to avoid.

A long moment of silence settled. Angie finally released the man's shoulders and when she was certain there was no more danger, she broke her protective circle. The blue light winked out in her mind's eye.

Sebastian finally turned away from contemplating the smudged chalk line. "Everyone alright?"

The man drew the back of his hand across his mouth. "That was my daughter's only chance. That's what she told me. This would help."

Angie exchanged a look with Sebastian.

"She who?" Angie asked quietly.

She'd automatically kept her psychic touch sense controlled when she'd grabbed the man, a reaction more instinct than anything these days. When she had to work actual magic, when there were demons around, she'd learned to keep her psychic senses extra controlled and not let accidents slip through. Touching and reading someone involved in demon summoning, or in any of the things around demon summoning, could be pretty horrible. And since she'd been caught twice by demon objects a month ago, she was extra careful now.

But closing off that sense meant she had to ask questions and hope for answers from people. Like a normal, non-psychic witch.

The man glanced at her, blinking as if he'd only just noticed her. "Her. The woman. She told me not to say her name, but... She calls herself Marta. She said the demon would help, was the only thing that could save my daughter."

The name struck Angie in an instinct, and she narrowed her eyes. Why was she reacting to the woman's name? She didn't recognize who it might be. Still, something felt...off. Suspicious.

"Marta didn't mean for you to succeed," Sebastian said. "She drew the circle?"

The man nodded.

"She left a weak spot, a place where the demon could have escaped. That's why I'm here."

"I don't understand you, any of this." He looked between Angie and Sebastian, tears thick in his eyes but not running down his cheeks anymore. "She said this would help. Why would she want the demon to escape? How does that help my daughter?"

Good questions.

"Do you have a way to contact her?" Sebastian asked.

The man shook his head. "She found me. She…knew things. About my daughter. My family. She knew my brother-in-law's money wasn't helping. She knew who he was, even though I don't discuss him with people. She said… She said she was a nurse at the hospital."

"Could you tell us what she looked like?" Angie asked, as that instinctive something niggled at her.

The man shrugged. "Ordinary. Brown hair, eyes." He put a hand to his own head. "About this tall, I guess." He shrugged again. "Pale. Sounded like the Puerta Ricans. Looked like a nurse."

A generic description that could be half the people in this city. Less helpful but the description raised the same worrying instinct that had reacted to the woman's name.

She set that aside for now and asked, "If you can, will you tell us what's wrong with your daughter?"

The man shuddered. "They don't know. Cancer maybe, but they can't find the answers. She's in hospital a lot. My wife is desperate. Me too. She's our only baby."

Angie's heart twisted. She hated the woman who'd sent this man to a demon with false hope of helping his baby. "What's your name?"

"Ivan. Ivan Meknikov."

"I'm Angie. This is Sebastian. You were open to the idea

of demons. Would you be open to help from witches instead?"

She wasn't sure the healer friend she knew from work could do much, but maybe Cindy could at least give the doctors a better idea of what was wrong with the girl so she could be helped. Magic could do a lot of amazing things, and her healer friend was capable of miracles. But she wouldn't give false hope the way this Marta person had. She'd offer help. Not miracles.

Ivan narrowed his eyes and took a little step away from her.

He was okay with demons, but witches scared him? Humans were weird.

"What would these witches do?" he asked.

"I have a friend. A healer. I'm not making promises. Medical doctors are still your best hope. But my friend might be able to help the doctors with a diagnosis, since they can't find the problem. My friend might be able to pinpoint where the doctors should be looking, what they should be doing for your daughter. Knowing what the problem is will give them a direction to treat her."

Ivan was nodding before she'd finished. "Yes. Yes. We need answers. No one can do anything until we know what the problem is."

"If I can arrange a meeting with my healer friend, would you take it?"

"Yes. Yes. Please." He gestured to the now smudged chalk circle—Sebastian had continued to run his foot over the white line while they spoke and a good chunk of the chalk was now so faint, it had nearly been erased. Definitely no demons sneaking back now. "I did this for answers. We need answers. A witch can't be any worse."

Angie kept her mouth shut, but barely. Being told she couldn't be "any worse" than a demon was not the compliment Ivan thought it was.

"Give me your contact information. My friend will be in touch. Her name is Cindy Wong. She will not look like a witch when you meet her."

Cindy was a full-figured fireball of a woman who refused to play into the witch stereotypes, even at work. Angie played up the bohemian, dramatic witchy thing at work, despite it not being her personal esthetic, and many of the others at Dana's Cauldron—her place of work and her home away from home in the city—dressed the part because it fit their personal taste and style. Cindy was not one of those witches.

She dressed high fashion glamour, perfect makeup, perfect hair—thanks to some truly spectacular wigs—and always looked more like a sexy movie star than a practicing witch and healer. More than one mundane client had refused to believe she was an actual witch. Cindy delighted in those moments.

Ivan motioned toward the front of the garage. "I have a paper and a pen up here."

She and Sebastian followed a few feet behind him, after Sebastian gave the chalk one last scrub with his foot and Angie had one last look around to see if she could find any books or papers Ivan—or Marta—might have used to summon the demon.

As they returned to the front of the narrow garage, Sebastian whispered near her ear, "Can your friend help his daughter?"

"She can get some answers. Help…" Angie sighed. "Depends on what's wrong. Magic has limits." Everything had limits. One of the more frustrating realizations she'd come to as she aged.

Ivan stood over a small desk, just inside a narrow box of a booth not far from the garage's door, where the locked cabinet for the car keys was tucked against a plane wood wall, and a few dusty pieces of soccer memorabilia and an old clock decorated the shelves above the desk.

He handed her a folded piece of paper. "My brother-in-law is…a man of prominence. He has a lot of money and power. He's been unable to help my daughter. I thought… If someone rich and powerful can't do anything, nothing on this earth could help. Marta convinced me there were things not of this earth that I could turn to." He let out a long breath. "A witch healer won't demand my soul?"

"No," Angie said, tucking the folded paper with Ivan's details into her jeans pocket so it wouldn't get swallowed and lost in the depths of her large purse.

"Then a witch healer is better than a demon."

Any day, Angie thought. "I'll ask her to call as soon as possible."

"My wife's name is Petia. She will probably answer the phone."

Angie nodded.

"If Marta returns," Sebastian said, "and offers to help you summon another demon, I'd recommend turning down that help."

"You said she set things up so the demon would escape. Would it have killed me?"

"Yes," Sebastian said. Not pulling punches.

"Then I will not be taking her help again."

His eyes narrowed and for a moment, Angie wasn't sure she liked the look in Ivan's expression. Probably better Marta, whoever she was, stayed as far away from him as possible. The woman wouldn't receive a friendly welcome anymore.

"Good," Sebastian said. "Then you aren't likely to see us again. That would be best for all concerned."

He turned toward the still closed garage door, but Ivan stopped him with a hand on his arm. Sebastian didn't flinch or pull his arm away, which surprised Angie. She wasn't sure why.

Ivan did drop his hold the minute Sebastian faced him. "Thank you. Thank you for not… My family needs me."

Sebastian nodded, his only comment.

Ivan opened the garage door from the attendant's booth, the metal slow rolling upward against the ceiling as they waited. Sebastian didn't turn around as they stepped out onto the sidewalk. But he did pause as the door closed again, waiting for it to settle into place before heading back in the direction of the subway.

CHAPTER SEVEN

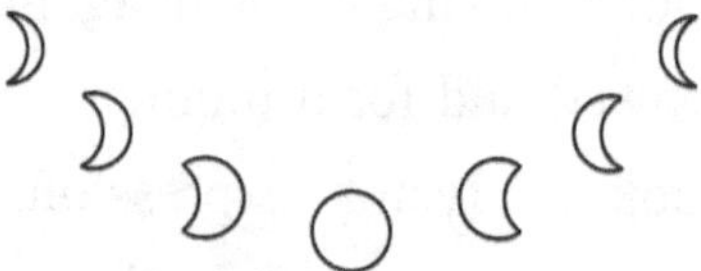

*D*arkness settled over the city now and the sidewalk lights slowly came up, though they were still dim in the evening gloom. Angie remained silent as she and Sebastian turned onto the main road and walked toward the subway entrance.

Ivan's story bothered her. Not his part, which she understood, but the woman who'd helped him summon the demon. Something about this mysterious Marta person…

"Marta is an issue," Sebastian said.

"But what kind?" she returned without missing a beat. "Is the name familiar to you? Do you know who she is?"

He shook his head, but he was still frowning as they went down the stairs into the station. He must not have been making any effort to look innocuous to those around them, because several people looked up, startled, and moved to the opposite side of the narrow stairwell, leerily walking around Sebastian.

She glanced at his face. Yeah, he looked pretty fierce. She found it sexy, not scary, though. That probably said things about her.

When they were on the platform, he finally turned to her. "Thank you for your help. The distraction spell worked well. And it's always nice having someone to keep the mundanes safe from themselves."

She chuckled. "You're welcome." She only hesitated a moment before saying, "You want to come back to my place so we can finish our earlier conversation?"

They'd managed to spend time together without falling into old habits, without letting feelings overwhelm common sense. And they did have a lot to talk about. A diner or restaurant might be safer. She would keep her hands to herself in a public space. But the things they needed to discuss also needed privacy. And since he'd just had to exert so much will fighting a demon, it seemed selfish to demand he use more for her convenience. Having him in her home was a risk she could probably take. Especially since the things they needed to talk about made her mad, not randy. That helped.

He held her gaze for a long moment, a speculative look in his expression. Then he nodded. And quietly said, "I hadn't thought you would…agree with the council's plan." His gaze flickered away briefly. "Or mine."

"I haven't and I don't. With either plan. But… Well, that's what we need to talk about."

She was going to take up the council's… She couldn't really call it an offer. Threat more like. And knowing they only wanted her to train as a demon hunter because they figured she'd get herself killed trying to do a job she wasn't suited to pissed her off mightily. As much as them thinking they could force her to do anything. But she needed time. Stalling time. To figure out how best to handle them without causing chaos and disarray among the hunters.

Their job was so necessary, so essential to the world balance. The incident with Ivan a perfect example. Angie's witchy instincts were all about balance. Things had to balance. And the demon hunters were part of that. This evening, once again, showed just how essential they were. She didn't want to bring down this council if it meant upending such a necessary force for good in the world. Sebastian's reassurances that it wouldn't do what she feared didn't sooth her worry, though.

She wanted, *needed*, a better plan. But she needed more than a couple of weeks to come up with one. More time, but also more information. She wanted to see this council face-to-face. All of them. Take their measure. Maybe even shake a few hands. Given they were all demon hunters themselves, with enough will to control what leaked through to a psychic, the handshakes probably wouldn't give her much. But she could hope for someone getting careless and forgetting that, despite their best efforts, she was actually a witch.

She also had questions she wanted answered before she made a decision on what to do about the council. Questions raised by the job that had brought Sebastian back into her life this time.

First among them…

What the hell was a demon witch?

The subway roared into the station with a blast of hot air, rushing past before stopping hard. Oh good, one of those drivers. They got on for the short trip and transfer that would bring them to the stop closest to her apartment.

They didn't talk during the journey. Which gave Angie's mind time to churn through her various concerns and questions ad nauseum. By the time they reached her apartment, she was starving—always bad—and sick of her own thoughts.

"We're ordering Mexican food," she said as they walked into her living room and she let her large purse clatter to the floor near the couch.

She sighed as the comfy familiarity of home settled around her. She loved this apartment—the wooden floors, the red brick detail on one wall, the non-working fireplace she decorated with little flowering cacti, her permanently set up altar near the large, street-facing living room windows. It was a long, narrow apartment, the bedroom and bathroom close to the front door, the living room and open kitchen at the front of the building. The view took in the convoluted streets of the Village, full of colorful shops and people, the trees leafy green in the summer and bare twigs in the winter.

No trees with natural V's splitting their trunks anywhere in her neighborhood.

She was within walking distance to Dana's Cauldron, a

subway station, and one of the best Mexican food restaurants in the city. A little dive place that people didn't notice if they didn't know what they were looking for. And the Mexican food restaurant delivered. Angie tipped well, ordered from the place at least once a week, and the owner she talked to most often on the phone knew her usual order by memory.

Tonight, she needed that familiar ritual, even if she'd be shaking up her usual order with extra food. And she needed the comforts of being in her own space, even if that kept Sebastian temptingly close to her bed.

"Make yourself comfortable," she said, going to her landline and hitting the quick-dial button for the restaurant. "You want a burrito or tacos? This place makes great burritos, but their carne asada tacos are a gift from the goddess."

"Tacos. Two orders."

She grinned. After a fight, he could eat as much as a shapeshifter. She just ate that much naturally. "And we're getting loaded nachos. Just this once, I'll share."

His chuckle tickled along her spine. Dangerous. So very very dangerous having him here.

"You have any Tequila left after our last drinking session?"

She gestured to the little liquor stand on the outer counter of her open kitchen. She always kept Tequila on hand. Just in case. One could never have enough Tequila.

As she waited for the restaurant to pick up, the phone braced between her shoulder and ear, she played with her bracelet, running her fingers along the smooth white beads, pressing the little silver pentagram inside a circle against her thumb until she felt the shape imbedding in her skin.

When the restaurant answered, Angie made her order, exchanging pleasantries with the owner, taking a little ribbing when he noticed she was ordering more food than usual. She relaxed her grip on her pentagram as she settled into the casual chat, and the anticipation of good food. But when she hung up, the reality of big, strong Sebastian standing in her living room, looking at the little cacti decorating her fireplace, got her nerves jumping again.

She nodded at the couch. "They'll be here in thirty minutes. We might as well get comfortable." She noticed that despite having asked about the Tequila, he hadn't actually gone and gotten any. "I thought you wanted a drink?"

"After dinner, maybe. I just wanted to make sure you weren't out."

Something inside her grew warmer and softened. "What would you have done if I didn't have any?"

"Stepped out to get you more, of course."

Her heart flipped a little in her chest. "Of course."

He held her gaze for a long moment. Having him here was a bad idea. She knew that. Even the anticipation of Mexican food couldn't fully squash her desire to move closer to him on the couch. To cup his face and run her thumbs over his cheekbones, feel the rough evening scruff against her skin. See what it was like to kiss him now that he had that goatee.

Memories of his hands on her, his arms around her... So familiar and so missed.

She swallowed hard and leaned against the couch arm, away from him. Wanting him and being able to have him were two different things. Being with him now would complicate what was an already complicated situation with the demon hunter council.

Breaking up with him, leaving to come to New York, had been one of the hardest things she'd ever done in her life. For six months after, when he showed up to drag her back into his world, she hadn't been able to resist going back into his arms either. And every time made the separation after harder. Every slip back to the old ways, made going forward without him so much more painful. Reopening the wound over and over again.

He claimed he wouldn't have kept showing up in those first six months if the council hadn't been forcing his hand. He claimed he would have given her the space she'd asked for, that he'd have handled the last two years differently. And she believed him. On that at least. Those six months hadn't been easy on him either.

They'd go right back to that pain now if they let their guards down. Right back to...to feelings that were complicated and messy. Loving him was so fucking easy. But being in his life was not.

And now that she was going voluntarily back to the demon hunter world, this time to find a way to keep the council off her back permanently without starting an all-out war with them, returning to her relationship with Sebastian seemed impossible to resist. But she'd be going back for the wrong reasons, under the wrong circumstances.

Wouldn't she?

She sighed. "Complicated and messy," she said aloud.

"Complicated and messy," he said with a nod. As if he knew exactly what she was thinking. As if he'd been thinking the same thing.

Maybe he had.

"We should talk about me agreeing to train as a demon hunter," she said.

"We should."

Tension she hadn't noticed he was holding in his shoulders eased as he settled back against the opposite couch armrest, leaning away from her the way she was leaning away from him. He let out a long breath. She wasn't the only one struggling with their current predicament and all those old feelings. That didn't make things easier.

"When did you decide to go along with my plan?" he asked.

"I'm not going along with your plan." She pulled her legs up and wrapped her arms around them, resting her chin on her knees as she met his gaze. "I'm not interested in destroying the council unless they force my hand. But I don't know what to do about them yet. Which means I need time. I will agree to their pointless attempts to train me as a demon hunter to stall. To gain some time, maybe even some leverage to use to get out of this world forever." She blinked a few times, forcing her mind away from the thoughts of being out of Sebastian's life forever. "And I have some questions I need answered before I make a final decision about the council."

"What questions?"

"For one, Carmen called me a demon witch. I want to know what that means."

Carmen was one of the people involved in the case that had brought Sebastian back into her life after eighteen months. A woman who'd been using demons against people she deemed reprehensible—and if the one Angie had met was any indication, Carmen wasn't wrong about them. But Carmen's revenge plots—getting these greedy bastards to summon demons, make deals they couldn't keep, and get themselves killed—had, at least in this last circumstance, dragged a mother and daughter into the situation and nearly gotten them killed, too. Angie understood Carmen's motives. But her vigilante efforts were deeply dangerous to innocent people caught in the crossfire. Something Angie couldn't abide.

When Carmen had seen her accidentally open a breach between this realm and a demon realm, she'd called Angie a demon witch. It wasn't a term Angie had ever heard before, even during the years she'd been working with Sebastian and studying demon related stuff. And Sebastian had been evasive when she'd asked about the term.

She needed those answers now. If he couldn't provide them, she had a feeling the council could.

She'd start with him, though. "What is a demon witch?"

"I don't know what Carmen was talking about. I haven't heard the term demon witch before."

She flinched. "You can't lie to me if we're going to do this thing with the council. Not to me. If you can't tell me, say so. But don't lie."

He let out a sigh and ran a hand over his eyes, then roughly down his face. He stared at her fireplace cacti for a long silent moment. Until she was sure he wouldn't tell her what he knew. But he had to be honest about that, about not telling her something for whatever reason, or she wouldn't be able to trust him either.

And that would change everything.

"Demon witch isn't a term I've heard before," he said finally. "It's not…not the one the council uses. But the other thing she called you, a realm splitter, that is the term the council uses. It's the term used by our history keepers."

Angie straightened, letting her hands drop from her knees to her ankles as she stared at him. "The history keepers have a term for me? They've encountered people like me before?"

She wasn't sure why that should surprise her. Her trait was extremely rare. She couldn't find much written about it except in a few oblique references. Certainly not whole terms to describe her skill. She'd assumed there was no name for it, it was so rare. Because of that, she really had been half convinced most of her life that it was some kind of curse on her ancestors that came back to bite her in the ass.

But people like her had existed in the past, and it shouldn't have surprised her that the demon hunters had records of those people, knew of them. It shouldn't have surprised her they had a term for her.

She could release demons into this realm. She could open a portal between demon realms and this one. All of that would, of course, be of great interest to demon *hunters*.

Still, the news took her by surprise. Shocked her even.

Not so much that they had a name for her, or that they'd encountered people like her before... But that no one, not even Sebastian and Aidan, had thought to *mention* this information to her at any time before this moment.

What the absolute hell?

"Why haven't you told me before?" she said. "Why didn't Aidan tell me there was a name for this? That the history keepers had...historical records of people like me? Why didn't either of you *say* anything?"

He didn't look at her when he said, "Realm splitters haven't had a...good history with the hunters."

"What does not good mean? Exactly."

He shook his head, as if he wasn't going to answer. But he did. "In all other encounters kept in our history, the realm splitters have been on the opposite side of the fight with hunters."

He finally met her gaze. And the little flicker of red in the depths of his brown eyes was brighter, just a little more obvious. She caught her breath.

"Every realm splitter the hunters have ever come across in the past," he said slowly, "was actively working to release a plague of demons on this realm."

CHAPTER EIGHT

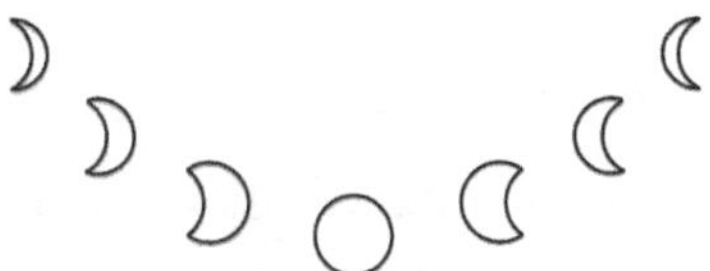

The buzzer for the downstairs door startled Angie out of her shocked silence. "That's the food," she muttered, unfolding herself from the couch to go let the delivery guy up.

Her head reeled as she paid for the food, tipped her usual delivery guy, Manuel, asked the usual questions about his night and his family before waving goodbye. All of it mechanical and rote because her brain, her ability to think clearly, had stepped away from the room for some air.

She set the bag of food on her coffee table, staring at it without moving until Sebastian leaned forward and started taking out the aluminum foil containers, their plastic covers revealing the different dishes. He laid the food out, opened the containers, so that the scent of melted cheese, beans, and spices wafted around Angie. Then he got up and went to the kitchen. She was aware of him moving around, but she couldn't rouse herself enough to see what he was doing.

The food smelled good enough her stomach grumbled. Even in shock she was still starving and needed to eat. The instinct to fill the hole her gut had become would kick in soon. She could eat no matter what was going on around her. And forgetting to eat wasn't really an option most of the time. But in that moment, she was just…frozen.

Every person like her, through all of the demon hunters' recorded history, every one of them had actively tried to bring down destruction on this realm.

No fucking wonder they wanted to lock her up!

"Fucking hell," she muttered, and was surprised by the deep, raspy sound of her own voice. She only ever sounded like that when she was working big magic.

"It's a lot," Sebastian said from the kitchen.

No closer. She looked up and he was standing next to her, holding out a glass tumbler with a finger of Tequila in it. The bottle of Tequila was in his other hand.

"One shot before food. Then you need to eat before you get shit faced."

She snorted. "I have to go into work in two hours. I can't afford to get shit faced." But she could afford the one shot to warm extremities that had gone very very cold.

Their fingers brushed when she took the glass from him. He was so warm she sucked in a breath. That heat to her cold skin stung in a delicious way. Like stepping into a scalding hot shower after being out in the snow. Which only made her want to step into him so she could forget what she'd just learned and concentrate on warming herself up.

Except she couldn't forget. And taking Sebastian to bed instead of facing this wouldn't solve any problems. It would just complicate things.

She gulped down the shot in one, letting the familiar flavor slide down her throat. Her cheeks warmed instantly. The rest of her slowly followed. First her chest, and then slowly, out to her limbs until she no longer felt like an immovable ice block.

"Thanks," she murmured, setting the glass down on the coffee table beside her taco and tostada combo meal. The lure of melty cheese and seasoned meats warmed her further and she finally picked up a taco and started eating.

Sebastian stood a beat longer, before setting the Tequila bottle down by the nachos and returning to his place next to her on the couch. They ate mostly in silence, after Sebastian's eyes rounded at his first bite of taco, and he gave her that emphatic nod he used when the food was especially good. She was through most of her meal, working on the nachos, digging for still-crunchy chips at the sides to scoop up all the cheese, beans, and guacamole piled at the center of the container, when she finally felt settled enough to speak.

"I'm not going to unleash a plague of demons on this realm."

"I know that. Aidan knows that. But the others… History doesn't support our instincts in this."

"I thought demon hunters lived by their instincts." Second only to their will as a necessary part of the job.

"They do. We do. And normally, they'd trust Aidan's instincts."

Aidan was Sebastian's mentor and a literal legend among the demon hunters. She was the one who'd come to save Angie when Angie had, at five years old in a church parking lot, accidentally opened a portal into a demon realm and released a bunch of demons. Aidan had even helped Angie's mother find Angie's first magical mentor, Esmerelda. Aidan vouching for Angie with the council should have been enough, as far as Angie was concerned. Obviously, they were determined to see her as a threat despite Aidan's support.

"I have gone out of my way to avoid the demon world," she said. Except for the years she was with Sebastian.

But even then, that had started when Aidan and Sebastian had come to her for help with a demon-related problem. She hadn't had any intention of messing around with demons, and had actively worked to ensure she could avoid accidentally opening a portal again. She'd done everything to stay out of this world before *they'd* come to her.

"My path is magic." She felt the need to keep reminding everyone this because so many seemed to forget. She was, first and foremost, a witch. The realm splitter…thing, curse or talent or…yeah, curse. That was a part of her but not who she was or what she wanted to be. She'd ignore the skill, outside of making sure she had control of it, if everyone would just let her.

"The others like you were all witches as well," Sebastian said. "That must be where Carmen got the name demon witch."

"How did she learn about it? When I haven't seen it and when your people have a different name for someone like me?"

"I don't know. I don't know how she heard the term realm splitter. I'll see if the council has questioned her."

Carmen disappeared after that incident nearly a month ago, but the woman from the council who'd shown up afterward had assured them Carmen and her thief associate would be arrested by human police and charged with fraud. Angie hadn't thought to ask if the arrests had happened. Where the two in jail or out on bail? She should probably ask more questions about that.

She didn't, though, because she needed to know more about these other realm splitters. "How do you know all these others were also witches?"

"It's written in the history. Aidan would have known you'd be a witch, even if you and your family hadn't already known."

Her family was, almost entirely, mundane. Only her mother had a touch of magic. It wasn't much, not like Angie's, but it was enough that she knew what was going on with Angie when she'd spark little fires with just her fingers and a muttered word, or when sparkling faery butterflies danced around the dinner table, appearing out of nowhere, or when it would suddenly rain out of a cloudless sky after Angie had a tantrum trying to get something she wanted.

Angie hadn't had the spells or control then. But the raw magic was there. It popped out in weird ways that were impossible to ignore or hide. Or predict. So the entire family knew she was a witch.

In the beginning, her mother had been able to help her control that magic. But her mother's skills were more kitchen witch level—good with potions and herbs and small magics. She wasn't strong enough, or knowledgeable enough, to train Angie's type of power. She'd been looking for someone to train Angie when Aidan had come into their lives.

The touch psychic skill, fortunately, hadn't manifested until after Esmerelda was in Angie's life. Otherwise, Angie wasn't sure she'd have stayed sane long enough to find someone to help her with that particularly ability. It was hard to go through life without touching anything.

"What did the others being witches have to do with their ability to open portals into demon realms?" She was very curious about this point, so this wasn't a defensive question. The fact that they were all also witches was significant. It had to be. She just wasn't sure what it meant. But her own instincts insisted that connection was important.

"No one really knows for sure—that they've told me. I haven't been allowed to see the specific records on realm splitters."

"You haven't?" She thought the hunters all had access to their history records. All of them. Because they might need that information in a fight at some point in their lives.

"There are some things… Some things the council deems too dangerous for more than a handful of people to know."

She stared at him, her chin lowered. "Too dangerous for…you. For a *demon hunter* to know?"

What the hell could those things be? Given what Sebastian did, what he faced regularly, she had no idea what kind of knowledge could be more dangerous than the demons themselves.

Obviously, to the council, information about people like her was more dangerous.

Which was absolutely terrifying.

"Does Aidan know any more? Has she seen the records?"

"If she has, she hasn't told me."

Would Aidan tell him if it was important? Angie wasn't sure. Aidan was his mentor, and as far as Angie knew, Aidan trusted Sebastian. But Aidan was also enigmatic and hard to read. She knew more than she let on, Angie was sure. How much and what…? She'd have to ask Aidan that one day, she supposed.

"Where is she right now, anyway?" she asked. Right after Sebastian had shown up in New York, Aidan had had to leave for France for another issue. She could be anywhere by now.

"I haven't heard from her," he said. "No idea where she is now. She'll be in touch if she needs to be."

That was the way of it with hunters. They touched base with each other here and there, but mostly, they worked alone, traveled alone, and spent most of their time alone. And most of them preferred that. Sebastian had semi-settled in New Mexico with her, when they'd been together. Always returning to the apartment they shared. When he had to travel, she went with him, most of the time. To have his back. They'd worked together, hunting demons. And returned to their apartment at the end of the hunt. That wasn't a normal life for a demon hunter. But they'd made it work.

Until she couldn't take it anymore. Until she couldn't get the nightmares under control. Until being with him caused too much pain.

She pushed those thoughts aside. Dredging up old pains —current pain—wasn't helping.

"Being a witch is somehow tied to the realm splitter skill. Which comes first? Magic or realm splitting? Or are they interwoven? Part of the magic? Not something to view separately?" She wasn't looking for answers from Sebastian since he'd already said he didn't know. But she had to ask aloud as she worked her way through the things she needed to learn. "I wonder if my touch psychic skill is tied into all this, or just another talent not linked to the others."

She remembered having a thought, one half-formed and almost forgotten not that long ago. The way her regular magic took effort and work. Casting spells, performing a scrying, the occasional potion, all took work, study, and investment of her internal magic. But both the touch psychic skill and opening portals into demon realms just…happened. There was no required effort to do those things. In fact, she had to actively work to prevent them from happening. Both of them. She'd had to train hard to *avoid* reading easily just by touching things. And she'd had to work at not looking into just the wrong kind of tree shape.

There was something there, in that connection. There had to be, right?

Or it could just be a coincidence and she was looking for patterns that weren't real. Damn it.

"I need more answers," she said. "I need the information your council thinks is too dangerous. They know more about me and my skills than I do and that strikes me as a very bad idea. And foolhardy. With more information, I'm more likely to manage my skills better."

"And that's precisely what they're worried about," Sebastian said. "That you'll manage your skills by unleashing a plague of demons." His gaze flicked away. "Or that someone will manipulate you into doing that."

"Are they worried about you?" She was appalled by the idea. He was a superb hunter. He'd never purposefully try to bring demons into this realm.

He smiled a little. "Not that I'll encourage you to unleash a plague. They wouldn't have tolerated our relationship if they were worried about that."

According to him, at first, the council were against the romantic part of their relationship. But it had placed him in a unique position to "keep an eye on her"—the thought of that being the point of their relationship always made her snarl; Sebastian claimed that wasn't the reason for him, and she believed him. Mostly. Still, the fact that the council had started encouraging the relationship because they assumed he could control her if they were together was enraging.

One more thing to enrage her.

"They're worried about you for other reasons, though?" she asked.

He shrugged. "My…position with the council has been fraught for a while."

"Because of me."

He nodded, meeting her gaze as he did.

She wasn't sure how to feel about that, so she set it aside. "If I play along with this attempt to make me a demon hunter, do you supposed they'll give me more information about the demon witch thing? Give me access to their history? Knowing what happened in the past, with the others, could help me ensure it doesn't happen again."

While she didn't actively want to unleash a demon plague on this realm, it was one of her greatest fears. That she would do it on accident. That she'd stumble and not be able to pull herself away from the brink, and without meaning to, cause massive destruction in her own realm. Very Pandora-holding-the-still-unopened-box. But she wasn't afraid her curiosity would cause the catastrophe. She was afraid she'd fall and drop the box, letting it spill open before she could stop it.

That was her deepest fear.

"They've deemed the information too dangerous to know. For hunters. But it's always possible they'll see sense and show you what they've keep in the history."

"You don't sound hopeful about that."

"I'm not. Especially with…certain members of the council. But we can ask."

Ask. Yes, probably best to ask first. She was supposed to be playing along and pretending to train as a demon hunter.

An alarm on her phone broke into their conversation with a surprising beeping sound issuing from the depths of her bag where it sat by the base of the couch. She huffed out a breath and dug through her purse to retrieve the phone.

Turning off the alarm, she looked at the time. "I have to get ready for work. That's what the alarm was for. We'll have to talk about this more later."

Her first client tonight didn't arrive until seven thirty, and she only had four readings scheduled, but she couldn't afford to be late or it disrupted the whole flow of the night and one of her clients would get their session cut short. She hated doing that to any of them. Especially since her last client was a lovely man who came in regularly. They all deserved her complete attention, and their full sessions.

She tucked her phone back into her purse. "You can tell the council I'll meet with them tomorrow. Not too early or they'll be facing a seriously grumpy witch. Not a safe thing to do when she's already under duress."

He chuckled, as she'd hoped. But sobered again quickly. "Are you sure about this?"

"Yes."

"Knowing at least one of them, maybe more, probably wants you dead?"

"Yes. The whole keep-your-enemies-closer concept is good advice. And maybe I'll get more answers."

"Don't strike my idea off entirely. We might still have to bring them all down to keep you safe."

"Only as a last resort."

She walked him to the door. Paused when he turned to face her again. They were standing too close, and he smelled delicious, clean soap and Mexican food. A combination hard to resist.

He smiled a little. "You made it through that conversation with only one shot of Tequila. I'd call that a win."

She snorted. "If I didn't have to work, I wouldn't have been so restrained."

He reached up, as if he intended on touching her, but then fisted his hand and drop it to his side. "I'll call around at noon. Late enough?"

"Should be. But don't complain if I'm grumpy."

"Wouldn't dream of it."

Another long pause. Another moment when it would be so so easy to fall into old habits. Her gaze dropped to his mouth. She could feel his heat seeping into her, and it wouldn't take much to take that last step, to close the space between them, to wrap her arms around his neck. Her gut tightened and her skin tingled.

She sucked in a deep breath, let it out slowly. Then she met his gaze again. "Have a good night. Thanks for the Tequila."

"Thanks for the Mexican food."

He hesitated just a moment longer, then stepped back and out the door. She didn't watch him go to the elevator. She firmly closed the door and went to get ready for work.

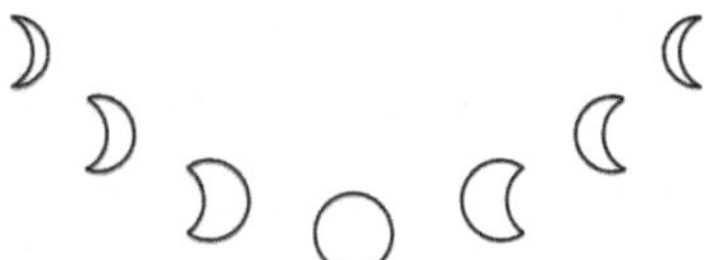

ana's Cauldron was Angie's home away from home. From its funky Village location amidst other unique boutiques, to the ground floor ode to all things pagan, to the café on the second floor that carried her favorite tea and some excellent sandwiches, to the rooms on the third floor where she met clients and did her readings. The owners were delightful witches, careful to look after their employees, the full-time employees were kind and generous, and the other psychics were fun and supportive.

The place worked for Angie on so many levels. She felt as comfortable here as she did in her own apartment. Maybe more so. Which always made coming in to work a delight rather than a chore. Not much more a person could ask for than actually enjoying their work.

She stopped at the register on her way in to say hi to Laura Fuentes. Laura had been at Dana's since the sixties, when the store had first opened. She was as much a part of the store as its glass cabinets filled with crystals and tarot cards and the posters of various world goddesses on the walls.

As usual, she wore bell bottom jeans, a flowing pagan shirt, this one decorated with little flowers, and her brown leather choker embossed with a pentagram, a little shark's tooth hanging down from the leather. The choker had been a present from friends when she'd first come out as trans in the early seventies, before her transition. The shark's tooth was a recent addition she'd bought in a cheap jewelry store a few blocks away—though she liked to tell costumers a shark she'd communed with in the Pacific gave it to her. She had her steel gray hair pulled up into a bun today instead of the usual thick braids, a style Angie always thought did great things for her cheekbones.

The scent of patchouli permeated the air at Dana's, at least on the main floor, but Laura's little section of the store, behind the checkout counter, boasted an undercurrent of sage from the smudging she'd just finished.

"Keeping the place clean, I see," Angie said with a smile, nodding to the remains of the sage sticks burning in a little green clay container lined with sand. The smoke curled into the air, visible against the muted orange light from a lava lamp sitting just behind it.

"We've had a lot going through here in the last month," Laura said, leaning against the counter and crossing her arms. "Not just that fellow walking with the demon a few weeks ago."

Angie winced. The situation that had brought Sebastian back into her life had also brought a human carrying a demon inside him into Dana's. And Angie had not been happy at all about that. Laura had been assuring her ever since that she was all right and that seeing the demon's aura hadn't done anything bad to her. Laura's ability to see and read auras was unmatched, but Angie still worried.

"Anything I can help with?" she asked. She'd been responsible, obliquely, for a demon managing to get into Dana's. She felt a deep need to balance that with help where she could.

"Nothing you need to worry about," Laura assured. "Just a few customers with hinky auras looking for the kind of magic books we don't carry. And a woman who managed to hide her aura from me, who's presence was a little strange, I guess."

"She hid her aura from you? That's..." She was going to say unprecedented, but it wasn't entirely. Laura was very good. Reading auras was her strongest skill. But there were a few people who could hide even from her. It had happened a few times without any of it necessarily meaning anything. Still, after the last few weeks, and the day she was in the middle of, she was edgy and seeing danger in every little thing.

"Did the woman say or do anything to bother you?" she asked.

Laura shook her head. "Just wandered around, looking at things. Asked about the readings upstairs but didn't go up or book anything. Bought a package of Frankincense sticks and some red candles." Laura shrugged. "She was friendly enough. But she hid her aura really well, from the moment she stepped into the store. Like she knew she'd need to. Some people are like that."

Angie frowned a little, but she let it go. In a store that catered to all things witchy and pagan, a lot of different kinds of people came through here. Most of them were harmless. And the owners had a special circle set around the place to help discourage those who meant harm from even coming inside. It wasn't full proof, of course. Especially since they were a storefront open to the public—they couldn't have their protections and wardings keep everyone out or they wouldn't have a business. The circle discouraged those with ill intent and made being inside the store uncomfortable for them.

Most of the time, that was enough to keep dangerous people out. From Laura's description, this woman was comfortable here, even if she kept her aura blocked. So she likely didn't mean harm. Probably just someone powerful who didn't want to freak anyone out. Dana's got as many ordinary mundane humans and magicless witches as it did people with actual magic. A powerful witch keeping things low key made sense.

Something about the woman still poked at an instinct for Angie, but since she couldn't pinpoint the reason for her unease, she let it go.

"You've got room four tonight," Laura said nodding toward the wooden staircase at the rear of the store, the little neon sign next to it pointing up to the café, and a wooden sign under that directed people to the third floor for reading rooms.

"Thanks." She headed up, sliding between the tables stacked with books and candles and incense pyramids.

She paused on the second floor to get a to-go cup of tea, something to offset the single shot of Tequila. She wasn't feeling the alcohol anymore, even a little bit, but she preferred to ensure she was clear headed for readings. She owed her clients her full attention and that included not being sleepy from food and alcohol. A psychic drifting off to sleep in the middle of a reading would be bad.

The cafe was busy enough, people hiding from the colder weather outside, stalling before a late dinner reservation, or treating themselves to tea and desert after an early dinner. Angie liked being here this time of night. When it was dark outside and the Village came to life, even on a cold autumn night. There were only a couple more weeks until Halloween. She couldn't wait for that, and for the parade.

So long as her situation with the demon hunters didn't interfere.

She passed Bianca and Rachel, two of the other psychics, on the way up to the third floor and paused to exchange hugs and greetings. Bianca was a bouncy, curvy blonde, who's personal life was an ever-revolving door of happy men and enthusiastic appetites. Her "uniform" of flowing black velvet and silk skirts, and a black bodice sinched tight enough to push her curves to extremes, made her pale skin paler in the dim lighting on the stairs to the third floor. Her jewelry jingled as she hugged Angie.

Rachel was a study in contrasts to Bianca tonight, dressed in a flowing white gown that slipped elegantly across her subtle curves and brought out a glorious glow in her dark brown skin. She had a white scarf wrapped around her head, keeping her long braids tucked up, and the style showed off her perfect cheekbones and long neck. Her jewelry was less jingly than Bianca's, consisting of chunky, smooth woods, and blocks of colored glass.

Both women's makeup was dramatic and perfect, Bianca wearing a signature smokey-eye, Rachel a mauve lip color that popped even in the low light.

Clients expected the dim lighting on the third floor. And their psychics to look like psychics. So they all dressed more dramatically for work. But where Bianca favored the black and dynamic materials even on her off time, and Rachel went in for trendy, modern clothes when she wasn't working, Angie preferred jeans or business casual to the flowing skirts and poet shirts she wore for work.

"Busy tonight," Rachel said, nodding back up the stairs. "We've had a bumper crop of people coming in for spontaneous readings."

"Guess we get to keep our jobs a bit longer," Angie said with a grin.

"You still seeing that delicious hunk you had here a few weeks ago?" Bianca asked, her eyebrows raised. "Haven't seen him around."

"Oh, who is this? I missed him?" Rachel leaned in a little for the gossip.

Angie sighed. "He's still around. I'm not *seeing* him. Technically. It's complicated." Very very complicated.

"Huh." Rachel straightened and gave Angie a look. "Like that, is it?"

"Mm hmm," Bianca said. "Got that last time, too. Complicated."

"I don't want to talk about it," Angie said.

"Fine. When you do, we're here, though," Rachel said with a wink. "I'm sure the entire coven will be delighted to hear all about your complicated personal life." She chuckled and glanced at Bianca with a knowing look.

"My personal life is not complicated," Bianca said. "It's quite straightforward and simple. It's just always on the move."

"And so are the men in your life," Rachel said.

"But they always leave happy."

"And exhausted," Angie added.

Bianca just grinned. Angie wasn't sure she'd ever known anyone who so fully and completely embraced life like Bianca, and it never ceased to awe her.

They continued on to the café and Angie went upstairs to get ready for her first client. She only handled drop-ins when she had space in her schedule, but tonight her time was filled with scheduled regulars. She liked that, though. New clients, or spontaneous drop-ins, could be a more draining experience. Most of her regulars were more interested in talking and counseling than future predictions. And since Angie had gotten a psychology degree in college and had considered traditional counseling as a career option, she was happy to accommodate her clients. Her ability to touch them and read where they were in life and what their real underlying problems were helped a lot too, enabling her to give them some solid advice for handling their difficulties.

Room four was one of the smaller rooms, which Angie liked, the center taken up by a round wooden table large enough to seat four comfortably but no more. The chairs were wooden but topped with thick black velvet cushions embroidered with stars and moons in silver thread. The entrance was covered with multi-colored beads that gave the room privacy and yet ensured those inside weren't completely cut off from the outside hallway. The owners believed in safety for their employees. That included a camera on this level to record people coming in and out, and reading rooms that didn't allow a psychic to be completely closed off from potential help.

One of the reasons Angie had taken this job was the fact that the owners were both real witches with actual magic who used magic *and* technology to look after the safety of their people. They were also old friends with Angie's earliest mentor, Esmerelda, so the personal recommendation helped.

At the time she took the offered job, she'd also needed to get away from New Mexico. From Sebastian. From the demon hunting world. She run away to New York City. Not for fame and fortune, but for a quiet life reading palms in Greenwich Village. Her hope for a quiet life had gone out the window, though, thanks to the demon hunter council. And she resented that mightily.

But she had to let that outside world worry go or she wouldn't be able to do a good job for her clients tonight. After setting her purse and coat aside, she sat at the table and took a few deep breaths as she settled and prepared for her first client, a man named Sam who had a complicated family life and who just liked someone to listen to him when he talked. Angie wanted to ensure Sam had her full focus and attention, so she made the effort to clear her thoughts in the same way she would before working big magic.

The person who stepped through the beads a few minutes later, though, was not Sam.

Angie blinked at the man a few times, frowning. He was tall, slim, dressed in a black suit but no tie. His black hair was slicked tight to his scalp and collected at the base in a low tail, his skin was pale, his dark eyes glittered slightly in the dim overhead light. She didn't recognize him. And he didn't look like their usual drop-ins—those were mostly tourists and locals looking to try something new. He definitely wasn't one of her regulars.

"I think you have the wrong room," she said in her most professional tone.

"Angela Jordan?"

She stiffened, something in his voice putting her on alert. No one here called her Angela. "Yes?"

"I've been sent to talk with you."

"Sent by whom?" she asked.

He stepped farther into the room, closer to the table, and Angie got a better look at his eyes.

And the hint of red in their depths that could have been written off as a trick of the light if she didn't know better.

But she knew better.

"You're a demon hunter."

CHAPTER TEN

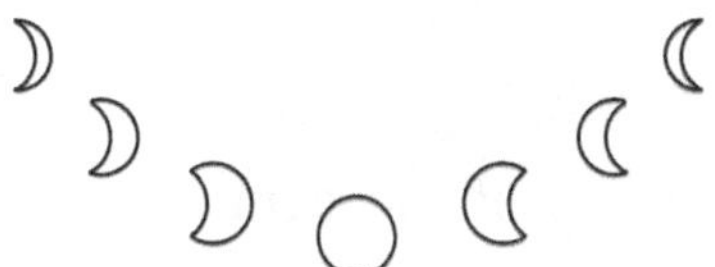

Angie sighed loudly because she was irritated beyond all measure and also a little nonplussed that someone like this had gotten past Laura—hunters could hide their aura from her, but she recognized them even faster that way. And Laura wouldn't have let this guy come up and ambush Angie. Not without good reason. She had either been too busy with something or someone to notice him walk past, or she'd assumed Angie would want to talk to him.

Either way, she blamed the man standing in her reading room for that.

"What the hell are you doing here? This is my place of work, and I'm working. You need to get out of here. We'll speak when I'm ready. Who sent you? The council?"

She kept her voice low, but she was so monumentally angry she was hissing her words.

He blinked once when she mentioned the council out loud. A reaction she wasn't sure he meant to give her.

"May I sit?" the man asked, gesturing to the seat across from her.

"No. I have a client due any minute. One of my regulars who's a very nice man and I don't want you here when he arrives. State your business and go."

He paused a moment longer.

"My name is Jacob."

She nodded. Most of the demon hunters only went by their first names. Especially the older ones. She wasn't even sure Aidan remembered the family name she'd had before becoming a demon hunter. Sebastian said he remembered his, but he didn't use it.

"I'm not from the council."

That was interesting. She waited in silence, staring at him. Waiting him out.

He lifted a brow at her silence. Then said, "I have an interest in you…not becoming a hunter."

"Talk to the council about that. They're the ones who want me to be one."

"You've decided to take them up on the offer, though."

"What makes you say that? And it wasn't an 'offer' so much as a threat."

Another slow blink. "You went on a hunt with Sebastian today."

"Just in the wrong place at the wrong time."

She noticed he wasn't whispering or keeping his voice

particularly low. But this wasn't the kind of conversation he'd want just anyone to overhear—especially the mundane humans filling this place. And since she'd warned him she had a client due at any moment, she had to assume he realized there were humans just beyond the beaded curtain. If he wasn't worried about keeping his voice low, that meant he was exerting will to keep the conversation private, to keep anyone outside from overhearing them. That was as interesting as his slow blinks.

"You worked with Sebastian for years."

"Two years. Yes."

"You'll work with him again."

"How is this your business?"

"As I said, I have an interested in you remaining…out of our world."

"Ha. So do I. An interest in not dying. But since *your world* keeps dragging me back, I'd like to know why you're personally interested in keeping me out? And why aren't you telling this to the council?"

"I have. And my personal interest in this is…nothing you need to worry about."

She snorted. "Right."

"It doesn't directly concern you."

"Then why do I feel like I'm smack in the middle of it?"

"Peripherally. But a distraction."

"Again, you need to take this up with the council." Whatever *this* was.

She'd never really thought of the demon hunter world as

particularly political because most of them were such loners. They only gathered once a year, rarely worked together, and outside of the mentoring period where one demon hunter ensured a new hunter could survive long enough to learn the job, they did the job alone. There hadn't seemed any need for politics.

But then, she hadn't known the council existed until just a few weeks ago. If there was a governing body, and power was involved in being on that governing body, then of course there was politics and machinations and all the crap she avoided by being a solitary witch. She'd never been particularly keen on coven politics either.

"I'm asking you to turn down demon hunting and continue on as you have. It's what you want anyway."

"I'm not being given a choice in the matter."

He smiled. A surprisingly charming smile. "I doubt you can be forced to do anything you don't want to do."

Little did he know. "What makes you say that?"

"You're too powerful to be pushed around."

"Flattery doesn't work on me." And she had been forced to do things she didn't want to do. Starting with leaving Sebastian. But that wasn't something she was going to mention to a stranger with an agenda.

"Interesting," Jacob said.

"What?"

"You really aren't vain about your power. You do realize how…extensive it is, don't you?"

"Do you?" She knew herself and her power well enough. She also knew that all her mentors since Esmerelda had been telling her she was holding back and could do more than she thought. But there was no way this stranger could know that.

"Extensive enough you don't have to worry about the council."

"Interesting," she echoed him.

"What?"

"That you'd tell me that while trying to convince me to defy your council."

He blinked slowly again when she said "your council" and she wondered at that. He had to realize those slow blinks were telling her things. Didn't he? A hunter couldn't survive without complete control of their will, and by will, complete control of their body and the impressions they gave others. Was he attempting to give her information? Or attempting to make her think she was reading his body language?

To what end?

The whole conversation was strange.

"It's important that you don't attempt to become a demon hunter," he said, his voice lower now, more intent. "It's not your calling."

Damn right about that.

"And it will be better for everyone if you remain… separate from us. You'll survive longer."

Ah, but wasn't that the point? To kill her when she didn't have the will to beat a demon in a fight? "Was that a threat, Jacob?"

"Not from me."

"You think I don't know at least some of the council wants me dead?"

Unlike before, he didn't do the slow blink this time. In fact, his expression remained exquisitely neutral. No response or reaction to that statement at all.

Got him! The blinks had been on purpose. An attempt to make her think she was reading him.

"Then you understand why refusing their job offer is imperative."

"They aren't taking no for an answer. Any suggestions on how exactly I'm supposed to turn them down?"

"Stay away from demons?"

"Ha. Ha."

"They'll likely argue at your meeting with them tomorrow."

Either Sebastian had already set up the meeting, as she'd asked, or Jacob was guessing. The fact that he might know there was a meeting before she did was irritating. But in this conversation, she had to assume he knew how she'd react to his statement and was trying to manipulate her.

Damned manipulations and machinations. She hated this shit.

"What will they argue about?"

"You."

"What do you expect me to do, Jacob?" she asked. "Spit it out soon, because my client is likely here." Probably confusedly standing in the corridor trying to remember what he was doing here and where he was going thanks to Jacob's will. That thought irritated her further.

"Demon witches can't be hunters," Jacob said, his voice

lowered more. "Remember that. It's better for you to stick to witchcraft."

Sebastian had said the hunters didn't use the word demon witch. That that was something Carmen had probably made up. The hunters called people like her realm splitters. The fact that Jacob used demon witch instead made her heart pound for reasons she couldn't pinpoint. She took him using that phrase as a threat. On a bone deep, lizard brain level. And she had no idea why.

"I'll let you get back to work," he said, and his whole demeanor changed. His shoulders relaxed, his expression lightened, the intensity she'd only barely noticed to that point vanished. Suddenly, he was a relatively ordinary man in a suit, looking around like he'd walked into the wrong room. "Thanks for hearing me out."

He pushed the beads aside and left without looking back. Leaving her staring after him with a sense of dread tightening her chest.

She had to take several long, deep breaths to settle herself as Sam stepped into the room a moment later, looking befuddled, his glasses reflecting the dim light as he glanced around the room.

"Sorry I'm late," he said, taking the seat across from her. "Not sure what happened. Thought I was on time, but then…" He lifted his hands and glanced around as if he'd find the explanation for being late in the corners or hanging on the walls.

"Don't worry. It's not a problem. We'll still get the full

session in." She smiled, forcing herself into the moment so she could give Sam the time he deserved.

But the encounter with Jacob hovered in the back of her mind.

She had to talk to Sebastian before the meeting tomorrow.

Things were a lot more complicated than they'd guessed.

CHAPTER ELEVEN

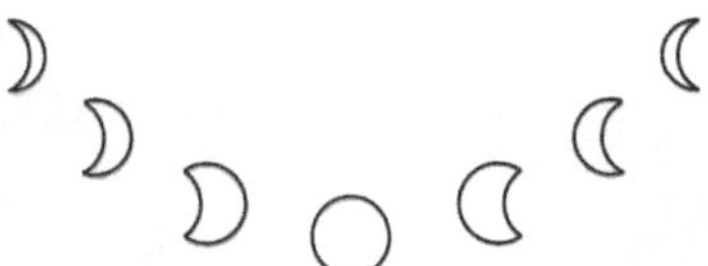

During a break between clients, Angie went back downstairs to get a tea and talk to Laura. The demon hunter had slipped past while Laura had been ringing up a customer, but because he was who he was, and Angie had been hanging out with one of his kind of late, Laura had assumed he wasn't an issue.

Laura was very careful not to actual use the words demon or hunter. For which Angie was very grateful. While they stood in the middle of a pagan shop with books on all manner of witchcraft and otherworldly stuff, and while some of these people would absolutely know that demons were real, it was one of the few topics Dana's didn't cater to. Another reason Angie loved it here. There were theological books that contained references to demons. Books about myths and legends where some of the main deities were referred to as demons. But no books on demonology. No aids for summoning demons. It was a personal quirk of the owners to leave all the demon side of things to other stores. And Angie was forever grateful to them for it.

So carefully not mentioning demons when there were mundanes who could overhear was good.

Fortunately, this demon hunter hadn't actually been trouble. At least not yet. But now she had to decide if everything he'd been telling her was some sort of complicated hunter political scheme, or if there was another motive.

"Fucking politics," she muttered.

Laura snorted. "Gets into everything doesn't it? Like sand when you're fucking on the beach."

Angie laughed. She considered Laura a moment. "My… my aura reading is pretty bad. I can manage vague impressions. Sometimes. But nothing like you. Would you be willing to teach me how to get a better handle on it?"

"You sure? The touch isn't enough?"

She thought about the hunter, and how he wouldn't have touched her, knowing who and what she was. "Aura reading means I don't have to get too close to someone."

"It's never going to be as precise as your touch. And we both know there are people who can hide their auras."

Angie heard the silent *like demon hunters* at the end of that sentence.

"But I can teach you how to improve it. At least how to bring it more under your control, more consistent." She tiled her head. "You've never wanted to learn aura reading before. This something to do with…with them?"

She leaned against the counter carefully, cradling her to-go cup of Earl Grey tea as she looked around the ground floor at the dozen people shopping. It was getting later, and things were quieter now, but a lot of the pagan community that frequented Dana's were night owls, so there was always someone here right up to closing, even on late closing nights on the weekends.

"I just think it'll be a useful skill to build," she said after a moment. "Never want to stop learning, right?"

Laura smiled. "You get old if you stop learning."

"So you don't mind teaching me?"

"No. We can start whenever you're ready. My next day off is Saturday."

It was Thursday so that would work. So long as the meeting with the council tomorrow didn't turn into a massive clusterfuck. Which wasn't guaranteed.

"Saturday should work so long as nothing goes…wrong."

"Given your current visitors, yeah. We'll keep it flexible."

"Thank you."

They chatted a few more minutes, then Angie gave Laura a quick hug and went back upstairs to get ready for her last two clients. She should have asked Laura to help her improve her aura reading skills a long time ago. It was a useful ability, didn't require Angie get too close to someone she wanted to read, and Laura was superb at it. Until just recently, Angie hadn't thought it a skill she really needed to work on. Practicing spellcraft took enough time and focus already. But she was starting to think if the demon hunters wouldn't leave her alone one way or the other, if she was going to have to spend time in their world again, having as many skills in her repertoire as possible could only help her.

And not just with demons.

HER LAST TWO READINGS WENT WELL, NO PROBLEMS, NO more demon hunters arriving. She was exhausted and ready to go home by the time she left, though. The day had been a lot longer, and involved a lot more than she'd expected when she'd decided to treat herself to the planetarium that morning.

Had it only been that morning? Seemed like days ago now.

The chilly air cooled her cheeks when she stepped outside, a pleasant contrast from Dana's warm interior. She sucked in a deep breath, pulling in the distinct scents of tarmac, traffic, and the pizza restaurant across the narrow street. She walked home, as she did most nights after work, letting the strain of sitting and listening for so many hours go, shaking out her muscles. The area was quiet enough, fewer people walking along the narrow side street than there had been earlier in the evening. A lot of the stores and boutiques were closed or closing. Street lights turned everything white-ish yellow.

She liked walking the Village at this time of night. The little spark spell that came to her so easily and instinctively now was a good deterrent to anyone trying to hassle her or steal her bag, and after two years here, she knew the people working the places that stayed open late on her route home, like the family-owned bodega, and the parking garage attendant who had the night shift, and the tattoo parlor's three artists, and the weekend bouncer at the drag club. People she could go to and at least stand around talking to if she got into trouble.

Not that the mundane humans could help her with any magical trouble that might step into her life. But they were helpful against ordinary human trouble. And she only had magical trouble now because of the demon hunters.

When she reached her apartment building, she half expected to see Sebastian waiting for her. The mixture of disappointment and relief were strong enough to make her a little shaky as she unlocked the outer door and let herself into the building lobby. She couldn't think properly when he was around. He was too distracting. Too…familiar. And yet after being away from him for a year and a half, she was also a little edgy around him. As if being with him was new. Like in the beginning, when she'd wanted him, but wasn't sure that was a good idea, and wasn't sure if the feelings were returned, and didn't know what to do with her hands when she was with him.

She knew her feelings were returned now. But she still didn't know what to do with her hands around him—mostly because keeping her hands to herself was so difficult.

She'd missed him over the last year and a half. Missed him enough that she wasn't even mad at him anymore for coming back into her life, for dragging her back into the hunters' world. She hated this world, but she loved Sebastian.

Still. And she had no idea how to deal with that. How to make those two things work. She'd tried before. All it had gotten her was almost dead.

Inside her apartment, she changed out of her work clothes —the long, black velvet skirt covered in moons and stars and the white embroidered shirt that slipped off her shoulders were quite comfortable, really. While her work clothes weren't to her personal aesthetic, they weren't hard to wear. But when she was home, she wanted to live in her own, everyday clothes. And in this case, that included less jingly jewelry, flannel pajama pants, and a t-shirt.

She left on her little hanging moon earrings—they'd been a present from her brothers, a nod to her love of astronomy more than her witchiness—and her pentagram bracelet which she never took off. But everything else associated with work-witchcraft went into the laundry basket, the closet, or back into the appropriate drawer. She took a quick shower to rinse off the day. Slipped into her pajamas and t-shirt. Then went out to her altar.

The visit from the hunter tonight, the demon fight this afternoon... Something about the day was nagging at her instincts. She couldn't put her finger on what was bothering her. Just that she was more edgy and uneasy than she'd been when she'd gone to the planetarium that morning. She needed some sleep, because tomorrow was going to be a stressful day, but she also needed a few minutes to see if she could figure out what her instincts were trying to tell her.

Not that her instincts were always helpful in the demon

world. But the niggling of unease wasn't something she could ignore.

Part of her thought it was just the fact that she intended to meet with the hunter council tomorrow, tell them she'd let Sebastian train her. That was more than enough to get her nerves jumping. Especially since she knew at least one person on the council wanted her dead, and getting her to hunt demons was a very efficient way to accomplish that.

But some of the hunters—well Jacob anyway—wanted her to stay out of the demon world. A new and interesting twist that changed her perspective on the meeting tomorrow.

She dropped the large pillow she sat on at her altar onto the floor at the base of the small wooden table. It was more a cabinet than a table, with a few shelves underneath were she kept some of the fundamentals she needed—candles, salt, incense and incense holders, sand, a few pieces of wood and some smooth rocks. The things that she set out onto her altar depending on the work she did here.

Tonight, she didn't intend on working big magic. Tonight, she just wanted to open herself up to guidance. Her particular brand of psychic skills didn't lend itself to random visions not prompted by touch. And in this case, there was nothing to touch. Nothing precise enough for that. Just this vague unease that she was missing something important in all this.

An unfortunately familiar sensation around the hunters. And another reason she should not be doing the job.

But even without touch, if she set herself up right, she could still help her instincts dig up what they were trying to tell her. Not a vision proper, usually. But a little spark of insight to help.

Any help she could get leading into tomorrow was worth the effort.

She lit a single white candle in the center of the pentagram etched into the top of her wooden altar, the inlaid wooden five point star surrounded by a circle of the same inlaid wood reminded her of the charm on her bracelet. She set up a stick of incense, a blend of cedar, cinnamon, and sandalwood, inside a long, green porcelain holder next to the candle, letting the smoke rise and mix with the candle's gentle smoke. At the top of her pentagram she set a little wooden bowl of salt. At the base of the circle, a little stone bowl of water. For tonight's working, that's all she needed. Simple and bare but all the elements in place to aid her.

After a few calming breaths, she closed her eyes and mentally drew a protective circle around her workspace. She hadn't always made the effort to include this extra precaution. Especially when doing the kind of mediative work she intended to do tonight. But with demons back in her life, she didn't dare take any chances.

When she brought the ends of the circle together in front of her altar, she felt the sacred space snap closed, and in her mind's eyes, the flare of blue light as a cone of light rose over and around her, keeping her inside a space where she was safe from outside interference and dangers. She let that safety and comfort flow through her for several moments, keeping her eyes closed, soaking in the peace, filling her breath with the scents of candlewax and incense.

As the sense of safety and peace settled over her, she opened her eyes, staring directly at the candle's flame, her gaze soft. She murmured a soft prayer to the goddess to guide her. And then she whispered a spell for clear sight, her fingers twining into the pattern that set the spell.

A tingling along her shoulders and skin, that slight sensation of the fine hairs on her arms rising momentarily before settling, let her know the spell had worked.

She placed her hands on her knees and watched the flame through half-closed eyes. The dancing colors swirled into a blur of red and orange, the central yellow a brighter spark in the midst of that swirl. Then deeper into the colors, things darkened, took on a richer red color, then a deep purple. The colors moved from purple into black. A sense of the candle still, but her vision was all darkness.

No sounds. Not a first. Then a scream. Someone shouting her name. Sebastian? No. A woman. Not Aidan. Who was that? Then the chittering sound of approaching demons.

Temptation to snap out of the moment, to run from that chittering noise.

She forced herself to stay, to listen, wincing as the noise neared. Her heartbeat pounded. She let out a slow breath. She was safe inside her circle. This wasn't the approach of real demons. They couldn't meet her here. She was safe.

The chittering seemed so close it was right at her ear. If she turned her head, she'd see a demon, looking at her, smiling, ready to strike. She resisted, but fear coursed through her blood, and panic made her breathing harsh, her pulse hammering so hard she felt dizzy.

The chittering cut off abruptly. So fast, her ears rang in the silence. And then she saw a spark in the darkness. And a pattern forming from iridescent blue light. Light like magic, circling and crossing in long thing lines. A pattern like a web, a beautiful web dotted with pearls of blue light, glowing in the darkness. The web snapped into place, flaring, and then settled.

Then a red line started, near the center and spreading out the length of the web. From that single line, another line turned red, this one circling the entire web. Like an infection, seeping through the bright blue magic, the red moved into another line, and another ring.

But then stopped. Held. Didn't infect more of the web. And the whole thing settled into a glow that didn't change for long moments. A complex web. Her vision zeroed in on the center of it. She sat there, as she sat in her apartment, circled by blue, glowing with the magic. The line of red emerged from her chest, spiking out into the web, flowing out of her as freely as the magic did.

The image of herself in the center of the web opened her eyes suddenly, staring back at Angie as Angie stared at the woman that was her. Then the image change. No longer her own face looking at her, but…

"Carmen?"

The woman whose revenge schemes had started a cascade of trouble, a woman who was supposed to be, even now, in jail for…something. The hunter from the council had said Carmen would be taken care of, that she wouldn't get away.

Why was she in the center of Angie's web?

And why was she also surrounded in blue, with a line of red coming from her chest. The red pouring from Carmen was thicker though. As Angie watched, that red light turned viscous. Became blood. Poured from Carmen. Too much for a human. Too much blood. Coming from Carmen's chest. Spilling out of her mouth, leaking from her eyes. Filling the web. Turning the lines of blue light into rivers of blood.

The chittering started again. Right next to Angie's ear. She heard someone call her again, over the chittering. This time it was Sebastian. His voice a beacon in the red coating her vision.

She turned away from the chittering demon at one ear, looked for Sebastian in the opposite direction. There. Reaching for her. Pulling her out of the demon realm she'd been dragged into. His hand solid and real even as the demons surrounded her. Her hands scrambled against the glass sharp rocks under her, reaching for him, grasping his strong, warm hand. He dragged her out of the hellscape, pulled her back into the fresh air and sharp crisp scent of pine trees.

Angie took in a deep breath as that image faded, though the scent of pine sap stayed with her. She hadn't opened a breach using a pine tree. They didn't grow into the natural V shape she needed. It had been a different tree. But there had been pines in the woods, too.

Her vision darkened again, but she still felt Sebastian's arms around her, holding her as the blue spiderweb brightened around her again. She was no longer looking at it from outside, seeing herself in the center. Now she sat in the center, the web extending from her in all directions. And now she felt the magic, the flow of it. The power. And that red line coming from her chest, spearing out into her magic web. Only a single line, this time. Not blending into the blue magic. A single thread of red, separate but part of the complex design.

That red line felt powerful, too.

What would happen if she tugged that thread? What would happen if she took hold of it? Would the rest of the magical web react?

She could almost feel that reaction, just about sense it at the edge of her awareness. As she sat cross-legged in the middle of the web, the vibrations of it subtle against her skin. She was alone there, at the center of the web, but still sensed Sebastian's arms around her. She reached out and touched the line of red coming from her chest with one hand, keeping her other hand wrapped around a thread of blue.

A gentle tug, a mere tightening of her grip. The red line flared brightly.

Angie gasped. Power poured through her web, through the blue and red lines. The red didn't spread farther into the blue, but both now brightened, glowed so sharply she couldn't see around the glare. All blue with a streak of red through the center.

In the distance, demons chittered. Someone whose voice she couldn't place called her name. Power poured through her, until she thought she might explode from all the magic filling her up, soaking into her pores, into her bones, into her cells.

She breathed it in, held it. Ah. So much power. It felt amazing. And dangerous.

And *hers*.

Darkness snapped over her again, with a suddenness that left her breathless.

Then the flickering glow of the candle flame. Reds and oranges rising, normal shapes on her altar returning. The smoke from the incense mingling with the smoke from the candle. The little stone bowl of water at the base of the altar. The wooden bowl of salt at the top. The inlaid pentagram surrounded by a solid circle.

She let out a long, slow breath, her pulse slowly returning to normal. The feel of all that power that had poured into her, through her, still a tingling along her skin. But everything else was normal. Her home. Her flannel pajamas. Her altar. Her cushion. The sounds of traffic outside, a constant background hum even this late at night.

Blinking a few times, she let the real world settled around her again. Letting the normality of it reintegrate into her awareness.

She sent up a silent thank you to the goddess, to the elements who'd watched over her as she'd worked. Then she softly blew out the candle. Its smoke swirled and danced upward on invisible air currents. When those died away, and the last of the incense burned out so only a streak of ash and a bit of wooden stick remained in the holder, she cut her circle.

For a long time, she sat on her cushion and stared at her altar, not really seeing it. That was more of a vision than she'd been expecting. But not like what happened when she touched something and got a vision. Similar, she supposed. But not the same. The feel of it had been different. More… personal.

And it raised more questions than it had answered.

Which sort of defeated the purpose of the exercise.

She rolled her eyes. So much for clear vision. She cleaned off her alter, replacing everything to the drawers underneath the table except the candle and incense holder. Those she took to the kitchen sink where she'd leave them overnight, just in case. Living in an apartment building had made her hyper aware of fire dangers, so she was always over-the-top careful with her supplies after she'd spent time at her altar. The ash would go into the trash in the morning when she was sure it wouldn't spark. The candle would go back inside her altar then as well.

After she picked up her cushion and tucked it behind the altar, she closed the living room curtains, cutting off the light from the street below. A wave of exhaustion tugged at her. Not just the ordinary long-day-tiredness. Bone deep exhaustion like she'd been awake for days.

Her eyes were already blinking shut as she stumbled into her bed and collapsed onto her pillow, sinking into a deep sleep.

CHAPTER TWELVE

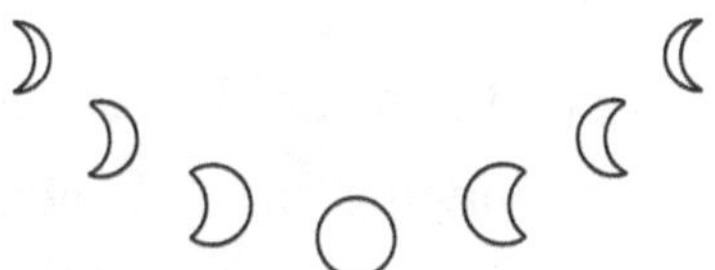

The combined sound of her phone alarm going off in the living room and someone knocking on her door brought Angie out of a groggy sleep. She groaned and desperately wanted to put the pillow over her head, ignore the knocking, and sleep more. What the hell time was it? Too early for visitors based on how sleepy she felt.

But the knocking was persistent. And a niggling of worry hit her. Something must be wrong. Maybe in the building? She pushed out of bed and stumbled to the door. Her head was a little woozy, like she'd had a binge night on Tequila. Not enough to be properly hung over but enough to feel the effects the next day.

Since she hadn't had any alcohol before bed, the sensation had to be down to lack of sleep.

Whoever was at the door would not stop knocking. "Hang on, hang on," she grumbled.

She worked through her locks and got the door open to see Sebastian standing there, a phone in one hand and a slightly frantic look on his gorgeous face.

He tucked his phone in his jeans pocket, took her face in his hands, and set his forehead against hers, breathing out a curse.

"Fucking hell, Ang. Are you okay?"

She blinked. "I was sleeping."

The feel of his hands on her, his forehead against hers sent a little shiver of longing through her. For a dizzying instant, she wanted to press against him, brush her lips against his, feel his fingers flex on her cheeks. His scent wrapped around her, clean soap and musk, and it was so familiar and so delicious, she sighed.

He leaned away from her, his chin tucked back as he held her gaze, pulling her away from the dangerous direction of her thoughts.

"It's three thirty in the afternoon," he said, his English accent prominent. "You're not answering your phone, returning my texts. And I've been knocking for twenty minutes."

She straightened a little and he dropped his hold on her. She missed the contact, but the information about the time of day distracted her. Three thirty in the afternoon? That was later than she'd expected. Especially given how sleepy she still felt. She'd gone to bed a little late she supposed, but not late enough to require sleeping all day. She hadn't looked at the clock before collapsing in bed, though. Maybe her spell work last night had taken longer than she'd thought? No, that wasn't right. The incense stick was just burning out when she'd come out of the vision. If she'd been under too long, the incense would have burned through and been cold. The candle burned lower.

"I could have been at work," she said, but she was looking past him, frowning.

"I tried Dana's when you wouldn't answer my texts," he said. "Can I come in? You took a few years off my life and I need to sit down."

She rolled her eyes but let him in because she was a little surprised, too.

"Are you hurt?" he asked.

"No, of course not. I could have been at a doctor's appointment, Sebastian. I could have been at the grocery store and forgotten my phone."

"I've been trying to reach you for four hours, Ang. At some point in that time you would have gotten back to me. No matter what you were doing." He looked at her a little closer. "Are you hung over?"

"Rude." She made a face.

That broke his scowl and he finally smiled a little. "You still look gorgeous. But there are circles under your eyes and you look a little rough."

"No benders. Not drunk. Not hung over. Didn't even have a drink." But she felt a little like she had.

And she definitely didn't feel like she'd gotten more than thirteen hours of sleep. She did sleep in after working a night session like she did yesterday, but she was still usually up by noon.

The feeling reminded her quite a lot of her early years formally studying witchcraft. The days when she'd push herself hard and use a lot of magic. Like a muscle, magic needed training, and it could be pushed too far. And in the early years, working most big magics left her drained and exhausted. In those days, she did sometimes sleep for thirteen or fourteen hours after doing something that pushed her abilities.

She rubbed her head, a faint headache behind her eyes also reminding her of those early days. When working big magic left physical side effects like headaches, not just exhaustion.

But all she'd done last night was use a clear-seeing spell. It wasn't the kind of spell that pushed her powers, her skill level. Even in the early years, clear-seeing wasn't the kind of spell that drained her or caused any physical side effects. It was basic and didn't require a lot of magic to make it work. In fact, witches without any innate magic could make a clear-seeing spell work.

"Fucking hell," she muttered, echoing Sebastian's earlier comment.

"What?" he asked. "You look like you need to sit down, too."

He set a hand to her lower back and guided her down the long hall past her bedroom door and into the open living room. She didn't protest. Her curtains were closed but bright autumn light still leaked in around the edges. She plopped down onto the couch, trying to think through what had happened last night, why she felt a magic hangover.

Sebastian quietly went to the kitchen and put the kettle on. Got down a couple of mugs and the tea boxes without having to ask where everything was. She might have been annoyed by that but she needed the tea and she was still too befuddled to care. At the moment, his familiarity with her home was good.

"I'm feeling…a magic hangover," she told him. Clarifying, "Like when I was young and pushed my magic too hard and it wore me out. When I did something big and it drained too much internal magic. I'd get exhausted, have to sleep, sometimes get a headache. But that hasn't happened in a long time." She had good control of her magic now, and she'd been training for most of her life, so her stamina and recovery was good, too. "And the spell I worked last night wasn't the kind of thing that should have drained me."

"Will you talk about it?"

"I can. Yes."

He nodded, then didn't ask more as he finished making them each a cup of tea—his a good quality English Breakfast that she kept on hand for sentimental reasons she wasn't going to admit to at the moment, hers an Earl Grey with a drop of milk and too much sugar for his snobby English taste. In the past, just to tease him and make him wince, she'd add even more sugar than she needed.

He handed her her mug then sat down on the couch next to her. "Tell me," he said.

She started with the spell work, and the vision she'd had. "I wasn't expected anything quite like a real and proper vision. Just some insights from my gut that I hadn't been able to see clearly. I wanted to understand what my instincts were trying to tell me."

"And do you now?"

"No! I've got more questions now than answers. And that's just irritating." She told him about the spiderweb and the line of red in it. "The power flare when I tugged that thread…" She shook her head. "I've never felt anything like that in real life before."

"You supposed that's why you feel like you do this morning? Why you're so exhausted?" He sipped his tea, then gave a little happy sigh at the flavor.

She smiled. She couldn't help it. "Such a tea snob," she murmured.

"I appreciate you have the good stuff around."

For him. But she wasn't going to say that out loud. "The vision shouldn't have had a physical effect, though," she said, answering his question. "My visions come with sights, sounds, sometimes smells. I get a lot of emotion in them. But even the future flashes don't drain me. None of it does." Bit like when she opened portals to demon realms. It took…no effort. It just happened. Like her visions.

And she was still half convinced there was something to that. Something that connected those two aspects of her nature and her powers. But she couldn't see what it was. She couldn't understand the connection.

She'd have to think about it more. Not another clear-seeing spell, though. Until she figured out what happened with this one, she was not going to risk draining herself again.

"The vision wasn't the only strange thing about yesterday." She told him about the hunter who'd cornered her at work, everything he'd said about not wanting her to become a hunter. "He introduced himself as Jacob. Anyone you know?"

Given how small the hunter community was, she'd be surprised if Jacob and Sebastian hadn't crossed paths before. Even if only at the annual history-keeping meet ups.

Sebastian nodded but his gaze was turned inward. He didn't immediately comment.

She waited him out, sipping the rest of her cooling tea. She was going to need another one of these. Maybe even something stronger like coffee. And food. Now that she was awake—though she was dragging enough she could have gone back to sleep—her stomach announced she'd gone too long without food and she would hear about it if she didn't put some protein into her system soon.

She stood, leaving Sebastian to think while she boiled the kettle again, made more tea, and hunted her cabinets and fridge for something to eat. She needed to go to the grocery store. The last few weeks had been... Chaotic was the most encompassing word. She had a few protein bars, two eggs, half a loaf of bread, and the usual condiments and canned goods that, combined, didn't really make a meal. She didn't even have any leftover Mexican food from last night's dinner —which felt a really long time ago now—because between her and Sebastian there was rarely any food left over. She dug out a protein bar. It would have to do for now. She could eat the eggs but there wasn't enough for Sebastian and that felt rude. He hated protein bars, so she was safe bolting that down without leaving him out of the meal.

By the time she'd finished the bar and making their second cups of tea, Sebastian was facing her again.

"Not the turn of events I expected," he said as she handed him his mug. "Things with the council have been complicated for a few years. But the most consistently agreed opinion between them has been that they want you... monitored. And brought into the fold."

"Jacob is on the council?" He'd said he wasn't, but she took everything a stranger said to her with a grain of salt and, in these cases, a touch of suspicion. She probably should have remembered that when she'd met Carmen for the first time.

"No, no. He's not. But he's been around a while. And is...influential among the other hunters. When he wants to be."

"So..." She narrowed her eyes as she took a sip of her now hot tea. "Probably there are more hunters who don't want me anywhere near demons." She couldn't blame them for that. She didn't want to be around demons either. Or demon hunters for that matter. Just one hunter really—well, technically two if she counted Aidan.

"I'm sure there are. Though most of them wouldn't talk to me about it."

"Why not?"

He met her gaze. "You have to ask?"

"Oh." She took a bigger gulp of tea. Let the awkward moment slip past because she didn't know what to say to the look in his eyes. Instead, she said, "Jacob implied I was a peripheral distraction. There's more going on there than just hunters not wanting me to be part of the group."

He nodded, but didn't comment.

"So… What do I do now?"

"Now. We go see the council. And try to get some answers."

From the council?

She snorted. Right.

CHAPTER THIRTEEN

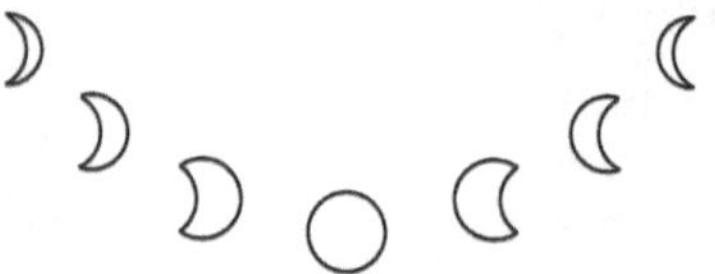

"I should have eaten more," Angie murmured as she straightened her jacket.

"I'll get you a kebab on the way home," Sebastian said.

She chuckled. She hadn't had a kebab in years. Not since Sebastian, even though there were carts and little restaurants all over the city where she could have. But the smells of them reminded her too much of her time with Sebastian, so she avoided that particular food. Avoiding things she liked because they reminded her of Sebastian seemed less important when he was standing right next to her, warm and delicious smelling and comforting.

Her stomach danced in nervous circles, which left her feeling a little nauseated. Between the nerves and her empty stomach, and her magic hangover, she wasn't in any shape for this meeting.

If she were smart, she'd turn and walk away now. Claim

she would see them tomorrow. Stall until she felt better. But she'd stall for weeks already. She needed answers. Any she could get. And she needed them sooner rather than later, magic hangover and empty stomach be damned.

They stood outside a relatively ordinary black painted door in an office building that was just one of many lining the streets of Midtown. It wasn't one that stood out for unique design. No Lipstick Building or Empire State here. Just an ordinary twenty story rectangle with a black glass façade and no distinct or interesting elements on the outside, squatting in the middle of the block. A pharmacy took up half the ground floor. A heavenly smelling coffee shop was open next door. An appetizing Italian restaurant across the street.

She'd veered toward that restaurant once they'd gotten out of the cab before she'd even thought about what she was here for. Her stomach grumbled at her for not heeding the call of garlic, tomatoes, and pasta. She really should have eaten more.

The door they stood in front of wasn't marked with any company logos or a name plate. This was a strictly commercial building. No apartments on any of the floors. According to the directory outside the elevator bank, there were a whole bunch of businesses in the building. Lots of doctors and a dentist and a few psychologists as well as the usual Something Financial, and Something Something Inc, all names that meant nothing to her and didn't particularly illuminate what the businesses actually did. She assumed the ones with "business" or "financial" tacked on to the end probably dealt with money. But that was the extent of her guesses.

This particular suite hadn't had a listing in the directory. And the door itself was so innocuous that she might have assumed it was just a storage closet. The only identifying feature was a little suite number at the base of the door. Fourteen zero one. Not a particularly ominous suite number either. No sulfur smells permeated the hall from beyond the door. No smells at all filled the hall except for the mild cleaning product used to keep things polished and dust free. Nothing magical or spooky leaked from behind the door.

The sheer innocuousness of the place gave her the creeps. Ordinary, harmless-looking, from the outside. But so aggressively unobtrusive—look over there! nothing to see here!—that she was edgy and suspicious and her nerves were jumping.

And she really needed to eat.

"I promise I'll take you to dinner after," Sebastian whispered. "Can you survive that long?"

She made a face. "I'm fine. I'll be fine. But I will eat an entire restaurant after this."

"Should have fed you first," he muttered.

She huffed out a laugh. "Let's get this over with."

"Still going to go along with their job?"

He hadn't asked her that again today, even with the new information about Jacob and whatever the other hunter's interest was in her not becoming a hunter. Sebastian hadn't asked if she was now going to refuse the work, if she'd changed her mind about anything to do with the council.

Which was good. Because right up to that very moment, she hadn't decided.

"I'm going through with my original plan." Do this to gather information. Decide what to do with that information once she had it.

Without knowing what the hunters knew about "demon witches"—and why Jacob had used that term but Sebastian hadn't heard anyone else use it—she couldn't plan farther than accepting the job. She needed to know what the hell was going on. Stay alive long enough to figure it all out. Then decide how to deal with it. All so she could go back to her witchy life reading people's futures and practicing her skills and *not* dealing with demons.

She ignored the final part of that decision tree—what to do about Sebastian.

Straightening her jacket, adjusting the strap of her huge purse over her shoulder where it angled across her chest, she took in a deep deep breath, let it out slowly, all the way, until she felt hollow. When she breathed in again, she nodded.

"Let's get this over with."

Sebastian opened the door for her, and to her surprise, it opened easily. Either that was a hunter trick, or the hunters didn't feel the need to keep the door locked. Could she have just opened it?

Could she have read something if she'd tried?

Door handles were tricky, and could be overwhelming if she opened to them, so probably better she hadn't tried.

The interior of the suite was just as ordinary and mundane as the exterior. No smells beyond faint cleaning products, the space was bright, with ordinary overhead florescent lights. A little too bright for Angie, a little too ordinary office workplace. There were a few windows opposite the door, adding some natural light to the open entryway, which helped keep the place from feeling claustrophobic.

Not that it was small and closed in. The entrance was large, with high ceilings, plain white walls, and a grayish blue carpet—the industrial kind that wasn't particularly soft and comfy looking, but it did cushion the sound of footsteps. There wasn't anything else in the open entryway. Just a lot of space. No desk or receptionist or seats. It almost looked like the place was still being set up and they hadn't gotten around to adding some of the internal features yet. There was a single, closed door to her left, two halls branching off from the entryway, and that was it.

"Do we wait for someone to come get us, or do you know where we have to go?" For reasons that felt a little silly, she kept her voice low. Even then, there was a faint echo. The carpet helped, but the room was so open and empty, an echo was inevitable.

"Thank you for coming," a voice from the hallway said, answering Angie's question.

"Not sure I was given a choice," Angie said, not speaking loudly, but not whispering now either.

The woman who came around the corner wasn't the sort to stand out in a crowd. She was average height, average weight, maybe a little thicker around the middle. She was dressed in black work slacks and a button down, pale blue shirt with a very starched collar. Her heels were low, easy to walk in, very professional. Her steel gray hair was pulled back into a braid and wrapped into a bun at the base of her neck. Her light tan skin showed a few creases around her eyes and mouth. Her age wasn't obvious, but she gave the impression of older rather than younger, and the impression of control rather than grace.

She was the kind of woman you might expect in a place like this, an office still in the middle of becoming an office. And until you looked into her dark brown eyes closely, you wouldn't guess there was anything particularly interesting about her.

But that little glow of red in the depths of her eyes was hard to miss, even under the florescent lights.

"Angela. Sebastian." She greeted in her deep, smokey voice. No smile or show of any emotion with the greeting.

Angie had expected her to say something about how long it had taken, or how they should have been here weeks earlier. This was the hunter who'd insisted Angie meet with the council. A council member herself. This was the hunter who'd taken the bone lanterns into custody, to ensure they were safe. And she was the one who had issued the ultimatum that was the reason Angie was here.

She'd also never given Angie her name. And neither had Sebastian.

She returned the greeting with a slight nod, since she didn't know the woman's name, and kept her mouth shut. If the hunter wasn't going to bring up that Angie had been stalling, Angie wasn't going to draw attention to it either.

"If you'll follow me." The hunter gestured down the hall she'd just come from. "The council is waiting."

Angie exchanged a look with Sebastian, but she couldn't tell what he was thinking. He had remained carefully quiet, too. She wasn't sure if that was good or bad. They followed the hunter without comment. But Angie did start murmuring a spell under her breath, a little protection circle ready to snap into place if she needed it.

"You won't need it," the woman said, without looking back. "You aren't in danger here."

Angie didn't comment. She didn't stop setting up her spell either.

When she had the spell one gesture away from being able to initiate it, she turned her attention to her surroundings. Not that there was much to see.

The hallway had the same gray-blue carpet. There were a few closed doors. No windows or glass looking inside the closed rooms. The soft pearl-gray colored walls were hung with non-descript landscape paintings, nothing that looked fancy or expensive. Although, to be fair, Angie wouldn't know. She spent a lot more time at the American Museum of Natural History than she did at the Met. Her art knowledge was sadly lacking.

Because all the doors were closed and there weren't any windows into the offices—or whatever they were—the hallway was lit only by the overhead florescent insets running the entire center of the ceiling. Bright and neutral. Everything was very bright. And very neutral.

She was tempted to touch something on the way past, one

of the door handles specifically, just to see what she could pick up. If she could pick up anything. Given these were demon hunters she was dealing with, she couldn't be sure they'd leave anything of themselves on the door knobs. Which would leave her with nothing to read.

But it was still tempting.

The hunter led them to the end of the long hallway and another ordinary-looking closed door with nothing about it to distinguish it from the others around them. It was just a door with a little metal knob. No signs or numbers. No lock to keep others out. Just…a door.

The woman didn't open it right away. She stood before it for a beat longer than would have been necessary if there really wasn't anything special about it, and then she turned the knob easily and swung the door open, stepping aside for Angie and Sebastian to enter first.

Angie gave her a look, ducking her chin. Right. She was really going into that room first.

The woman shrugged and passed through the open doorway ahead of her. Sebastian set a hand to Angie's lower back. Next to her ear, he murmured, "Still time to change the plan. We can back out."

"If that were true, we wouldn't be here in the first place," she murmured back.

They followed the woman into the room, Sebastian sticking close to Angie. The knee-jerk, almost instinctive, reassurance that gave her was a little humbling. She didn't pull away from him, though.

The room was larger than it looked from the outside. And

darker. Not dark. But not the headache-inducing, artificial office brightness of the hallway. She couldn't see the source of light at first because the it took her eyes a moment to adjust to the dimmer room. When she could see better, she noticed a curtained window with the curtains drawn tight, only a little light leaking around the edges. More light came from a series of soft lamp sconces on the walls around the perimeter of the room.

The carpet here gave way to polished, inlaid hardwood floors. There was decorative, square-panel, dark wood wainscotting, and above it the walls were painted a peach color that took on a pink hew in the dim light. Fancy white crown molding above that. And though they weren't on, there were two large crystal chandeliers hanging from the ceiling, a ceiling that was higher than it should have been relative to the hallway and the entryway.

Across from the door was a large fireplace. The kind of stone monstrosity a full grown human could actually step into. It was surrounded by gargoyles and other things etched into the gray, polished stone that she didn't look at too closely because she was afraid she'd see demon faces. And for a moment, looking at the fireplace from the edge of her vision, she got the impression of a gateway.

Which was interesting.

In front of the fireplace were scattered six large leather chairs. Just the sort of thing she might expect to see in front of a fireplace in a manor house or large estate. Two of the chairs faced the fireplace directly. The other four were angled so Angie could see three of them were occupied and one wasn't. The woman who'd led them into the room sat in the empty chair without a word.

No one invited Angie or Sebastian to sit.

Angie wasn't sure she wanted to sit anyway. Especially so close to that fireplace which was, she was certain, not a real fireplace. She did want to get close enough to touch it, to see what it really was, and she was sorry she hadn't started her aura reading lessons with Laura yet. Laura didn't read objects, just people, but Angie thought given her innate skills, she might get the techniques to transfer to objects. She'd need to test that theory, though. Up to now, her aura reading skills were so minimal as to be non-existent. And if she couldn't read people, reading objects through an aura would be impossible.

Still, she was tempted to walked to the fireplace and touch the large stone mantle just to see what the four seated people in the room would do.

Instead of causing an immediate uproar, she took a beat to study the others—obviously members of the council.

Frankly, she'd been expecting more of them. She wasn't sure why. But she'd expected this demon hunter council to be larger. To have more than four people on it. She glanced at the two empty seats. Maybe it did. Maybe these were just emissaries of the larger group, since she wasn't technically a demon hunter yet and therefore shouldn't even know the council existed.

Maybe the others were on the other side of that fireplace.

The woman who'd accompanied them from the lobby gave a good indication of what the others would present. All of them were dressed in business casual—slacks, button-down shirts, mostly in dark, neutral colors with sharp creases and starched collars.

The man sitting next to their escort had black hair feathering back from his face with a streak of gray coming away from his left temple. His eyes were nearly black in the dim light. His skin tone pale brown. Like the woman, he wasn't too handsome or too distinctive or too anything in particular. Except for the gray streak in his hair, he was a relatively ordinary looking human. She couldn't even see the flash of red in the depths of his eyes. Which was interesting.

He gave her a brief nod, but his expression was as neutral as his overall look.

Across from him, sat another woman. She had sharp features and white-blond hair styled in a short bob that cut across her jawline. Her blue eyes showed the hint of red more distinctly than the hunters with brown eyes, a little bit harder to pretend it was a trick of the light. But the flashes of red were muted and faint. She wore more makeup than the other woman, her lips a brighter red shade, her lashes extravagantly long. But other than that, she was as ordinary looking as the others. Like a woman doing the best with what she had but not the sort to turn heads on the streets. Precisely the kind of look hunters cultivated.

The person sitting next to the blond woman gave the impression of being a little older than the others. With creases around dark brown eyes and bracketing a soft mouth. Dark brown hair swept back into a short, simple braid. The hint of red in their eyes a little more obvious. They were the only one wearing jewelry—a simple gold necklace and three gold rings on their long-fingered hands. Paler than the others, they wore no makeup either. And rather than the neutral expression of the others, this hunter smiled a little before nodding a greeting to Angie.

Angie returned all of their faint greetings without a word. Waiting for one of them to speak first. Blinking at them each slowly as they sat silently, probably to see if she'd start the conversation. She was a witch whose spells took time to build. She'd trained in psychology at college and worked with jumpy clients all the time. She was patient. And she knew they were playing a game with their silence. One she didn't intend to lose.

She didn't smile when one of the hunters spoke first. But it was a close thing.

"We're sorry the others couldn't make the meeting," the man with black hair said, gesturing at the two empty chairs. "They've been called away."

She gave a little nod, though she wanted to ask how many "others" there were—just two to fill the empty seats? Or more? She wanted to ask a lot of things all at once. Instead, she kept her tongue. Growing up with two brothers had taught her a lot about the power of silence. As much as her psychology work had.

"You know why you're here?" the blond woman asked.

She nodded again, meeting the woman's gaze but remaining silent. This was their meeting. Time for them to give a little instead of demanding so much from her.

"We have a lot to discuss," the black-haired man said.

More silence. She wanted to wave a hand for them to get on with it. But she let out a slow breath and held on to her patience. She also needed them to reveal themselves. And her silence would get that.

Finally, the woman with the steel-gray hair grunted an irritated noise. "This isn't a game," she said, looking at Angie.

Angie raised her brows.

"We're here to discuss you becoming a hunter," the woman said. "Becoming one of us. Part of our fold. And you just stand there?"

"Waiting for you to state your peace. What else would you like me to do?" Her voice sounded a little deep to her own ears, a side effect of her annoyance. And her anger at being forced into this situation.

The woman opened her mouth to say something, then snapped it shut.

"Perhaps introductions are in order," the black-haired man said.

"Helpful," Angie said. Then waited again. They already knew her name.

"I'm Steven," the man introduced without pausing or waiting on Angie for anything. "This is Gabriella." He gestured to the steel-gray haired woman beside him. "Karen." He nodded to the blond woman. "And Jess." A half smile for the final council member.

They all stared at her for another long moment after the introductions. She stared back, wondering why all the delays and hesitance to speak. They'd brought her here. This was their idea. She wasn't a petitioner requestioning something from them.

"Will you join the hunters voluntarily?" Jess asked. The first they'd spoken and cutting right to the chase.

Angie appreciated that. "Let's call it forced voluntarily and we'll be closer to the reality."

"You don't wish to become a hunter?" Jess asked.

"I'm not a hunter. I'm a witch. I've always been a witch."

"You're a realm splitter. You deal with demons regularly." This from Karen.

"First, only learned the term realm splitter a few weeks ago. In all the years I was…with Sebastian, why didn't I know that term before?"

"It's kept closely guarded," Steven said. "Quiet. Those unaffected by the realm splitters don't need to know about them."

"And for those who *are* realm splitters?"

"The less they know the better," Gabriella said.

Angie met her gaze. "You think so, do you?"

"Yes," she said without hesitance. "I've read the history."

"I'd be interested in that history."

"You aren't a hunter. Yet."

"When I am? Will I have access?" She finally glanced at Sebastian. "He didn't know everything."

Gazes were exchanged. She narrowed her eyes.

Karen said, "The full history isn't for every hunter either."

Interesting they admitted that to her. She glanced at

Sebastian again, but he showed no reaction to the conversation, his expression neutral and calm and…careful.

"Why do you want me to be a hunter?" she asked, facing the four council members again. "I worked with Sebastian for two years without any pressure to become an actual hunter from you. Why now?"

"You left Sebastian," Steven said. "You left hunting."

"And was content to remain a quiet witch going about her business having nothing to do with demons," she said, holding herself very very still as the anger surged in her gut. She kept as much of it out of her voice as possible, when she said, "I would have continued quietly with my life, without ever being an issue for you again. You kept dragging me back. You want me here. Why? I'm not a hunter."

"But you are," Karen said. "If you weren't, you wouldn't be here."

"Hunters don't turn down the job," Jess said. "It's who they are."

"Which is how I know I'm not one," Angie said. "I am a witch."

"A demon witch," Gabriella muttered.

"A woman who wasn't one of the good guys called me that not too long ago," Angie said. She kept the fact that another hunter had called her that just last night to herself. She'd hold that encounter close until she'd figured more of this situation out. "Sebastian had never heard that term before."

Or so he'd said. Since two hunters had used it now, she wasn't so sure anymore. But she'd deal with that later.

"What do you mean when you use that name for my… ability?" she asked Gabriella. "Why is realm splitter more commonly used? If I'm to become a hunter, I need to know what you know about my ability. Lack of information hasn't helped this situation even a little bit."

And she was getting angrier and tenser as the conversation continued. She could feel the anger as little electrical sparks along her skin. She breathed in and out slowly, letting the static settle, letting calm encompass her. But she was still a little wobbly after her magic hangover, and she was mad she was in this position, and it was tempting beyond measure to finish her protection circle and set up a safe space for herself in this room so she could sit on the floor and have a good pout.

Mature and reasonable? No.

Getting more desirable by the moment? Yes.

She let out another slow breath. Steady. Steady.

"You have agreed to join us," Jess said. Both a question and a statement.

Angie answered the question part. "I have. Reluctantly. I don't think I'll make a good hunter." She watched them all closely, wishing the other council members were here, as she said, "It seems like I have to prove that to you. So I'll train to be a hunter. And when it doesn't work out, you'll let me quit again. And this time, you'll leave me alone."

Yeah, there was a reaction to that pronouncement. Several. All of which were subtle and hard to read. But there was reaction. And given they had such control over themselves, they could will themselves not to react, she figured she'd said a very…impactful thing to get them to show anything at all.

Interesting.

"Hunters don't quit. Or retire," Jess said softly. Their voice had been soft from the start, but now, they spoke with a tone Angie heard mostly reserved for holy spaces. Reverence and resignation all rolled into one.

"It's happened before," Gabriella said to Jess, her mouth flattening, her eyes narrowed. "Just not often. And not in modern times."

"There haven't been any demon witches in generations, either," Angie said. She let her gaze move over all four of them. "When I prove I'm not a capable hunter, I'll expect you to stop trying to drag me back into this world."

"You know too much now," Steven said, sounding almost resigned. "You are part of this world. Like it or not, Angela."

"Not," she said without hesitance. "But that wasn't my point. I will train. I will try. And when it doesn't work, because I'm a witch not a hunter, I will leave. And you will let me go."

A flicker of movement from Gabriella and Steven, as if they'd say something, do something, respond in some way to her statement. Jess stared at her without comment and with an unreadable expression, but their head tilted to one side in a way that left Angie feeling studied. Karen looked toward the fireplace, a crease tightening lines along her brow.

Angie flicked a glance at the fireplace, too, but only a passing glance as she looked between the four hunters. She didn't want them to know she had any particular interest in the fireplace. She didn't want anyone to know.

"Let's not discuss failure before we've begun," Steven said. "You don't know how you'll fair as a hunter."

"I worked with Sebastian for two years." She shivered, the chittering in her ears a memory she worked hard to suppress. "I am not a hunter. I would have known."

"You weren't properly trained," Gabriella said, lowering her chin to stare at Angie, her irritation a physical thing between them. "You weren't encouraged to work *as* a hunter. Just with one. The training will change that."

"You believe that?" She shook her head. "I suppose I wouldn't be here if you didn't. But as I said, I will try." She shrugged. "And I will gloat when it turns out I'm right."

Another very telling exchange of looks. Angie filed that away. She knew—or at least strongly suspected—that all this was some sort of elaborate assassination attempt. They saw her as a threat and wanted her out of the way. Some of them at least. And the best way to get rid of her was to have her fail in a demon hunt and die. Easy. No blame. No pointed fingers. No getting their hands dirty with assassination.

Being able to pretend they hadn't committed murder.

Angie had no intention of dying. Of letting them win. And she needed them to know that, even if saying it outright wasn't going to happen yet.

"Your training begins tomorrow," Gabriella said.

"With Sebastian," Steven added. "You know and trust him. He'll be able to show you everything you need to know and teach you all you need."

"You will *not* half-ass this," Gabriella said.

Not a question. A command. But there wasn't any will in the command. None of the hunter tricks to compel her to do as they wanted, think as they wanted. She wondered for the first time if this was something they couldn't will into being. If willing someone to take up the job of a demon hunter was somehow against the rules. Persuasion and manipulation and outright blackmail were obviously fine things to use.

But maybe will was the one thing they couldn't?

"I don't half-ass important things," Angie said. And learning everything she could from Sebastian would be necessary for her survival until she could get out of this. "But I need more information about what I am if I'm going to make this work. Keeping me ignorant isn't the answer here."

There were no exchanged looks this time. But she got the impression that took effort for all of them.

"Once we're assured you're on the correct path," Gabriella said, her deep voice stern and uncompromising when she said "correct." "Once we're happy that you're making appropriate progress, we'll speak of the realm splitters again."

Right. She was taking that promise with a hefty bowl of salt. "Fair enough. We'll start tomorrow."

Steven shrugged. "You could even begin now. Tonight."

She tried not to wince. She was too tired and still feeling the effects of whatever she'd done to herself last night. She needed to explore that first before she'd have the focus to do demon stuff. But she'd discuss that with her new trainer. She glanced at Sebastian out of the corner of her eyes, a funny little tingle of panic settled into her gut. She tried to ignore it.

"And we'll judge when you're ready for more information," Gabriella said.

"We'll speak again soon," Jess said. "To assess progress."

"Will I meet the other council members at that time?" She was extremely curious who these other hunters were. And which one was the one instigating all this.

"Perhaps," Steven said. "It depends on schedules."

Interesting excuse.

"For now," Karen said, "we're content that you have decided to join us, Angela Jordan. You will make a fine hunter. Whether you believe that or not."

Angie didn't snort her response to that assessment out loud. But she was snorting with derision in her head, big time.

"Until we meet again," Steven said.

"You can find your way out?" Gabriella to Sebastian.

"Of course." The first time he'd spoken since coming into the room.

Angie had so many questions for him after they left.

They exchanged head nods with the council members. And as she turned to leave, Angie thought she caught sight of movement inside the fireplace. She didn't react to it, or try to look closer. But she filed away the memory of that fleeting flash of motion.

There was a lot going on beneath the surface here. She was positive now.

None of this was what it seemed.

CHAPTER FOURTEEN

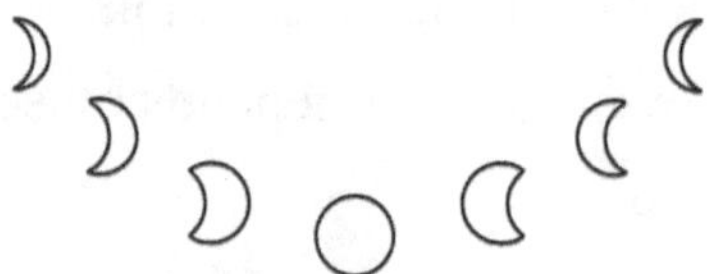

Angie breathed in the scent of warm asphalt and too many cars rushing by on the Midtown avenue, letting the sounds of the city sink in and settle the agitation that made her insides jumpy. The night felt cool and calming, the city air refreshing and sharp after the meeting. The lights from still-open buildings, sidewalk lamps, cars, and street level stores. The crowds of people pushing past. The honking and shout of drivers unhappy with the pace of traffic.

"I still have too many questions," she said. "But I guess I'm committed now."

"Kebab first," Sebastian said, taking her hand. "Discussion second."

She didn't pull her hand from his. And didn't question why she wanted the contact.

A part of her still questioned his part in all this, his motives. She wanted to trust him. She had before and thought she still did. But there was a suspicious little voice deep down whispering that he knew more than he'd told her. And she couldn't trust him.

She couldn't tell if that voice was instinct or insecurity, though. A very big difference in this situation.

They wandered south, in the general direction that led toward the Village. She wanted to walk all the way home instead of taking the subway back. She might feel differently later. But a nice long, exhausting walk through the city sounded lovely just then. Mostly because it put her out of touch with anyone who might want to reach her. Her phone was turned off in her purse. No one would know where she was. No one could bother her.

Her stomach growled, though, so definitely food first. They went into a small Kebab restaurant with a half dozen metal tables near the front, a counter at the back, and three rotating columns of meat hanging behind the counter. She got a pita filled chicken kebab, because she balked at eating lamb. Sebastian went with mutton. They sat at a rickety metal table near the front window, watching the pedestrians pass as they ate mostly in silence.

The food was delicious, and she was so hungry, she finished her sandwich before Sebastian. She was considering a second one when he finally finished. She wasn't super hungry anymore. But the magic hangover left more than just the exhausted after-effect. It also left her ravenous and in need of a lot of energy replacement.

Sebastian studied her a moment through narrowed eyes, then without a word, got up and got them both a second sandwich. She chuckled when he returned and put the food in front of her.

"You might know me too well," she admitted.

"I've never seen anyone stare so longingly at a kebab counter before," he said. "I was afraid you'd cry if I didn't feed you more."

She laughed. "Right." She gobbled up half her second sandwich before saying, "Do you want to talk and walk? Or take the subway back to my place."

"You're not too tired to walk all that way?"

She'd have been insulted if she didn't know he meant her earlier magic hangover. "The food's helped a lot." And letting go of the nearly-formed circle spell that she hadn't, in the end, needed to invoke helped restore some of her energy too.

"Walk then. I need to stretch my legs."

"Did that go the way you expected?"

"Not entirely. I was expecting…" He cut himself off and glanced around.

No one was paying any attention to them. Four of the other tables were occupied, two with men sitting alone, one with three women dressed in business clothes, and one with a woman and a baby in a stroller pushed close to the wall. One of the lone men was reading a newspaper. The other stared out the front window at the pedestrians. The woman with the baby had her face in the stroller, making funny faces at the baby. The business trio were leaning over the table having an intense conversation.

All so very ordinary and normal, she thought with a sigh.

Even with no one looking in their direction, Sebastian said, "We can discuss it more as we walk." He refocused on her. "Was that enough? You want a third?"

"I'm good." She was contently full now, finally. She might be hungry again after the long walk, but that was a worry for after she got home.

They tidied up their trash and rejoined the push and shove of Midtown foot traffic as many of the office workers emerged to hurry toward subway stations and catch taxis. Angie had never, in her entire life, wanted to work in an office and have regular nine-to-five hours. She wasn't built for that kind of life. But there were moments where the ordinariness of it, where the predictability—and the fact that there were no demons involved—really appealed to her. This was one of those times.

"We will start training tomorrow," Sebastian said. "Tonight is too soon. But better not to push this out any longer."

"So we can get it over with?"

"So you'll be safer."

Well. That was interesting. "I have as many questions now as I did when I went into the meeting." Though she had learned a few things. None of it really answered her fundamental questions. "Why weren't the entire council there?"

"Good questions," he muttered. "The one I told you about, the one that's been…manipulating the council into more active control over hunters? He wasn't there. I expected him, at the least, because he's been the one pushing for this. For you to become a hunter."

"He's the one who wants to kill me then."

"Probably. One of them anyway. Don't trust Steven or Karen either."

"Jess? Gabriella?"

"Don't trust any of them," he said, his mouth flattening for a moment. "But Jess and Gabriella are the ones who think you were meant to be a hunter and will succeed at being one. Gabriella in particular has been bothered by you not coming into the fold."

"She didn't always feel that way."

"No. But after we started working together, she changed her mind."

Angie nodded, falling silent so they could move around a clump of people stopped in the middle of the sidewalk contemplating a map. She tried not to let her irritation out. Why people couldn't just move out of the way when they had to stop… Grr.

When they were free of the congestion, she said, "I would have liked to meet the one who's trying to kill me. He'd know better than to let me shake his hand?"

"Yes. But you wouldn't likely be able to read him anyway."

Worth a try, though. And maybe, if her training with Laura worked, she'd be able to read an aura or two. She had no idea how much the council knew about her, but she had to assume they knew all of her skills at this stage. They'd been "keeping an eye on her" for years. Aura reading wasn't one of her strengths, though. So they might not think to hide their auras from her. At least not at first.

"Was the absence of this particular council member the thing that bothered you," she asked, "or was there more? And what the hell is this guy's name?" Seemed like she should know the name of the man trying to kill her.

"He'll have to introduce himself. Hunters are weird about their names."

She'd never noticed that before. But then again, mostly she'd dealt with Aidan and Sebastian, and they'd both introduced themselves. Aidan had never mentioned anything about hunters being careful of who knew their names.

"It's because you're a witch," Sebastian said, answering her unspoken question.

The fact that he'd known the direction of her thoughts bothered her a little. She was either too predictable, he knew her too well, or both things were true and that was unsettling.

"They don't want their names getting to witches. Even if the names they use aren't their power names. No one but the individual knows that name anyway."

"You have power names?" That was new information too. Fucking hell. She was starting to think she knew nothing about demon hunters at all.

Which meant she hadn't ever really known Sebastian at all.

"Do you have one?" she asked, not looking directly at him. "You don't need to tell me it, obviously. But... Do you have one?"

"Yes." A long pause as they waited at a traffic light and a

lot of people crowded in around them. Once across the street and free of the tangle of humans, he said, "And I won't tell you the name because no one knows it. No one at all. Not even Aidan. I don't know Aidan's power name. They're used for specific purpose, during hunts, and aren't spoken aloud."

She let out a sigh. "Fair."

That sort of thing had a place in many witchcraft traditions, too. A lot of witches took power names, or secret names, or a variation on that theme, and they didn't reveal those names to anyone either. They were used within the context of spellwork and when dealing with whatever elements or deities or spirits the witch might commune with. She couldn't feel hurt that Sebastian didn't share this particular secret with her when she knew full well the reasons behind it from her own tradition. There was, well, power in knowing someone's power name. Extremely dangerous power.

She said, "I only get to know this now because I've agreed to train."

"Yes. And everything I'll teach you now are things you cannot reveal to anyone else. I know this isn't… That we're doing this to stall, and to gather information, but I'm going to teach you as if you were on your way to being a demon hunter. You'll learn things that are, for lack of a better word, sacred to us."

He snorted a little under his breath. She wondered at that reaction but didn't question him.

"At any rate, for the safety of us all, the things you learn now will need to remain secret. Revealing any of this to someone who is not a demon hunter could get all of us killed. Or worse."

"What's worse than getting all the hunters killed?" she asked, genuinely appalled at the thought that there might be something worse.

"Loosing a demon plague on the world with no one left to stop them."

Ah. Yes. That did sound quite a bit worse. Or maybe it sounded all together worse. "Isn't that what they're worried I'll do anyway?"

"The hunters would still be around to do something about the demon plague if it's just a you-issue."

She made a noise somewhere between a laugh and a derisive sniff and rolled her eyes.

Sebastian glanced at her from the corner of his eyes, smiling a little. She kept her attention focused ahead so the impact of that little grin only hit her in her peripheral vision.

"At any rate," she said, to ensure they stayed on track, "I am good at keeping secrets. I will keep the demon hunters' secrets. No one here wants a demon plague unleashed."

A voice from behind, a voice Angie did *not* expect to hear ever again stepped into the conversation.

"Oh, I don't know about that."

CHAPTER FIFTEEN

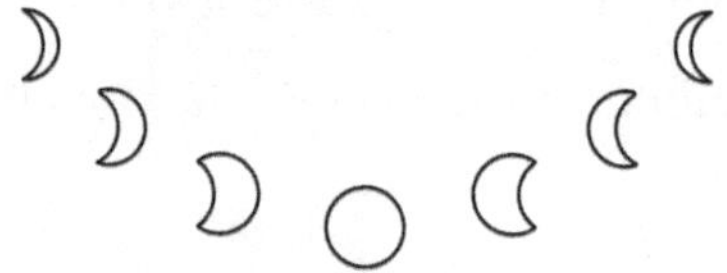

ngie and Sebastian both spun to face the person standing behind them. Angie was a little appalled she hadn't sensed the woman approach so close, but she was even more astonished Sebastian hadn't noticed.

Carmen was truly a scary impressive…whatever she was.

But how much of their conversation had she overheard? Had they just revealed some of the secrets Sebastian had told her couldn't be revealed?

Fuck.

"Wasn't expecting to see you again," Angie said, even as she started to mentally murmur the spell for a protective circle. She'd let go of the one she'd built for the meeting with the hunter council. And was now irritated with herself that she hadn't kept the spell in standby until reaching the safety of her apartment. Dumb mistake.

"Thought the demon hunters would catch me? The

cops?" Carmen laughed. "I've been dodging and avoiding them for decades now. I've got a lot of practice."

"That's not a reassuring statement."

"Ellen and Mara were fine in the end, weren't they?" Carmen said. "And Grant got what he deserved." She shrugged. "All worked out just fine."

Angie wasn't going to argue that point again with Carmen. It almost hadn't "worked out fine." Angie had been possessed by a demon and had nearly unleashed a demon hoard, and she was still reeling from that experience. She had no forgiveness for Carmen putting her into that situation in the first place. And Ellen and Mara hadn't survived because of anything Carmen had done.

Rather than argue, Angie studied her. She hadn't changed her look much in the weeks since she'd last seen her. Though she was no longer making herself look smaller and more innocuous—they'd met while she'd been pretending to be a maid for a rich white man and had been playing up the part. She was a woman of medium height, dark hair and eyes. Dressed in jeans, a dark blue t-shirt, and a thigh-length black leather jacket tonight. She'd kept her hair up in a bun most of the previous times Angie had seen her. Now her hair was loose around her shoulders. And there were a couple of white streaks in it that hadn't been visible before.

She still looked like the sort of person who just blended into her surroundings. There wasn't anything about her to draw attention. Just another New Yorker, making her way home after work.

Carmen had so very much in common with the demon

hunters. Including a will strong enough to deal with demons for years without getting killed. Not stronger than Sebastian's will. But still formidable. A human who could have been a hunter under different circumstances.

Unlike Angie.

But there was more to Carmen. Angie was sure of it. More than just a strong-willed vigilante. More under the surface that she hadn't revealed yet. And it was that unrevealed element that made Carmen especially dangerous.

"What do you want?" Angie asked. "Why are you here? Just to show us you escaped justice. Because that might not go as well for you as you think."

Carmen laughed. "Escaped justice? That's funny. Since I'm the one doling out justice."

"Sure. Justice." Grant had been a horrible person. He deserved a lot of bad things. But even he hadn't deserved what the demons had done to him. No one did. It was… Well, what demons did was the stuff of Angie's nightmares, so she tried not to think about it too much.

"Did you get my message?" Carmen asked.

"No."

She smiled. "I think you did. You'll figure it out soon. You're a smart couple of sheep. When you're ready to learn more about your…nature, come talk to me."

"Which part of my nature are you talking about? Since I have multitudes."

Carmen's smile turned knowing. "You're a rare bird, chica." She glanced at Sebastian. "And I, for one, want to see you master all your talents."

"I find that hard to believe. But what makes you think I haven't?"

"That night in the trees outside Ellen and Mara's apartment? Pretty sure you didn't mean to show me that… particular skill."

Well if that wasn't the fucking truth. Angie had made a mistake, let the wrong kind of tree catch her out in the dark, not careful enough, and Sebastian had had to help her, pull her away from disaster. Again. But too late to hide the mistake. Carmen had known what she'd done. Carmen even knew the names the demon hunters used to describe her skill. Not Angie's finest moment. Not least because it gave Carmen way too much information about her.

"Rare bird indeed," Carmen murmured, still smiling. "When you're ready to talk, let me know. Enjoyed watching you two work together yesterday, by the way. You make a good team."

She turned and walked away, disappearing into the crowds, before Angie could comment. Probably for the best because her comment would have involved a lot of cussing.

"She set us up, the bitch. She set up that poor man, used his daughter's illness to lure us out. She's Marta. Bitch."

This was the second time, that Angie knew of, that Carmen had used a child in her plots. Angie might have no interest in having children of her own, but she loved kids. And using kids was the height of evil as far as she was concerned. Carmen gave justifications for her actions with nonsense about the children not actually being in danger. Whether Carmen believed that or not, Mara had been in serious danger from Grant. And Ivan's daughter was ill and using that illness and his vulnerability was just…

Angie snarled at the spot where Carmen had been.

Sebastian set a hand to her arm. "She's trying to goad you."

"I know. It's fucking working. Let's get back to my place. I'm dangerous like this."

She was, too. Her control over her magic was excellent. She'd been practicing that since the age of five. But Carmen pushed her buttons. Buttons that shouldn't be pushed. Made her want to cast spells best left unuttered. She didn't do curses or revenge. On purpose. She believed in the witchy concept that what you put out you got back. Especially in the realms of magic. So she was very careful how she used her magic.

But anger, and in particular anger at injustice, stretched her control. Carmen did very bad things in the name of "justice." And Carmen's bad things could push Angie down that same destructive path. Since she did not want to even step onto the path behind Carmen, she needed to calm down and release her anger.

Without unleashing a revenge spell of her own.

CHAPTER SIXTEEN

hen they got back to her apartment, Angie called Cindy Wong again. She'd left a message with the healer yesterday, giving her Ivan's contact details, but she wanted to talk to Cindy and make sure she'd been able to get in touch with him. By the time she got off the phone, Sebastian had settled on the couch and had two gently steaming cups of tea sitting on the coffee table.

"Feel better now?" he asked as she flopped down next to him.

"Sort of. I feel better that Cindy is helping Ivan. And that she's already seen his daughter. Hopefully, there's something she can do. I didn't want to raise his hopes yesterday, in case she can't do anything. But if any human healer could help, it's Cindy."

"Good."

"Carmen set that up. She set us up."

"Yes."

"To see how we worked together."

"And to push you. To see what you would do."

Angie scrubbed her hands over her eyes. "We were in a garage. Did she think I'd open a realm breach in a garage?" She dropped her hands to her lap. "No trees."

"She's seen you open a portal already. I doubt that was her motivation."

"What then?" She picked up her tea and took a sip. Then gave Sebastian a look. "Chamomile?"

"You needed soothing. Chamomile is soothing."

He was right. On both counts. And it was probably better than Tequila right now.

She sipped some more before saying, "This has been a hell of a day for pushing my buttons. I'm already a little edgy after my reaction to the working last night. Between the council and their mysterious agenda and Carmen showing up to gloat that she's still free and able to manipulate us, I'm not a happy witch."

"Good thing you aren't working tonight, then."

She snorted. "So now what?"

"Depends on what part of the day you're asking about."

"Council first."

"Easy part. Already decided. We start training tomorrow. When you're rested and not so edgy. You'll take to the early lessons better that way."

She made a face. "The Carmen part?"

"I'll get in touch with Gabriella tonight. Let her know

Carmen's on the loose and still teaching people to summon demons."

"And setting them up so their circle isn't solid enough." Angie cursed into her mug. "She was there somewhere. In the garage. She purposefully set that man up to have a weak circle. What if the demon had escaped before we arrived? What if we hadn't been the ones to arrive? What if another demon hunter had shown up?"

"Answer to that's simple enough. She would have just set up another scenario that required a demon hunter. But she gambled with good odds that I'd be the one called to the situation. Outside of the council, there aren't any other hunters in the city."

"There's Jacob."

"He's…a different case."

"You said he wasn't on the council."

"He's not. But his position is complicated. Let's just say, he wasn't likely to have shown up."

"Fine. But what if you'd had to leave for another hunt? Carmen couldn't guarantee you'd still be here."

Unless she'd found Angie's home. Or wherever Sebastian was currently staying—Angie had purposefully refused to ask where he was living at the moment because she didn't want to be tempted. Finding where a hunter slept was difficult unless the hunter wanted to be found. But Angie hadn't been making any attempt to hide her home from anyone. And she walked home from work.

Carmen knew where she worked. One of her associates had even gone to Dana's to find Angie.

"Son of a bitch. She followed me from work." Angie hadn't thought to cover herself, hadn't even occurred to her to look out for someone following her. She even had a spell for that! She just hadn't thought she might need to use it.

"And saw me here," Sebastian said. "She knows where you live."

There was a growl in his voice, a show of anger. He'd been keeping his anger carefully to himself before that. Probably so as not to make hers worse. The fact that he couldn't keep his emotions hidden anymore emphasized the problem.

"This is not good."

She stared at the cacti in her fireplace. Having Carmen know where she was, how to get to her home, was bad. Dangerous. She'd need to set up some protections on her apartment now. Things she hadn't bothered to do before because she hadn't needed to. Protecting an apartment was a lot more complicated, and took more power, than just putting in a circle around a house and adding a few wards.

But with the demon hunter council out there with at least one member of it wanting her dead, and now Carmen knowing where her home was, she needed to do something. Setting a preemptive circle might work. Something she could activate when she was home maybe? Except when she was gone, someone could always sneak in. She didn't have any illusions that a locked building would stop Carmen. She'd tell someone she lived here, and they'd believe her and let her come in with them because Carmen was a consummate actress. Bitch should have been on stage.

Angie took a deep breath, let it out slowly. Her anger was getting to her again. She was starting to get that little vibration through her body that meant she was gathering power. Doing that when she wasn't trying to was dangerous.

Frowning into her tea cup, she considered how much trouble she was having with that today. The day after her vision. Her anger didn't usually dent her control like this. She got pissed off all the time—she'd been extraordinarily angry with Sebastian when he'd come back this last time and dangled a child in danger in front of her to get her to help him. And yet she hadn't had any trouble at all controlling her power. None of this unintentional gathering of magic.

But she'd had a hell of a time with it today.

After she'd had that strange vision last night.

After she'd tugged the red line running through the blue spiderweb.

"Your frown's changed," Sebastian said. "What's wrong?"

"Besides Carmen knowing where I live and at least one demon hunter hoping I'll die?"

"Yes, beside that."

He said that so matter-of-fact, she glanced at him and huffed out a laugh. Her humor didn't last, though. "I… I've been having a little trouble keeping my power from rising today. Keeping my magic under control. Every time my anger rises, so does my power, like I'm about to cast a spell. Except I'm not calling it up. I'm not trying to gather the power for use. It's just happening. And I have to make an effort to relax and let the power dissipate again."

He studied her. "And that doesn't normally happen?"

"No. Not ever. Well, it might have when I was first learning. At five. And I know there were a few years of, shall we say volatility, when I was a teenager."

He raised his brows and she shrugged. All teenagers were prone to drama. Hers had just required an extra bit of control so she didn't turn Sarah McKenna into a snake for kissing Bobby Henderson, who was supposed to be Angie's boyfriend, when they were in the nineth grade.

"Point is," she said, "I haven't had my magic rise unbidden in years. Never like this. Where my emotions call it without my conscious effort."

Once again, she thought about that minor epiphany she'd had, that both her touch psychic skills and her ability to open demon realms were things that just happened. Things she'd had to learn to control and/or avoid triggering. Her magic had never been like that, just happening. She had to call up the power, and she had to work it into spells with very specific words and hand gestures. She couldn't cast spells on accident. She couldn't use most of her power without making an effort. Except for the touch psychic and realm breaching power.

She let out a breath as she stared at Sebastian. He wasn't a magic wielder. He hadn't studied magic per se. At least not anything that wouldn't be used to summon demons. He wasn't likely to understand what all this meant any more than she did. But he might have a different perspective, something that could help.

And despite the moments of wondering how much he was

still keeping from her, how much he wasn't telling her, she found she still trusted him. Probably because she still loved him and saw him through that love. If she were less emotional about him, she might also be more suspicious of his motives in all this.

Maybe a part of her was.

But she wanted to talk to someone about these connections. And the only person she wanted to talk to was Sebastian.

So she told him about the realization she'd had.

"There's something there," he said after a long silence. "You're right. There's something in that."

"But not a clue what that something is, huh?" Well, she hadn't really thought he'd have any great insights. It felt good to have discussed this with him, though, to get out the idea so she wasn't the only one considering it.

"No," he said with a little shrug. "Wish I had answers."

"Would there be something in the council's information about demon witches?"

"Might be. Hard to say without having seen the records myself."

She set her empty tea mug onto the coffee table, then sat back and ran her hands through her hair. "I was kind of hoping the meeting today would give me more information."

"It was never going to be that easy. And I still think my way is better."

"I'm not writing off your way." Maybe the council did have to be brought down. She didn't know enough yet to make that call. But until she did… "I'm just not going to put energy into destroying them without knowing if its necessary first."

He didn't argue, which she was grateful for, but he did study her for a silent moment and his scrutiny left her uncomfortably edgy. Though she wasn't entirely sure why.

"I'd better leave now," he murmured. "You look tired."

She was tired. She was exhausted. It wasn't all that late. Some days she'd still be at work at this time of night. But despite sleeping until three in the afternoon, she felt like she could fall asleep again easily.

"The exhaustion is strange," she said. "I haven't done anything that should have me this drained. Not today."

"Whatever that vision of yours was about, it really took a lot out of you." A furrow formed on his forehead, between his brows. "Maybe don't work that spell again until we figure out what it all meant."

She snorted. "You think?" She smiled a little to take the sting out of her sarcasm. "I'm sure I'll be fine after a normal night's sleep. Just need to refill the well a little."

Except her magic didn't feel drained and in need of replenishment. She actually felt like she had more magic bubbling through her. The way it kept rising without her conscious effort like…like there was so much it was going to overflow.

The thought was a little terrifying. So she squashed it down. She was out of sorts, off balance, too much had been happening in the last few weeks. She just needed a little more rest and recovery from the magic hangover. Then she'd be able to think clearly and see clearly what was going on. She'd have control of her magic again.

"I'll come back tomorrow," Sebastian said, still frowning a little at her. "Round noon? We can get some initial training in before you have to go to work."

"Sure. Sounds good." She rose to walk him to the door, her thoughts spinning. Worry was taking up residence in her gut. Which made letting Sebastian leave more difficult than it should have been. "Be careful," she said. "With Carmen out there and…everything."

He brought his hand up to cup her face, a gentle caress of his thumb along her cheekbone. "Worrying about me?"

"If you get killed, I'll lose my inside man with the demon hunters." She tried for casual, but her voice sounded a little too breathy. His palm was warm against her skin, and the gentle rub of his thumb made her want to leaned into his touch.

With so many of her defenses jumbled up, and her balance already off, the thought of pulling him back into the apartment, of leaning in those last few inches and pressing her lips against his… So so tempting. So dangerous. But so tempting. And so easy.

Kissing him would be so very very easy.

"Ang."

His voice was quiet, almost a whisper. She heard the question in it, as well as the longing. Longing that matched hers so perfectly, it was almost like pain.

She met him half way, him leaning down just a bit, her

moving her up just a bit. The first brush of his mouth against her was soft, gentle. A coming home. But also with that zing of the new. His facial hair tickled a little. She'd managed to stay away from him for a year and a half. And since he'd come back into her life, she'd made an effort to keep some distance between them. Now, she had trouble remembering why. Why she'd left in the first place. Why she hadn't done this sooner.

Kissing him was all she wanted to do. He smelled like heaven and tasted like tea and he was everything she'd ever needed in life. She wrapped her arms around his waist, settling against him, softening into that remembered feel of him. Wanting to remember every inch of him. His hands flexed against her jaw, still gentle, and then he ran his fingers up into her hair, cradling her head, holding her in place as they deepened the kiss.

The progression from gentle to intense moved fast, sweeping her legs out from under her. Need overwhelmed her. She dragged her nails over his back, and smiled at his shiver. Gasped when he spun her so her back was to the wall. Groaned when he kissed along her jaw and down her throat.

He seemed to remember all those places that made her knees weak, that made her moan. The soft spot where her shoulder and neck met. The pulse on the side of her throat. That tiny, delicate area at the base of her skull toward the back. Ah goddess when he brushed that spot with his lips, she saw stars.

Restless for more, she gripped his shoulders, his waist, his back, trying to feel all of him at once. He'd worn jeans and a button-down shirt to the meeting with the council, a nod to more formal attire, she supposed. But she'd always lost her mind for him in a button-down shirt and now that she had her hands on him, ripping the buttons to get him out of the shirt seemed imperative.

She had her hands up under his shirt, her fingers on his skin, letting his heat seep through her, her body craving that fire. The exhaustion from earlier faded into the background. So did her worries. Having Sebastian pressed tight into her was all that mattered. That and stripping them both out of their clothing.

She assumed he intended to do just that when he eased away from her, leaving just a little space between them. But he stilled her hands on the buttons of his shirt and set his forehead against hers. His breath was ragged, brushing her lips. She could feel his heart pounding against the hand he'd pinned to his chest.

"Ang," he whispered. The sound of his voice rough and gravely.

She shivered and tried to close the few inches of space he'd put between them. Everything in her demanded she get as close as humanly possible and then never let him go again.

And even as she had that thought, she recognized the way this complicated things. The way this would make everything…even more impossible.

"I'd better leave," he murmured, though he didn't let go of her hand, still pinned against his chest, and he didn't lift his forehead from hers.

"If I asked you to stay?" She wasn't sure why she asked that. They both knew it was better if he didn't.

"I'd stay," he said. "I don't want to let you go again."

With her free hand, she cupped his cheek and sighed. "So complicated."

"So simple," he agreed.

She smiled. He was right. He needed to leave. She wasn't ready to throw the last couple of years away yet. Not when she was still so uncertain about her future. If they managed to get her extricated from the council's machinations, if she could put the demon hunter world behind her permanently… Where would that leave them? Could they work, could they be together, if she wasn't part of his world?

The reason she'd left in the first place—the fact that she desperately wanted away from all things demon—hadn't actually changed. Her hand was being forced. She was back in his world and his life. For the moment. But for how long? She'd only agreed to the training until she could get some answers and then get herself out of this mess.

If she did, she might have to give Sebastian up again. And every time she had to do that, it destroyed a little more of her.

She let out a resigned sigh. "I know you're right," she said. "I'm just not happy about it."

"Me neither," he said, with feeling.

Ah it would be so easy to wrap herself around him again, strip him naked and take him to bed. So so easy.

So so complicated.

"I'll be back tomorrow," he said. "Sleep well. Put a ward up on your door after I leave."

She smiled. "I will if you promise to be careful, too."

"I will." He finally lifted his head from hers and leaned back to meet her gaze.

The silence and history stretched between them.

Then he pulled in a sharp breath and finally let her go, stepping away. Leaving her feeling hollow and cold.

She locked her door behind him. Then took the time to put a ward on the door frame, murmuring the spell as she pressed one hand to the frame and made a series of finger gestures with her other hand over the door. A discouragement for anyone who got too close. A warning to her if someone did get too close.

When she finished, she stumbled to her bed, exhaustion sweeping through her again. The spell on the door hadn't been enough to drain her, so she assumed the exhaustion was still a hangover from last night's casting and an effect of the day she'd had.

Whatever the cause, she was asleep an instant after her head hit the pillow.

She dreamed of a glowing blue spiderweb.

With a single, pulsing red thread.

CHAPTER SEVENTEEN

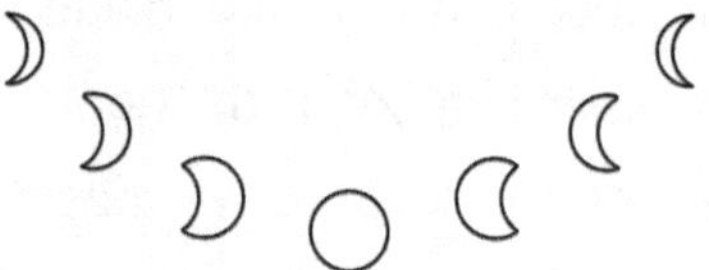

Angie had worked with Sebastian for two years. More if she counted the times he and Aidan had requested her help before that. She'd watched him face down demons with little more than his will, and occasionally a sword he pulled out of thin air. He'd never told her where the sword came from, either where he'd gotten it or where it went when he wasn't using it. It was just something he had when he needed it.

But as often as not, he didn't even use the sword to physically fight a demon. Most of the fighting was done with will. A will that had to be stronger than a demon's.

Watching a hunter use their will, being present at the fight, opening a portal into a demon world so they could rid this realm of that demon more easily. Using her magic as backup to Sebastian's efforts... None of it was the same as *being* the hunter.

She'd gone into all those fights with Sebastian, she'd fought alongside him in her way, but her way wasn't the demon hunter way. Learning the demon hunter way was an entirely different skill set.

And she was not happy with the process.

"I'm not happy with this process," she said aloud.

"I'm well aware," Sebastian said, his expression carefully neutral.

Though she thought that lip twitch might be him trying not to laugh, and if he was laughing at her right now, she was going to poke him with the spark spell she used to use on her brothers when they annoyed her too much.

The thought of using a spell sounded so pleasant and straightforward and instinctive. She nearly whined again. But that would just be embarrassing.

"Let's try it again," she huffed.

Their "training" wasn't what she'd been expecting. She was used to training with witch mentors and teachers. The active sessions, when practicing a new spell, involved quieting the mind, setting a protective circle to keep the magic in and anything that might cause harm out, a teacher talking her through a spell she'd been memorizing for weeks, practicing the various pieces of the spell, the different finger gestures, until she could get everything precisely right and coordinated. All of that advanced practice and reading and learning happening before going into a circle with her teacher to work the full spells. Her kind of witchcraft took time, learning, patience, practice, and occasionally failure so she learned what not to do.

As far as Angie could tell, even outside the witchy world, most training in a new field involved a similar strategy. Although maybe with less protective circles required.

Demon hunter "training" was…not like that.

The little imp demon inside the summoning circle in the middle of her living room glared at her. She glared back.

It was a small creature, only about three foot tall, with disproportionately long arms and legs, its long, claw tipped fingers scrapping the ground even as it stood its full height. Its skin was an orangey-red color, and there were patches of iridescent black scales covering its skinny thighs and the tops of its hands and feet. Thick knobby joints were covered with scruffy clumps of red fur. Its head was small compared to its wide, thick shoulders, with pointed features, a stubby nose over a mouth too wide for the sharply angled bottom of its face, and eyes too big for the narrow top of its face.

Those giant, round, black eyes were narrowed, its wide mouth stretched into a frown, even as it tapped its spike tipped tail on the hard wood floor. As if impatient.

She rolled her eyes. Was it her fault they *needed* a demon for her to will away?

Apparently, according to Sebastian, the only way to practice banishing demons was to work with an actual demon. Learning the various ways a summoner could call a demon, the ways to reverse those ceremonies, the types of bargains a demon might attempt, the loopholes to watch out for in a demon challenge fight…none of that background learning helped at all if a hunter couldn't master their will to overcome a demon's will.

"It's just an imp," Sebastian said. "Your will is definitely stronger than its."

The imp laughed. "No witches sends me back. No witches can out will me!"

"Shut up," Angie said. "Or I'll make it rain on your head." Given it had come from one of the hot realms, a cold wash of icy rain water would feel decidedly… uncomfortable.

The imp glowered. But, wisely in her opinion, shut up.

"You're still thinking like a witch," Sebastian admonished.

"Cause I am one. Because I've been trying to tell your people that from the start."

"I know that. And you know that. But until we can convince them, you have to learn this." He gestured at the imp.

They'd pushed aside her couch and coffee table, edged her cacti farther back into the fireplace, and tucked her altar into a corner to open up the center of her living room as much as possible. The apartment was longer than it was wide, and there wasn't a lot of width to work with, but Sebastian had said it was enough for their purposes. The summoning circle drawn on her wooden floor in white chalk wasn't particularly large, but for a demon imp it really didn't have to be.

They'd set up a few red candles around the circle, and Sebastian had drawn a few archaic symbols around the candles. But most of the set up was for show, he said. She was a witch, used to working with symbols and candles and sacred objects in her formal sittings. He thought having them on her first day of training might help.

The nod to witchy ceremonial magic was not helping.

"I'd rather just dump icy water on it and be done with this," she said, still glaring at the imp.

"No no nos the water," the imp said and stomped its foot. "Not part of the deal!"

Before summoning the imp, Sebastian had explained it was one of the "cooperative" ones. A creature that agreed to help the hunters train in exchange for protection. What kind of protection and how they conferred that protection Sebastian said was part of a later lesson. Which had earned him one of the many glares she had readily available to dole out today.

"Everything in its time," he said. "I'm taking you through the training just as Aidan took me through it. Trust me."

She'd grumped, but she's acquiesced. She knew he wouldn't steer her wrong in this. Her getting it right was too important.

Her first lesson wasn't off to a rousing start, though. The councilmember or members who wanted her dead were probably on to something with all this.

"You're blocking your own will," Sebastian said. "Your...habits in wielding magic are interfering. You're trying to use gestures and words to support what you want to accomplish."

She snarled. She couldn't help it. Her hands just...moved when she was trying to cast—

Except she wasn't trying to "cast" anything here. She wasn't doing spellwork.

"Think about it this way," he said quietly. "Think about it like your touch psychic skills. That just comes to you right? You open to it, touch something, and read it."

She nodded, frowning but with less snarl now.

"Your will works the same way. Open to it, and let it flow through. Let it fill you. Gather it around you like a…like a shield, but…" He glanced away. "It has to just be. To exist. And you have to use what is there and exists to send the imp back."

"I'm sure everything you just said makes sense in your head," she said, "but a lot of that was 'blah blah blah no spells blah blah' to me."

His lips twitched again, and she still couldn't tell if it was humor or annoyance.

She released a loud breath. "But I get what you mean about needing to open to it, rather than trying to make it work." She faced the imp. "I think."

She was trying to wield her will like it was magic, like she did when casting spells. She was putting effort into the process and she *was* trying to use gestures and words the way she would with a spell, even if she hadn't been trying to do that on purpose.

He was right. She needed to think about this the same way she thought about her touch psychic skills, maybe even the way she opened realm breaches. She had to let the will flow through her and let it do the work. She just had to open to allowing it to happen.

In theory.

Maybe.

"I'm very resistant to this idea," she said, but without heat and annoyance this time. She was trying to analyze the problem now. "My instincts aren't convinced this will work. That's not helping. My instincts are insisting I need…" She let out a little huff that was almost a laugh. "Insisting I need the props."

People always assumed they needed the props to summon and control a demon. The props helped them get into the mental space they needed to make the connections to demon realms and demand a demon come to attend them.

But all demon hunters knew those props were unnecessary. A simple circle and will were the only necessary elements. And the circle was just to ensure the demon wasn't accidentally freed into this realm. The circle kept the demon contained and connected to its realm, kept it in a limbo type position that ensured it couldn't run free through the human world.

Other than a containment circle, none of the props, spells, charms, incantations, sacrifices, none of it was strictly necessary.

She was still, mentally, insisting the props were required. She was falling back to witchy props, but still props. Since she knew better, on an intellectual level, the fact that she was falling victim to that way of thinking on an instinctive level was a bit embarrassing.

Sebastian nodded. "You need to internalize that the props

aren't important. You could hold up a unicorn stuffed animal and it would work as well as a skull."

"No no nos stuffed animals," the imp said, stamping its foot again. "Theys scary."

"You're scared of stuffed animals?" she asked.

The imp shivered. "Stuffs them. Stuffs them is hurts."

She was about to point out that these weren't *real* animals being stuffed—that was a different thing all together—and that even in taxidermy the animals weren't alive while being stuffed so there wasn't any pain involved. Then she realized the imp was from a realm where stuffing a living being probably did happen because demons liked pain and torture, even inflicted on other demons, so to the imp, stuffing probably did equate to hurting.

She kept her mouth closed. She really didn't need any more details on that subject.

"When you take someone's hand," Sebastian said, "during a reading, and open to them, how do you do that? You don't need props or spells or hand gestures. Think about that now, how that part of your nature works."

Angie nodded, her gaze on the imp. The imp stuck its long, forked tongue out at her and did a little jig. If it meant to distract her, it was working. The jig was ridiculous and for some reason she wanted to laugh. Probably not the imp's intent.

She pulled in a deep breath, filled with the hint of sulfur mixed with the ordinary smells of her apartment, the faint smell of tea and candle wax, the tease of Sebastian's scent so very close. She let all that wash over her, through her. Then she let in sound, The background hum of traffic outside. The imp's tail clacking on the wooden floor. Her refrigerator turning on. Then she allowed herself to be aware of the air around her. The cool flow of it, warmer in the direction of the imp, cooler at her back. She let her senses open and take in everything around her.

Then she thought about starting a session with a client, taking their hands gently, letting her psychic sense open. Relaxed. Open. Aware.

She stood with that feeling for a long moment, letting it flow through her. How it felt to open and just take in what she needed. To let the thing happen. Not try to make it happen.

Her eyes drifted almost shut as she connected with the sense of flow. The imp laughed and stepped closer to the edge of the circle, the claws on its toes clicking against the floor. She watched it move but kept most of her attention on catching the sensation of flow, of magic moving through her without effort. That was her will. That was what her will had to do. Flow through her. Be a part of her.

Even with her eyes half closed, she still noticed when the imp pressed a hand against the air where the containment circle kept it enclosed. She let him test the circle for a beat, no more, before snapping her eyes open and saying, "Step back. Now."

The imp jumped away from the circle's edge, fast. Like she'd shoved it.

She ignored the imp's curses and said, "Return to your realm. You aren't welcome here. Go. Now." And she let her will pour into the words, holding the image of her abilities flowing through her without effort.

The imp screeched. "No no nos." And stomped both feet this time. "Likes it better here. Staying this time. Gonna stays."

The whine was…effective. She felt sorry for it and wanted to let it stay. She worried it would get hurt in its realm. She worried about hurting it herself.

And the sense of will flowing through her waned.

The imp grinned and jumped to the edge of the circle again, making Angie gasp and step back.

Her turn to curse. "Damn it."

"You almost had it," Sebastian said. "You let your sympathy for it get in the way this time. But at least you were using the full force of your will before that."

"What little good it did." She put her hands on her hips and hung her head. "I know this will take time. Of course it will. Learning a new skill always does. I can't expect to get it right the first day."

"But you wanted to."

She laughed. "I wanted to. I want to get this over with and mastering this part is the first step to not getting killed. I'd rather not get killed."

"I'd rather that you didn't as well. We'll keep practicing until you've got it. But, you're right, it will take time. Give yourself a break."

"Ha!" She looked up, shaking her head.

The imp stared at her, smiling, its row of little pointy teeth doing a great job of dampening her sympathy. She stared back at the imp, tempted beyond all measure to pull out a spell of some kind that would be impressive enough it would wipe that grin off the imp's face.

"Enough for today," Sebastian said. "We'll practice more tomorrow. And believe it or not, we have made progress."

"Learning all the ways to not do a thing first, are we?" She was only half-joking.

"Precisely," he said, straight-faced.

She chuckled. "Fine. What do we do with…" She gestured at the imp who was still grinning at them.

"Home you go," he said to the imp. And the imp jerked backward, again like it had been pushed.

"No no nos!" It tried stomping its feet again, but it couldn't get as much oomph into the motion this time. "Nos, I say! I want to stay."

"We're done for now," Sebastian said, and this time even Angie felt the flow of his will. So casually done. So powerfully easy.

"Show off," she muttered.

"Return to your realm," Sebastian said, his voice deeper, the command holding power even without the will pouring in behind it. "Now."

The imp screeched loud enough to hurt Angie's ears, then spun in a quick circle, so fast it blurred into a red wash of light.

Then with a little popping sound, it disappeared.

Leaving its last cry of protest echoing in her living room.

CHAPTER EIGHTEEN

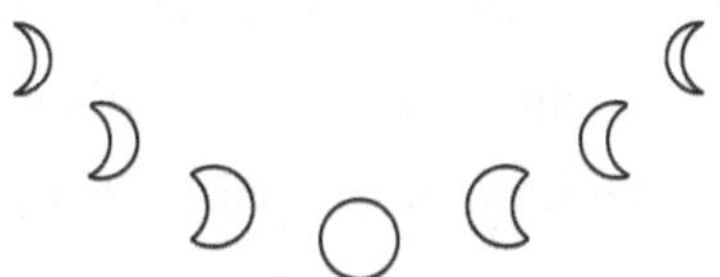

"Well that was fun," Angie muttered, staring at the now empty containment circle chalked onto her living room floor. "The imp is gone?"

"You tell me," Sebastian said.

She flattened her mouth, but she did allow her senses to open again, testing the area in and around the containment circle. She couldn't sense the imp there, hiding or trying to trick them. Because she was having a bad day learning demon hunter stuff, she gave in to the urge to just be a witch and touched the air where the containment circle barrier was, letting her normal, well-trained instincts take over. Nothing came back through the circle. No lingering imp energy or malevolence or threat.

Confident the imp was gone and she wouldn't accidentally turn it loose in this realm, she smudged the chalk circle with her foot, breaking the containment circle and the connection between the demon realm and her own. She kept smudging the circle until chalk had been fully erased in one section. Then she went to get her mop so she could scrub out the rest of the circle.

"You did good, Ang," Sebastian said.

"Right." She shook her head. She held the sponge on her mop under the sink water to get it thoroughly wet. "I managed to shove the little bastard backward a foot and then lost my will when it whined a little. That's not helpful."

"It's helpful to know your empathy is an issue."

She supposed he was right about that. "I wouldn't have thought empathy would be a problem with demons. But here we are." She scrubbed the chalk off her floor easily, the mechanical process helping her settle and release the frustration of the session.

"They're tricky bastards all right. And the imps are particularly good at that kind of thing. That's another reason we use them in training. They are a little scary looking, but also a little harmless sounding. They provoke feelings of empathy and protectiveness when they drop hints about how scary their realm is. And we fall for it. Every time."

"Everyone falls for that act?" She raised her brows, hopeful.

"A lot of training hunters do."

"Guess I don't feel too bad, then. But…" She took the mop back to the kitchen and rinsed the sponge as she considered what he said. "Empathy is, in most circumstances, a good thing. How do you get around the empathy to do what needs to be done without killing it entirely?"

She hadn't considered her empathy as something that could be killed off, but as she considered the task ahead, she could see how a hunter might lock off all emotions, including sympathy for a bullied demon, in their quest to ensure those emotions didn't interfere with the hunt. But doing that, closing off all emotion, felt almost as dangerous as the demons.

What happened when you stopped having at least some sympathy for the human who'd summoned the demon?

They were sometimes horrible people, like Grant had been. But sometimes they were like Ivan who'd just been looking for a way to help his kid. Too many were like Ivan. Almost as many as people like Grant. She had no sympathy for Grant and what he'd done, but she wouldn't have wished the death he'd had at the hands of demons on anyone. Not even him. And her sympathy for Ivan meant she cared even more that the demon he'd summoned didn't escaped and didn't kill him or anyone else.

It felt like a very complex balancing act, one she hadn't had to consider before.

One that explained a little better why so few hunters got involved in long term relationships.

Having partners, having someone to love, even having kids, wasn't exactly forbidden to them. Most just didn't do those things. Their lives were constantly moving, constantly at risk. Their concentration and will had to be absolute. And having a weakness of any kind that could be exploited by a demon was dangerous, potentially deadly. So most hunters didn't allow those potential points of weakness into their lives. Relationships were casual. Loving families were admired from afar. Love was more a concept to uphold than an emotion to get deeply involved with.

She and Sebastian had ignored this general practice of hunters when they'd gotten involved. Their relationship was…unusual. Always had been. Sometimes she wondered if that was part of the problem.

"We don't cut off our empathy," Sebastian said. "We just don't allow any for demons. It takes practice, though. The bastards are tricky."

"Sympathy for the humans, but none for the demons?"

"Only way to survive. Even the demons who might deserve some sympathy, the ones just trying to get by and not get eaten by bigger and badder demons. Because those big bad demons will use the crack of sympathy for the lesser ones to kill a hunter. They'll pretend to be one of the weaker ones. They'll manipulate your feelings. And then they'll happily gut you. There's no room for sympathy for demons because you'll never know for sure if it's an act or not."

He was right. She knew he was right. Hell, she'd seen demons attempt to manipulate using sympathy. She hadn't been the one in the way of their efforts. She hadn't been the one who'd had to hold onto the will to banish them in those moments. So she hadn't thought about any of this before.

Her witch's heart, and the part of her that had trained in psychology, who recognized her job reading people's futures was mostly just being a counselor through a more unconventional method, balked at the very idea of the distance required to be a hunter. And the cynicism.

She was a little surprised by that last. She was a pretty cynical person. Couldn't do what she did, see what she saw, and not harbor some cynicism. But she was a cynical optimist, if that sort of oxymoron existed. The required depth of hunter cynicism might be beyond her.

"Think of it as skepticism," Sebastian said, almost as if he'd followed her unspoken thoughts. "Always always remain skeptical of a demon and their motives. Does that help? Not so much a lack of sympathy, just a deep, and usually justified, suspicion of their motives."

"Yeah. That helps. I can use that perspective." She hoped.

Because while she wasn't in this for the long haul, she did have to get good enough at demon hunting to fool the council and survive until she could get them off her back.

"When do we train again?" she asked.

"Not too tired?"

"Not like I was the other night." She still hadn't figured out why that vision spell had left her exhausted. When she'd dreamed of the red thread running through the glowing blue spiderweb around her, when she'd reached for the thread in the dream, she'd woken before she could touch it. And she hadn't been tired at all today.

So she suspected there was some sort of connection between her exhaustion and that red thread in the web. She just wasn't sure what it was yet.

"We'll do more tomorrow, then," Sebastian said. "Let the lesson sink in a little before we try again."

She huffed out a laugh. "Want some dinner?" She hadn't meant to ask that. They were spending too much time together already. More training together. More casual meals after. Too easy to fall back into the old routines. The old habits.

The missed relationship.

He opened his mouth, closed it. Ran a hand over his short hair. "I probably should go."

She wanted to argue even though she knew he was right. Instead, she said, "I'm working with Laura tomorrow on my aura reading. She's agreed to help me train that, get better at it."

"Sounds like a good idea. Never hurts to have more arrows in your quiver."

"Exactly." Even if they were witchy arrows and not the arrows she was supposed to be developing at the moment. She frowned a little. "Have there ever been witch demon hunters before? Hunters who were also trained witches?"

The training for both was specific, long term, and not exactly easy. Witchcraft in particular was something she knew she'd be studying and practicing for most of her life. There was too much to learn, and she'd never manage to take in all that information and wisdom in her one human life. She kind of liked that part. That there was always more to learn, more to study. She had the impression demon hunting was a similar skill. Always something to learn. Always things to study.

Could anyone be good at both? Or did the practice always come down heavier on one side of that equation?

Not that she'd be studying to be a hunter long term. She

was a witch in her blood and bones. But she was curious if any other witch had managed the balance.

Sebastian didn't meet her gaze. He kept his attention on moving her furniture back into place as he said, "Not that I know of. But it's possible I missed someone like you in our records. There are quite a lot of them."

Said to make her laugh and to distract her. She wasn't distracted. "There haven't been people who could successfully be both witches and hunters. A choice between disciplines is always necessary. Is that right?"

He did more, unnecessary, couch straightening, which conveniently kept him from having to look at her. "Can't say for sure since I haven't heard of anyone attempting to do both."

"Mm hmm." She crossed her arms over her chest and stared at him until he looked up at her finally. "You probably need to tell me what you aren't telling me."

He sighed and shook his head. "Can't get anything past you," he mumbled.

"If you really wanted to, you could. Something about this topic has you conflicted. You want to tell me, but don't think you should. You might as well, or I'll just badger you until you do."

"You really should have become a counselor," he said. "You're very good at reading people. Cutting through the bullshit."

"Which I'm gonna do again now. Compliments don't distract me."

He shrugged. "Worth a try."

"Spill, Seb, or we're going to have a problem."

He held her gaze for a moment, his mouth set in a line. Despite his compliment, she actually couldn't read him very well in that moment. Couldn't tell if his hesitance was something she needed to be worried about, or just him trying *not* to worry her. Which was, ironically, worrying her.

"I don't know if anyone has tried to train a realm splitter like you to be a hunter because I haven't seen those records." He spoke slowly. "I haven't lied about that."

"Then what?"

"There have been cases of hunters with other skills. People who were born with both some innate magic and the will to be hunters." He frowned a little. Let out a sigh. "Those… The combination isn't always a successful one."

"Sometimes? Or never successful?"

"If they come to hunting first, before learning to control their magic, the magic gets away from them and…"

He shrugged a little, but he didn't have to go into detail. She was well aware what happened to magic wielders when they didn't learn to control their magic. The results depended on the strength of the individual's innate magic, but it was never good. For anyone.

"Does the magic get them or the demons?"

"According to the history keepers, it's been a little of both. But always during a fight, so, you could say it's always the demons in the end."

Her stomach tightened as a crawling anxiety worked through her. She tamped it down to ask, "When they come to the magic first, and have control over it?"

"They default to it," he said, his tone flat. "The way you do."

"And never master using their will?"

"For a period of time, they can be successful hunters. But… In the end, they've always defaulted to their magic."

"Results?" She had a feeling she knew already. Where she still had her arms crossed over her chest, she found herself squeezing tighter, hunching her shoulders, an attempt to protect herself from the information she knew was coming next. And her fingers twitched to rub the pentagram on her bracelet.

"Fighting demons with magic is…complicated," he said. Which didn't answer her question. "Possible, obviously. Plenty of non-hunters in the world have had to deal with demons, for one reason or another. Some of the summoners are magic wielders."

"But someone trying to fight a demon as a hunter, who defaults to earlier magic training… What happens, Seb?"

"None of them have been as powerful as you," he said, still not directly answering her question. "The records indicate their magic was… Not as powerful as yours."

"They died, too. Like the ones whose hunter training came first. They all died during a fight."

"Ang," he sighed out her name. "All demon hunters die during a fight. We don't retire."

"But some of you survive decades and decades fighting. Like Aidan. You aren't killed because some other skill complicates your hunter training."

There was a reason most hunters were humans. Not

beings from other, more magical, species. Not even shifters. Everyone defaulted to their innate natures. Shifters would, even with training, eventually fight like shifters—a tactic that didn't work over the long term with all demons. Magic wielders defaulted to magic. Fae defaulted to glamour and trickery. Vampires to mesmerism and strength. Everyone defaulted to their nature.

And those weren't the natures of a demon hunter.

"The…the other things interfere with the focus of a hunter's will," she said. "That's right, isn't it?"

"Will isn't the only way to overcome a demon," he said. "It's just our way. It's what a demon hunter fight comes down to."

"Yes, but, for those of us not demon hunters? Our other natures get in the way."

He shrugged. "They can."

"All the time?"

He glanced away, then met her gaze again. "Most of the time."

"Any case of a witch becoming a successful hunter? Even one?"

"I'd have to see the records of someone like you, a realm splitter, to say for sure."

"The others. The ones not like me. Did any of them succeed as hunters?"

"No."

She nodded. She knew the intent of all this was the council trying to get her and her dangerous skill out of their hair. But at the very least Gabriella, maybe Jess, thought she could succeed. Yet if none of the previous witches turned demon hunters survived…

What made her so different? Being a realms splitter? Did being a demon witch really make that much of a difference?

"Even Gabriella has to know this is a nearly impossible ask," she said. "Everyone in that room today has to know the odds are against me being a successful hunter."

"They do. But if we paid attention to odds, we wouldn't be able to do our jobs. The odds of having a stronger will than a demon seems pretty astronomical. Don't they? How many humans can actually *will* a demon away?" He spread his hands wide. "Yet here we are."

She nodded, but not because what he said made her feel better. She didn't. She felt worse. This wasn't going to work. Even as a show until they could find a way to get the council to leave her alone.

"It will work," he said, slowly approaching her. "This will work. Because I'll be with you. And because we both know you're not going to be a hunter long term. We'll find a way out of this. Until then, you need the skills to survive. You will get this. There's no one I know stronger and more capable." He ducked his head a little to meet her gaze, standing close enough to touch but not touching her. "And I was trained by a literal legend."

That startled a snort of amusement from her, even though she didn't want to be amused.

"Don't get discouraged after one session," he said. "This part will take time. It does for everyone. Even those of us who fought our first demon instinctively."

He rarely alluded to how he became a hunter. None of them talked about it. Not directly. There were things said, implied, hinted at. But none that she'd met had ever come out and talked about their first hunt, their first experience with a demon, when they realized they could be demon hunters.

"Will you finally tell me…how you got here?" she asked quietly. "What got you into this job?"

A long pause. He didn't look away from her direct gaze, but the little flare of red in the depths of his eyes brightened momentarily before fading back to something that could be mistaken for a trick of the light.

"One day," he said. "I might be able to talk about it. One day."

She nodded, a fast and jerky motion. His phrasing told her a lot. Being able to talk about it. That was the hard part. Being able to discuss those memories aloud.

In the silence that followed, she wondered how much she'd ever really known Sebastian. She'd loved him. Still did, despite herself. But there was an awful lot about him she didn't know.

Every time she was reminded of that, she worried about this plan they'd concocted.

And her heart broke a little more.

CHAPTER NINETEEN

Angie sipped her tea, standing at the counter on the first floor of Dana's Cauldron, talking with Laura as they watched the customers peruse merchandise. She'd finished two readings already and had an hour free for walk-ins if any appeared. Until someone did, though, she was happy standing around talking with Laura, Astor, and Moon Star—the other two working the floor that day—and giving herself time to be herself and be comfortable in her own skin.

She'd been missing that over the last few weeks, after being plunged back into the demon world. She'd missed just feeling like her ordinary witch self.

Her first session with Laura on bettering her aura reading had gone a lot more smoothly than her first demon hunting practice. She didn't have the same barriers to deal with. The defaults were already in place. She just needed to stretch herself. Practice with a master. The skills were within her normal range of practice, the kinds of magic she was used to dealing with.

And it was such a pleasure, such a relief, she knew in her soul she wasn't cut out to be a hunter.

To be fair, she'd always known. But the way she'd walked away from her session with Laura buoyed and happy even though she hadn't made much progress yet, while the session with Sebastian had left her frustrated and restless… The contrast couldn't have been clearer.

She'd chosen the right path when she'd made her decision to honor witchcraft. Nothing the council said or did would change that. She was a witch.

Just a witch with one unusual skill in her arsenal.

She'd considered discussing the dreams she'd had with Laura during their session. And as she stood watching the handful of customers in Dana's, she considered it again. She could trust the older woman with the details of her vision and the dreams that had followed. Laura had been around for a long time, and while her primary skill was aura reading, she knew a lot about a lot of things, including dreams.

But outside of the demon hunters, Angie hadn't told any of the people at work, any of her friends in the city, about her ability to open a demon portal. Laura knew Angie sometimes dealt with demon things. But not the details.

No one knew the details.

She'd kept that part of her life to herself, though, mostly because she'd wanted to put the demon world behind her. And, if she wanted to be completely honest, she was a little worried the owners of Dana's Cauldron would fire her if they knew. She loved her job and she loved working here. There were no demon things here. The owners didn't want any. And she was afraid they'd consider her one of those demon things if they knew the truth.

"You can talk about it, you know," Laura said. "I know you have your secrets and I respect that. But… You have something you want to discuss."

"You should be upstairs doing the readings," Angie said with a huff.

"No." Laura raised her hands and shook her head, though she smiled when she did. "I did my time at the table. I don't have your innate sympathy for the ones who just need to see a therapist. Not enough patience in the world for that."

Angie chuckled. She cradled her to-go cup and considered the decks of expensive tarot cards inside the glass counter next to the register without really seeing the exquisite artwork. "Suppose I have a lot on my mind. And some of it I can't discuss, but… I had a strange experience the other day. It'd be good to discuss it with someone familiar with witchy things."

"As opposed to the deliciously handsome…man you've been hanging out with?"

"He's not a witch," she said with a shrug. "He understands my life and magic, as much as he can, but he's… He's not a witch."

"I'm listening."

Angie smiled and then sighed. "I had a vision. I'd just set an intention and cast a spell for clear seeing. I wasn't even supposed to invoke a full-blown vision. But I had one. And one element of it keeps coming back into my dreams."

A customer walked up to the register, so they paused their quiet conversation while Laura rang the person up.

When the man walked away, his book and candles neatly wrapped in plane paper, Laura said, "Tell me about the element that keeps coming up in the dreams. That's obviously the crux of the vision."

Angie explained the spiderweb, the glowing blue threads, her at the center of the web. No spiders. But one long red thread that radiated out from the center of the web, from Angie's chest.

"When I tugged the red thread inside that first vision, I got a flash of... It's hard to describe. Power. Probably the easiest way to say it. Lots and lots of power pouring into me."

"Overwhelming you?"

"Not...in a bad way. And it felt like *my* power, not an outside thing. But it also felt like so much that it would just spill out of me. Like an overfull cup."

Laura nodded, but remained quiet.

"The next day, I was hungover like I'd done a major working. But, Laura, even major spells don't exhaust me that way anymore. I haven't given myself that kind of a hangover from anything but Tequila in a long time."

Laura's lips lifted a little at the Tequila comment, but her gaze was turned inward. She absently rubbed the pentagram inset in her leather choker. "Interesting."

"Any ideas?"

"A few. Obviously, the red is some untapped part of your powers."

Angie had been afraid of that.

"And if you embrace it, take it up like you did in the vision…" She whistled softly. "Sounds like you'll be in a position to level up power-wise. So to speak."

"And if I don't want anything to do with the power inside that red thread?" Because she didn't. She really didn't.

Because she was pretty certain that was the power, the thread, that led to her ability to open demon realms. The thought of what more she could do if she did embrace that magic was terrifying. The possibility of releasing a plague of demons was bad enough.

Laura shrugged. "That's always a choice. You asked for clarity. You got it."

"Not so clear. Just raised more questions."

"Only the question of whether you want to accept all of your nature, or if you want to continue trying to cut yourself off from that single part of your magic. You'll have to cut the thread, probably not metaphorically but literally for you, if you want to separate yourself from that part of your nature." Laura met her gaze, her fingers still on her choker. "I wouldn't recommend that, though. Denying your full nature and cutting yourself off from a fundamental part of what makes you you is…dangerous. For ordinary people. But even more so for witches."

Without knowing what that red thread meant, what power it led to, Angie wasn't so sure Laura was right about that. In this particular instance, cutting herself off from the ability to open demon realms seems prudent.

But she understood Laura's point. Cutting herself off from her magic, even the stuff related to demons, might have knock-on consequences she wasn't prepared to pay. Like taking away her touch psychic skills. She lost those and her ability to do the job she loved went out the window. She wasn't the kind of psychic who could read someone at a glance. One aura reading lesson with Laura didn't make her an expert there. She didn't read tarot, use a crystal ball, any of the other prop-based options for helping people. She shook their hand, got a handle on the real situation, then let them talk and found a way to guide them toward a solution to their problem, or at least a better understanding of the problem. She loved her way of "counselling" and she sure as hell didn't want to cut that part of her nature off on accident.

She also didn't want to risk her other magic. A spiderweb was a delicate balancing act of different threads and when everything was in place the delicate became strong. If she cut one thread, she risked unraveling the entire whole.

No longer able to open breaches between realms. But maybe no longer able to do magic either.

That thought made her want to throw up. She was a witch and had been since she could remember. She *liked* being a witch. She liked her magic, her powers—even the ones that had taken her awhile to get under control—and her community of fellow witches. The community wouldn't abandon her, she knew. A lot of pagans and even some witches didn't have actual magic. They were still embraced by the community.

Still, she'd feel separated from it, and from herself, if she no longer had magic.

But could she continue to risk what her realm splitting powers were capable of? Did she want to go her whole life being careful around trees and worrying about accidentally unleashing an apocalypse?

"Damn it," she muttered.

"Not sure what to do?" Laura asked, her brows raised.

"Not even a little bit."

"Then don't do anything yet. Give it time. These things don't usually have to be resolved in a day or two. Something large can take...years to work out. Let yourself mull the options."

"Thanks. And thanks for listening. Saying this out loud helps."

"You'll probably still have the dreams for a few days. Don't let that push you into a hasty decision."

"I can deal with bad dreams," Angie said. She'd dealt with those her whole life. "I won't be hasty."

Her biggest problem was going to be stalling too long to make a decision. If she didn't have to decide, she'd be happier. But if the decision was made for her, she'd be pissed. So she needed to take this choice into her own hands.

Before someone made the choice for her.

CHAPTER TWENTY

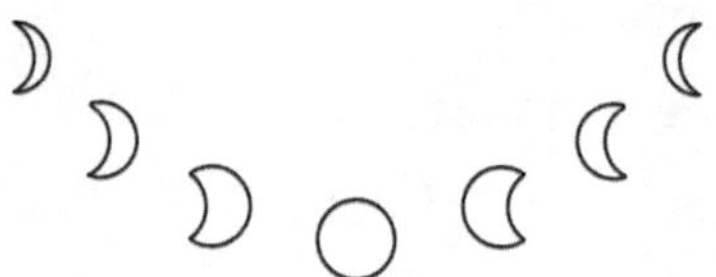

When the tall, lean, wiry man walked into Dana's Cauldron a few minutes later, Angie spotted him instantly. He wasn't exactly trying to blend in. He was a white man, age hard to judge but she'd guess around mid-to-late forties, with thinning blond hair and sharp brown eyes, which were narrowed as he took in his surroundings. He wore black suit, white shirt, and black tie, all well-tailored and starched.

A passing glance and he might have looked like a business man in a new environment. They got those types sometimes. Someone looking for a present. Or wandering in to see how the other half lived. She would have put him in that second category, just based on the way he scanned the store and his brow crinkled with his frown. Not exactly hostile and disgusted, but not open to the adventure of Dana's either.

He was the type she usually let the floor staff handle. Astor was on his break, but Moon Star and Laura had a lot of experience with these tourist types of customers and could handle them well.

But something about this guy set off warning klaxons in Angie's head. She wasn't sure what it was. Something about his bearing. Something about the way he looked down his nose at his surroundings. Not just arrogance. But a dangerous arrogance.

"His aura is not good," Laura said quietly. "The circle should probably be making him itchy by now, though. Hopefully, he'll leave soon."

He didn't leave. He searched the store with a sweeping gaze, spotted the cash register, and headed toward Laura and Angie.

Angie carefully set her mostly empty cup behind the countertop so she'd have her hands free if she needed to deal with the guy. Moon Star, standing across the store working with a customer, gave her a look. Moon Star's parents had been hippies long after the hippy-era faded and had literally named their only daughter Moon Star Mackenzie on her birth certificate. Moon Star was a bespeckled pagan by theology who's big curly hair was currently tamed by a scarf and her star-speckled orange pants complimented her namesake well. But she wasn't one of the witches with magic that worked at Dana's. She was just a happy, out-of-time moonchild more comfortable here than at an ordinary mainstream retail store.

Moon Star made a move toward the register, but Angie shook her head slightly. Since she didn't know what kind of person this guy was, she didn't want anyone non-magical in his way. Plus, it was better for someone to stay out of the direct line of this guy's attention, whoever or whatever he was, just in case they needed to go upstairs and get backup.

She wasn't entirely sure why she felt like there might be trouble. The man wasn't yelling, or glaring, or in any way indicating that he was here to fight.

But she felt the impending trouble in her bones.

She gave her bracelet charm a little rub, her fingers skimming the dangling silver pentagram, as the man stopped at the desk.

Laura put on her polite but reserved smile and said, "May we help you with anything?"

"I'm looking for a woman named Angela Jordan." The man's Russian accent was slight, but there, and his tone was business-like. Not aggressive. Unlike his bearing when he'd stepped into the store.

"May I ask what this is in regards?" Laura said. "If you'd like to schedule a reading, I'd be happy to help."

"A reading?" He glanced around. "She's one of the tarot readers?"

"Are you looking for a reading?"

"No. No. Just a conversation." The man faced them again, his gaze skimming them both. The look was distracted, cursory. His brow creased as he refocused on Laura.

Moon Star had crept a little closer, close enough to hear the conversation while still attending to the handful of customers milling about the store. Angie motioned her with a subtle hand gesture to stay where she was. The man wasn't giving the impression he intended on attacking at the moment. But something about him was still off.

And both she and Laura knew the last time a stranger had come into the store specifically looking for Angie, that person had been possessed by a demon.

"I can leave her a message," Laura said.

"Yes. A message would be good. May I leave my card?"

"Of course."

The man lifted a card out of his front pocket and left it on the counter top for Laura to take. He frowned a little at the selection of crystals and tarot decks, but didn't comment. Instead, he said, "Please let her know Mr. Gregory Sokolov would like to speak with her about a favor she did for his brother-in-law."

"Does his brother-in-law have a name?" Laura pulled out a little pad of paper and wrote the note, even though Angie was standing right there to listen.

"Ivan Meknikov. She was able to provide him the name of a…specialist who is helping his daughter."

"I hope his daughter is doing well?" Laura kept her gaze on the notepad as she asked.

"There is hope where they had not been," the man said.

Angie wanted to smile, wanted to sag with relief. She knew Cindy was good, but it was a relief to know Ivan's daughter was getting appropriate help without having to summon a demon again. And she was relieved whatever Carmen's scheme had been, it hadn't worked. At least it hadn't killed anyone. She was afraid it had worked for calling out her and Sebastian. But no one had died and Ivan's daughter was getting help.

"My brother-in-law informed me that she helped with… another matter as well. For which our family is very grateful. Please let Ms. Jordon know that we are in her debt."

He put a strange sort of emphasis on that last word.

Angie wasn't sure she liked that emphasis. But she wasn't sure why either. She let her gaze soften and attempted to read Sokolov's aura, the way she'd been practicing with Laura. Laura had said his aura wasn't good. Angie just picked up a muddy collection of colors she couldn't tease apart and interpret. Nothing in the layers that would have given her any information about Sokolov. There was a single flare of color and then it faded back into the muddy mix. But because it had happened fast, and Angie wasn't very good at this yet, she really didn't see what the color was. Maybe Laura had.

"I will let her know, Mr. Sokolov," Laura said, as she finished her note. She looked up and smiled politely. "Is there anything else we can do for you today?"

"Please ask Ms. Jordan to call me. I would very much like to talk to her personally."

"I will let her know you've been here."

"Thank you."

The man gave Angie another cursory glance and a slight nod. He hunted around the store again, as if trying to take it all in, then gave them both another nod and headed out.

"That was interesting," Laura said. "I presume you understood some of it."

"Some. Not all."

"Will you call him?"

"Maybe."

She did want to check on Ivan's daughter's progress. But she could talk to Cindy about that. If all the man wanted to do was thank her, the note was more than enough. She had too much going on to deal with a stranger thinking he was in her debt. Especially since the whole demon summoning thing was an idea Carmen had given Ivan just to lure Angie and Sebastian out. Might be better to let it go.

Moon Star stopped close to the desk. "Everything okay? You both got pretty tense there." She might not have any innate magic, but she had a great natural ability to read body language. Her skills with reading people without any help from magic always impressed Angie.

"Everything is fine," Laura assured her. "He just wanted to leave a message."

"Looked a little scary," Moon Star said, glancing back to the door and pushing up her glasses as they sagged down her nose. "Not sure why."

Angie wasn't sure either. The whole thing had felt... Contradictory. No, that wasn't quite right. She just had a weird feeling about the exchange, but she couldn't place a name to the weird feeling.

"Probably the suit," Laura said. "We don't get a lot of suits in here this time of day."

The suits usually came in on Friday nights, or after eight pm on weekdays.

Angie returned to her small reading room on the third

floor when a walk-in customer came in and asked for a reading. Getting out of her own head and concentrating on work was good.

But the strange visit hung at the back of her mind for the rest of the night.

CHAPTER TWENTY-ONE

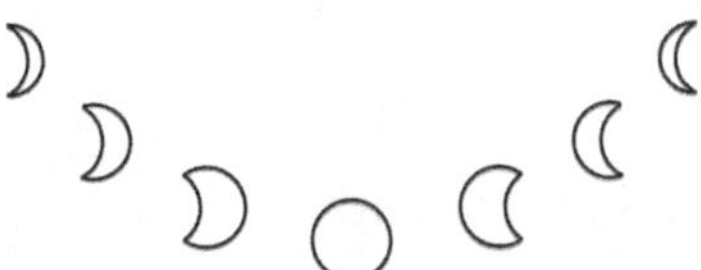

Sebastian was waiting for her when Angie finished work and came downstairs in her "street clothes" —a pair of jeans and a long sleeved, turtleneck t-shirt under a thick wool coat against the increasingly cool temperatures. October in New York was always tricky. It could go from freezing cold, to pleasant autumn, to spring time hot over the course of a week, sometimes in a single day. Right now, the city was swinging cold and her lighter jacket hadn't been enough for the late night walk home from work.

She had not been expecting to see Sebastian tonight. And his arrival after the earlier encounter with Ivan's brother-in-law seemed suspicious.

"What's up?" she asked him, stopping at the counter where he was talking quietly with Laura. "Wasn't expecting you tonight. Anything wrong?"

"Nothing wrong. Just thought I'd walk you home." He

smiled, but the expression looked tense, the muscles along his jaw and around his mouth stiff.

She wondered if he was showing her that tension on purpose. And did Laura notice. When Angie glanced at the older woman, though, she wasn't giving Angie a speculative look or any indication that she knew something was not quite right. In fact, she was smiling a little secretive smile. Like she knew something Angie didn't.

Angie was tempted to try reading Sebastian's aura, but since she'd be doing so without his permission, that felt wrong. She hadn't had the same compunction when trying to read Gregory Sokolov's aura earlier. She'd have to discuss the ethics question with Laura at their next lesson.

For now, she kept her—granted still a work-in-progress—aura reading skills to herself, and said, "That was nice of you. I'm ready when you are."

Laura waved them off.

Astor fanned his face behind Sebastian's back. And Moon Star gave her a wink, exaggerating the gesture ridiculously behind her big round glasses. Angie rolled her eyes at them both and walked out the door Sebastian held open for her.

Once they were safely away from Dana's and engulfed in weekday pedestrian traffic, Angie said, "Okay, what's really going on? You don't show up to walk me home from work unless there's a problem."

That wasn't technically true. But when he'd shown up the first few times after the incident with Grant to walk her home, she'd asked him to stop. At the time, she was still sorting through what to do about the council, and she'd felt pressured by his presence. He'd never spoken about the council and her training to be a hunter on those walks. But still, she'd felt like he was just waiting on her decision.

She'd also liked those walks too much. Liked him meeting her after work, walking with her through the Village. She'd wanted to hold his hand and pretend to be a couple again, an ordinary couple who only had to worry about little things like what to order for dinner and what they'd do with their day off. The fantasy had been so tempting and delicious, it had felt like pain. Like a cut she kept salting and adding a little lemon juice to just for good measure.

So she'd asked him only to meet her at work if there was something wrong, something important. And he'd honored her request. She'd missed walking home with him the first night he hadn't shown up. Hurt enough she knew she'd made the right decision.

"What's wrong?" she asked again when he didn't answer.

"You don't know?"

She scowled at him, but he was frowning just as fiercely at her. "What am I supposed to know?"

He looked away, shaking his head. "You can't feel the call? The need to…go?"

"Shit. There's a demon about to break loose somewhere, isn't there?" She realized why he looked upset now. "And because I'm in training, I should have felt the instinct to hunt."

"Yes," he said. "Come on. We'll figure it out after the demon is contained."

"I already know the answer," she said, draping the strap

of her giant purse over her head so the strap stretched across her chest. "I'm not really a hunter. And I'm not meant to be one."

His mouth flattened but he didn't comment.

"How much time do we have?"

"Feels like something that will happen in a few hours. We have time to get there. It's outside of the city. New Jersey."

In the two years she'd lived in New York, she wasn't sure she'd been to Jersey. Not even to go to the airport. She'd driven into town when she'd moved here, so she'd passed through New Jersey then, she supposed. But she'd only flown home to New Mexico once for the Winter Solstice, and then she'd flown out through JFK.

"How are we getting there?" Trains would take time. A taxi was expensive. But Sebastian had ways of doing these things…

Ways she'd have to figure out, she realized. At least in the short term.

He stopped beside a car parked a block from her apartment. "Taking this."

"A rental?" And how had he gotten street parking? He'd have had to circle the block for hours waiting for someone to pull out. Or, more likely, he willed a spot somehow. Impressive.

"Easiest option." He held her door for her as she slipped in, then moved to the driver's seat.

The car itself was an innocuous mid-sized, four door Toyota with nothing about it that stood out. It was clean. It was dark gray. And it was one of thousands. To be fair, Angie thought most cars looked too much alike these days anyway, but she was certain this one was *supposed* to look like every other car on the road. Another hunter instinct—to blend in as much as possible.

Since she hadn't driven in New York since selling her car, the drive to the Holland Tunnel was an exercise in patience and not cringing and flinching at every impatient horn honk. A weeknight meant a lot of traffic even at almost nine p.m., so the going was slow. Once in the tunnel, traffic picked up and they emerged into New Jersey in a rush.

With the traffic behind them, on a freeway not so packed with commuters, she relaxed a little. She didn't ask Sebastian where they were going. He was following instinct and probably didn't know the exact location either, at least until they got there.

She was very aware of the fact that she *didn't* feel any driving need to go anywhere in particular. Her stomach rumbled for dinner. She was a little sleepy after a day's work. And the traffic had left her tense. But she didn't feel a pull toward anything but her own bed.

Which was worrying. She couldn't fool the council into thinking she was taking the hunter track seriously if she had no idea when she was needed for a hunt.

"Is it because I'm new and still training?" she asked, grateful she didn't have to clarify even though her question came out of nowhere after a prolonged silence.

"Possible. I remember feeling the tug early on. But it's been a while. I can't remember if I felt it in those first few weeks after… When I started training with Aidan."

She let his slip go without comment. "So it's possible I'm just too new to this, right? Possible I didn't feel anything because there was a more experienced hunter around, and I would have been out of my depth going in alone?"

"Possible," he said quietly.

But she heard the hesitance. Not quite doubt, but… uncertainty. And uncertainty was very dangerous for a hunter.

She was tempted say, *I told you so*. But he wasn't the one that had earned her I-told-you-so's. That was the council.

They pulled off the freeway and drove down a wide street running through a smallish town, the road bracketed by small shops, two car washes, a gas station, a library, a large hardware store, and some restaurants, most of which were closed, except for a drive through fast food place. A few more turns, and they pulled up to a house in a nice-looking neighborhood.

The surrounding houses were largish for the east coast, two stories with enough space in front for a decent patch of grass and driveways leading to detached garages. The street was lined with large, thick-trunked trees—none with split trucks she was happy to see—and the street lights were dimmed and infrequent, making the area darker than the main streets had been.

Sebastian parked on the street in front of their destination, then came around to stand on the sidewalk next to Angie as they studied the house.

Two story and ordinary-looking, like every other house on the block. Narrower than some of the larger houses in the neighborhood, like there were two rooms in front and two in back and not much more. Painted a light color, maybe gray or light blue, though it was hard to tell in the orangey-yellow street lights. The curtains on the lower floor were pulled closed, but there didn't looked to be any lights leaking past the curtains. No light visible through the windows bracketing the wooden front door either. The top floor was as dark as the bottom, at least on this side of the house. There was a little stone fence enclosing a simple grass-covered yard, with decorative wrought iron bars above the stone. The wrought iron gate had an arch over the top with swirling designs in the metal.

Angie glanced around the neighborhood. If she listened carefully, she could just hear the TV from one of the neighbors. And there were lights on in most of the houses. It was after ten at night now, a little late maybe, but not so late for a weekday night. Still, the house in front of them looked either empty or the occupants had gone to sleep. There weren't any sounds coming from inside, that she could hear, and not even a motion sensor light flickered on when a squirrel darted across the small stone porch in front of the door.

Sebastian walked to the corner of the stone fence and glanced around the house. She went in the opposite direction, seeing if she could see anything from that angle. Just a small, pale colored shed in the back that could have been a garage since there was a concrete driveway leading to it. But it was a small enough building, it could also have just been a tool shed. She didn't see a car anywhere. And there were no cars parked directly in front of the house, other than Sebastian's rental.

From the outside, the house looked empty. No one home.

But even as she walked back to the front gate to rejoin Sebastian, a crawl of anxiety went down her back.

"Now what?" she asked, staring up at the front door again.

He didn't say anything for a moment. Then, "We knock."

CHAPTER TWENTY-TWO

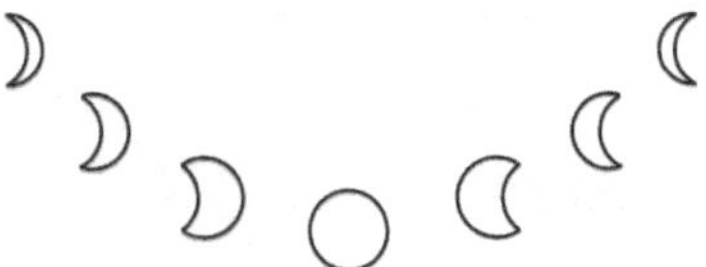

ngie stopped Sebastian's hand as he reached for the front gate, that crawl of anxiety in her gut getting worse. The thought of Sebastian touching the gate blocking the way to that ordinary looking house left her breathless with fear, and she had no idea why.

"What's wrong?" he asked, easing his hand back to his side.

The farther his hand was from the wrought iron rails, the more her breathing and heartbeat normalized. The panic hadn't just been her imagination.

She let go of his arm and scowled at the gate, but looking at it directly wasn't telling her anything. It looked normal enough. Still, her instincts were humming and she could practically feel the crackle of…something on her skin.

Instead of answering Sebastian, she turned her head a little to the side, softened her gaze, and looked at the gate through her peripheral vision, opening to seeing whatever was there.

A weird flickering at the edges of her vision. Just there. Blue light. She turned back and tried to look at the light directly, but she couldn't see anything. She angled her head away again, turning just enough…

Blue light shimmered around the wrought iron gate. And the arch over the top of it pulsed with light and what looked to be runic symbols, though without being able to look at them directly, she couldn't tell for sure.

She hissed. "There's magic here," she said quietly, even though there was no one else on the sleepy residential street. "The gate. Probably a security spell of some kind, a complicated ward, to keep unwanted visitors out."

"Something you can break?" he asked, his gaze on the front door.

She frowned, taking in the gate, seeing it without the magic flicker. "Let me see what I can do."

Breaking spells required knowing what they were and how they'd been crafted. She'd studied this a little over the years, but it hadn't been a focus. Mostly, she'd learned how to break a damaging or negative spell thrown at her by another witch. Which hadn't actually come in handy much over the years because Angie hadn't gotten on the wrong side of any of the witches she'd met since she started her training. Her more solitary leanings, with only a single mentor or teacher at any given point in time, and keeping the other witches and psychics and otherworldly types in her life as friends instead of people she did magic with, had probably helped with that. She hadn't put herself into the position to piss off many other witches.

So her skills in following a magic spell in order to break it were rusty.

She let her eyes drift almost shut, though not fully, and angled her head until she could see the blue light again. "Watch my back," she murmured to Sebastian, probably unnecessarily. Then she let herself sink into the magic encompassing the wrought iron, touching it mentally rather than physically, letting her own magic reach out to tentatively touch the lines of power.

The sensation of buzzing insects against her skin was instant and decidedly uncomfortable. A manifestation of the spell she suspected. She let her breath out slowly, let the sensation give her information rather than instinctively running away from it.

Yes. The spell was designed to repel visitors. To make people uncomfortable knocking or touching the gate. Worked at the primitive lizard brain. Specific to humans, she realized. Nothing here for vampires or shifters or Fae or any other otherworldly beings. Not even demons. Strictly for keeping humans out.

For casual visitors, she thought as she followed the threads of the magic, running the "finger" of her own power along the lines without pulling or tugging at them. Just getting the feel of the spell's "knot." The pattern wasn't as complex as she'd feared. She picked up a flavor of Eastern European magic. Definitely witch magic, though. Not wizard or Fae. Not particularly ancient magic. The spell hadn't been designed using rare knowledge. No elements beyond its base magic to complicated things.

As she studied the spell, she realized that while it was strong, created by a powerful magic wielder, and solid as a rock, it wasn't actually a complex spell. Not built to confound a witch's ability to break it. Not mixing multiple types of magic disciplines to make things more difficult. Just a straightforward warding spell, designed to ward off human visitors.

And only human visitors.

That struck her as a little strange since they were here because Sebastian sensed a demon about to get loose from its summoner's control. The people inside knew enough about magic to ward their gate and enough about demons to summon one.

But they only protected their home from human visitors. And the ward they'd used wasn't designed to stop a witch.

That made her think either the witch who'd set the spell was poorly trained. Or the spell had been bought by the people who lived here and they didn't realize another witch would see it and could break it.

Or the witch who'd sold it to them hadn't warned them.

For reasons Angie couldn't precisely pinpoint, she thought of Carmen. She wouldn't have said Carmen was a witch, though. A woman intent on using demons to exact revenge against people she deemed deserving. Someone who knew how to use ceremonies and spells to deal with demons. But not a technical, magic wielding witch, like Angie. Angie hadn't gotten the feeling of "witch" from her at all.

Either that had been a grave oversight on her part. Carmen was more dangerous even than she'd suspected. Or she was looking for links to Carmen because the woman was on her mind.

Whichever was true, that was a problem for another time. First, she had to unknot the tight twists of the gate's warding spell.

Following the threads through their pattern, she murmured a detangling spell, which helped her see the connections better. No surprises. The unweaving took longer than the weaving would have, because she didn't want to set off any unexpected alarms or surprises. But less than five minutes later, she had the threads untangled and the spell dissolved in her metaphysical hands.

She kept her eyes mostly closed, looking at the magic to make sure it faded, the power inside the spell grounding harmlessly into the earth. She took a deep breath, let it out slowly. Waited to make sure she hadn't accidentally set off any backup spells.

"Nope," she murmured. Then opened her eyes fully. "All clear."

She glanced up at the sky. If she had tried to brute force the spell, she would have brought down rain. Elements went a little wonky around her brand of brute force magic. But the autumn night sky remained clear, the air crisp and colder out here away from the city.

The surrounding neighborhood remained relatively quiet, too. No one left their houses or arrived, parking on the streets. No cars rolled passed, slowing to investigate the people just hovering outside one house gate.

"Keeping it clear," Sebastian said under his breath, letting her know he'd been willing the street to remain quiet. "Wanted to give you time to work."

"Thanks." For some reason, her chest warmed at both his faith that she'd get the spell undone and his help in giving her time. He was no doubt a little impatient to get inside and stop an impending disaster, but he hadn't tried to rush her.

She appreciated that. But it was also a reminder that he knew her and her witchy ways. That he understood how her brand of magic worked. That he knew *her*.

She pushed the unwanted rise of feelings aside. "We should head in?"

"Still not...sensing anything?"

She shook her head. Outside of the spell, she had no instinct to go into the house, to investigate. There was no push to get inside and make sure a demon didn't break free into this realm. If, as a demon hunter, she was supposed to feel that sense of impending doom, she was an utter failure.

And she wouldn't have minded if she weren't currently trying to fake her way at being a hunter.

Sebastian frowned at her, but then glanced at the house and said, "Let's go."

They pushed open the gate slowly, but it didn't squeak or announce them in any other mundane way. Another pause inside, on the lawn. No sounds of barking dogs coming around the corner. No lights came on inside the house. No noise.

Angie was tempted to ask if this was the right house. But the magical ward on the gate had given it away. Otherwise, the silence was so absolute, she might have worried Sebastian had gotten this wrong. She searched with her mind's eye as well as her actual eyes, checking for more magical spells and wards. While she couldn't sense the impending danger like a hunter, she could at least use her witch skills to help.

They reached the front door without setting off any alarms, and then, just as he'd said he would do, Sebastian knocked.

Angie gave him a look, raising her brows.

He shrugged. "Easiest way to get inside. If they don't open it, I will."

"Surprise might have been a useful tactic."

"Maybe."

He didn't sound even a little repentant or hesitant about his plan. She sighed and started to prepare a shielding spell, just in case.

A minute passed, long enough for Angie to get her spell into the holding place where all it would take was one last hand gesture to bring it up. Long enough for her to think no one would answer.

Then the door slowly creaked open, stopping when the inside chain reached its max. An eye looked out the narrow gap between the door and door frame. "Can I help you?"

"We didn't wake you, did we ma'am?" Sebastian asked, letting his English accent roll out a little stronger.

"No. I think you have the wrong house, though." The woman glanced at Angie, then back toward the gate.

The gap between door and door frame wasn't large enough for Angie to get a good view of the woman. Especially since the lights inside the house remained off. She was a little shorter than Angie's own six foot height, though not by much. Her eyes were dark brown, and in the dim light thrown by the streetlamps, she looked paled-skinned, probably a white woman, with light brown hair. Her age was impossible to judge yet, though her voice was strong enough. She wore a t-shirt and jeans, her one visible foot bare, no socks.

Angie couldn't tell if she had anything in her hands, but she didn't get a sense of magic from the woman. Nothing screamed at her to throw the shield up and protect herself and Sebastian from bad magic. There could be a gun behind the door. Or a knife. But at least there wasn't magic to contend with.

"It's late," she said when she refocused on Sebastian and Angie. "Is something wrong? Are you the cops?"

"Not the police," Sebastian said, his tone soothing. "We're here because you're about to have a problem, and we need to stop it."

"What problem?"

"May we come in?"

"No. Why are you here?"

"The demon you've summoned is about to escape."

The matter-of-fact way Sebastian said this made the

woman draw up, pulling back from the door as if he'd poked her with something.

Silence for a long moment. Then the woman moved closer to the door again. "I don't know what you're talking about. You should leave."

"If we leave, there'll be no one to stop the demon from breaking free of your control and killing you." Sebastian's tone was still remarkably gentle and soothing.

Angie couldn't tell if there was any will in his voice, backing up the sound, willing the woman to open the door for them. She actually wasn't sure his will would work that way. Though she'd probably need to ask. She'd watched him talk himself into a few houses over the years. Typically, he'd just needed his charm and his accent to do it.

The woman wavered, glancing between Sebastian and Angie again.

"I don't know what you're talking about," she repeated, but there was less certainty now, and her voice trembled just a little.

"Please let me help you," Sebastian said quietly. "The demon will not go easy on you should it enter this realm."

The woman stared up at Sebastian for several long long moments. Then, "Who are you?" Asked to both Sebastian and Angie.

"Friends," Sebastian said. "People used to dispatching demons back to their realms."

"And if we don't want that?" the woman asked, then hissed under her breath. She'd given herself away and was not happy about that.

"The problem," Sebastian said quietly, "is that the demon you've summoned is about to escape your control. And it will kill you and everyone in this house if it does."

The woman's eyes widened with each word. "How can you know? You can't know."

"It's what I do. I know." He spread his hands. "I'm here to keep you alive. One way or the other, I'll stop the demon. But I'd rather you were alive afterward."

"You don't know me. Maybe I'm evil."

"Maybe. I'd still rather you were alive."

Angie watched the woman closely. She could be evil. She could be luring them along, only to try and kill them in the midst of her demon ceremony. But Sebastian was telling her the truth. He wanted her alive at the end of the night. Having to clean up an escaped demon after it had already killed the human summoner wasn't his favorite task. Wasn't any of their favorite tasks.

"I don't know what you're talking about," the woman said again, but she glanced behind her now, toward the interior of the house.

And if Angie concentrated, she could hear some shuffling behind the woman. She couldn't identify who—or what— was making the noise, but there was definitely someone else in the house.

"It's okay if you want to keep denying it," Sebastian said. "But denial won't stop the inevitable. It just makes the inevitable harder."

He was doing that thing where he made himself look harmless and non-threatening. Ensuring there was nothing about him that might scare the woman. On the one hand, looking non-threatening didn't make his claims to be able to stop a demon very credible. But on the other, the woman would be less jumpy if the large Black man standing outside her house didn't come across as threatening. A delicate line to walk for a hunter.

Another glance back into the house.

And then a noise from deep in the home, like a scream cut off. A gasp or grunt. Some gurgling. The woman cursed, and hurried away from the door—

Leaving the chain in place.

CHAPTER TWENTY-THREE

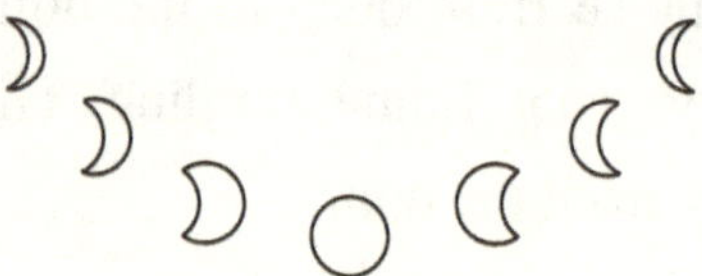

"Well, that's not helping," Angie murmured, gesturing to the chain holding the door closed.

From inside the dark house, she heard the woman calling someone's name and what sounded like footsteps on stairs. Another ominous gurgling sound answered the woman. And the footsteps quickened.

"Sounds like they're in trouble," Sebastian said. "We can't wait."

He put his shoulder against the door and pushed, hard, until the chain stretched and strained under his weight. Normally, this wouldn't budge a security chain. But there was a demon about to break loose, one that might have already broken free. A chain wouldn't stop a hunter.

This was one of those times, though, when Angie envied those with telekinesis. Being able to just move the chain would have been handy. And less strain on Sebastian's shoulders.

The wood door cracked, splintered. And the entire chain lock panel came away from the door frame with a suddenness that had Sebastian pushing through the door in a whoosh. He didn't stumble or lose his balance as he followed the door inside, though Angie reached for him to catch him if he did.

Without a word, he headed deeper into the house. Following the sounds of gasps and shouts now. Angie stayed with him, knowing she should be preparing to use her will alongside Sebastian. She was supposed to be a hunter now.

Instead, she queued up two spells—her little fire spell, and an illusion spell. Just to be on the safe side.

The interior of the house was as dark as it had seemed from outside. No lights on. All the curtains pulled. The central hallway led straight back to a visible kitchen at the back out of the house, and there were two open rooms on either side of the hall. A stairs near the kitchen led up to the second floor.

In the dark, everything appeared neat and tidied, but lived in. Shoes under the table in the entryway near the door. The coffee table in the one room covered in magazines and some left over food cartons. The table in the opposite room containing two empty wine glasses and an open bottle of wine.

Angie walked behind Sebastian, scanning the house, the rooms, looking for anyone, or anything, that might complicate the coming fight. She was more than a little relieved not to see any signs of kids. She hated when someone involved kids in demon summonings. It was never ever good. Though, more than one hunter had come from just such a circumstance.

More gurgling shouts came from a door next to the staircase. The door was open, the space beyond pitch black.

"Basement?" she asked Sebastian, keeping her voice low.

"Basement."

Why was it always basements? No one ever summoned a demon in their front living room. She supposed that made sense by way of not wanting to be seen and caught summoning demons by a nosey neighbor. Still. Always basements…

Basements left so little room for the humans to escape.

She sighed and closed in tight behind Sebastian, wondering if her fire spell was such a good idea in the confines of a basement with few exits. She dissipated the spell without triggering it, making sure it dissolved completely. Then murmured a new spell. She had a shield spell. And she could form a circle to keep the humans downstair safe. But none of that helped Sebastian. He had to face the demon without a shield, without anything between him and his will.

And, Angie realized, she was supposed to be doing that as well.

The magic came instinctively. Her go-to response to a dangerous situation. It wasn't a habit she was likely to break any time soon. She wasn't even sure she wanted to. But somehow she had to try, or at least give a credible appearance of trying.

Sebastian paused next to the wide open basement door for several moments before easing around the edge of the frame and down the dark stairs. Below, it wasn't as dark as it had first appeared though. The ominous—and predictable—red glow of the demon below gave the stairs a strange, eerie sort of illumination.

More gurgling. That didn't sound good and it sent Angie's adrenaline spiking. Her instincts screamed to hurry, to save the person making those noises.

But rushing into a situation with a demon like that was almost always deadly.

She forced herself to ease quietly down the stairs without breaking into a panicked run. Running away or running forward. Toss up, really. Her heartbeat hammered the deeper they went. Every time. She never quite got over the fear when she had to face a demon. Not even during the years she'd worked with Sebastian. She'd never gotten used to walking into a strange place and confronting the beasts.

This moment was no different. When they reached the bottom of the staircase, her pulse was a loud rush of blood in her ears, and sweat trickled down her back under her coat. The strap of her purse over her shoulder and across her chest felt too tight, and the weight of the bag dragged at her. She had to force breath in and out so she didn't pant, or worse, stop breathing all together and pass out.

The basement was a wide open space with the corners and edges cloaked in dark shadows. In the center of the room, a white chalk circle had been etched in the concrete floor and candles circled the outer edge. Between line and candles, another circle of symbols drawn with salt. Runic symbols. A spell for containment. A witch spell.

More witch magic involved.

Was that significant, or a coincidence.

The woman who'd answered the door stood just outside the candle circle, trying to physically pull a man back out of the circle. He was held above the chalk line and runes, not smudging the protections fortunately.

But since he was being held above the circle by a giant fist wrapped around his throat, that wasn't a lot better.

The demon was wide, and squat, red skinned with a series of scales and feathers running down thick arms and over the top of his giant thighs. Hooved feet. Horns like a bull. Face a combination of bull and eagle features—bull nose over a sharp beak beneath beady black eyes with pupils of glowing red. Around the bull horns on its head, tentacle like hair waved in an absent breeze. And when it opened its beak mouth, a forked snake tongue flickered out to lick the man it held in one large fist.

The man gurgled a little more and gripped the demon's wrist tight. The demon's laugh was a piercing screech.

"Let him go, let him go," the woman cried, trying to drag the man back to her without knocking over any candles or smudging the chalk and salt.

At least she was trying to keep the circle intact. But with the man already in the demon's grip, the circle had broken somewhere. The demon had gotten through.

Sebastian had vanished into the basement shadows almost as soon as they reached the bottom stair. Angie didn't bother to hunt for him in the darkness, knowing he was there somewhere. If she concentrated hard enough, she could practically feel him, feel the pull as he gathered his will for the fight.

Something she should be doing.

Instead, she hurried close to the woman, looked up at the demon and said, "Let him go, beast." She used her best hunter voice, infusing as much will as she was able into the command.

The demon screeched a response that was so piercing in the confined area, she worried her ears might bleed. She murmured a sound dampening spell, a quick twist of the fingers, and the sound no longer cut her so deeply. But the woman dropped her grip on her companion to cover her ears.

A move the demon took advantage of, dragging the man fully inside the circle. Right toward its wide open beak.

The woman screamed. Angie surged forward, trying to reach the man's flailing limbs.

From the opposite side of the circle, Sebastian's voice echoed around the basement. "Stop!"

The demon stopped. It screeched again, but it seemed to be unable to drag the man closer. For the moment. Angie used the pause to trigger her illusion spell. Around the basement, smoke started to curl toward the circle's edge, a stalking fog filled with little sparkling lights. The demon glanced around at the fog and its beady eyes narrowed.

"What trick is this, hunter?" it said.

The voice didn't come from its beaked mouth, though. It took Angie several moments to realize it spoke through a second mouth, located on its forehead. A mouth she hadn't see amidst the tentacle hair.

She wracked her brain to identify the demon. She'd studied the different species, knew a lot of them now, but she had been actively avoiding that study for the last year and a half and she was rusty. Not a Molder demon, like she'd faced a few weeks ago, thank the goddess. But something in the back of her mind poked at her. A warning.

Her illusionary fog also caught the woman's attention. She pushed up against Angie, as if trying to prevent the fog from touching her. Angie held her position, her gaze on the demon's.

"What trick is this?" it demanded again as the thickening fog collected outside the circle, obscuring the candles' dim and flickering light.

"Poison for a demon," Angie said, with as much bravado and confidence as she could muster. A lie. But demon's lied so much, their ability to tell the difference between a lie and truth wasn't as honed as it could be.

"You lie. There are no poisons in this world that could affect me." Another screech and it jerked the man closer to its face again.

"Stop!" Sebastian again, his voice deep and rumbling with his will.

The demon froze again, and its forehead mouth snarled.

The illusionary fog continued to pile up just outside the circle, creeping higher now, water piling up against an overturned glass.

"Let the human go," Angie said, letting her voice go deep.

"Or what? You cannot stop me when they have agreed to a sacrifice. It is the bargain. The bargain must be kept."

"We didn't," the woman said, frantically tugging at Angie's arm. "We didn't make the bargain."

"Your man did," the demon said, though it kept its beady eyes on Angie.

She had a moment to wonder why it wasn't paying just as much attention to Sebastian behind it—the real hunter in the room. But since its focus on her meant it wasn't currently crushing its victim's throat, she wasn't going to draw attention to the fact that it was looking at the wrong hunter.

"He didn't," the woman insisted. "We were still negotiating."

"Negotiation is done." The demon opened its beaked mouth and screeched again, even as it said through its forehead mouth, "Sacrifice of blood."

CHAPTER TWENTY-FOUR

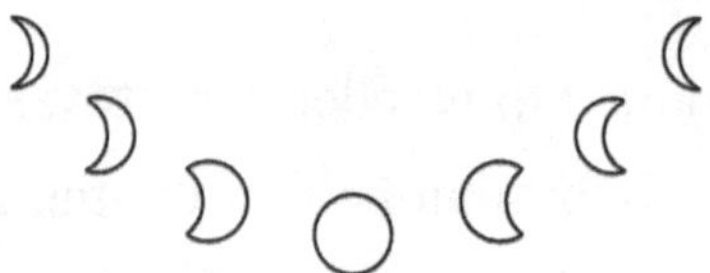

The woman bellowed a denial that made Angie wince as it echoed around the basement. The demon laughed at the woman's reaction and jerked the man closer.

"For what?" Angie demanded from the demon, trying to distract it, to keep it talking so it didn't have a chance to eat the human in its grip. "What bargain did you set?"

"The one they agreed to," the demon said, its voice a screeching nails-on-chalkboard irritation along Angie's skin.

"What was it?" Angie asked the woman now, though she kept most of her attention on the demon.

"We just…we just needed time. That's all. Just a little time." The woman tugged at her arm again as she spoke, as if that would help Angie understand.

"Time for what?" Angie asked.

"Time for…" The woman swallowed audibly. "Time for

the money. To get the money. We could get it. We would get it. But we needed more time."

"What was your bargain? Specifically. What did you agree to?"

"We didn't. We didn't." Panic in the woman's voice made her sound breathless now. "We didn't set the bargain yet. You interrupted, knocking on the door."

"The bargain has been set."

The demon attempted to drag the man close again, and again Sebastian said, "Stop."

The beast froze again. But its face contorting as it fought Sebastian's will, the man hanging from its grip only inches from its face.

"Let the man go so he can reveal the bargain," Angie said, and she attempted to put some of her own *will* into her voice. She held the demon's gaze, willing it to drop the man. Willing it to follow her command as it had followed Sebastian's.

Her sparkling fog formed a barrier against the demon's containment circle now. The illusion showed clearly where the weakness in the circle was, where the demon had managed to grab the man. It could only have taken him if there was something in the bargain that gave it permission, though. The containment circle hadn't collapsed yet. But it was weakened and would collapse soon.

Freeing the demon.

They didn't have much time.

Though she didn't look away from the beast, she watched her illusionary fog's progress from her peripheral vision. The mists had started to slide through that weakened part of the containment circle, tiny tiny curls of gray puffing past the chalk line. It was still just an illusion. The fog wasn't real. Wasn't really inside the circle. The fog couldn't do anything. But it was as useful as throwing sand at an invisible man— she could *see* what she needed to see now.

She could see where the demon would strike.

She shifted her position to stand in front of that weakness. The demon turned to follow her movements. The woman scrambled to the side, trying to both stay out of the way and continue to tug on Angie for understanding. The tugging wasn't helping Angie's mood.

"Drop. The. Man." She filled her voice with her will, even as she let her magic rise.

The man gurgled something unintelligible. But he released one had from his death-grip on the demon's wrist to reach in Angie's direction. Like he thought she'd take his hand and simply pull him away. Wouldn't work like that. Couldn't work like that without breaking the circle.

Angie hadn't made the demon's bargain. If she crossed the line, she'd break the line.

The demon screeched from its beak again, but its grip on the man loosened. Giving Angie a surge of hope. She tried again to fill her voice with the will that would force the demon to do as she said, "Drop him. Now."

Behind the demon, Sebastian repeated her words. And she *felt* his will. Felt it in her bones.

The demon loosened its grip farther and finally dropped the man to the ground. The man sprawled onto the concrete floor with a bone-jarring thud. Then he started scrambling for the edge of the circle, for escape.

"No," Angie said, pointing at him while staring at the demon. "Don't move. If you cross the line from in there, you'll free it."

"It's going to kill me," the man said, his voice pinched and squeaky with his panic. Probably made worse by the demon's previous grip on his neck.

"What was your bargain?"

"Nothing. Not made yet."

The demon chuckled and made a move as if to reach for the man.

Sebastian's voice rolled out to echo in the enclosed basement. "No."

The demon's forehead mouth snarled as it froze mid-motion.

Angie could see it struggling against Sebastian's will, see it trying to reach for the man through their combined wills. She could almost feel the pressure of it pushing back, willing *her* to allow it its prey. Her instincts screamed to throw a protective circle of her own, encircling her and the woman to keep them safe. She didn't.

"Stop prevaricating and tell me what deal you struck," Angie hissed. "We don't have time for lies."

At least not the man and woman's lies. She would happily lie to the demon to keep the humans safe.

"Like Vera said. We just needed time." The man's voice still squeaked. He whimpered and curled himself onto his side. Edging closer to the chalk circle despite Angie's warning. "If we didn't repay the money, they'd kill us."

"Summoning a demon is going to get you killed," Angie pointed out.

The demon chuckled.

"She said this would work," Vera whined. "She told us it would give us the time we needed."

The hairs on Angie's neck rose. *She*?

Angie wanted to look at Sebastian but she didn't dare let her attention stray from the demon.

"Demons don't control time." Time didn't work the same for them. But they couldn't actually stop it for a human. They could twist a human's perception of time. And they definitely moved through time differently, especially in their own realms. But they couldn't stop it. "Why didn't you ask it for the money you need?"

"She said the bargain would be too high, then," Vera said, once again tugging Angie's arm.

Angie wanted very much to shake her off. She didn't just yet. But she really didn't want the woman touching her any more.

Not least because, she realized suddenly, exerting her will on a demon meant her control over her other powers—her touch psychic power in particular—felt more precarious than usual. And she did not want to have an unintended vision of the woman's life right now.

She hadn't considered that before. Hadn't worried about it. But the will she was shoving at the demon to keep it from reaching for the man again was pulling her control into this tight focus and away from where she usually used it.

The realization that she used will as well as training to keep her psychic powers mostly controlled was a revelation she'd have to consider when they weren't faced with a demon who might escape at any moment.

"Let go of my arm," Angie said, her voice even deeper now.

The woman dropped her hold fast, letting out a little gasp.

Angie didn't know what the sound meant, or what the woman saw, but she couldn't worry about that now. "What was the bargain for time? What was the payment you owed in exchange? How did you think it would give you time?"

"She said…" The woman swallowed audibly. "She said the demon would distract the people we owe money to, giving us time to raise it. We have… We had a plan for that. We were going to sell some of the stuff my mom left us. But the…the man we owed said we had to pay him tomorrow or…or he'd break Bill's knees."

Broken knees seemed the least of Bill's problems now. "What did you promise the demon in exchange?"

"Nothing yet," the woman said. "Still negotiating. It wanted blood sacrifice."

"They always do. Because they're demons."

"We thought…" The woman made a sort of gulping, choking sound. "We thought…a chicken. A goat?"

"You were going to sacrifice a goat?"

That made sense at least. Animal sacrifice was used in a lot of different kinds of ceremonies and as religious offerings.

It was used with demons, too. Usually in the summoning, though. Demons rarely accepted animal sacrifice for the price of a bargain. Though they might lead a human to believe they would.

"Where's the goat?" she asked, really just out of curiosity, but also, they could use it to distract the demon.

"We…we were going to get one."

"You didn't come prepared to pay the bargain?"

"She told us…we could… We would be paying our part after… After the demon did its part."

"We're going to need to talk about this 'she' person," Angie muttered. But her brain was too busy working on the current problem. They needed to get the man out of the circle without breaking the circle.

Which meant sending the demon back.

And she hadn't even been able to do that with an imp demon. Not on her own.

She wasn't here on her own, she reminded herself. She had Sebastian. Sebastian knew what he was doing, was capable of stopping the demon with his will.

She wasn't alone.

CHAPTER TWENTY-FIVE

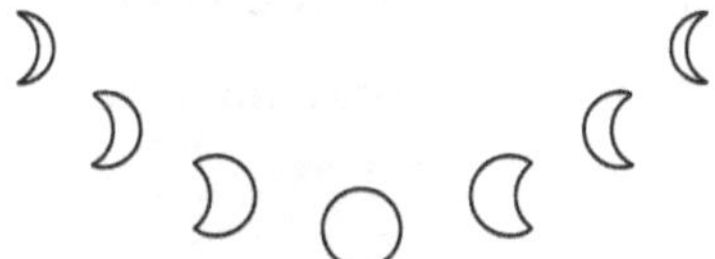

Angie let the panic subside. She wasn't on her own. Sebastian was here in this dank basement. His will was strong enough, even if hers faltered. They could do this.

"What did you agree to, Bill?" she asked, looking for the information they'd need to send the demon back. "While Vera answered the door. What did you agree to?"

Bill was still curled into a fetal position on the concrete inside the circle, whimpering whenever the demon pushed hard enough against Angie and Sebastian's will to move closer.

"Gotta answer me, Bill," she tried again. "Only way we know how to stop the demon."

"You cannot stop me." The demon rolled its beady black eyes at her, the red pupils glowing brightly. The mouth in its forehead grinned, and there were a lot of teeth there. "My will is stronger than a baby hunter."

"Baby hunter…?" Angie shrugged. "Possibly. But I'm not the only hunter here."

An annoyed screech emerged from the demon's beak. She winced, because it was impossible not to wince under the onslaught of that sound, despite her sound dampening spell.

"Come on, Bill. Spill. What did you promise?"

Bill whimpered again. But he said, "The demon said it could…could stop the men from coming after us, ever. That it could stop them so we didn't have to raise the money to pay them back."

"You were gonna let a demon kill the people you owed money?" Lot of sleaziness all around in this situation.

"No, no! I didn't agree to murder. I just wanted them stopped."

"How do you think a demon 'stops' people, Bill? Honestly." She shook her head. People worked themselves into knots to *not* know a thing they already knew.

"I didn't say kill them," Bill muttered. "Those words weren't in the bargain."

"You weren't supposed to agree to anything until I got back," Vera wailed. "What did you agree to?"

Thank you, Vera. That was the question.

The demon reached for Bill again, and Bill curled farther into himself, whimpering and crying a stream of, "No, no, no, no."

"Stop," Sebastian said again.

The demon froze and snarled with its forehead mouth. "I will have my price!"

"Fight me for the price," Sebastian said. "You want it, you have to beat me."

"I have earned my price already, hunter," the demon said, though it looked at Angie instead of facing Sebastian.

"No," she said. "You haven't stopped the people Vera and Bill owe money to. You haven't earned anything." Yet. But she decided pointing out the *yet* was a bad idea.

"I will eat them first then," the demon said, a strange, sly note in its tone. "Then I will return for my price."

Except there was no real way for the demon to go to the people Vera and Bill were unleashing it on without Vera and Bill cooperating. Bill and Vera would have to lure the people they wanted the demon to take care of to the demon, since the only way the demon could be in this realm was through a summoning, inside a circle.

"You have no intention of seeing through your part of the bargain," Angie murmured. "Or you wouldn't have tried taking Bill already."

The demon couldn't fulfill its side without cooperation from the humans who summoned it. Even if it intended to turn on those humans as part of its price for doing their bidding, it'd keep that to itself until it was too late for them to back out.

Taking Bill now was…odd.

"What was the wording of your bargain, Bill? You have to tell me. Aloud. Now."

"Just…" Bill whimpered again when the demon growled. "Just that it would give us time, and we would give it blood.

That it would slow down the people we owed money to in exchange for blood."

Angie considered that wording, rolling it around in her head, looking for the loophole. With demons, there was always a loophole. Always a way of interpreting the wording that served the demon's need for blood, terror, and destruction, a way that the humans making the bargain couldn't foresee easily.

"It would certainly slow them down if Bill disappeared," she said aloud. "Can't get money from someone you can't find."

"But..." Vera reached for Angie again, dropping her hands back to her sides when Angie gave her a look. "But they'd be able to find me. Try to get the money from me. That wouldn't slow them down. Technically."

She sounded less worried about Bill than the logic of the loophole in that moment. But then she glanced at Bill, her face contorted, and she took a step closer to the circle before stopping herself.

Strange relationship.

"If the demon made both of you disappear, it would frustrate all efforts by the people you owe money to to find you. Unless they went specifically looking for the demon who'd eaten you, which they wouldn't unless they knew more about demons than I hope they do. They'd be significantly slowed down from getting their money from you. The demon would have fulfilled its end of the bargain. And gotten the blood it was promised. All in one easy move."

Which was why it could reach through the circle to claim Bill. If Bill agreed to the wording of that deal, he'd have given the demon permission to reach him through the circle. Not necessarily break out of the circle. Just enough permission to fulfill its part of the bargain. Bill just didn't realize that he'd given the demon permission to eat him.

She sighed. "Always a loophole. Making deals with demons is stupid."

The demon laughed and screeched at the same time. Angie winced. That was a very irritating selection of sounds.

Vera glanced between the demon, Bill, and Angie. "No. That's not… That's not what we meant."

"Doesn't matter. Demons will twist your words, extract whatever meaning suits them." She didn't look away from the demon, because it was holding her gaze and she didn't want to risk freeing it to attack Bill. But she tilted her head toward Vera. "You'd have to be capable of outthinking the most cunning and manipulative beings in existence. Maybe even more manipulative than vampires. And unless you know that, you *will* make a mistake. And the demon *will* kill you."

"Vampires?" Vera asked.

Proving, as she latched on to the exact wrong point, that she was not thinking clearly enough to make bargains with demons.

Angie sighed again. "Never make deals with demons. They will eat you." There. That should be simple enough.

Bill whimpered again, curled tighter into a ball, and started to cry. "Didn't mean it, didn't mean it."

Her illusionary fog continued to back up against the circle, covering the basement floor outside the candles. More of the tiny tendrils of smoke curled into the circle through the weak point. One way or another, they were running out of time.

"A challenge," Angie said.

It was the only way now. Since the bargain was set, and killing Bill helped the demon fulfil its end, she and Sebastian couldn't just banish it. And they couldn't just demand it give Bill back. That broke the bargain. Which, in turn, made Bill's life forfeit and freed the demon.

Tricky fucking demons.

It hadn't escaped the circle yet, though. That attempt would come after it completed its bargain. If it got free, all bets were off and Angie and Sebastian could banish it—well, they could try. There was still the matter of the demon potentially having a stronger will than the hunter facing it. But the rules changed when the demon escaped, and banishment, with or without fulfilling the bargain, was possible.

They didn't have that option. And thanks to the stupid wording of the bargain, while the demon remained inside the circle, they didn't have the option of banishing it by reversing the summoning process. *It* was following the rules. So they had to.

This was one of the many, many reasons she hated dealing with demons and being part of the demon hunting world. She *hated* the way demons could manipulate things and the way hunters often had their hands tied by those manipulations.

"A challenge," she repeated. "Winner gets Bill and Vera."

"What?" Vera squeaked.

"Shut up and stay back," Angie said, her voice dropping deeper. Instinctively, she let her magic rise, let the power suffuse her, drawing strength from the earth beneath the house foundations.

"Ang?" Sebastian's voice was quiet.

"Will you accept the challenge from a hunter?" Angie said to the demon.

"I do not need to challenge," the demon said, its beak clacking together threateningly. "I have fulfilled my bargain."

"Not yet. And we won't allow you to kill the humans. We're at an impasse. Challenge is the only way out."

"You can't stop me from fulfilling my bargain," the demon said. "It was not set with you."

"We can interfere and delay and stall," she said with a shrug. Because that was true. They might not be able to simply banish it, but they could frustrate the hell out of it, in an attempt to keep it from eating Bill. There was nothing in the "rules" that prevented that.

"My will is strong enough to overcome yours, baby hunter."

She'd been hoping it would agree to the challenge without being specific about which hunter it would fight, so Sebastian could fight it. Sebastian had, technically, issued a fight challenge already. And she'd intended on using that as her own loophole.

But the damned thing was entirely too focused on her.

So she'd have to pit her will against its to end this and save Bill and Vera. Not her magic, already flowing through her. But her will.

And she was not ready for that fight.

CHAPTER TWENTY-SIX

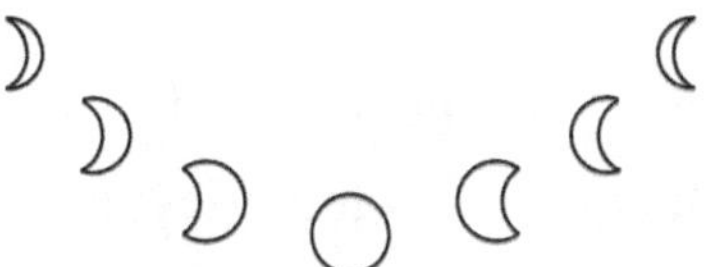

Sebastian's voice echoed loudly in the basement. "I issued the challenge. You must fight me."

His will was a solid thing in the air, his strength obvious. Angie desperately hoped the demon would accept Sebastian's challenge over hers.

Unfortunately, the demon wasn't as stupid as the humans who had summoned it.

"I refuse your challenge, hunter," the demon said to Sebastian, even as it continued to stare at Angie. "I do not need to accept. I can wait to fulfill my bargain longer than you can stall me. You will falter before I do. And then I will feast."

It clacked its beak together again, the sound making Angie's ears hurt.

"But," it continued, "I will accept the baby hunter's

challenge in exchange for the humans' lives. She has also issued a challenge. I will accept the terms of hers."

Well, fuck.

Either they stood here at an impasse, risked freeing the demon by breaking Bill out by force, or she fought a demon challenge and tried to will it back to its realm. Without a tree conveniently handy for her to open a portal so Sebastian could push the demon through.

This was not what she did. She did magic. And she occasionally, reluctantly—sometimes accidentally—opened breaches into demon worlds. She didn't *fight* them. Not in challenges. And in the years she'd worked with Sebastian, when the challenge came up, he fought it. She was only useful when they were in the open and near trees. Or when she could use her magic.

She narrowed her eyes at the demon. There was nothing saying she *couldn't* use her magic. She might be here, technically, as a hunter. But she was a hunter with magic. Elemental spells and illusions were some of her stronger talents, too. Her fire spell probably wouldn't do much to a demon. And a lightning strike in the middle of the basement was both complicated and dangerous for everyone here. Water was possible. But gathering enough moisture to make it rain inside was easier in the humid New York summers than the dry autumn. Wind had possibilities. But...

Illusions might work even better.

She straightened her shoulders. "Challenge accepted. The terms are set. I win, you leave and forfeit your bargain. And the humans' lives. They will be mine."

"And if you lose?" The demon moved its head in a swiveling motion that looked both snake and hawk-like.

She couldn't afford to lose. "You fulfill your bargain with the humans unimpeded." Which was an impossible outcome and she refused to allow it. One way or the other.

"No," the demon said, his forehead mouth spreading in a smile. "If you lose, I claim you."

"No," Sebastian said, and the force of his will made the demon straighten and loose a screech that pierced Angie's skull.

"I will only accept challenge on these terms," the demon snarled. "If the terms are not accepted, the challenge is null, and I will fulfill my bargain."

Angie glanced away from the demon to meet Sebastian's gaze across the circle. She could practically see the struggle in his hooded expression. They both knew she wasn't ready for a demon fight. She had barely begun training. She wasn't ready for this. No hunter would be ready for this at this stage. The senior hunter would always manage the challenges.

"If I fail, you accept the other hunter's challenge," Angie said.

"I do not have to do this."

"You will, or we will fight another way."

"Then we fight another way. I will simply wait you out."

"And I'll force you back to your realm like it or not. You have a chance of something this way."

"You cannot force me back without challenge, baby hunter."

"Believe that if you wish."

She kept her gaze on Sebastian even as she poked at the demon's ego. They were, in the end, as arrogant as they were manipulative. She hoped that arrogance got the better of it here.

From the corner of her eye, she saw the demon snarl and clack its beak, but the beak clacking was quiet and contemplative rather than loudly threatening.

She shrugged and turned her attention back to the demon, infusing as much arrogance into her own stance as she could manage under the circumstances. She smiled at it. "You have a choice. Challenge. Or I simply destroy you."

It laughed. A nails-on-chalkboard sound. "Humans cannot destroy one of my kind."

"Believe that if you wish. But I doubt you've faced a human like me before." Since there were, historically, so few of them, the odds were in her favor this was true.

"I have faced baby hunters before." The demon swiveled its head again in that strange move that reminded her of both a hawk and a snake. "I ate them as they screamed."

Bill whimpered and curled tighter in on himself. Vera reached for Angie again, but again thought better of it and aborted the move.

Angie applauded her restraint since, as Angie gathered her magic close, she would have shoved Vera aside bodily to avoid that touch.

"You assume I'm a baby hunter."

"I know you are."

"Has it occurred to you, I might be…more than just a hunter."

The demon titled its head, looking at her through narrowed beady eyes. The red pupils shrank and opened, reflecting the faint light from the candles around the circle. It scrapped its clawed feet across the concrete a few times in a restless movement that looked like it was walking in place. Since it didn't try to reach Bill, Sebastian said nothing.

"There is nothing *more* that can help you." But it didn't sound nearly as confident of that as it had a moment ago. It didn't know what her *more* meant. So it didn't know what to expect. And it couldn't tell if she was bluffing or not.

Since she was being perfectly honest, that confounded its ability to read her—it expected lies and she wasn't lying.

"Then accept my challenge and my terms," she said, shrugging. "If I fail, you kill me and only have one more hunter to face before you can claim the humans' lives. A small delay."

It clacked its beak and let out a noise halfway between a hiss and a screech, but quieter as it considered her offer. Then it straightened its shoulders, standing at a full, impressive height, its tentacle hair brushing the roof of the basement.

"I am hungry. I will enjoy feasting on two hunters."

"Challenge accepted?"

"Challenge accepted," it said. "I set the fight's form."

That was the way the challenge worked. Hunters issued the challenge. Negotiated the wins and losses. Demon determined the form of the fight. It couldn't be a simple physical fight because, in challenge situations, the demon was inside a circle still. There was usually some form of manipulation or riddle or sometimes simply will against will.

Bill scooted closer to the edge of the circle and Vera moved toward him. Without looking away from the demon, Angie said, "Bill, if you try to cross that line now, you will free the demon and this all gets more complicated. Do not cross the line. Vera, do no help him cross that line. You will both die if you do."

"They will die anyway," the demon said.

"We'll see."

"Why do you wish to save them, baby hunter?" the demon asked. "They offered me blood in exchange for killing their enemies."

Bill made a noise like he would object but then quickly shut up when the demon turned to look at him.

"I don't wish demon death on anyone," Angie said, sincerely. "Even my worst enemies."

"You know what kind of death we provide?"

"More than you might imagine." And it was the stuff of her nightmares. "Name the form of the fight."

She started murmuring an illusion spell as she waited, letting her hands twist together in the gestures that would set the spell, hoping the demon just thought she was restless and unable to keep her hands still. She kept her voice low, almost inaudible, her lips barely moving as she mentally chanted the words.

The demon tilted its head and moved closer to her edge of the circle, until it was so close she could feel the heat of it seeping out of the containment circle. It wasn't one of the beasts made of lava, or formed from heat and fire. But it was from a hot realm and she was sure it could still burn with a touch if it wanted to. The fact that Bill wasn't smoking only proved the demon had wanted to eat him alive.

Probably best Bill didn't realize that.

"The form," the demon said, "will be simple. No riddles for a baby hunter. No complicated tasks." It chuckled. "Your will is no match for mine. I am hungry and I intend to feed. So we will fight will against will. If you are forced backward by my will, I win. If I am forced backward by yours, you win. Simple enough? Baby hunter?"

"A distance," she said. "If you push me backward more than the length of my arm." This gave her some wiggle room. It gave the demon wiggle room, too, but she was less worried about that. "And if I push you backward by a distance longer than the length of your arm."

It wouldn't be able to resist that. Its arms were significantly longer than hers. It would assume that gave it an advantage. She was counting on that assumption.

She watched it take the bait, watch it smile with its forehead mouth as it pawed the cement floor again with one clawed foot.

"It is set. The battle form. The challenge terms. Agreed?"

"Ang?" Sebastian's voice from behind the demon.

"I've got this," she said, briefly shifting her gaze to look at him. "We've got this."

He nodded, though she saw the worry in his dark eyes. That worry was nowhere else in his expression. He nodded again, more firmly this time, and relaxed his stance, crossing his arms over his chest, taking up the pose of a man settling in for a wait. Not a man ready to pounce if something went wrong.

His show, even if it was only outward and for the sake of the demon as much as for her sake, was appreciated.

She faced the demon again.

"Agreed?" it repeated.

"Agreed."

The word was barely out before the battering ram of the demon's will slammed into her.

CHAPTER TWENTY-SEVEN

Angie willed herself to the floor. But she was forced back a step before she stopped the shoving force of the demon's will from pushing her farther. Her heartbeat hammered at the suddenness of it all. She should have expected as much. She should have anticipated it not giving her time to take a beat and prepare.

Too late now. She gathered her will and held her place, refusing to budge. Unfortunately, the focus, the will it took to resist the demon's will, took up all her attention. She couldn't finish her spell and loose the illusion she'd carefully built.

The demon shoved again, a harder push of will. She slid back an inch. Grounded herself more solidly again, willing herself not to move any further back, leaning into the demon's push.

But this wasn't how she'd win this challenge. She had to push back. Except it took everything in her to stay in place.

Damn it. She needed to focus, to concentrate. She needed her will.

A brush of something like fresh air. Not an open window. Just a hint of…strength blowing through her. She took a breath. Loosened her clenched teeth. Took in another deep breath.

And shoved.

The demon growled and leaned into her shove. But it didn't slide backward. Not even a little bit.

Like pushing at a goddess damned wall. She snarled, focused, and shoved again. Willing the bastard backward.

Now. This time. Move.

The beast leaned back, as if actually feeling her push.

But its feet still didn't budge.

More will. That fresh burst of energy from…somewhere. And she pushed again, growling under her breath as she did. Willing the bastard backward. Willing the demon away.

An inch. It slid backward an inch this time.

A surge of triumph flooded her system, feeding her. She pushed again, putting all her anger and determination into the heave.

The beast slid backward. Just a little. But it slid backward. Its clawed toes dug into the floor, leaving deep gouges in the concrete. When Angie shoved again, it didn't budge.

The demon laughed. Gave her another push.

And Angie fell backward another inch, despite willing herself to resist.

Fuck. This wasn't working. This wasn't her way. She

didn't have claw toes to dig into the ground. She couldn't do this.

Even as that thought flowed through her, the demon shoved against, and she slid a little more.

She was going to lose and everyone would die.

No. Damn it. No! She would not see anyone die. Especially Sebastian. He was right there. He was in trouble, too.

Another brush of that fresh, clearing air. Was that Sebastian? It had to be.

She pulled her scattered thoughts together and resisted the demon's push. Resisted moving any farther backward.

But instead of will, instead of stubbornness, she reached for something else. Instinctively. She reached for her magic.

She didn't have the focus for the illusion spell she'd intended to use. Couldn't form the last words or the last gesture. Not while holding off the demon. Her reach wasn't anything so focused or specific. She just grabbed for the magic that flowed through her. She wasn't even sure what she'd do with it, what she intended. The mental scramble for her own powers was all instinctive.

The image of the blue spiderweb rose in her mind, all those threads of powerful blue energy surrounding her, their faint vibrations tingling against her skin. She grabbed one of those threads. And power shot through her body. So much power she gasped.

Without thought, she used that power and shoved the demon. Heaved with all her might. Holding its beady little gaze as she forced it backward, using the strength that flowed through her, the power that filled her.

Faintly, she was aware of a blue glow in her peripheral vision. But all her focus now was on pushing the demon, using not simply will, but the magic that filled her.

No spells. No chants. No patterns.

Just pure, unfiltered power. And one physical gesture.

She pushed her hands forward, pushing her magic at the demon, shoving so hard, it slid across the floor. Despite its claws buried in the cement. Despite its roar of protest.

It pushed back, hit her with a will so strong it sucked away her breath.

She grabbed tight to her spiderweb thread of magic and held her place. The web vibrated more now. An insect at the edge of the web. Moving. Struggling.

Angie smiled.

She grabbed a second thread, holding both in her mind's eye. And so much power surged through her, she no longer felt like she needed to breathe. The power was all. It was everything.

It was her.

She didn't shove this time. She didn't need to. The demon was trapped, caught, done for. It was going back to its realm. Now.

Another roar of denial, so loud it pierced through the basement like a ricocheting bullet, destroying all in its path. Angie was vaguely aware of shouting. Of screams. She almost, almost turned her attention to the noise, to the screams.

The demon shoved at her again, just at that moment. The insect fighting against the trap.

She took the hit, didn't move. But her grip slipped on the spiderweb threads. She dropped one. The flow of power dimmed.

No. The beast wouldn't escape her. Not now.

She reached out, stretching for a second thread. Power poured into her again. Too much. So much she couldn't really see anything in the basement anymore. Only the demon down a long tunnel in front of her. And behind it…

Ah. There. That was where it needed to go.

Behind the demon…a breach. An opening into its realm. It didn't belong here. Time to send it back.

She shoved again. Hard. With all that blue magic swirling around her. Sent a pulse of power down the threads of her trap.

She saw the burst of red within the blue, a color so unexpected she blinked.

And then the demon screamed. An ear-piercing scream of denial. As it tumbled backward. Fell.

Into a hellscape realm.

Angie turned her head from the view into the rolling heat and red lava barrens, felt the realm breach close, suddenly and fully. Cutting off the demon's screams of denial with a snap that left her ears ringing.

In the silence that followed, Angie took what felt like her first breath in hours. Sucked in oxygen. Blinked back the spots in her vision. Slowly, very slowly, she released the threads of power she'd been holding. Easing her mental grip one finger at a time, letting the power gentle and settle back into place, into the web pattern.

There was no more vibrating through the web. The insect was gone. Devoured. No more. And the web settled back into a holding pattern. To wait for the next insect to stumble into its trap.

She blinked her surroundings back into focus. Vera and Bill were both on the ground, hugging each other. They'd smudged the white chalk as they'd slid together, breaking the circle. Angie wanted to drag her foot through it and ensure the circle was fully broken, but the energy to move wasn't there. She'd do more to ensure the connection to the demon realm was cut off in a minute.

Sebastian stood on the opposite side of the circle still, staring at her. She couldn't read his expression. Not even a little bit. That struck her as…unexpected. She could usually read something. Even if she couldn't interpret what he was feeling, she could almost always see *something*. But he was so closed off now, she couldn't even tell if he was experiencing any emotion.

She'd just fought her first demon challenge. And she'd won! She'd done it. She'd sent the demon back. Why wasn't he congratulating her? Why wasn't he by her side? What the hell was that stare about?

Even as the questions crossed her mind, a sweep of exhaustion rolled through her. She blinked. And next thing she knew she was on the hard ground, kneeling against the concrete floor. The ground was cold. She trembled.

She lilted to the side, heard Sebastian call her name, and darkness swarmed her vision.

A memory rose, a fact that hadn't occurred to her before that moment.

The threads she'd grabbed in her fight with the demon. The last one… The one she'd drawn a resurgence of power from. The one she'd pulled on just before the breach opened. That one…

Had been red.

The darkness took her and she knew no more.

CHAPTER TWENTY-EIGHT

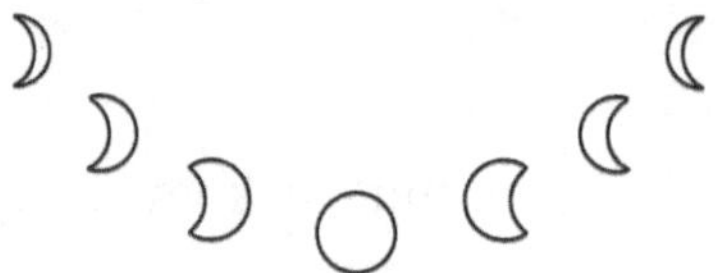

$\mathcal{A}$ ngie woke in the car, briefly, the vibration of movement and the dull sounds of traffic lulling her back to sleep. She was too tired to open her eyes and check where they were. She hoped they still had a ways to go to get home. She wasn't ready to wake up yet.

The next time she rose out of the darkness, she was in her own bed, a blanket pulled up over her, the room dark and warm. From the direction of her living room and kitchen she heard the soft clinking of mugs in the cabinet, some quiet shuffling sounds.

She knew that had to be Sebastian, so she didn't immediately jump out of bed in a panic. The panic came on more slowly, a growing tsunami wave about to roll over the top of her.

What the hell had she done?

She'd opened a portal into a demon realm without a tree.

Without the necessary shape anywhere. She hadn't thought that possible. She'd always required a tree, a tree with the right shape naturally formed into it. And though the process was wrenching because the world beyond was horrible, opening portals never exhausted her. Never bothered her at all, physically. Certainly didn't send her into an exhausted sleep.

And simply never happened if there weren't trees around.

What the hell had she done?

She pushed out from under the warm blankets, a little amused to see she was still wearing her jeans and t-shirt and socks. Sebastian had removed her shoes, her coat, and then tucked her under the blankets still fully dressed. She'd have been more comfortable without her jeans on. He'd seen her naked a lot, so that wouldn't have been new. But that wasn't their current relationship, and she'd been vulnerable. She appreciated that he hadn't crossed that boundary.

She changed into soft pajama bottoms and a clean t-shirt, then walked herself into the bathroom and washed her face, brushed her teeth, generally made herself feel less grotty and tired. Once she felt more human, more awake, she went to the living room.

He was on the couch, sipping from a mug—Earl Grey from the smell—and staring at the coffee table. He glanced her direction when she came into the room.

"Feeling better?"

"Not exhausted anymore," she said, sitting on the couch and folding her legs under her as she turned to face him. She leaned against the armrest and said, "You okay?"

"Not really." He went back to staring at the coffee table. "Do you know what you did?"

"Sort of. Not how or why I was able. I remember opening the portal."

"No trees in a basement."

"No trees in the basement."

"You don't know how?"

"Not how I was able to, no. I know what I did."

"Will you tell me?"

"Are you going to run and tell the council?"

"No."

She stared at the side of his face.

He finally turned to look at her and said, quietly, "No. They don't need to know until we understand the implications."

"They might not need to know even then," she murmured. "They know enough already to want me dead. At least some of them. This might drive the others over into that camp."

"Maybe," he conceded. Then took a sip of his tea. "Will I make you a cup first?"

"I'm okay for now.

"Does this have to do with the vision you had before? The spiderweb?"

"How did you guess?"

"That left you exhausted, too."

She let out a soft sound that wasn't quite a laugh. "I should have known you wouldn't miss that."

"What happened?"

"I reached for the magic. Instinctively. It's what I am. But instead of the usual way I use magic, I just grabbed onto the threads of the web. First one, then two. I was…shoring up my will, giving myself the strength I needed."

"Because you were losing the fight."

She nodded. "I wasn't ready for that kind of challenge yet."

"I couldn't help. It would have violated the challenge. The demon would have claimed victory. But…" He pursed his lips and stared into her fireplace, at the garden of cacti.

She frowned. "I thought you were helping. I felt… I felt your will. Or. That's what I thought anyway. You were giving me some of your will. Like you did when the Molder demon…" She swallowed and let the sentence trail off.

Thinking about having a demon take over her body was never going to be easy. Sebastian had helped her grab onto the will she needed to force the demon out, to not unleash an apocalypse of demons on the city. He'd fed her some of his own will and called her back from the void. She'd assumed he'd done that again in the basement.

"That wasn't me," he said. "What did it feel like?"

"A breath of fresh air. A breeze. Some space to breathe and regroup."

"It wasn't me," he repeated.

"There was no one else there."

"Could it have come from your web?"

"I…" She wouldn't have thought so. But then, she hadn't known the magic web even existed, hadn't had that image of her magic before. What the hell did she know. "I have no idea." She ran a hand through her hair, rubbing her skull to ease some of the tension building in her skin. "The thing is, remember I told you about the red line in my mental web of magic?"

"The one that you grabbed the first time and it left you reeling?"

"And exhausted like I had a magic hangover. Well, that's what I grabbed when I opened the portal. I didn't realize it until afterward. I didn't consciously grab that thread. I was just trying to hold on. To hold out. And trying to will the demon back enough to win the challenge. I'd slipped and let go of one thread, so I just grab the closet thread without *looking*. Then the portal opened."

He set his mug down and turned to more fully face her. "That's..."

"A little worrying? Yeah, I'm worried, too. I've never done anything like that. And I have no idea what it means."

"It means you aren't limited to portal breaches through trees."

"Is that good or bad?"

"It was good last night."

She glanced out the window. Wow. He was right. The sky was lightening as dawn sluggishly filled in the streets between the buildings. She shook her head. "Didn't realize I'd slept all night. Did you sleep here?"

"Your couch is as comfortable as the hotel bed where I'm staying."

"That doesn't sound like a great hotel, if that's true."

He smiled, but didn't elaborate.

"You want more?" She nodded at his cup as she unfolded from the couch. For some reason, knowing it was dawn made her crave the caffeine hit of a cup of tea. She'd been okay before realizing it wasn't still the middle of the night.

He nodded. "Thanks."

She took his cup and busied herself in the kitchen boiling the kettle again, making fresh cups. Trying not to think about the way she'd done something she'd thought impossible.

She handed him his mug before sitting down again, cradling hers between her palms and letting the gently pungent scent of English Breakfast seep into her senses.

"I don't want to be able to open breaches just anywhere," she murmured.

"But if you can, it makes banishing demons a lot easier."

"Also a lot more possibility for trouble. For demons to escape into this realm. For…"

No, she wouldn't go there. Almost being trapped in a demon realm had been one of the single most terrifying moments in her life. A memory that still haunted her. Filled her nightmares alongside the newer one of having a Molder demon take over her body. She couldn't think about that and still think logically about the treeless portals.

"I've been wondering if the council knew this was possible," Sebastian said quietly. "If something about this was in the histories. And if they knew…"

"That puts a new spin on them wanting me to join the hunters." She snarled into her cup. "If they knew and didn't tell me, I'm going to be pissed."

"Maybe they wanted to test you, see if you already knew?"

She shrugged, because that was possible.

"Or maybe they hoped you wouldn't learn the full extent of what you could do."

"Possible too." She certainly didn't like learning she could do this. "Why wouldn't they want me to know, though?"

"Dangerous as well as useful skill," he said, tipping his mug in her direction in a sort of half solute. "They're already scared of you."

"I wish they'd let me see their histories of witches like me."

"The council, as it stands now, seems to think the less some of us know the better. The safer."

"It's a dumb assumption. Not knowing what I could do could have put everyone in real danger last night. I don't like surprises."

He smiled a little. "I remember."

He'd tried to surprise her once with a birthday party. Her brothers had warned him it wasn't a good idea. They'd learned the lesson that she didn't like surprises the hard way, too. Though with something a lot less thoughtful than a surprise birthday party.

"You recovered," she said, rolling her eyes.

His smile deepened.

She fell into that smile, and better memories, for a moment. Then blinked and pulled herself out. She had things to deal with right now. No time to moon over her ex-boyfriend. Who was starting to feel less "ex" as the weeks progressed.

"The hunter who came to me, urging me not to become a hunter… Jacob. Do you think he knew what I could do?"

"Hard to say. Hard to know what he was after with that stunt."

"He said he was sent to me, so there are more like him."

"There are."

"I really hate so many people may or may not know what I'm capable of when I had no idea. It's irritating as all hell."

"I agree. Do you want to tell the council what happened?"

"Not unless they bring it up. Not until I understand what happened. But…"

But the council knew what realm splitters were, demon witches, which meant they had some information about her skills and she wanted that information and they weren't going to let her see it if she continued keeping things from them. Though, that was just fair since they kept so damned much from her.

"Will you have to report on my first official hunt?" she asked.

"Already had to," he said. "And no, of course I didn't tell them *how* you banished the demon. Knew we had to talk about that first. But they can be…persistent. So I told them you fought a demon challenge, won, and the demon was forced back to its realm."

"Thank you for not telling them everything yet."

"I'm on your side, Ang. Not the council's. Remember that."

She knew. He wanted to bring the whole council down. Though she still wasn't clear why, outside of it protecting her.

Still too many questions. More questions than she'd had before the demon fight. Her vision was supposed to have given her clarity of thought. All she had now was a new and terrifying skill and a heap ton more questions.

"What now?" she asked.

"You rest and recover from…whatever you did. I'll push again to see if we can get access to the information on past realm splitters. It'll be a futile attempt, but I'll try."

"And, if possible, we need more information on Jacob and his people. Whoever they are."

"And we need to find out who the witch is that helped Bill and Vera learn how to summon a demon."

Shit. Right. She'd almost forgotten about that. "You afraid she'll do it again? That they'll try it again?"

"Not them. But I've a bad feeling about the fact that yet another mysterious woman has helped someone summon a demon in the area lately. When you and I are conveniently around to stop it. There was a spell on their gate, but one you could spot. One a witch could spot. But not a hunter."

Angie was quiet a moment as she stared at him. "You're thinking its Carmen behind this, too."

"Aren't you?"

She'd had that suspicion. But opening a portal without a tree had overtaken her other worries. "Working with a witch, or is a witch and has been hiding it?"

"Probably the latter. But it's impossible to say without questioning her."

Angie let out a deeply angry sigh.

"She knows what you are," Sebastian said quietly. "She's testing you."

"I hate tests."

"I remember that, too. But why is she testing you? Why is she still even in the city when the hunters want her?"

"We'll have to ask her."

Angie was starting to think Carmen knew more about the realm splitter skills than Angie did. Bad enough the council knew more. Having a vigilante who liked to summon demons know more about demon witches than she knew…

If that were true, she was going to be so pissed.

CHAPTER TWENTY-NINE

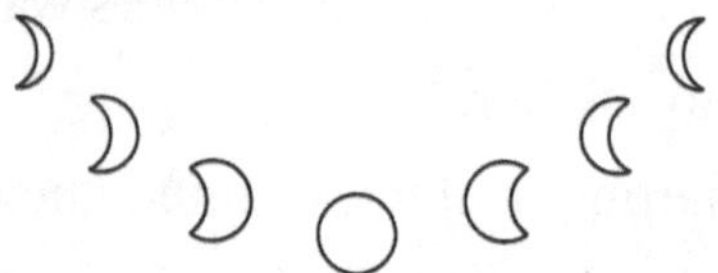

Angie took an extended nap during the day and woke up feeling a lot better. No more grogginess from tapping magic she wasn't used to using. That was a quicker recovery than last time. Not necessarily a good sign, though. She didn't want to adapt to using the magic in that red thread. Especially since she still didn't understand most of this.

Knowledge was a witch's power. Study and learning were baked into the life of a witch—something she'd always appreciated since she loved learning and study; not tests, but studying was fun. Lack of knowledge when working a spell, formulating a potion, even setting up an altar space, could have dire repercussions. And right now, she felt like her lack of knowledge could have deadly consequences.

But she had no idea how to convince the council to allow her access to their information about her kind. Not when they were scared of her and what she could do. They weren't just going to hand over their history records.

They didn't understand keeping her ignorant was significantly more dangerous than helping enlighten her.

Work that night was comfortable and ordinary. Which was a relief. Dana's was a place of comfort, where a lot of her friends worked, and where she felt safe. Too many people had come looking for her there lately. If that kept happening, she was going to dread going into work. And that would be a true and horrible tragedy.

Sebastian didn't meet her that night to walk her home. She wasn't sure if that was a good sign or not. On the one hand, no demon hunting required that night. Yay! On the other hand… She missed him. Missed his company on the walk. Missed having him there to bounce ideas off and discuss—ad nauseum and in circles—all the things she had running through her thoughts at the moment.

Mostly, she just missed coming home to him.

Their relationship felt like it was in a kind of weird limbo now. Not together. But not apart. She snorted. It was exactly what she'd told Rachel and Bianca. And Laura when she'd asked. It was complicated. Complicated in a way that wasn't likely to get less complicated any time soon.

She pulled her coat tighter around her as the October wind picked up, bringing an icy blast of air down the narrow Village streets. She missed the less complicated life she'd built for herself here in the last two years. Missed it almost as much as she missed Sebastian.

The streets were quiet as she made her way home, a few

people scurrying past, but it was a weeknight, and even the night owls that roamed this section of town were quiet. The corner store near her place was lit up, so she stopped in for a soda and a sandwich, chatting with Mr. Hadid as he rang up her purchases. The familiar patterns soothed her worry a little. Not a lot, but enough that she could find a genuine smile for Mr. Hadid as she left the store.

The smile dropped and her worries came rushing back when she saw Jacob waiting outside her apartment building.

She scowled as she stomped up to him, mentally preparing a shield spell even though she wasn't sure why.

"Good evening, Ms. Jordan," he said, his voice quiet. He pushed away from where he'd been leaning against her building's brick façade and turned to face her.

She snarled. "It was. What do you want?"

"To make sure you're okay."

"Meaning?" She wanted to look around, see if Sebastian was anywhere nearby. The fact that he wasn't, and *now* Jacob showed up, and all this after her first hunt where she opened a portal without the normally required tree with a V shape… None of it was coincidental. She was certain of that.

"Your first hunt." He smiled. "It went well?"

"I'm alive."

"Good point."

"You don't want me to be a hunter. Why do you care?"

"I don't want you dead either."

"Why?"

"Why don't I want you dead?"

"It's a fair question. I have no idea who you are outside of

—" she gestured at his eyes, since they were still on a public street even though the few people passing them weren't paying any attention to their conversation, "—and no reason to think you might want me alive, given…what I can do."

"I don't want you to be one of us, quite specifically because I don't want you dead," Jacob said.

"Why?" she asked again.

"What you can do… Pushing that skill is a mistake. Keeping it mostly dormant should be our priority. Not pushing to see how much dam— How much you can do."

"You nearly said damage. You're worried about what I can do." She wasn't asking. She was worried about it too.

But how much did Jacob know? How much did the council know? Did they suspect she could open a portal without the trappings, or was that not something buried in the records of her kind? Could any other demon witch do what she'd done last night? And what, exactly, did Jacob know about all this?

"I am," he admitted. "The council is making a mistake. And I'm not the only one who things so."

"How many?"

"I'd rather not say."

She snorted. "Of course not. You're speaking for them?"

He gave a shrug that didn't answer the question.

"Tell those other worried parties, they can back off. Unless I need help on a hunt, I don't need more of you in my life than I've already got."

"Are you sure? You may well need friends soon."

"Meaning?" She shifted from one foot to a more solid

stance and the words of several defensive spells sprang to mind, almost instinctively. She didn't start building anything more than the shield spell she'd already set, but she felt her magic rising nonetheless, readying for a fight.

"I'm not threatening you, Angela," Jacob said, his voice low. "I'm not a threat to you. I just understand the council is playing with fire. And they should stop. Now."

"Wish someone would explain cryptic statements like that," she said. "Especially when you consider me the fire. You know I don't want to burn the place down, right?"

"Fire never does. Fire doesn't *want* anything but to burn. And if it takes out everything in its path, it isn't intentional, or even considered. It's just fire doing what it does. I don't blame the fire, Angela. I blame the people lighting the match."

"Then go talk to them."

"They won't listen. They've already struck the match."

"You think you're the water?"

He shrugged. "Either that, or I'm the fire break."

She let her stance relax just a little. "I have no intention of burning anything down. Or letting someone else trigger a fire using me."

"No matter what you intend, things happen. Things beyond your control. Your only hope is to pull back and refuse to hunt anymore. Tell them you've tried it and you're done. Go back to psychic readings and witchcraft where you're happy."

"You say that like it's so easy," she murmured. "I'm tired.

And I'm hungry. And I get really pissy when I'm hungry. I've taken in your…warning? You can leave now."

"I know I'm not being particularly clear, and you don't have any reason to trust me. But please consider what I've said. There's more going on than you know. It's better for everyone if you're not in the middle of things."

"Are you going to explain what's going on?"

"No."

"Then we have nothing more to discuss. Goodnight."

He let out a sigh. Then he snapped down his suit jacket, gave her a little nod, and turned down the street. He didn't glance back as he walked away. She watched him go, not moving until she'd seen him turn a corner a few blocks away.

"He's lying."

The new voice had her spinning and cussing…

To face Carmen.

CHAPTER THIRTY

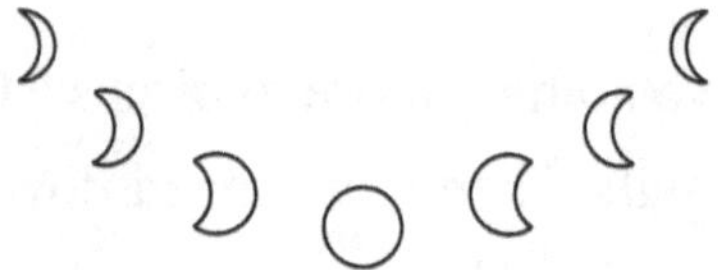

ngie cussed some more under her breath. How the hell had Carmen gotten behind her and she hadn't noticed? Again!

"What are you doing here?" She snarled at the woman.

"Checking on you," Carmen said, smiling as she glanced past Angie, in the direction the demon hunter had gone. "They all want you dead. He does. The council. All of them."

Shit. Carmen knew about the council? No one was supposed to know they existed. Had she known about them for a while, or had she just overhead Jacob mention them? Or had she overheard Angie and Sebastian talking about them?

Damn it. How the hell did Carmen know so much? Where was she learning these secrets?

"They hate your kind," Carmen finished.

"What kind?"

"Demon witch." Carmen's smile grew. "You can't trust any of them."

"Said the least trustworthy person I've ever met."

"I'm not pretending to be your friend."

"What do you want?"

"I want to see how you're doing after last night. Did you…learn anything on that hunt?"

"What do you know about all this?"

"More than you, it seems. But that's okay. I have time to see if you figure it all out or not."

"Figure what out?" She hated *hated* that Carmen seemed to know things she didn't. Hated it so much she actually growled. "I'm getting a little tired of all the dancing words and innuendos without information. Starting to think none of you know anything and are just hoping the vague hints and guesses will get me to reveal something."

Carmen shrugged. "Might be the case for that hunter. They're manipulative bastards. All of them. And you can't trust them."

"Because they keep sending the demons you summon back?"

"Because they think they know best."

"Wow. You can honestly say that with a straight face? The vigilante who things she knows the best way to take care of bad people?"

Carmen's mouth flattened into a line. "I know better than they do what it takes to stop bad people from doing bad things."

"You'll forgive me if I don't believe you, since I watched

you do bad things yourself and endanger a child. Children, if I count Ivan's daughter."

The tension that snapped into Carmen's shoulders and jaw could have cracked concrete. "I'm not here to talk about that."

"Then what are you here to talk about?"

"Your hunt last night. You did it, didn't you?"

"Went on a hunt?"

"Found your true power."

"I don't know what you're talking about." But her heartbeat kicked up a few extra beats.

Carmen's tension eased a little, but she didn't smile. "Don't let them know," she said, her voice low. "They already want you dead. They will kill outright you if they find out what you can do. That you've learned… They still think you have limits. You don't. And when you're ready to face that, you come find me."

"Why?"

"Because I can tell you everything you need to know."

"You set up that hunt last night." No longer a question. She was sure of it now. "You're a witch?"

"Not like you," Carmen said with a shrug. "If I was, I wouldn't have spent all these years using demons to do my work. But I can manage a few spells."

"Like the ward on Vera and Bill's gate?" That still could have been something another witch, someone working with Carmen, had set.

Carmen grunted a non-answer, neither confirming nor denying the spell had been hers. Then she glanced around, and raised her hand. An empty soda can clinking along the gutter flew to her palm.

Angie blinked, but held in her gasp. She was pretty proud of herself for that lack of reaction. The older woman had been hoping to shock her. She didn't want to give her that shock.

"And I can do this," Carmen finished, holding up the can. "Useful, but not exactly the kind of skill that helps put rich white bastards in their place."

"If you say so. Although it might have less collateral damage. Why Bill and Vera? What did they do to you?"

"Nothing. Conveniently owed the wrong guy money."

"And Ivan? What did he do to earn your attention?"

"Nothing again. He just has the unfortunate luck to be married to a mobster's sister."

"Mobster?"

"Rich white bastard named Gregory Sokolov." Carmen smiled a little. "Met him yet? Same rich white bastard Bill and Vera owed money to. Sokolov gets killed..." She shrugged. "I'm not going to lose sleep over it."

Angie had to work harder to keep her reaction to the mention of Sokolov's name to herself than she'd had to work to keep her reaction to Carmen's telekinesis hidden. She took a beat before saying, "The rich white bastard hasn't been the one in danger of being killed by demons. You've left the people summoning them vulnerable."

"You haven't figured out why?"

"Because you're a bitch who doesn't care about killing innocent people."

The smile flattened. "Because how else do you get a demon hunter to go to a summoning? They only go when the demon's about to escape."

"There could just not be any demon summonings. That's an option here."

"Demon about to escape. Local demon hunters show up. Newbie demon hunter gets to test her *real* powers. Didn't know you could do…what you could do. Did you?"

Angie's pulse sped and she felt the crackle of her magic under her skin. Then a flash, a memory, an image…

Carmen sitting at the center of a magical spiderweb, blood pouring from her.

She blinked away the memory. "Still don't know what you're referring to."

Carmen chuckled. "Right. Aren't you ready to discuss it, ready to find out what you can really do?"

"Stop pretending you know what I can do."

"I'm not pretending. I've known from the first time you opened that portal in the trees outside Ellen and Mara's apartment. See, I know a lot of things the hunters don't want me to know. I know exactly what you're capable of. What amazes me is that you don't."

"What amazes me is that you're still standing there, and I haven't called down a lightning bolt yet." She could even feel that spell just at the edge of her consciousness, feel the shapes of the gestures in her fingers.

"You're too nice for that kind of thing. You believe in right and wrong. Probably even believe in that crap about 'what you put out, you get back.'" She rolled her eyes.

"You don't believe in right and wrong?"

"Oh, I believe in it. I believe in it down to my bones, chica. I just don't think the human world knows the difference most of the time."

"You're human. Should I point out the obvious?"

"I do what I do to right the balance. Justice doesn't come for a certain type of human in this world. Got enough money, enough power, the right color skin, you can get away with anything. I just make sure some of them don't."

"And risk any number of innocent people getting killed on the way to this supposed balance? It's not your ideology that's the problem. You're right about these people. It's your methods of going after them that's the issue. You're not the good guy, Carmen."

"Well, I'm also not Carmen." She chuckled at Angie's raised brows. "Or Marta for that matter. Like the demon hunters don't want others to know their power names, I don't give out my real name. Wouldn't do to have a witch with an eye toward revenge knowing, would it?"

"I don't want revenge against you. I want you to stop endangering innocent people."

And she wouldn't mind some justice for Carmen—whatever her real name was—either. The woman's continued crusade had to stop, and she had to have consequences for the pain and suffering she'd caused, the people she'd endangered. The people she'd killed. Angie would consider that justice.

But she wasn't the one to dole out that justice. Unfortunately, in this world, she wasn't sure who could. Not like ordinary cops and judges had any jurisdiction over demon summoning. And Carmen seemed to avoid the demon hunters easily, so they weren't going to be a source of accountability either.

"How do you do what you do and avoid the hunters?" Angie asked, not expecting an answer but curious. Carmen was a good actress. She'd fooled Angie and Sebastian both the first time they'd met her, gave every appearance of being an innocent housekeeper caught in the nefarious plots of her employer. She'd been working her revenge schemes for years. Yet the hunters had never stopped her.

And they now knew she'd killed at least one hunter, years ago, when he'd tried to stop one of her revenge plots. The demon hunter council had to want justice for that crime. Yet Carmen was still walking around free right under their noses.

"Only came close to losing control of a demon a few times over the years," Carmen said. "Hunters only show up when the demon's about to escape." She made a face. "Unfortunately."

"Because it's usually about to escape one of the people you want to die at its hands?"

She tilted her head in a little half shrug. "Hunters get in the way. But they're predictable."

"You killed one of them."

"No one knew that until a few weeks ago, did they? No one looks at me and sees what I don't want them to."

"I did."

Carmen narrowed her eyes. "Almost fooled you, though. Almost."

"Why do you think I'd trust you to tell me anything about my supposed skills? You're a liar and a con artist and a murderer. Going by a false name even. I've got no reason to believe you know anything at all."

Now Carmen's smiled wide. "You are desperate for answers now. You think I can't see the signs? The fact that you're still talking to me? Haven't tried to call your boyfriend? Or that hunter who was just here? You want to know what I know. Just in case it answers some of those questions. Don't worry. I'll tell you everything. When you're ready to hear it." She looked around the mostly empty street.

Angie mentally started the fire ball spell, letting the shield spell she'd prepped for facing Jacob fall away. She needed something more offensive with Carmen.

Carmen looked back at her, her eyes narrowed. "We'll talk again soon."

She turned and disappeared down the street, going in the opposite direction from the one Jacob had taken, blending into the shadows besides the buildings so that she was hard to see as she turned a corner a block away.

Angie let the fire spell go without finishing it, murmuring the dissipation chant to ensure the spell was nulled. But she didn't go inside until she was sure Carmen was gone. She checked the streets, feeling like a rope being pulled in opposite directions by enemies with different agendas.

If she couldn't find a way to make them release their holds, she was going to snap.

And no one wanted that.

CHAPTER THIRTY-ONE

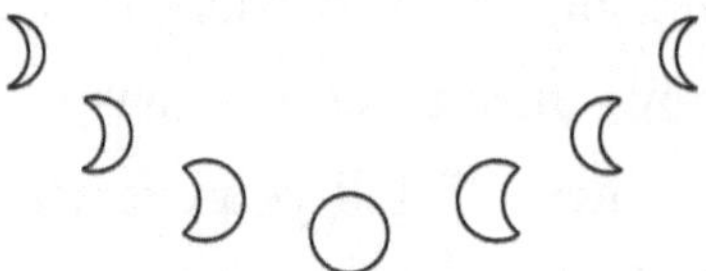

ngie was seriously considering calling Sebastian to come over as she waited in the lobby for the elevator. She wasn't sure calling him was a great idea for her on a personal level. Letting him leave kept getting harder, and the more time she spent with him, the worse that got. They were falling into old routines in so many ways, old habits that lead to other old habits. And eventually, she was going to give in to the longing that was never too far away when they were together. She was still a little buzzed from their kiss the other night.

But she needed to talk to someone about both Carmen and Jacob. There was no one else she could talk to, because none of her friends and work colleagues knew the details about the demon hunter stuff. She was reluctant to tell any of them, even Laura and Bianca, because she didn't want them in this world.

The elevator dinged opened in the lobby just as it occurred to her that she didn't have any really close friends here in New York. Not close enough she could call them and talk about Sebastian even. Not that she'd know what to say about that situation. Besides her repeated, "It's complicated." She'd been keeping people at a distance, without even realizing it. She'd been keeping herself just enough to herself that she didn't risk…

What? Getting hurt? Hurting others?

She wasn't even sure. But she'd been keeping all her friendships here at a certain level. Even the people she'd considered almost a second family—the people she worked with at Dana's. She was as close to them as anyone in New York. But, almost like she did with her real family, she kept a lot of her life from them, a lot of her history, so they wouldn't get hurt. And it meant, when she really needed someone to talk to about the big complicated stuff, she didn't have anyone to call.

Well. That was a shitty realization.

She might have continued mulling over that shitty realization too, but the minute she stepped off the elevator on her floor, her hackles went up and she stopped in her tracks.

"You have got to be kidding me," she muttered.

Gabriella stood outside her apartment door. The council member was wearing dark pants and a black wool coat, her steel-gray hair up in another painfully meticulous bun, her hands clasped in front of her, her expression serious but unreadable.

And her presence could only mean bad things.

"Why are you here?" Angie asked with a sigh.

"You had your first demon fight last night. A challenge. And your will bested the demon's."

"If you say so."

What and how much did Gabriella, and the entire council for that matter, know about what had really happened? Sebastian hadn't told them about the portal, but Carmen knew—or at least suspected—what Angie had done, which meant the council might know as well.

But then, Carmen knew a lot more about Angie's skills than even Angie did, thanks to the council keeping information from her.

That reminder just upped her irritation at seeing a member of said council outside her door.

"May I come in so we can talk?" Gabriella said.

"No." She paused beside her door without opening it—or releasing the ward spell on the frame. She hadn't managed to affix a full circle around her apartment yet, because doing that took time and energy and was complicated in an apartment building, and frankly, she hadn't had the time to figure it out yet. But she'd kept the warding on her front door and activated it when she left for work.

Turned out that wasn't a paranoid move.

"Talking in the hall where any of your neighbors might hear is…not convenient," Gabriella said.

"You can will them not to hear us. Do that." It wasn't like Gabriella was a vampire, where an invitation would open up Angie's home to her indefinitely. Angie just didn't want the council member in her apartment.

Gabriella made a noise in the back of her throat. "Waste of will when your apartment is right there with a convenient door and ward."

"Talk. I'm tired."

"Because of your hunt last night?"

"Because of work tonight. What do you want?"

Gabriella considered her a moment. "There's a member of the council who wants you dead."

"I know." Though she hadn't expected another member of the council to come right out and tell her. She refused to show Gabriella she was surprised, but she was. Not by the information but by who was discussing it with her.

"You know they want you to fail, and to be killed by a demon during a hunt?"

"I figured it out, yes."

"You haven't met him. He avoided the last meeting."

"Was he watching from that big ass fireplace?"

Gabriella's mouth flattened. "Not… It doesn't matter. He isn't your friend."

"Neither are you."

"But I want you to succeed."

"Why?"

"Because in the past, when we made enemies of other realm splitters, it was bad for everyone. And we're not learning from that past."

"You think I'm your enemy?"

"I think we're going to force you into that position by trying to get you killed."

"You want me to be a hunter."

"Yes. I want you to *succeed* as a hunter. It's your calling."

"No. It's not."

"It has to be. You wouldn't be able to do what you do if it wasn't."

"Then why didn't I have the instinct to go to the hunt last night?" She wasn't sure if Sebastian had told them that and she wanted to see Gabriella's reaction.

She wasn't disappointed.

Gabriella's frown deepened as her eyes widened. "What?"

"I had no idea there was a demon about to escape last night. I didn't sense it. I didn't have an instinct to go to that house in Jersey. Sebastian came and got me. That's the only reason I was there." Well, technically, she supposed Carmen was another reason she'd been there. Since Carmen had set things up so Angie and Sebastian would be forced to go on the hunt. Still, the point was the same. "If Sebastian hadn't come to get me, I wouldn't have had any idea a demon was about to escape. Those people would have died. And a demon would be loose in New Jersey right now."

She watched Gabriella's expression move through a series of emotions, though Angie wasn't entirely certain what any of them were. Confusion though. There was definitely confusion in there.

"That's…"

"Not the hallmark of a demon hunter," Angie finished for her. "I've been trying to tell you. Even when I worked with Sebastian and had his back, it was as a witch. I never got that instinctive knowing that I was needed somewhere. I just…

tagged along when Sebastian needed to hunt." She waited for Gabriella to look her in the face. "I'm a witch. Not a demon hunter."

"You're a realm splitter," Gabriella said. "You can open portals into demon worlds. If that's not a skill that belongs to a hunter—"

"What happened with the other realm splitters? What's everyone trying so hard not to tell me?"

Gabriella had just hinted. And the hint implied bad things. But Angie was tired of hints and innuendos. She'd been getting those all night. First from Jacob. Then Carmen. Now Gabriella. Her patience, already at snapping point, would not hold out much longer.

In fact, she could feel the bubble of her magic building, just under her skin, as if she'd need it soon. Crackling in her blood the way it had during her conversation with Carmen.

Damn it. She couldn't lose control of the one part of her life she'd always been confident in. Especially not now.

She took a deep breath, trying to sooth the irritation that was making her magic rise. But she was very tempted to mutter the spark spell and give Gabriella a little shock if she didn't start talking.

"We're not supposed to… We can't talk about that history with others outside the council. It's not for most hunters to know. The chances of any of them meeting someone like you are low anyway."

"Aidan knows?" She'd gotten the impression, from Aidan, that Aidan knew a lot more than most hunters. Maybe even the council.

"Enough to bring you to our attention when she discovered you."

"Saved me," Angie corrected. "She saved me." Saved her from herself.

"She knew what you were and what that meant. She agreed we should keep an eye on you."

"But she didn't think I should be a hunter. She knew I wasn't one."

Gabriella's mouth compressed again. "Aidan isn't one of the history keepers. She's not on the council. She doesn't know as much as she thinks she does."

There was some history there, between Aidan and Gabriella. But that was gossip she could plum latter. When she was no longer under threat from all these people.

"You're here to warn me that someone on the council wants me dead. Is that all? Because if you're not going to tell me why—the *real* reason why—then we're done here. I have to get some sleep."

If possible, Gabriella's pinched expression got even more pinched. "I'm not your enemy here, you know that right?"

"Too many people tell me things like that when they're busy getting me into trouble. You'll forgive me if I don't believe you."

Gabriella shook her head. "So stubborn. If you turned that will to this work, you'd be excellent."

"No. I wouldn't. I could have failed last night and gotten people killed." She wasn't prepared to calling Bill and Vera innocent—she didn't know enough about their situation to go that far. But no one deserved the kinds of deaths demons doled out. And Sebastian had also been there. If Angie had failed, he would have been in trouble.

She refused to think about that.

"You didn't fail. You beat a demon on the very first challenge you faced. Only true demon hunters do that."

"And most of those first challenges are what bring them into the demon hunter fold. They prove their will is strong enough *before* you all start training them. I failed with an *imp*. A lot. I am not a demon hunter."

"Fa!" Gabriella made a hand gesture so full of frustration, if she'd been a witch Angie would have assumed it triggered a spell. "You spend so much time protesting when you could just do the work. You sound whiny and childish."

Angie wasn't sure whether to laugh or initiate her spark spell as anger choked her. "I sound childish and whiny? I'm not the one pushing for something impossible. I'm not the one hounding a witch to convince her to be a demon hunter. Even some of your own people don't want me."

Gabriella straightened abruptly, like she'd been slapped. "One council member doesn't represent most of us."

"I'm not talking about the council member," Angie said. She wanted to know what Gabriella knew about Jacob and whoever he represented. Did Gabriella honestly think it was only this one council member that didn't want Angie involved with the hunters? "I'm talking about other hunters. One has approached me, twice now, hoping to discourage me from taking up your…offer to become a hunter. I get the impression he represents more than just himself in that request."

"Who?"

"Not my business to tell you. I don't trust him. But I don't trust you either."

"I'm here to help you. I wouldn't have told you about the hunter who wants you dead if I wasn't."

"I appreciate you telling me, and confirming what I had already guessed. Do I get the council member's name?"

She paused and looked around the hall.

"You're preventing eavesdropping," Angie said. "Or we wouldn't be talking so freely. No one will hear."

"He's…" Gabriella shook her head. "It's not…"

"If you're not here to tell me *who's* trying to kill me, why are you here?"

Gabriella didn't meet her gaze, so Angie couldn't see the flash of red in the depth of her brown eyes, but she was acutely aware of it, even without being able to see it. The quiet hallway, despite all the talk of demons and demon hunters, was proof Gabriella was willing the others on the floor not to hear this conversation. A handy hunter trick. And something Angie knew she'd never have the will to manage. Yet another sign she didn't belong in this world.

"Will you let me see the information you have on realm splitters?" she asked after a moment when Gabriella didn't answer. "I might better understand why you're so insistent I join the hunters, and why one of your colleagues is so insistent I die."

Gabriella made a face at that, almost like she wanted to roll her eyes at Angie's phrasing, but couldn't because it was the truth.

"It's not permitted." Gabriella raised a hand when Angie opened her mouth. "But I can tell you…a little."

"Talk."

"Can we please go in and sit down? It's a story. And as you said, you're tired."

Angie snorted. Trying to use her own exhaustion against her wasn't going to work. "There's a diner around the corner that stays open twenty-four hours. We can talk there. You a coffee person or a tea person?"

"Both, depending on my mood. What I could really use now is a Tequila shot, though."

Angie was proud she didn't react to that suggestion. But a part of her did warm to Gabriella in that moment.

She needed a shot of Tequila, too.

CHAPTER THIRTY-TWO

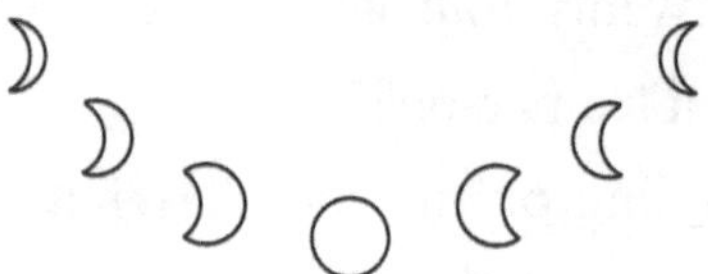

The diner was a long, narrow restaurant with a line of two person booths down one side, a long counter with turning stools along the other, and a small square space in the back with larger booths for groups. At this time of night, on a quiet weekday, the places wasn't packed, and there was no wait for a table, but it wasn't empty either. Five of the eight two-person booths were filled, most with just a single dinner. And one of the larger booths in the back held five people, a group of aging men loudly griping about co-op fees.

The smell of fresh French fries and coffee made Angie's stomach growl. She'd save her bodega-bought sandwich for tomorrow. If she was going to be in the diner anyway, she was going to do more than drink a tea.

A bored-looking woman in a neat skirt and blouse, showed them to a table and dropped menus in front of them.

Their small booth was near the front of the diner, and there was an empty booth between them and the next where a young man sat feverishly scribbling in a notebook while idly stuffing onion rings into his mouth.

"Good seat," Angie murmured when she and Gabriella were alone. She settled her oversized purse on the small bench next to her and shrugged out of her coat. "I'm eating while we're here. You can or not. I won't mind either way." Not much got between Angie and food. Especially not something as changeable as social expectations. And when something did interfere with her getting fed, that was usually bad for everyone involved.

"I'll be fine with a coffee."

They didn't talk until after the waiter had taken their orders—Angie's a veggie omelet with extra cheese, a side order of fries, and a tea. Gabriella a black coffee.

When the waiter left with their order, Gabriella said, "I haven't been here before."

"Been in many diners in the city?"

"A few. I've lived her a while."

"Get down to the Village much?"

"Occasionally."

This wasn't even close to the reason they were here, but she had a feeling Gabriella was waiting for the food to arrive before they talked about something more serious, so she kept up the small talk until after her eggs and fries arrived. Then for several moments, she ate in silence, too hungry to worry about conversation.

When she felt a little more settled, and could focus on

something besides the food, she looked at Gabriella. "You have things to tell me."

Gabriella's mouth flattened. She glanced around the diner. "This would be better in private."

"You have a hunt tonight you need your will for?" Angie asked. "Cause I'm still not inviting you into my home."

"I'm not a vampire."

"A joke I don't plan to engage with." She shrugged. "Though I did tell myself the same thing earlier. I'm still not letting you in my apartment. And we've had this argument already. I'm full now. Now's the time to talk, while my patience is high. Wait too long, my patience drains again, and I go home and go to sleep."

"You're the one who needs this information. You're the one who insists."

"True. But I also don't have the tolerance for this dancing around bullshit anymore. You claimed you were going to tell me. Let's go."

"Why you?" Gabriella sighed. "Why someone so resistant to just doing the job?"

"Good question. I could have done without the special, rare skill, too. I like my other skills an awful lot more." Her touch psychic skill had taken her years to train and been a pretty big inconvenience for a few years. But even that one she didn't mind anymore because it helped her make a living helping people.

The possible connection between that skill and her demon hunter skills niggled the back of her brain, but she didn't have the time and privacy to focus on that connection right now. She should though. Soon. She knew there was something there, some reason those two things came easily and she had to train *not* to use them. Unlike her other magic.

Gabriella didn't relax her stiff posture, but there was resignation in her expression. She glanced around the diner one more time, then settled against her seat and her eyelids drooped to half closed, her gaze turned inward. A moment passed, she blinked, and she picked up her mug of coffee again.

"There haven't been a lot of demon witches over the years," she said.

"Got that impression. Also, didn't think hunters used the term demon witch." She was proud of herself for not reacting to Gabriella's use of that term.

"We do. Just not with everyone."

Should she mention Jacob by name yet? No. Keep that close to her chest until she knew what Gabriella intended on telling her. "Carmen used it—the murderer you let get away."

"We didn't *let* her get away. That…woman has been avoiding the hunters for years while still working with demons. And she's still alive."

"Meaning her will is strong enough to both manage demons and hunters?"

"Demons certainly." She sniffed. "Maybe some hunters."

"I'd prefer she was in jail."

"You've seen her."

She wasn't asking a question, but Angie said, "Sebastian told you."

"He's upset she hasn't been taken into custody. I can't

blame him. I'd like her taken care of too. She killed one of ours and still walks around. That's…upsetting."

Simple word to describe some complex feelings that. "Carmen knows the term. I got the impression she knows more than I do. That's unacceptable." One more detail. Maybe it would push Gabriella to stop prevaricating. "She's offered to help me learn how to use my skill better. To train me. Implied she knows things." Angie leveled her gaze on Gabriella. "I don't like that someone like her knows more about me than I do."

Gabriella's mouth flattened into a line. "No. That doesn't seem wise. You were tempted by her offer?"

"I don't trust her enough to let her teach me anything. But if she's my only source of information…" Angie spread her hands around her mug before cupping it again. A subtle shrug.

"She'll lie to you. Tell you twisted versions of the truth."

"And you?"

"I'm going to tell you the truth."

"As far as it goes and while revealing as little as possible?"

Gabriella made a sound that was halfway between a choke and a laugh. The sound surprised Angie. She wasn't sure she'd heard Gabriella come anywhere near a laugh in any of their brief conversations. She got the feeling the council member didn't laugh all that often.

"I'll tell you what I think is safe to tell you," she said after a moment. "And when I trust you more, I'll tell you more. Will that suffice?"

"When you trust me more? Not if?"

"If, when… Either way."

Gabriella didn't give a lot away, but Angie wondered if the "when" was a slip. Did she really think one day she'd trust Angie? It hadn't crossed Angie's mind that one day she might trust Gabriella. Or anyone on this hunter council for that matter. Though her opinion of them was probably skewed by the fact that one of them wanted her dead.

"Tell me what you will, then," Angie said.

"Demon witches come around once in a few generations. No one on the current council has dealt with one in person. They've just read the records."

"Has Aidan?" She really had no idea how old Aidan was. The question might be absurd. Aidan couldn't be older than everyone else on the council, not old enough for what they were talking about. Still, she felt the need to ask.

"No," Gabriella said. "No living, working hunter has encountered a demon witch. And we make an effort to keep knowledge of them strictly limited. For the witches' sake as well as ours."

"Why their sake?"

"Do you want a freed demon to know you exist? To know your kind exists? There are freed demons in this world, here under treaty or given asylum, who are powerful and dangerous. You do not want them knowing your kind are more than a myth."

No. No, she didn't. Having the Molder demon figure out what she could do and then take over her body with the intent of using her ability to open a realm portal had been… Well, she had regular nightmares that weren't going away anytime soon. But the real fear came not from what had actually happened. It came from what *could* have happened. That crept into her nightmares. All the horror that could have ripped into this realm.

And it would have been her fault.

"So we don't discuss realm splitters, though as with everything, we do keep the records. And some hunters have had access to those records of course."

"What do the records say?"

"That every time a demon witch has been born, death and destruction have followed her."

"Always a her?"

Gabriella blinked. "Now you mention it, yes. Strange. Hadn't thought of that before."

Witch wasn't a gendered word. There were male witches, nonbinary witches, female witches, transgendered witches, cisgendered witches…any and every variation of human could be a witch. Witch described the type of magic available to a wielder. And sometimes it just described a religious theology, or someone without magic but with a great deal of knowledge about witchy things like herbs and potions. None those people had to be shes.

The fact that, in the records, all demon witches were females was…strange. She wasn't sure if it meant anything, but it was a curiosity she filed away to mull over later.

"It's possible it's a sampling error in the records," Gabriella said. "We might have missed other demon witches. There's really only a record of twelve named individuals and then discussions of more unspecified individuals."

"Fair enough. Go on."

"The records, from back that far, can sometimes be hard to interpret, but there's always dread and death around the demon witch. Always a release of demons, great battles fought to banish the hoards, the demon witch at the center of it all."

"On purpose or on accident?"

A brief pause. "The records indicate on purpose."

"You sure? Because that first time, I was five, and it was most definitely an accident."

"You were five. These are records of adult individuals who would be well aware of their abilities. They unleashed demons on this realm on purpose."

Well that explained all the hostility and mixed messaging she was getting from the people who actually knew about demon witches.

"Why?" she asked.

"Why what?"

"*Why* did they unleash demons on this realm on purpose? Why would anyone do that?"

Gabriella pursed her lips. "Details for some are too scarce to say. Or the records are too difficult to interpret. They go back a long time. Other witches were… There was no time to question them for their motivations."

"Demons killed them or hunters did?"

And tightening around the mouth.

Angie couldn't tell if her quick questions were throwing

the hunter off or if she was using the blinks and mouth tightening and pausing to organize her answers. If she was organizing her answers, was it because she didn't want to tell Angie everything, because she was about to lie, or because she didn't know the answers?

"A few, the demons."

"Others the hunters."

"A few."

Angie narrowed her eyes. "You're being quite vague. I have a feeling the deaths of these previous demon witches have been recorded in more detail, at least for the specific named individuals. Twelve of them, right. Even with difficult to interpret records, the ways and means of a demon witch's death will be recorded. In detail. How many *exactly* did the hunters kill, and how many were killed by demons?"

Gabriella sighed and glanced out over the diner. "It's complicated."

"So is life. We're here so you can tell me this information. You afraid I'll get upset and do something like hit you with a spark spell?"

Gabriella gave her a disapproving look. "I don't think you're a pouty child."

"You called me whiny and childish earlier."

"That wasn't what I meant."

"Not afraid of me either?"

She opened her mouth to retort. Then snapped it closed. "I'm not dignifying that with a response."

"You were about to, though."

"Why would you say that?"

"You know what I do for a living?"

"Read palms."

"It's more than that."

"Yes. You're psychic and a touch gives you insights to your clients."

"More than that. I got my degree in psychology."

"Are you telling me you're psychoanalyzing me?"

"I'm telling you I read body language very well, and I can hear the things people almost say in their body language." Angie raised her hand. "Would this be easier if you didn't have to force the words out aloud? Have you been keeping the secrets so long, you can barely admit them? A touch, and we can sort all that out."

"I don't think so."

Because Gabriella had more secrets than just the information about demon witches. Angie could only imagine what those might be. "Fair enough. Then you need to stop being vague when you don't have to be. It's just pissing me off. And if you don't think I'll give you a little zap with a spark spell because I'm supposed to be a grown up, talk to my brothers."

Gabriella's expression went through another of those indecipherable series of contortions, but Angie would swear the lip twitch was humor. That didn't seem right. She didn't think Gabriella possessed a sense of humor.

"Five of the twelve were killed by the demons they'd released," she finally said. "Most of those deaths were in the earliest records. The demons weren't the kind that…realized using the witches would be more useful to them. Three others were used by the demons they unleashed, their bodies taken over, possessed. Ordinary possession, not body swapping."

The thought of body swapping with a demon gave Angie shivers. Being possessed was horrible enough. You were still in your own body when you were possessed, just subsumed under the demon's will and spirit. Body swapping put you *into* the demon's body. And the idea of being in a demon body, being exposed to their thoughts and memories like that… She cupped her mug a little tighter even though it was no longer warm.

"The witches usually fought back for their bodies and that resulted in their deaths. Not that any would have survived long with a demon riding her anyway." Gabriella shrugged. Then fell silent as the waitress arrived to refill her coffee.

"Want more tea?" the woman asked Angie.

"Thanks." Angie kept her gaze on Gabriella. The waitress brought Angie more hot water and another tea bag. Then Angie and Gabriella were alone again. "Thanks for the break for hot tea." Gabriella had obviously willed the waitress here, or simply stopped willing her away. "Did you need the coffee, or did you need the break in conversation?"

"Both. The records of these various deaths were… difficult to read."

"I imagine. Keep going. Four more witches of the named ones weren't killed by demons in some way. They were killed by hunters?"

"One was killed by her coven. They fought back when she unleashed the hoard. Fought beside the hunters. And they took out their own. She's one of the few whose motivations we know for certain. Relatively recent—three hundred years ago. She was angry at the witch burnings. She intended on punishing the religious zealots leading the torture and murders."

"Why did her coven stop her?"

"The same reason we did. Once the demons are released, no matter the power of the witch, she will not be able to control them. Not all of them. Which means she can't direct who they kill."

"Innocent people die as well as those she wanted to punish." That was the whole problem with Carmen's way of exacting revenge on the people she saw as evil. There was always innocent collateral damage, innocent lives in danger, lives ruined, possibly lost, because demons could never be fully controlled.

"Some did," Gabriella said. "Including some fellow witches. That's why the coven stepped in to help stop her."

Angie understood both the motivation to unleash hell on the zealots murdering fellow witches, and the obligation of the coven to stop the murders since innocent people were being killed, too. Gruesome and horrible situation all around. And she didn't envy the coven their task.

"You don't have a coven," Gabriella noted.

"Prefer the solitary witchy life. That's a subject change."

"Not really. A coven could keep you balanced, keep you from giving in to the need to unleash a hoard of demons."

"First, don't intend on doing that. Second, the coven didn't help the witch from three hundred years ago. I'll stick to what feels right for me."

"You sure you won't unleash a hoard?"

"Positive. At least not on purpose. I have no wish to see my realm overrun by demons. Seeing the demon realms is bad enough."

"I haven't been to one, personally."

"I have. I don't recommend it."

Gabriella's mouth did a funny little twist and her brows lowered. She took a slow sip of her coffee, her gaze turning inward.

After a few quite moments, she said, "The council member who wants you dead... He sees your anger as dangerous. He thinks that anger is what will cause the trouble. Just like the witch trying to punish the zealots." Gabriella met Angie's gaze. "He doesn't see, or understand, your fear. It's your fear that's the problem."

"You think my fear will cause me to unleash demons?"

"No, no. It's what keeps you from going rogue. But it's also what makes you reject the hunter life."

"I reject the hunter life because I'm a witch and not a hunter."

"You were born to be both."

"No one is born to be both. When they try, they die."

"Sebastian told you that?"

"About ordinary witches trying to be hunters or vice versa, yes."

"You're not an ordinary witch." Gabriella leaned forward in her seat. "There's a reason the word 'demon' is in the name for your skill."

"But not because I'm meant to be a hunter."

"So stubborn." Gabriella fell back against her seat, shook her head and sighed harshly. "Fear. Accepting your destiny would be less painful."

"You people leaving me alone would be less painful." She held Gabriella's gaze. "I could have failed last night. I didn't sense the impending escape. I *am not* a demon hunter. And it's your fear and stubbornness that's causing the trouble."

Gabriella didn't look away but she didn't comment either. Angie looked at the tiny flickers of red in the depths of her brown eyes, and wondered about Gabriella. What had brought her here, to this diner, still trying to make Angie into something she wasn't? Why was Gabriella so convinced this was the right thing to do?

"What happened to the other three witches?" Angie asked after a prolonged silence.

"They were destroyed by hunters," Gabriella said. "Eventually. After much death and destruction."

"I understand why some of your people want me dead—given the records. But why would some just want me to stay away from the hunters? Why have I been told not to become a hunter, to keep being a witch, and to leave the demon world alone?"

"Who's told you that?" Gabriella narrowed her eyes.

"I'm more interested in discussing the why? Why warn me away, but not try to kill me? If I'm so dangerous?"

"Good question. Someone without a pragmatic streak, maybe? Someone who sees your right to live as more important than the threat you represent? Someone who doesn't believe you're dangerous if you stick to witchcraft?"

"You think that last is bullshit. You think I'm dangerous if I just stick to witchcraft."

"Not…precisely. I think you're dangerous period. I think everyone, *everyone*, will be safer if you accept your role in the hunter world and learn what you have to learn here."

"Then how do you explain the fact that I didn't sense the near escape last night?"

"I don't have an explanation." She flattened her mouth, the severe expression full of annoyance. "You should have sensed it. I…"

"I didn't because I can't be what you want me to be. Did any of the other demon witches attempt to work with hunters? Attempt to become one?"

"No. None. At least not any that are recorded. We thought a different tactic with you, since we'd found you so young, would…change history. Stop the eventual disaster before it started."

"You could have killed me at five."

"We aren't the monsters. We hunt the monsters."

"You didn't react as badly to that as I expected you to."

She gestured at the red in her eyes. "I'm very clear on who I am. What I do. But I realize my proximity to the demons, all hunters' proximity to demons, can call into question our humanity sometimes. It's our humanity that makes us good at what we do, though."

"You think 'humanity' is the word for the person or persons who want me dead?"

"Yes. He isn't thinking of yours, that's true. And that's a failing. But it's because he's thinking globally, of all humanity. I can't blame him for that. I just disagree with the way he wants to handle the situation."

"Not considering my humanity for the sake of a larger picture is a mistake. That kind of ends-justifying-the-means is what's driven people to do truly horrific things throughout history. It's what drove the witch wanting revenge against zealot witch burners. It's what drives Carmen. The problem with that kind of…selective humanity? It becomes entirely too easy to set humanity aside all together. And then innocent people get killed."

Gabriella nodded. "Yes," she said simply.

Angie hadn't expected the easy agreement. She took a sip of her milky, sugary tea while she let the moment of understanding between them settle. Despite herself, she might actually like Gabriella. A little bit. At least, she might learn to respect her. Eventually.

When Gabriella stopped trying to make her into something she wasn't.

CHAPTER THIRTY-THREE

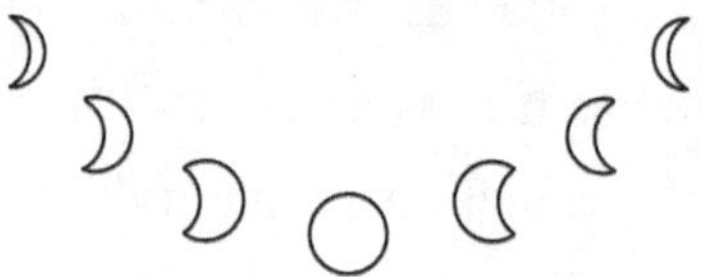

The clinks and quiet voices inside the diner filled the silence between Angie and Gabriella as they stared at each other. Angie thought she might understand the hunter better now, understand why she was so insistent Angie become a hunter. The history of demon witches was not good, and the idea of taking a different tactic with Angie, of trying to recruit her instead of killing her or waiting for her to go rogue, made sense.

It just wasn't going to work.

"I'll keep training with Sebastian for another three months. I will try. But after three months, when I have failed —because I will," she added when Gabriella opened her mouth, "—you will reconvene with the council and you will decide it's better to leave me alone and let me continue my quiet, witchy life away from demons."

"Three months is hardly enough time."

"Most hunters are identified as hunters right away and are able to do what they do immediately. They're...recruited, for lack of a better word, when their will overcomes a demon even before they've been trained."

Almost all hunters, as far as Angie knew, became hunters after someone tried to use them as a sacrifice to a demon, and they managed to survive. Usually with a hunter on hand to help. But the would-be-hunter demonstrates enough will in the fight to prove they're able for the job. And then they sense what to do next.

Aidan had explained that much to her in general, generic terms. Years ago, when she'd asked. But Aidan hadn't gotten specific about her experience. Or anyone else's.

"Three months is more than enough time to prove my point," Angie continued. "And in those three months, I want access to the information about demon witches."

"I've just told you everything we have."

"No, you haven't." She held Gabriella's gaze until the hunter sighed.

"No one on the council will agree to showing you the records. Specifically the person who wants you dead. He will assume you want to see those records to get ideas... Suggestions."

"He thinks I'll use the records to make a game plan for unleashing demons on the world?"

"Yes."

"I'd have to be crazy. I have no motivation to do that." Not even her anger and need to draw out the council member who wanted her killed was motivation enough for her to unleash a demon plague on this realm. She was *well* aware of what a disaster that would be.

Frankly, she had no idea why other demon witches would do it, how they could possibly think they could control all those monsters. Maybe some of them hadn't wanted to control the demons. Maybe some of them wanted the destruction simply for the sake of chaos and death. And maybe some, like the witch seeking revenge against the zealots, wanted to balance scales in some way.

But until she got to read the records themselves, see and understand everything the hunters had on her kind, she could never reassure them *she* wouldn't do what they feared.

It was always possible she'd never be able to reassure them. A possibility she'd have to consider if and when it happened. Until then, though, she'd do her best just to convince them she wasn't the real threat here.

At least now she knew *why* they feared her. And that Gabriella, at least, had no idea about Jacob and whoever he represented.

After a long pause, Gabriella motioned with a finger, and the waitress brought the bill, leaving it on the edge of the table. "After three months, we'll discuss your continued training. I'm not saying we'll see the benefit of you stopping that training. I'm saying we'll meet to discuss it. And I make no promises on you being allowed to see the records. We don't let most hunters see those records. Letting you see them will not be a popular decision."

"This...person who wants me dead..." She wasn't sure how to say this, at least say it without giving away that

Sebastian had wanted—still wanted—to destroy the council completely. "The council this size... I was under the impression the history keepers were a looser organization at one time. Not so formal. Not a governing body, per se."

"We weren't. Why?"

"Given the independent streak of most hunters..."

The phrasing made Gabriella snort.

"Given that independent streak, have you considered such a formal arrangement as the council is maybe... unnecessary?"

"I have. I've been out-voted. Why?"

"The dynamics of the council seem a little, well, toxic. You know that one of your own wants me dead. Is actively hoping I'll get killed during a hunt. That's not normal run-of-the-mill committee disagreements over a point of logistics or pricing or whatever. That's...bad," she said, because she wasn't sure any other word conveyed the unhealthy situation better. "What would this council member do if he knew you were here talking to me? How would he react to you telling me everything you have?"

"Badly. But I can handle him. And the workings of the council aren't your concern. Your concern is to survive. And, with effort, become a hunter to prove you're more useful to us alive than dead."

"I'm not on this earth to be *useful* to *you*." Angie tried very hard to temper the growl in her voice, but it slipped out anyway, and her voice dropped to a lower octave. To her surprise, she also felt her magic rising. She took a few deep breaths to let it settle again. Damn it, that was definitely happening too much. Something was wrong. And she needed to discuss it with another witch.

"If not delivered in those terms to the council, more of them will advocate for more extreme measures in dealing with you," Gabriella said bluntly. "You don't want that. You don't want a war with the hunters. Suck it up. Set aside your hurt feelings. And do what you have to do to prove you're not a threat. It's the only way forward."

No. No, it wasn't. But there was no point in arguing with Gabriella anymore. Angie had said her peace. So had Gabriella. And Angie did know more now than she had at the start of the conversation. Not a pointless hour—especially since she'd gotten a nice dinner out of it.

She let Gabriella pay for the food, because she was feeling petty, and waited for the hunter just outside the diner's front door. The sidewalks were empty now, most of the shops and businesses closed, the neighborhood falling quiet as night deepened. The tattoo parlor across the street was still open, it's neon sign above the stairs leading to its basement-level front door flickered a little. A cold breeze blew through the sidewalk trees, the orange street lamps giving the street a pretty glow.

She loved this neighborhood. She just wished the hunters had left her alone here.

All of them? a little voice in the back of her mind asked.

But she refused to think about that too much at the moment. She was too tired. Sebastian wasn't just a hunter. And her feelings for him, and about him being in her life again, were too complicated to sort out in a few minutes on a Village sidewalk.

Gabriella didn't walk back with her to her apartment. They parted ways in front of the diner, with Gabriella promising her they'd revisit Angie's work as a hunter in three months, and in the meantime…

"Watch your back and don't get killed. I'd hate for the council member who is not your friend to be proven right."

Angie watched the hunter disappear around a corner before walking back the three blocks to her building. This time, no one was waiting for her, outside or in. No one ambushed her. No one threatened her. She made it all the way home and inside her apartment, with the wards on her door refreshed and ready to keep her safe for the night.

She considered her altar. And she considered calling one of her mentors in New Mexico since the time difference meant it wasn't so late there. Then she thought about a shower and her warm, blanket ladened bed.

Conversations and altar work could wait. Everything could wait one more day.

Sleep called.

CHAPTER THIRTY-FOUR

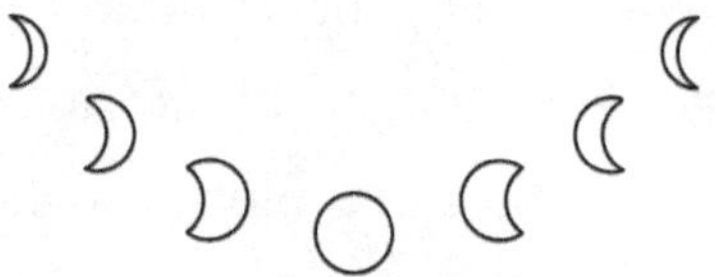

The next week passed without any new incidents, Carmen sightings, or drop-in visits from Jacob or Gabriella. And for reasons Angie couldn't seem to shake, it felt like waiting for the other shoe to drop.

She trained with Sebastian and the imp—little bastard. She did manage to will it away twice, finally. And she challenged him once, but the imp had picked the most ridiculous challenge form, so she sort of felt beating him had been luck—he'd suggested the first person to scratch would lose. He'd lost.

She practiced aura reading twice more with Laura, and that had gone well. She liked those sessions because it was witchy work.

Work itself had been busy in the days leading up to Halloween—a lot of people seemed to come down to the Village looking for paranormal experiences this time of year

—so she hadn't had much time for brooding or worry. She worked hard, whether with Sebastian, Laura, or her clients, then was able to collapse in exhaustion at the end of the day with no intruding demon hunters or demons.

The quiet was worrying though. Carmen was out there somewhere. And while the council was leaving her alone to work with Sebastian, she was acutely aware one really did want her dead, and she hadn't just been paranoid. The mysterious motivations of Jacob also hung out there, a complication waiting to happen. And all of this while she felt a little less control over her magic than she usually had.

She hadn't dared sit at her altar. She was afraid of what she'd find if she opened herself to any visions there again. Keeping all her visions reserved for her clients felt safest. But she was aware of that avoidance, and the longer she did, the more she felt something looming over her. Something waiting there to pounce.

Something that felt a little like a spiderweb.

The night before Halloween was a work day, thankfully too busy to let herself wallow in her worries. But she was edgy and jumpy for reasons she couldn't pinpoint. In between clients, she'd restlessly stalk through Dana's, getting tea, chatting to the other psychics, even helping Laura and Moon Star on the floor, even though that wasn't part of her job. She straightened shelves and reordered books and even did some dusting.

Laura was frowning hard at her when she returned the duster. "What's wrong with you this evening? You can't stand still?"

"I have no idea," she said, tapping her foot as she stood near the counter. "Restless."

"Something about to happen?" Laura worked with psychics. Premonitions often manifested in strange behavior.

"Not sure. Just…" She shrugged. "I'm restless."

She scanned the crowded first floor, all the people who'd come in to prepare for Halloween, tourists and locals alike. Some were even wearing their costumes already. Others seemed to be looking for party essentials. They'd been doing a lot of crystal and tarot card sales all day, according to Laura. There was nothing in the place that drew her specific attention though. No individual that caught her eye and made her instincts hum. She was just…restless.

"No other word for it," she murmured. "No idea what's wrong with me."

"How many more clients are you seeing tonight?"

"One more. Due in soon. Then I'm done for the night."

"Maybe you should go for a run or something to work off all that energy."

Angie chuckled. She was a long walk kind of person, not a runner, but maybe she would take a long walk. Maybe that's what she needed. She felt like she had so much energy about to burst from her, she was afraid she'd walk to the Bronx and back and still not feel better.

So strange.

She was able to settle during her last reading. The focus and attention on the young woman who was on her second session with Angie, and in desperate need of career advice— to Angie's way of thinking from a real mentor and not a psychic, but she did her best for Arabell—helped keep Angie centered. Using her magic seemed to calm some of the restlessness, too. She didn't feel the need to come out of her seat when she was opening her psychic skills, feeling her way through the readings so she'd provide her clients with the best possible experience.

But the minute Arabell left, the restlessness swamped her again. An itching, irritating need to *go*. To do…something.

She was dressed in her street clothes, dropping her bag over her head, when she realized what was driving her to distraction.

"Demon."

Shit. Demon about to escape. Somewhere. Nearby. Close enough for her to reach.

But…if that was the case, where the hell was Sebastian? She was too new a demon hunter to go in alone. If she felt this—and she couldn't believe she did since she was still convinced she was absolutely not meant to be a hunter—then Sebastian should.

Maybe he was downstairs waiting for her.

She rushed out, with only perfunctory goodbyes for Bianca and Rachel—who were between clients—and hit the first floor expecting to see Sebastian by the register charming Laura.

He wasn't there.

She stopped long enough to ask Laura if she'd seen him.

"No. He hasn't come in." She motioned to the crowded shop. "Even in this mess, he'd be hard to miss." Laura gave her a look. But before she could ask any questions a customer came up to the desk to check out. "You need help?" she managed to ask Angie, vague as possible.

"I'll be fine," Angie said, forcing a smile. "See you tomorrow."

She left before Laura could ask more, the itching need to move overwhelming her manners and desire to reassure her friend.

Outside, the cold air slapped her in the face. The temperature had dropped in the last two days, sharp and crisp with autumn and hints of winter to come. The cold felt good, brisk enough to calm some of her rising panic. The neighborhood was crowded, people filling the narrow streets and threading through traffic whenever a red light stopped the cars. The spicy scent of an empanada cart at the corner made her stomach growl.

But for once, the need for food was overwhelmed by her need to move.

She pressed through the crowds, not sure what direction she was heading, just following the instinct to get... somewhere. Music spilled out of a nearby bar. Restaurants were filled, some with waiting lines outside. The tattoo parlor a block down from Dana's was also crowded, with people hovering outside looking through art books while others were in chairs and on beds inside as the artists worked on them.

The neighborhood was hopping, busy with locals and tourists alike. There were even people on the street in Halloween costumes already. Groups of laughing zombies. A couple of people in matching doll costumes—which were frankly terrifying—and a family dressed up like planets—

which she loved. There were animal costumes and vampire costumes and "sexy" versions of everyday job costumes.

Considering Halloween was tomorrow, she was a little surprised to see so many people dressed up. But if her instincts weren't pushing her so hard to get…somewhere, she'd have really enjoyed the spectacle and maybe joined the drag queens outside the drag bar as they shouted compliments at everyone for their looks.

The neighborhood felt energized and…happy. Everyone was shouting, singing, talking loudly. Cars honked but even that seemed timed to be a cheer instead of an irritated "get moving" noise.

All the eager energy and goodwill should have delighted her. She loved when her neighborhood got like this.

But for some reason it only made her more antsy and anxious to reach her destination. And the crowds were in her way. Holding her back. Blocking her from getting where she had to go.

Why the hell were so many people in her way?

She dodged into the street to avoid a group of drunk tourists, got honked at by a passing car which missed clipping her by an inch, got back onto the sidewalk, only to have to push through a group of people spilling out of a Korean-French fusion restaurant and stopping in the middle of the sidewalk to figure out where to go next.

The drag queens gave her thumbs up and exaggerated waves as she passed. She returned the greetings and said hi to Ms. Tander Son and Jems Tone—they were both friends and occasional clients—but she didn't stop to talk as she might on a normal night.

Instincts drove her deeper into the heart of the Village, away from her own apartment but still in the neighborhood, through the narrow, twisty streets that were not designed to make navigation easy. She reached a place cut off from traffic, where only pedestrians could walk because of some road works, and broke into a jog.

She had to get there, she had to reach…

She came to a screeching stop just outside a three-story building.

Not an apartment building. There were businesses on the first floor, a bookstore, a coffee shop, and a pet food store—all closed. The second and third floors were dark, no lights anywhere. One window was boarded up, but the rest were just lights-out. A quick glance at a sign next to the glass door that led to a small lobby showed the top two floors were a shared work space, where people could rent rooms by the hour or day for meetings or just a quiet desk.

Glancing around, she realized that while there'd been crowds and traffic and noise and chaos slowing her down, keeping her from getting here earlier, the particular side street she was on now was dead quiet. The noise still wafted down from the cross streets. But the immediate area was empty. No crowds, no pedestrians, no traffic. None of the various shops and stores on this section of street were open. And the surrounding buildings were mostly dark or showed only a few scattered lights on the upper floors.

The change from too-crowded-to-move to empty was…

Well, if her instincts hadn't driven her here, she might not have noticed. But now this felt purposeful. Planned.

She pushed at the glass door that led inside, expecting it to be locked. She wasn't able to will locks open the way Sebastian could, so she wasn't sure what she'd do if it was locked. Instead of resistance, though, the door gave way easily and without even squeaking. A quiet woosh open to a dark, narrow lobby and a narrow set of stairs going up.

A single overhead light came on when she stepped inside, giving her a better view. Nothing much to see, though. A scuffed black marble floor, walls painted a pale color that could do with a refresh, and some brass mailboxes set into the wall.

The black marble stairs remained shadowed and dark. No light leaked down from upstairs.

Her heartbeat pounded hard, strong enough for her to feel it against her chest now. Her breathing sounded loud and harsh in the quiet, small space. She tried to calm her pulse and breathing, but that only made things worse.

Instincts drove her to go up those dark stairs. That was where she needed to go.

She really didn't want to go.

She adjusted the strap of her oversized purse across her chest and gave the pentagram charm on her bracelet a reassuring rub. If this was a demon about to escape, it was up to her to stop it. No Sebastian as backup. No other hunters appearing to help—she even glanced back out to the street to see if anyone had arrived. Nope. No help.

Her will and her magic and that was all she had to face a demon fight.

She hated this with every ounce of her being. She hated demons. She hated this world. She couldn't believe she'd agreed to do this.

And she couldn't believe she'd have to forgo saying "I told you so" to Gabriella. She'd been looking forward to that conversation.

She gave her charm another rub, pressing her fingers into the little dime-sized pentagram, taking strength from its protective spells. Then she started to murmur a spell of her own as she stepped onto the black stairs and started up.

CHAPTER THIRTY-FIVE

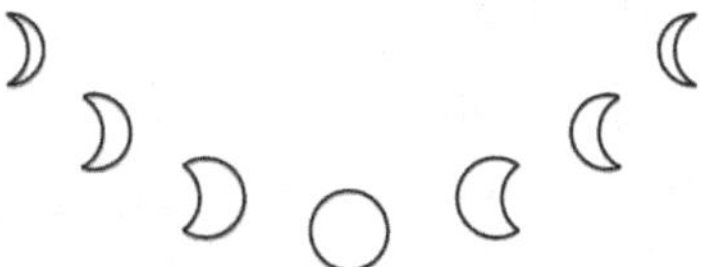

The stairs remained dark as Angie climbed them, slowly, listening intently for any sounds either ahead or behind. She'd half expected motion sensor lights, like in the little lobby, to turn on as she moved upward. But nothing. Just darkness that got darker as she went.

She leaned against the railing to keep her balance so she could keep her hands at the ready and complete the finger gesture part of her spell. A defensive shield spell. Nothing that would stop a bullet or knife or physical attack. She didn't have that in her repertoire, the magic beyond her powers. She knew very few witches who could build shields capable of fending off mundane weapons. But her shield would protect her from any magic thrown at her.

And it would hold off any demon magic. At least long enough for her to survive an initial attack.

She had no idea what her instincts were leading her into.

Only that she felt an imperative to get up these stairs and stop whatever was happening above. A demon must be about to break loose. Or maybe already had? Since she'd never experienced this instinct, she wasn't sure if she was supposed to be able to tell the difference between an imminently escaping demon and one that had already broke free and was on the loose.

Not knowing what she was walking into set her nerves on edge. Her gut so tight from anxiety, she wanted to throw up. She'd never gone into one of these situations alone before. She'd always had a proper hunter with her.

She didn't want to be alone now, either. Where was Sebastian? If she felt this, he did. So did the other demon hunters. Someone else should be here, right? At least Sebastian. He'd know she wasn't ready to do this alone. Hell, he'd assume she couldn't sense this. She hadn't been able to before. He had no reason to think this time would be different.

But no one else was there.

They could already be up there, but then she didn't think her own imperative would be so strong. They could be called elsewhere, in which case there was way too much demon activity going on tonight—and maybe there was because it was the night before Halloween and humans were idiots.

Or maybe any possible backup had been...detained or deflected?

Maybe Sebastian was in trouble?

That thought brought her to an abrupt stop on the stairs as panic seized her and she almost couldn't breathe. No. She shook her head. No. He was fine. He had to be. This was something else. Just her hunter instincts kicking in finally, despite her not believing she had any.

Unless this wasn't hunter instinct.

What if this was an instinct to get to Sebastian? Because he needed her. Because he was in trouble.

Not hunter instinct. Instinct that the man she loved needed her help.

Angie wanted to scream and race up the stairs. She didn't dare. But the thought made so much more sense than her suddenly having hunter instincts, it left her trembling.

She made an effort to slow her breathing, to take the steps slowly, quietly. No matter what was ahead of her, if she panicked and went charging in, she would help no one and likely get herself killed before she even knew what was happening.

No matter what—demon about to escape, Sebastian needing her help—if she didn't concentrate, focus, and act smartly, no one would come out of this alive.

At the landing for the second floor, she paused and listened. No noise. No windows to cast light, but enough street light leaked through from the glass door at the base of the stairs she could see the small landing. There were two doors, one to her right, one next to the second set of stairs going up to the third floor. No light came from under either door. And her instincts urged her up to the next floor. So likely nothing here to worry about.

Still. She couldn't tell what or how much was beyond the doors, if they lead to more of the building or were small apartment-sized areas. They each had little brass numbers on them, set underneath a peephole, but no signs to hint at what was beyond. No plaques on the walls to indicate if these were businesses, private residences, or storage closets. Since these two upper floors were supposed to be part of the shared workspace business, there could be whole corridors lined with offices and meeting rooms beyond those doors.

She set her shield spell into a holding pattern, and took the time to set a ward on each of the two doors. Not to keep things out of the rooms beyond, but to sound an alarm if either of those doors opened. She'd get a mental warning, a ripple through the magics, if someone—or something—came out of those doors.

Once she'd set the wards, she continued up the narrow stairwell. So dark now that no light from below leaked through and her night vision could no longer penetrate to show her anything. The stairs to the third floor were so pitch black there could have been someone standing halfway up and she wouldn't have seen them.

She opened her other senses, listening so intently it hurt, her skin prickling as she tried to *feel* the heat and presence of anyone above. She even dragged in a few deep breaths in an attempt to catch any errant smells that might give away someone's presence.

She heard nothing. Felt only the cold air of a narrow stairwell with no space heaters to keep it warm. Still no windows to provide any ambient light from outside. And the glass door below was no longer even visible. The only smells in the stairwell were a sort of generic stale coffee and dust smell. Not exactly clean, but not piss-soaked and choking.

She couldn't smell anyone else's sweat but her own. And —was this a good or a bad sign?—she couldn't smell the insidious scent of demon sulfur.

No ominous red glow from ahead either.

Either she wasn't where she needed to be yet and the red glow and sulfur smell would hit her soon. Or she'd been wrong about this being a demon escape instinct.

But if she was wrong about that, if this wasn't her hunter instincts kicking in, it had to be another instinct. And the only one that made sense was that Sebastian was in trouble, and that's what had driven her here.

She never thought she'd hope for an escaping demon.

She reached the third-floor landing and paused, listening so hard her ears hurt. Half closing her eyes, she let her gaze soften and scanned the area for signs of magic, hunting for the tell-tale blue light of a spell. Like at Vera and Bill's house, she wasn't expecting magic because magic outside a summoning circle wasn't normal. Very few witches summoned demons. They had other things at their disposal to get what they wanted. Dealing with demons was tricky and almost always deadly. Any witch in her right mind stuck to dealing with magic and leaving the demons to the stupid.

So when she spotted the faint glow of blue light around the doorframe of one of the two doors on the top landing, she was both surprised and strangely resigned.

Without knowing what was beyond that door—be it a corridor leading to many offices or just one room—going through was always going to be dangerous. But the magic spell on the door wasn't helping.

She considered that, though. There were only two ways to go. And the magic was only on one door. Which made it a great big blaring announcement. This Is The Way. She supposed that could have been done on purpose. Whoever was behind all this might know she'd look for magic and rig this specifically for her. If whoever was behind this knew *she* would be the one to show up.

How they'd know that, if they'd guess that, and who was behind all this were questions she'd only get answers to by picking a door.

The question was, did the door with the magic represent the real way forward? Or was it a trick? Maybe even a trap?

She glanced at the door without the magic spell circling the doorframe. She couldn't hear anything from beyond either door. The one without the spell looked the same as the two downstairs. No light leaked through. There was a brass number on the door under a peephole but again no sigh or plaque to indicate what lay beyond. That direction seemed innocuous enough.

Considering the bespelled door again, she let her eyes unfocus and tried to read the spell. There was definitely a deflective kind of magic in it. Not an illusion, per se, but a kind of "don't look this way" to the spell. The magic was flavored with hints of bruja magic, but only a sprinkling. There was more underlying Celtic tones. A strange mix she hadn't seen used before. And completely different to what she'd seen at Vera and Bill's house.

But like at Vera and Bill's house, this spell wasn't particularly complicated. It was a straightforward spell to make someone look the other way. A spell to make someone who couldn't see magic not even look at this door.

Okay. So, the question still remained. Was that the whole purpose—just to deflect anyone who might stumble up here? Keep them from whatever was happening behind that door? Or had whoever was behind all this known a witch would show up? A witch who would see the spell and know its purpose.

And if that was the plan, for her to see the spell, was it intended to make her think the real danger was behind the door not spelled? Or to fool her into thinking the warded door was the door she had to use because it wouldn't be spelled otherwise?

She rubbed the little pentagram charm on her bracelet and considered the two doors. Considered what she'd encountered at Bill and Vera's house in New Jersey. Considered what had been happening the last few weeks.

Which direction should she go?

She let her eyes drift down again as she continued pressing her fingers into her charm, and opened her instincts, the ones that had been urging her here, letting them guide her, opening herself to clear sight.

To her surprise, the spiderweb vision popped into her mind, those threads of running blue light all circling out from her into a strong, symmetrical pattern. The single red thread that arrowed down one line of the pattern from the center of her chest.

With no time to considered the whys of all this, she concentrated on the image of the web, feeling as much as seeing it in her mind's eyes.

There. One thread vibrated. One thread moved just a little.

She opened her eyes.

And went through the door without the spell.

CHAPTER THIRTY-SIX

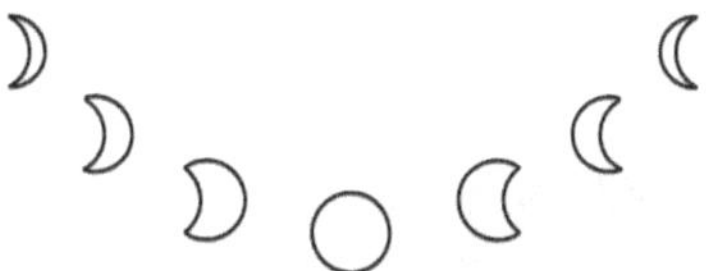

The space beyond the door was a corridor that curved and head toward the back of the building. There were a few closed doors on either side of the corridor before the bend. The lights were off, but at least here, a window at the far end of the short hallway let in ambient light from the street, so she could see without having to make a light source of her own.

She wanted to avoid that so she didn't give her position away. Though, she suspected that whatever was going on, whatever she was walking into, her presence probably wasn't a secret anymore.

Pale walls, pale linoleum-covered floors, and the smell of cold coffee and tea. No real art on the walls except a few generic motivational signs. A nondescript space with what she assumed, based on the size of the building, were a bunch of small offices off the corridor.

Still no sulfur scent.

Still no idea what she was walking into.

The fact that the door had been unlocked wasn't lost on her. Had she made the right decision or the wrong one? Picked the right door or not? She'd gotten inside easily, no lock, no nasty surprise spells, nothing to keep her from coming this way. In fact, this way was the easy choice.

And now that she as here, she was rethinking her decision.

But instinct had pointed this direction, so she'd keep going. Hopefully toward the trouble and not toward a trap.

Some answers about what was happening would be good, too.

She stared at the two doors on one side and three on the other that lined this part of the hallway.

Should she open them and check inside before moving on?

She should open them and check inside.

Then maybe take the time to ward them like she'd done downstairs. Her instincts were still pushing her to hurry, but if she charged off and left a bunch of unsearched rooms behind her, she risked letting someone dangerous trap her from behind.

The first three doors opened on well-oiled, quiet hinges onto small rooms with single desks, a rudimentary desk chair that didn't look very comfortable, and some plugs and wires for connecting computers and internet cables. Searching each room was quick and easy because there were no hidden corners or cubbies. She didn't even have to go inside.

The two exterior rooms had windows letting in ambient light. The third was an interior room with no window, but she opened her cellphone and used it like a flashlight to see inside so she didn't have to use magic or the overhead light.

She put quick wards on each door, so she'd be warned if one opened, before moving on.

The fourth door she opened turned out to be a storage room, not office space. It was the second interior room and without turning the lights on, she couldn't see anything too clearly. But the light from her phone showed boxes stacked high and tight. Unless she was willing to move boxes around to check behind them—which would give away her presence anyway—she couldn't tell if anyone might be hiding in the closet. She stood still and listened, but couldn't hear movement or breathing.

She'd have to chance it. Instincts were still rushing her, telling her she didn't have much time left. She closed the door and put a ward on the frame and hoped she wasn't leaving something or someone at her back.

The final room in the corridor was another larger office space, or maybe a meeting room was a better description, with six or so long tables set up in a square, and folding chairs stacked against one wall. Open curtains enabled her to see the larger space clearly, though. Empty.

Another ward on the door frame, and then she considered her next move as she stared at the bend in the corridor, moving back toward the side and rear of the building.

The absolute silence had her nerves stretched tight, her gut churning with anxiety. While the instincts that had brought her here screamed at her to hurry, the logical part of her brain was pointing out that everything was quiet. No noise. No sulfur. No one jumping out to grab at her.

No danger so far.

And yet her nerves were tight with anxiety and fear, her heartbeat hammered and she had to work to keep her breathing even so she didn't hyperventilate. Not her imagination, all this. She was too attuned to her own instincts. She wouldn't have imagined herself here. Something was definitely wrong, but…

Damned if she could tell what.

Not her imagination, the ward on the other door outside. That had been real.

She eased up to the bend in the corridor and looked around, down yet another door-lined, nondescript hallway.

And there, there she finally spotted a light.

Under the third door on the left. One of the interior rooms. So the light wasn't coming from an open window. It wasn't bright, like the florescent lights inside the room were on. If it was someone here working late—which she supposed was a possibility—they'd have the room's main lights on, wouldn't they? They'd hardly be working in the dark by minimal lighting. But what leaked from the bottom of the door wasn't bright. In fact, if the corridor hadn't been so damned dark, she probably wouldn't even have noticed it.

She wanted to take her time with the other doors, searching before warding, but now that she'd seen that light, everything in her pushed her toward that room. She compromised with her need to rush by warding the doors without searching the rooms. Someone was in them, she'd hear them coming. That would have to be good enough for now.

Adjusting her purse strap across her chest, she pulled in a deep breath through her mouth so she wouldn't make any noise. She finished the shield spell words and hand gestures, rising one hand in front of her to hold the shield up. Hoping it would be enough for whatever was on the other side of that door.

She approached on quiet steps, her ears straining to pick up any sound. The corridor was so quiet. Since these were office rooms, she assumed the doors were somewhat soundproofed. Still, the silence was oppressive. A weight in the air, pushing her into the floor.

She paused in front of the closed door for a long moment, staring at the handle, trying to see if any spells had been placed there or on the frame. Nothing she could spot.

Another deep, quiet breath, she took hold of the door handle, pushed it down. The click boomed loud in the quiet.

She swung the door open.

Inside, candlelight flickered from candles arrayed in two circles right next to each other.

In the center of one circle, the man who'd come to Dana's looking for Angie. Ivan's brother-in-law. Gregory Sokolov. The man Carmen claimed was a mobster. He was dressed in another neat suit, and bound to a metal folding chair with duct tape. Nothing covered is mouth, but he didn't say a word when he looked at her.

In the center of the second circle…

Sebastian.

CHAPTER THIRTY-SEVEN

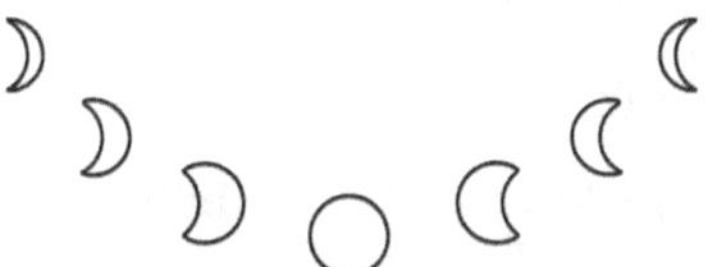

Angie started toward Sebastian, but stopped when he shook his head. He was sitting on the polished wooden floor inside his candle circle. Nothing bound him. No duct tape or even a metal chair. His mouth wasn't covered either. But, like Sokolov, he didn't say anything to her. Just that head shake to keep her from running to him.

Frowning, she looked around. The door behind her closed with a snap. She jumped, despite herself. And cursed when she saw Carmen walk from the corner shadows to stand between the circles.

Carmen smiled. "Took you a while to get up here," she said.

"I'm a careful witch."

"Maybe too careful. But I understand in this case."

"What's going on?"

Angie edged closer to the circle with Sebastian. She kept

her shield in front of her, but knowing Carmen had telekinesis and could throw something at her back made the shield feel a little useless. At least against the other woman. Depending on what the circles were for, the shield might still come in handy.

"You were finally able to really grab onto your powers," Carmen said. "At the house in Jersey, finally embrace them enough to really use them."

"No. Not embrace."

"You need to learn to embrace them."

"Why?"

This felt like the same argument she'd had with Gabriella. But Angie was fine going about her life as a witch, never accessing the deeper powers that marked her as a demon witch and kept getting her dragged into this world. The last thing she truly wanted was to open herself to a deeper connection with the demon-related magic. That red line in the middle of her bright blue spiderweb.

"Because if you don't," Carmen said, "those powers will grow beyond your control and you'll bring down a plague of demons on this planet." She smiled. "Happened before. Few times. And the demon witches never met nice ends."

"Why do you care if I meet a bad end?"

"I don't. I just don't want the demon plague. I've worked with them a lot, remember. A lot of them unleashed into this realm would be a disaster."

"You've spent the last…month, maybe longer, ensuring demons nearly escaped. Talking people who wouldn't consider summoning demons into summoning them, and then leaving them with either wrong information or damaged containment to ensure the demons got out. You'll forgive me if I don't believe a word out of your mouth."

"I wouldn't have risked the demon escapes if I didn't know there were a few convenient demon hunters in the neighborhood." She shrugged. "But we've been through this part."

And they didn't have time to argue about it now. Angie gestured with her free hand to the candles. "What are the circles for?"

She glanced at Sebastian. His eyes drooped to almost closed, but not fully closed. His gaze, now that Carmen was out of the shadows, was focused on the floor in front of him, not Angie.

She wanted to ask him if he was okay, but he looked so concentrated, she was afraid to break that concentration. When a demon hunter, when *Sebastian* looked like that, there was a damned good reason.

The fine hairs on the back of her neck prickled.

She glanced at the other man. Sokolov glared at the room, his gaze mostly focused forward. He still wasn't speaking. Carmen had seen fit to bind him to the chair, wrists and ankles, but not gag him? Why? And why wasn't he speaking, protesting, looking for help, cursing…? Any of the things she might be doing in his position just then.

Carmen stepped a little farther forward, bringing her face more fully into the candlelight. She was dressed in jeans and a long-sleeve t-shirt again. Nothing fancy. No elaborate jewelry or costuming. She'd pulled her dark hair up into a bun, which let the light and shadows carve out her cheekbones, making them more distinct and sharper. She looked sharper, like a knife ready to slice. Calculating. Balanced on her toes to move fast if she needed to. Her slight smile cold.

"Why bind this man and not Sebastian?" she asked.

Carmen didn't answer.

Angie glanced at Sokolov. "Can you speak?"

"He can't right now," Carmen said.

At least it was an answer. "Why not?"

"I needed them both quiet while you and I talked."

"How?"

Carmen waved her hand in a little gesture that encompassed the two circles. "There's a lot that can be done within the confines of a containment circle. You know that right?"

She did, but she didn't respond to Carmen's taunt. She just stared at her, waiting.

"We needed to talk," Carmen said after another long pause. "And I needed you motivated. But I also needed your boyfriend occupied."

She waved a hand again and murmured a few words in Spanish that Angie didn't catch.

The candle light pulsed. Angie blinked.

And there was a demon in the room. Inside the circle with Sokolov.

Shit.

CHAPTER THIRTY-EIGHT

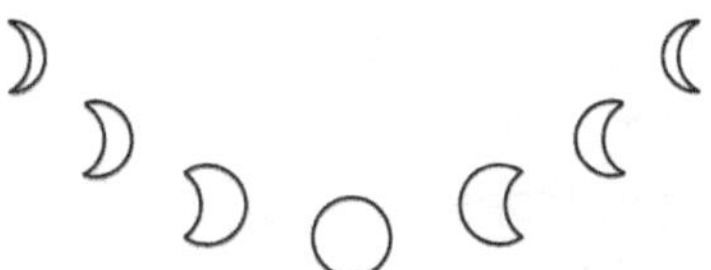

The demon wasn't one of the more sentient types. It was what Angie had heard described as more animalistic—which always struck her as an arrogant comment given how animalistic humans also were.

The Ychiktas was a snarling beast, with six long arms, talon tipped fingers, and a spiked tail that arched up over its head. The head was part boar, part bull, with pointed ears angled forward and razor sharp, pointed teeth the size of paring knives. Its skin was thick and reddish, with spots of yellow boils scattered between patches of white and yellow scales.

It was such a mixed hodge-podge of animals familiar to humans, but all mashed together into something grotesque. And it was much more vicious than any Earth animal—including humans.

The beast had one taloned-tipped hand wrapped around the Sokolov's face, covering his mouth. Which made clear now why the man wasn't talking. But the fact that the beast had been able to remain invisible, inside the circle, while holding Sokolov, was terrifying. She hadn't known the Ychiktas could do that.

She glanced at Sebastian, afraid to see one of the beasts in his circle, but his space was demon free.

What was happening?

Her gaze jumped from Carmen to Sebastian to the man in the demon's grip, back to Sebastian. His distant, concentrated look finally made sense.

He was holding the demon back. Willing it not to tear Sokolov apart. And doing it with two containment circles in his way.

"Only way to save them both is to send the demon packing," Carmen said with a smile. "Your hunter can't keep the demon from ripping Sokolov's head off and drinking his guts indefinitely. No one's will is that strong. And he's been at this for… Oh, a couple of hours now. I'm impressed he's lasted this long to be honest with you. Especially since, at the same time, he's holding off another demon from dropping into his circle."

No. That was too much. Hours? How had he been keeping this up for hours? Panic coursed through her and she took an involuntary step toward him.

Carmen stopped her with a sharp hand gesture and a growl. "You *have* to learn to embrace your power," she hissed. "If you don't, you *will* destroy this world. It's the fate of the demon witch. You know the history now."

And how the fuck did Carmen know *that*? Her ability to spy on Angie, without Angie having a clue, was both unnerving and infuriating.

"If you don't learn control," Carmen said quietly, "don't learn to embrace all your magic, the magic will overtake you, and leave a waste land in its wake."

"How do you know any of this?"

Her gaze kept slipping to Sebastian. He was sweating and his hands on his knees trembled. Goddess, she had to do something.

"The hunters want you dead because of this. But if you can *control* the magic, none of them will have the power to stop you. In anything you want to do. Remain a hunter. Leave the hunters behind. Anything. You will be too powerful for them to coerce."

"And what are you trying to do but coerce me?" She gestured at Sebastian.

"To embrace your power!"

"To what end? What do you get out of it?"

"My world keeps spinning. It's a selfish motivation, I'll grant you that. But helping you avoid ending the world serves my own best interest."

Angie doubted that was the sole reason. Carmen wouldn't be going to all this trouble without getting something out of it for herself. But she couldn't worry about that now.

She looked at the demon with its hand around Sokolov's face.

She wasn't sure she could do this again. She'd managed it once. But every time she took hold of that single red thread in the spiderweb of her magic, she risked losing control of it.

Or letting it take over.

Another memory from her vision, of red light bleeding into blue, seeping through the web.

A warning? Or a premonition?

Carmen relaxed her stance, leaning back a little as she shrugged. "You do it. You learn what you can do. Here and now. You can save them both. You fail. Everyone dies."

"Even you?"

"Even me."

"*Why*? Why this? All the tests, all the pushing?"

"You won't accept your nature without it. You've been avoiding it for how long now? Decades? Oh, I've heard the stories. I have…acquaintances who are very interested in the demon world who know all about you. They've told me everything. How you've tried to avoid the hunters, tried to stay out of this world. Some of my acquaintances think that's best. They argue you're too dangerous and the less you know, the farther you stay from this world, the better. I don't agree."

For some reason, Angie thought of Jacob and his warnings that she not become a hunter. And how Carmen had shown up at her apartment right after Jacob. Did they know each other? Was Jacob one of Carmen's "acquaintances?" Was that how she knew so damned much about the hunters? How she'd avoided them all these years while still summoning demons right under their noses?

Or was she seeing conspiracies where none were because she felt cornered by other people's machinations?

"If I do this, then what?" Angie said, her gaze jumping between Sokolov and Sebastian. "What happens if I rip open a portal to a demon realm inside this building and then can't control it?"

"You'll control it. And then you'll know what you're truly capable of."

"And then I just let you walk out of here without consequences? You get to go about your business of revenge without facing justice?"

"Don't worry about me," Carmen said. "I'm a survivor."

"That's what worries me," Angie muttered.

Carmen smirked. The expression brought out Angie's more violent side, and she was tempted to slap that smirk off with a spark spell. But she didn't have time.

Carmen was right, Sebastian couldn't do this forever.

She turned all her attention to the Ychiktas. Sokolov's eyes were narrowed, and he was also sweating.

That demon first. Then she could better help Sebastian.

She assessed the containment circle as she let her gaze soften and she opened herself to her magic. The shield was useless to her at the moment, so she dropped the spell, and then gathered her will.

If she could just will the demon away without opening a portal, she could keep from taking that last step. She didn't want to do what Carmen wanted her to do, because she didn't trust Carmen even a little bit. If Carmen thought this was a good idea, Angie *knew* it was a bad one.

But she still didn't feel like her will was strong enough on its own.

The Ychiktas weren't the sort of demon to bargain or engage in challenges. They were all brute force and would only respond to brute force. Will. She had to will it to leave.

She had no idea what ceremony Carmen had used to summon it. That would have helped. She could find her way into the process to send it away if she had a spell to mutter or a ceremony to reverse. Something familiar. Something she could feel in her witchy bones.

Since she didn't have any of that, she started a banishing spell. It wasn't for demons of the actual physical sort. It was for banishing dark magic spells, negating harmful spells, banishing bad energy. But it was a way in.

She moved her hands in the familiar pattern, comforted by the gestures as she took hold of her magic. She visualized the spiderweb. And there it was, in her mind's eye. Glowing blue. The intricate threads woven into a symmetrical pattern around her.

And there. The red thread. Coming from the center of her chest. Thicker now. Brighter. Spreading out into the nearest filaments of the web.

Seeping, just a little, into the blue.

She grabbed onto one of the blue threads, felt the jolt of power rush through her. Ah, yes. That was familiar. That was *her*. She added that to her spell, and focused on banishing the evil that was the demon. On breaking him apart. On sending him back to his realm.

On willing him away.

The demon screeched, a sound that set her teeth on edge. It snarled at her, it's body vibrating as it strained against her spell, her will. And Sebastian's. She felt Sebastian's will there, too. Yes. Together they could do this. She finished her spell and forced more will into it, twisting her magic to make the spell do more than it was meant to do.

"You will be gone," she said, and her voice was an octave deeper as she pulled on more of her magic.

The demon thrashed and released Sokolov. It started to smoke and tremble and scream in an ear-splitting pitch. It thrashed out with all six arms, reaching for Sokolov. Angie willed the beast away from him, felt Sebastian willing Sokolov away from the beast.

The Ychiktas body began to pop, the boils oozing yellow acidic gore that smelled like death. She forced herself to ignore the stench. But her throat closed and she had to take a tighter grip on her magic, on the effects of her spell. She concentrated on the blue threads, on holding them as she willed the demon back to its realm.

It fought. It flailed. It spewed acid that burned the hardwood floor and came perilously close to Sokolov's chair. She couldn't drop her concentration on the demon long enough to build a shield around him. The only thing she could do was get the demon banished as fast as possible.

The man shouted something. His chair scrapped across the floor as he cursed.

She sent more will at the demon.

Its tail whipped out, smacking toward Sokolov. But stopped, like it had hit a wall.

Sebastian, Angie thought.

She pushed more power, more will, through her web, and the demon started to vibrate harder, shrinking and twisting as it was called back to its real. Smoke filled the circle, surrounding the demon, the stench even worse than the demon's acidic puss. The Ychiktas compressed, twisted, growing smaller inside the smoke.

But it fought, pushing against her will with a violence and unrestrained brute power that stole her breath. She gripped the mental threads of her web tighter. Forced the demon smaller. Away. Forced him back to where he'd come from.

Too late she saw the movement of red into her blue thread. Too late she saw the creep of that red over the blue she gripped.

She'd avoided the red thread on purpose. But somehow it moved to her.

That red magic pierced through her, filling her with fierce and violent power.

She wanted to scream in denial. But it was too late.

A portal to a demon realm ripped open in the middle of the circle, at the Ychiktas' back.

Too late, too late.

She shoved the demon through with her will, desperate to close the portal as quickly as possible.

But the red had her now. She didn't control it. It had wrapped around her grip on the spiderweb of her magic, holding her in place.

Keeping the portal open, even though every sane part of her screamed to close it.

And then…

A sound. Distant but moving closer. A sound out of her nightmares. Closing in on her portal…

The chittering of approaching demons.

CHAPTER THIRTY-NINE

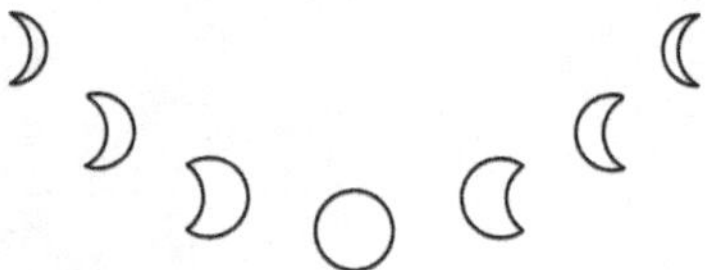

Someone screamed. Angie couldn't tell if that was her or someone else in the candlelit meeting room. Her throat was raw enough it could have been her. The demons were coming. Her nightmares approached.

And she was holding open a portal into their realm.

She had to close it. Had to stop this. If she let demons out into this world…

No, she wouldn't do that again. Hadn't done that since she was five. Wouldn't do it now.

But the red magic crept farther into her web, turning the blue magic a strange shade of purple in places. Almost like Fae magic. But, oh, this didn't feel Fae. This felt like her magic. Like her. And yet not.

The familiarity of it, though. That was almost the worst part.

Beyond the portal, the hellscape belched flames from

rocky ground. Ash coated the air and blurred the red sky. And in the distance, she saw a line of demons, not Ychiktas, but another of the lesser demons, the brute ones that would not make deals. They only ate and destroyed and spread fear and destruction in their wake.

The Ychiktas who she'd pushed into the portal tried to crawl back through. She willed him back into the hellscape, a mental push she barely had the strength for. She winced at the demon's screech of protest.

Could anyone else see this? Hear this?

No one saw the breaches she opened in trees. But this wasn't her usual portal. This wasn't even shaped in a V. It was an oval shape, longer than wide, and the edges shimmered with the red of her magic.

But also a little of the blue, she realized. Some of that blending, melding purple shimmered at the edges.

The distant demons approached, rushing forward over the lava rocks now. The chittering joined by a sound like hisses and grunts. The stampede of hundreds, maybe thousands, of feet against the rocky ground. They swarmed forward, heading for her portal.

Close it, damn it!

Was that in her head or had she heard it aloud? Had she said it? Someone else?

She couldn't tell. Her whole body seemed to be attached to the portal, a part of her. If she turned away, if she averted her gaze, this time the portal wouldn't close. Not like her usual breaches. Not like the one at Vera and Bill's.

She knew in some instinctive part of her fed by the red

magic. She couldn't close this one without willing it closed. Without taking hold of the power surging through her.

Easy and not easy at all.

And oh that power. So much of it. Feeding her. Filling her up. She'd never felt anything like this. All that strength, now at her fingertips. She could do anything with this magic. Anything at all. So much power.

Why had she been afraid of this? Why had she avoided seeing it, embracing it?

The power was magnificent.

She blinked at the opening, at the demons approaching, and murmured a spell. Calling down the lightning. But not here in her realm.

Inside the hellscape.

There was no moisture in the air. No water rain. But there was electricity. There was fire and heat and sharp, crisp static.

She drew at that static, that fire and heat, wound them into her spell, and dropped a bolt of fire-tinged lightning into the middle of the approaching hoard.

A demon screamed as it erupted into flames, taking a direct hit from the lightning. All around it, the shockwave from the strike sent demons flying. A wave of sound and pressure blowing them outward.

More chittering. The hairs on her neck rose. She pulled on more of her purpling magic. Another lightning spell, fed by the hellscape. Another direct hit on an approaching demon.

The Ychiktas tried to climb through the portal again

while she was playing target practice with the demons behind it. With her attention divided, she didn't have the focus to push it back through. It climbed over the shimmering red edge, its taloned hands grasping at the edges as it stretched and reached into their realm.

She hissed and tried to form the lightning spell again, but the Ychiktas was too close and she risked hitting a spot inside the room if she aimed for it.

Hellscape built lightning striking into the human realm would be bad.

She pulled herself from the spells, focused on her will.

And then someone behind her. Warm hands on her shoulders. Familiar breath near her cheek.

"I've got the Ychiktas," Sebastian murmured. "Keep the others away until you can close the portal."

"I'm not sure I can this time," she said, panicking a little as more of the Ychiktas pushed into their realm.

Her voice was so deep, she barely recognized it. And there was…power there. Power she hadn't heard in her voice before. Power she'd never felt before. All of it flowing through her from her spiderweb of magic, which was pulsing in her mind's eye with more and more purplish light.

"You can. You control it. You can close it. Concentrate on that, then. I've got the demons."

She swallowed, finished one more lightning spell, and unleashed it into the approaching hoard.

The Ychiktas, screaming in protest at a decibel that made her eyes hurt, flew back through the portal as if caught by a string. A long spiked tail whipped back at the portal, coming through, but then that vanished, too.

Angie had no idea what beast that spiked tail belonged to. It hadn't been the Ychiktas. And it wasn't from the approaching demons.

Which meant there were probably demons closer to the breach but outside the view she had of the hellscape.

Fuck.

"Close it!"

This time she knew she heard the voice aloud. Carmen. And there was command in her voice. Not panic. Not fear. Command. And will.

"Control it!"

Angie wanted to curse more, but she focused on the spiderweb. On the red creeping through her blue witch magic.

She still wasn't holding the original red thread, even though the power from that thread had spread out, encompassed the area she held.

Her attention slipped from the portal and farther into the vision in her mind's eye. She grunted with the effort, but she forced herself to release one of the blue threads. The surge of power around her felt like electricity and heat.

Sebastian's hands, still on her shoulders, flexed.

Had he felt the heat? Was she hurting him? Had she lost control?

No. No. She had to focus.

She grabbed at the red thread, taking hold of it in one hand. A blue thread, still pure blue, in the other.

And power surged again, but this time it felt… Balanced. Controlled.

Hers.

She refocused on the portal. More demons moving closer. A clawed hand gripping the edge of the breach. She murmured the lightning spell and threw the strike into the middle of the hoard. Catching five beasts at once as multiple bolts lashed off from the central stalk, like branches.

She realized if she had more power, she could make more lightning. Felt that in her bones.

She pulled on the web's power, on her magic, and formed the spell again.

More lightning. More arching bolts in tendrils spreading and striking throughout the hoard.

She smiled. And did it again.

But even this, even destroying so many at once. They still kept coming. She could hold them off, but not indefinitely. Just as Sebastian couldn't control the Ychiktas indefinitely.

She had to close the portal.

Or everyone would die.

CHAPTER FORTY

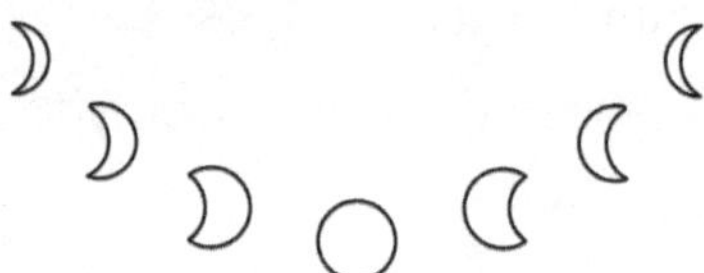

How? How? How did she close the breach?

Angie continued striking lightning down into the hellscape even as she started to panic again. All that power, surging through her, and it still wasn't enough. She couldn't *see* how to close the portal. Couldn't *see* how to control it.

It was part of her, she was physically linked to it. And the thought of cutting it off felt almost like she'd be forced to cut off a part of herself.

Not cut off. Close. Control.

The stench of burning brimstone, the sulfuric taste coating her tongue now. The chittering so loud she was sure the whole neighborhood could hear. Even from this empty building.

She wasn't grateful to Carmen for much of anything at all, but the fact that the woman had picked an inner room, with no windows, was one of the very few not-bad things about this situation.

Angie was very aware that somewhere close, somewhere just outside the portal, Sokolov was still duct-taped to a chair. She had no idea why Carmen had chosen him specifically for this, why he was here. But he was a life Angie had to protect.

Sebastian's hands on her shoulders confirmed he was still behind her, solid and sure. She could even sense his will rolling past her, into the breach, holding back the beasts surging toward the opening.

Toward their unprepared and unprotected world.

She hissed out another lightning spell and slammed it down into the middle of the hoard, forming multiple branches to take down as many demons as possible.

And still they surged. So damned many. Too many. They would overwhelm her and Sebastian soon.

Another will seemed to join Sebastian's. Unfamiliar. And yet…

It could only be Carmen.

Confirmed when Carmen said, "You have the power to close that breach. You *have* to close it. Control it. You *have* to take hold of it."

"Got any good ideas how, I'd love to hear them," she muttered, but most of her attention was on another lightning strike on the hoard.

She followed it with a quick illusion spell, forming dancing lights and dodging distractions that captured at least some of the demons. Sending them charging off away from the portal.

But not enough.

Not enough power. She needed more. She couldn't pull any more from her inner magic, though.

There was all that magic around her, encircling her, all those threads of power. Mostly blue, some purple now. And the red she held firmly in one hand. Balanced by blue. The balance felt good. Right.

But it wasn't enough. She could only force so much through her body at once. She could only grasp so much. She needed…

More hands?

She wasn't limited in the metaphysical plane to her physical body. She could grasp more. She needed to grasp more.

But it had to balance or she'd lose control.

Spiderweb.

Spiders had eight limbs. Eight places where they gripped their webs.

And stay balanced.

One more lightning spell. Then she diverted her attention to the mental vision of her web. It pulsed, the power flowing through it in waves like watching electricity pulse through nerves or water fast-flowing through clear pipes.

All of that hers.

Hers to hold and control.

It hardly seemed possible and yet she felt it in her gut. All of that was hers to access. To control.

And balance. And use.

She pulled in a deep breath, let it out slowly. Then, let

more "hands" stretch out to the web. She took hold of a third thread. And power poured into her. She gasped. Momentarily overwhelmed. Tilting. She took hold of a fourth thread.

This time the power slammed through her so hard she felt her knees wobble.

Sebastian's grip moved from her shoulders to around her waist, holding her upright. "Ang?"

His voice was tight. Worried.

She sucked in air so she could speak. "Fine. Here. Working on…"

The magic rushed through her with such strength she could barely feel herself anymore. Not her physical body. She was aware of Sebastian's arms around her. And yet even that felt like he was just another part of all this and none of it was physical.

She focused on the portal because she had to close it. Four was enough. Four threads was so so much magic.

But balanced. Stable. Under her control.

She sensed into the portal, concentrated on the pulse of red magic in one "hand." That very specific magic that held open the portal. How? How did she close it? What was the spell, the gestures? The words?

No. Never words or gestures with this magic. Instinct. No effort. Never effort. Effort to *not* do it, yes. But like her touch readings, this just happened. This was just who she was, what she did. She opened portals without effort, just by looking.

And she closed them by looking away.

She blinked. She'd been convinced, just moments ago,

that looking away wouldn't help. The portal was part of her, tied to her. Looking away couldn't close it.

But she'd been focused on looking away with her physical eyes, the way she did with trees.

Pulling away with her physical eyes had always been an effort, but also… Easy when something outside herself distracted her. When she was startled into looking away.

This didn't have to be hard, she realized. This was, like it or not, her. Like her ability to control when she did and didn't read someone by touch, she could just…

Close the portal. Close off this part of her. Not cut off. Close. For now.

She could look away.

She leaned into Sebastian, absorbing the very physical sensation of him against her back, the warmth of his arms around her. The way his heat and scent formed a safe cocoon for her. Oh she loved that feeling. She loved him so much. That surged through her, too. Those feelings. She loved him.

She turned her head to see him, his face right next to hers.

And in her mind's eye, gripping the red magic thread and its flow, its portal magic, she turned her "gaze" from the opening. Thought…

Close.

And blinked back to this realm.

CHAPTER FORTY-ONE

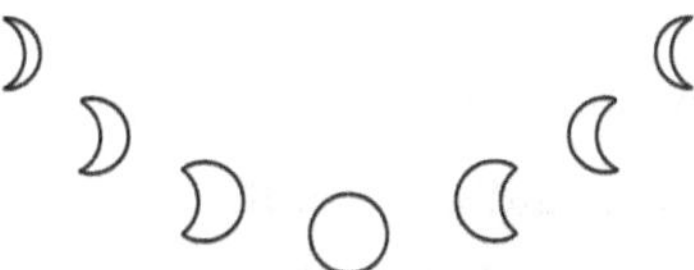

The portal didn't whorl closed or do anything dramatic. It didn't thicken and slowly rebuild a barrier between the hellscape and the human realm. The portal quite literally just…stopped being. Angie heard the echoes from the other side, the chittering, the screeches of protest. The faint scent of sulfur wafted through the room.

But all that was left were four humans blinking in the quiet darkness, with only a few remaining candles burning at the edge of the circle where the portal had been.

Slowly, because she didn't want to create a backlash, Angie concentrated on letting go of the threads of her power, releasing first the red, then one at a time, the blue. The spiderweb settled, easing back into its symmetrical pattern around her. The red that had bled into the lines of blue was still there, though, faintly purpling some of the nearest threads.

She'd have to look at that more closely, maybe with a mentor, to see what she'd done to herself.

Since no one had died and she hadn't unleashed a plague of demons, though, she'd worry about the magical consequences later.

"You okay?" Sebastian murmured against her cheek.

She nodded. "You?"

"I am now."

Carmen's slow clapping made Angie snarl.

"I told you you could control it."

"You nearly got us all killed, and I could have unleashed a hoard on this world." This was the second time Carmen had pushed her and almost caused a disaster.

"Without this, you would have unleashed that chaos sooner rather than later."

"What makes you think I won't now?"

Carmen shrugged. "Now, you know how to control the process. That's what they didn't tell you. I'm sure they didn't."

"What?"

"Control was always the issue. That's why some of them don't want you to be a hunter. And some of them do. And all of them want you dead. Because no demon witch has ever fully controlled her demon magic. It always overcomes them. One way or the other."

Ah, but Angie still didn't feel like she had complete control. She'd overcome one challenge. Balanced the power in four metaphysical "hands." But what if... What if she took hold of that power with all eight spider "hands?"

"You think this is done?" she said. "You think I'll be less of a threat now?" She wasn't even sure about that herself. Frankly, she preferred remaining cut off from her demon witch magic. But she couldn't see any chance of that now.

"If you are a threat now," Carmen said with a smirk, "it'll be because you mean it." She glanced at Sebastian. "Sorry about all that. Had to test her."

Sebastian growled. A sound Angie had never heard him make before. She glanced at him, a little worried what he might do.

But before she could talk to him, Sokolov stomped the floor and snarled at them. "If someone doesn't get these bindings off me now, I will ensure you're all killed. Slowly and painfully. I don't care what you did for my brother-in-law."

Carmen glanced at him and said, "I wouldn't untie him if I were you. He's as much of a monster as the demons. Pretty nasty guy."

Sokolov snarled at Carmen. "You will pay for this. For this betrayal. You will pay."

She ignored him and looked at Angie. "Why do you think I used his brother-in-law, two of the people who owe him money?" She made a sound that was almost a laugh. "Brought him here without any backup. No problems. Such hubris. And no one would have cried if he'd had his head ripped off by that demon."

Sokolov cursed at Carmen, issuing threats that would have turned most people's hair white.

Carmen still ignored him. "I couldn't be sure how long

your boyfriend would hold out, and how long it would take you to realize he was in trouble. Didn't want to kill anyone who didn't deserve it."

"You have got to stop this," Angie said. "You are playing with fire. Risking…everything. Including your own life. And for what? Just revenge?"

"Maybe one day I'll tell you a little more about me," Carmen said with a slight smile. "You wouldn't keep trying to stop me if you really understood."

"Let me touch your hand, and I'll see it all. You won't have to explain."

"No." Carmen chuckled. "But good try."

"He's going to kill you the minute we untie him," Angie said, nodding to Sokolov.

"I'm not waiting around." She turned toward the door.

"Wait!" Angie took a step toward her, only to come up against another circle she hadn't seen Carmen draw. She snarled at her. "We're not done yet."

"We are for now," Carmen said, her smile smug. "But don't worry. You'll see me again."

She left the room before Angie could form a spell to keep her in place.

Angie let out a snarling huff. "Son a bitch."

She stared at the open door Carmen had slipped through. She wasn't sure if she should even use her magic yet, not until she knew what had happened to it when the red magic leaked into the blue. So a spell for keeping Carmen in place probably would have been a bad idea.

Still, watching Carmen get away—*again!*—was not pleasant.

"We'll deal with her," Sebastian said. "Soon."

"I'm more worried about her dealing with us." She turned in his arms and wrapped hers around his neck. "You're sure you're okay?"

"I'm fine." He shrugged. "Tested my limits there a little. Been keeping the demon from killing Sokolov for most of the day."

"Fuck. I'm sorry. I didn't know you were in trouble earlier."

"The demon almost getting out. That brought you here."

"No." She cupped his cheeks. "Not the demon hunter instincts. I knew you needed me."

He kissed her, and it never once crossed her mind that she shouldn't kiss him back.

A loud and obnoxious throat clearing from the still-taped-to-his-seat "mobster" broke things off sooner than Angie would have liked.

She and Sebastian faced Sokolov.

"How did Carmen get you here?" she asked. "And without help?"

She dug into the depths of her oversized purse and pulled out a nail repair kit. Inside was a tiny set of scissors. She glanced at the duct tape and sighed. Cutting through that with her tiny scissors was going to take half the night.

"Why didn't you tell me who you were at that witches' store? When I asked for you?" Sokolov said.

She squatted down next to one of his hands, where it was

tapped to the metal arms of the folding chair. "I didn't know who you were and what you wanted?" She nodded toward the door Carmen had just exited. "And as you can see, I have some…acquaintances with untrustworthy intentions."

"You… What you did… What that monster was…"

"Very confusing, yes."

"No. My brother-in-law told me how you saved him. I'm not unfamiliar with demons."

"That's probably not something you want to admit in front of him." She nodded to Sebastian who was standing a few feet away, glaring down at the man, his arms crossed over his chest, looking extremely intimidating. But also Angie kind of liked it. Wrong moment to notice. She shook her head a little.

Careful not to touch Sokolov in case she accidentally read him, she nip nip nipped through the tape, little snips at a time, trying to cut through the thick mass. Carmen had used an entire role of duct tape.

"You kept the demon from killing me," Sokolov said to Sebastian. "Thank you. I am in your debt."

"No. No debts. From anyone, to anyone here."

His phrasing made Angie think there was something she didn't know. She'd ask when they were alone.

"Still, I would like to repay you. Somehow." He glanced down at Angie. "You are quite powerful. If you ever need a friend who is also…powerful in a different sphere perhaps, you may come to me. And if you'd like…" He glanced at the door before looking down at her again. "I can take care of your…acquaintance."

"No," Angie said firmly, looking up to hold his gaze. "No. I don't want you anywhere near her again."

"You think she could harm me a second time?" He sounded smug and also very very dangerous.

"Maybe. Or you'd harm her. Either way, no. Leave her alone. It's better for everyone."

She wasn't sure why she was trying to dissuade a possible mob boss from going after Carmen. Not like he wouldn't do exactly as he saw fit. And not like Carmen hadn't brought down any repercussions Sokolov saw fit to hand out. But she didn't want Carmen killed on her behalf. She didn't want Carmen killed at all for reason that were complex and a little confusing. She'd have to consider that reaction. But she knew she didn't want this man going after Carmen. One way or the other.

"Is that how you wish me to repay you for saving me? By *not* killing the woman?"

"There's no payment or repayment here," Sebastian said, again, his voice deep. "No deals being made."

Angie blinked and looked between Sokolov and Sebastian. That phrasing… That was more like something he'd say to a demon.

She let her finger hover over the man's hand, a breath away from touching him. She could. She could see everything if she did. But did she want to see that much?

Sokolov held Sebastian's gaze for a moment before looking away and focusing on Angie. He said, "There's a little red in the depths of your eyes. That wasn't there the other day at the witches' store."

She sat back on her heals.

"I think, sooner or later, you will need help, young one. I will be there when you need me."

"I've heard that before. Carmen just said she was helping, too. I have more than enough help as it is. Thank you anyway."

Sokolov smiled a little. But he didn't say any more.

The little scissors finally sawed through the tape after about five minutes of working at it, freeing one of his hands. With his help, she was able to break through the rest of the tape easier. She avoided touching him, despite the temptation. Her nerves were popping now, overstimulated from all the magic. If she opened to her psychic skills, she wasn't sure what might happen. Better not to find out.

When he was free from all the tape and standing again, Angie contemplated the circle Carmen had left them in. She looked at Sebastian. "I'm afraid to try…anything just yet. After…" She waved vaguely in the direction where the portal had been.

"I can take care of the circle for you," Sokolov said. "At the least, I can do this. As a thank you for your help."

"No deals. No bargains," Sebastian said. He still hadn't stopped staring at Sokolov.

"No deal," Sokolov repeated. "No bargains." He held Sebastian's gaze as he spoke.

Angie started to regret not having touched Sokolov's hand. Because she had the feeling there was something deeper here, something she was missing. Something important. She seemed to have missed a lot in the last few hours.

Maybe her magical spiderweb wasn't the only web involved in all this. She was starting to feel a little like the insect caught in someone else's web, too.

Sokolov walked to the edge of the circle and closed his eyes, stretched a hand out, and murmured a finishing spell. He paused for a moment, then made a sharp cutting gesture with his hand. There was a flash of blue light in her mind's eye, but in the real world, nothing obvious happened.

He faced them and gestured to the door. "We should leave this place now."

Angie carefully walked up to the edge of what had been Carmen's containment circle. And stepped through without issue. Sebastian joined her and stayed close to her all the way out of the offices, back to the stairs, and back down to the street. On the way down the stairs, she paused at each landing to remove the wards from the doors. The last thing she'd need tomorrow was repeated nudges as people came and went through these doors. Especially the shared workspace areas.

Out on the street, Sokolov considered Angie for a long moment. "I obviously did not approve of her methods." He rubbed a hand across his neck and scowled. "But I think perhaps the other witch has done something…powerful for you. I will look forward to seeing more from you, Angela Jordan."

"Probably best if you just take care of your family and

maybe we don't see each other again," Angie said. "Better if Carmen forgets you exist."

And better if Sebastian did too, she thought, glancing at the side of Sebastian's face and the way he stared at Sokolov. Under the streetlights, she looked a little closer at Sokolov, looking for the tell-tale signs of red in his eyes. Nothing but deep brown and a deceptive kind of cunning looked back at her. She had no idea what had gone on between him and Sebastian upstairs, but she got the feeling it was best the two men avoid each other in the future.

Sokolov did take a moment to return Sebastian's stare. Then he gave them both a brief nod. "Enjoy Halloween tomorrow night. I don't usual go, but I hear the Village parade is fun."

They watched him walk away until he'd disappeared from sight.

The side street remained remarkably empty as she and Sebastian stood there in the silence.

She blinked a few times. The slow, steady creep of her exhaustion finally catching up with her after adrenaline had kept her going for so long. She sagged a little and Sebastian's arms were around her instantly, catching her and supporting her weight.

She sighed and chuckled at once. "Better get home. I'm gonna fall asleep walking."

"You mind if I stay on your couch?" Sebastian asked as they turned toward the larger street ahead of them and back toward her place. "I want to make sure you're okay."

"And we have things to discuss," she said, nodding even

as her eyes drooped. "Do stay." She leaned into him. His arm tightened around her waist. She smiled.

She was too exhausted tonight to do anything but sleep. But tomorrow… They had things to talk about, yes. But she thought, maybe, she might want to do more than just talk.

What was complicated between them seemed a lot less complicated to her now.

She loved him. That wasn't going away. And neither was the demon world. At least not yet.

Carmen would claim he was Angie's weakness. She wouldn't have gone rushing to help him tonight if she didn't love him. Carmen wouldn't have used him in her machinations if she didn't know Angie would come running for him. He was a point of vulnerability for her.

And he always would be.

But wasn't that what love was? Being vulnerable for and with someone? He might be a sort of weakness for her. But he was also her strength. Their love was their strength. He stood at her back and helped her when she'd needed him tonight. She'd come to his aid when he'd needed her. And this wasn't the first time they'd done this for each other. They'd done this for each other…always. Right from the start.

No matter what, he had her back. She had his.

And they always would.

It wasn't any more complicated than that.

CHAPTER FORTY-TWO

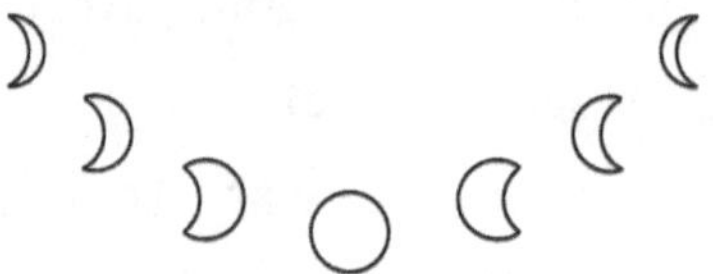

They came back to her apartment after the parade, laughing and happy and talking about all the outstanding dance routines and costumes they'd seen. Angie had a bowl of candy set outside her front door, on a little footstool, surrounded by fake cobwebs and pumpkins and some LED candles to give the setup atmosphere. The building kids had done a fair job of taking half the candy in the bowl. Good. She'd have some leftovers, but not too much.

She snatched up a mini Butterfinger bar before she and Sebastian headed inside.

"I'll leave it out another few hours," she said when he asked. "Give the teenagers time to get some."

She might have encouraged door knocking from trick-or-treaters in a regular year, so she could see everyone's costumes. But tonight, she wanted to be alone with Sebastian, without interruptions. So she left the grab bowl of candy and locked the door behind her.

Then she melted against him, wrapping her arms around his neck.

He blinked down at her, frowning slightly. "Ang?"

"I love you," she said. "I can't stop. I won't keep trying."

"Are you sure? Because if you come back to me now… I love you. So much. If you leave again, it will break me."

She cupped his face in her hands. "Last night. It wasn't the near demon escape that called me. I didn't sense that. I sensed you. You needed me. You were in trouble. I rushed there for you." She set her forehead against his. "That's not going away. And I don't want it to. Before… I knew you were okay. Alive. Safe even fighting demons." She took a shuddering breath. "And last night, you wouldn't have been in danger if it weren't for me and for what Carmen wants from me." Whatever that was. "But knowing you'd been in trouble, knowing you needed me…" She shook her head. "What if I'd been too far away to reach you?"

Her voice hitched, and she felt the pinch of tears behind her eyes. But she didn't want tears tonight.

He slid his hands up her back, wrapping them around her shoulders. "This world, my world, has put you in so much danger. Carmen wouldn't know you existed if not for me."

She leaned back, ready to reject that, but he placed a soft finger over her mouth.

"It's true," he said quietly. "And I hate that it's true." He kissed her cheek. "I want you in my life. I want us to be together. I want you safe from the demon world."

She closed her eyes as he brushed his lips across her cheekbone, nuzzled against her neck. "We can manage the first two of those things at least." Her breath shivered out of her. She leaned into him, pressing tight. "The demon world won't leave me alone. If I have to be part of it, I want you by my side when I face it."

"I don't want to be anywhere else," he said, and kissed her.

This time, she didn't make him sleep on the couch.

Angie rolled into Sebastian's heat and warmth. Savoring having him in her bed again. She'd missed this. More than she would have admitted even a month ago. A month ago, she'd still assumed she wanted distance. What she really wanted was for them to be together forever.

She just had no idea how that would work.

"You hungry?" he murmured, his eyes closed, his warm palm gliding up and down her spine.

"Always, apparently," she said, which made him smile. She traced a finger over his lips. "I like your smile."

"I like your appetite."

She laughed. "For you or for food."

"Oh, both. Of course."

She lifted up for a kiss.

When she settled her head back against his chest, she said, "Carmen is working with hunters, isn't she?"

He didn't even hesitate. "She is, I'm afraid. And we'll

have to find out which ones. That's not an alliance that's good for the hunters. For anyone."

"Someone on the council? She knows it exists, even though she shouldn't."

"Maybe. I have a hard time believing someone there isn't protecting her."

"Would explain why she's been able to do what she's been doing for so long without them stopping her." She paused. "She killed a hunter, though."

"We hunters are sometimes too pragmatic a lot," he said, his voice hard and harsh. "There are some who would consider that a means to an end."

"What end?"

"She goes after bad people. I don't like her methods any more than you do. But others…" His shrug lifted her head.

The fact that he was right did not make her feel any better. "Sokolov."

"More there than appears, yes."

"I think he was working with Carmen. At least before the other night. That's how she knew his brother-in-law, some of the desperate people who owed him money. I think there's a connection there." She paused, then, "You were very specific with him, that there were no deals or bargains being made. That's the kind of language needed with a demon. He's not a demon?"

She was asking because it *was* a possibility.

There were freed demons who'd negotiated sanctuary on Earth, in this realm. A few of those were stupidly powerful and dangerous. Only slightly less dangerous than they might have been because of the deals they'd made with the hunters. But they were still demons, at the end of the day.

Sebastian was quiet for a long time. "He's… complicated."

"Meaning?"

"Meaning he's the servant of a freed demon."

She took a moment to process that. "A mob boss who serves a freed demon?"

"Yes."

"That's maybe a little too…" She sighed. "On the nose?"

"He's been serving a particularly cunning demon for years. It's how he's gotten to the position he's in."

"How does this fit in with Carmen? Where does she come into it?" Angie had half assumed, based on the way Carmen talked about Sokolov and what she'd done to Grant, that Carmen probably went to Sokolov as part of a revenge scheme. Maybe taught him to summon demons since he claimed to have experience with them. But knowing Sokolov was the servant of a freed demon seemed to contradict that idea.

"This particular freed demon apparently hates Carmen for reasons to do with her former demon associates. Sokolov isn't working with Carmen. His master wants Carmen dead."

"Neither of those sides are good guys."

"No, they're not."

"How is this demon Sokolov is enthrall to able to keep working? He's obvious influencing a bad person doing bad things. Isn't the demon breaking some sort of rule?"

"He hasn't been violating any of the terms of his

sanctuary. Demons, at the end of the day, still do evil things. It's what they are. The powerful ones anyway. This one… mitigates his culpability by working through humans. The humans have a choice to work for him. Hunters can't interfere in those choices and what the humans do as a result of those choices. So the more dangerous freed demons use that."

"How did we end up in the middle of them?" She winced. "I meant specifically you and I, not the hunters."

"Good question. But unless any of them are open to talking about it, I'm not sure we'll get answers."

"We do have to find out which hunters are working with Carmen."

"That. And what Jacob wants from you."

"The next few months aren't going to be easy." She'd promised Gabriella three months. Three months to prove she'd make a terrible demon hunter. While trying not to get killed making that point. And thanks to Carmen, she now knew she had access to power at a magnitude she'd never imagined before.

Magic she was more than a little afraid of.

Sebastian rolled to his side, and met her gaze. "You're still sure about this? The training. What you did the other night…"

"Was something I need to understand better. But I'm going to get help with that from a witch mentor. Not the hunters. I don't trust any of them right now. Except you."

"You can trust me. The only thing, *the only thing*, I want is for you to be safe."

"Same," she said. "So we give the hunter council their three months. I try not to get killed—by demons or my own magic—and we work to figure out how to extricate ourselves from whatever mess we're in the middle of."

"And then what? If we get you free of the council's machinations, with or without destroying the council, if we get you freed from the hunters' world… What then?"

She ran her fingers over her jaw, across his chin, playing with the texture of his beard. Her bracelet fell down her wrist a little, the pentagram dangling between them.

"I don't know," she murmured. "I only know that when that happens, when I'm free of the demon world, I still want *you* in my life. I won't let you go again. I won't push you away. And I won't let anyone separate us. Not the council. Not Carmen. Not the hunters. Not the demons. No one will make me let you go again." She shrugged. "And the rest, we'll figure out."

He nodded. "I can live with that." Then he kissed her.

She sank into the kiss, believing, even if only for this one moment, that together they could both live with that.

Thanks for reading SPIDERWEB WITCH! I hope you enjoyed this second novel in the Demon Witch Series. Angela Jordan is first introduced as a secondary character in one of my other romantic urban fantasy series, the Cary Redmond Series. The Demon Witch series arose out of my interest in exploring Angie's past and the mysterious links to demons she hints at in Cary's series.

For those of you reading the novels, if you haven't tried the short prequel stories yet, these go even farther back into Angie's life. I'm writing them out of order (sorry for those of you who like chronological order!), so the most recent novella, published in August 2022, is actually the earliest story. *Howling Dreadful* is the story of Angie's first meeting with Sebastian. When sparks, and demons, fly. Keep reading for a short excerpt from that story.

For a chronological reading order, SO FAR, the order is *Howling Dreadful*, *Moonlit Strange*, BONE LANTERN WITCH (Book 1), SPIDERWEB WITCH (Book 2). Obviously, there are more novels ahead for Angie. But if she decides to show me some more adventures from those early years, I'll have more short stories and novellas too. I'll keep the reading order updated at my website for those of you who like chronology.

Also, if you like the hints about the demon hunter Aidan, I have a collection of short stories releasing in October 2022 with a short story featuring Aidan, and another short story in that collection that deals with some of the consequences of one of the historical demon witches mentioned in this book! The collection is called HAUNTS AND HOWLS WHERE DEMONS DWELL and as you might guess, features short stories with a demon theme. So, of course, demon hunters and demon witches get a shout out.

If you'd like to stay-up to-date on my releases and news, the best place to do that is my newsletter. All new subscribers get a free, exclusive short story from my paranormal romance Tiger Shifters series, which was originally written for an erotic romance anthology so, forewarned, it's hot. Subscribers also get an exclusive short story from the Cary Redmond series as well.

For those who prefer not to join newsletters, you can catch up on all my news and releases at my website. You can also follow me on my author page at your favorite book vendor or on my author page at BookBub (Kat Simons). You can also find me on Instagram (@IsaboKelly) and Facebook (Kat Simons Author).

Thanks again for reading!

~Kat

Howling Dreadful

HOWLING DREADFUL

A DEMON WITCH PREQUEL STORY

EXCERPT

CHAPTER ONE

ngela Jordan knew, since the age of five, that she had a unique gift. A gift that wasn't her witchy magic. A gift she wouldn't exactly call a "gift."

The demon hunter who'd rescued her that first time in the church parking lot, Aidan, called it a gift. Angie thought her ancestors had done something millennia ago to piss off a druid and all these centuries later, she got stuck with the curse.

Trees. Trees were the problem.

And at that moment, she was surrounding by them.

On purpose. Because Aidan had asked.

She was not a happy woman right now.

"I am not a happy woman right now," she muttered.

"So you've said," Aidan said quietly. "A few times."

A small snort from Aidan's protégé, Sebastian, didn't help.

Angie was trying very hard not to think too much about the demon hunter's protégé.

Sebastian was… Well, he should have been one of the most ordinary people she'd ever seen. Aidan was. Aidan had ordinary brown hair, currently pulled into an ordinary braid. She had an ordinary build. Was an ordinary average height. Had an ordinary pale complexion with no distinguishing facial marks like freckles or moles. Had an ordinary average face. She wasn't too attractive or too unattractive to draw attention. She wasn't too tall or too short. Her ordinary brown hair brushed her shoulders, when it was loose, always in a non-descript hairstyle. She didn't have any obvious scars, tics, disabilities, or extraordinary attributes. She didn't dress to stand out in a crowd. She didn't draw attention to herself in any way.

The demon hunter was as unremarkable, as easy to overlook, as any person Angie had ever met.

Until, of course, you looked into her eyes.

And really, unless you knew what you were looking at, it was pretty easy to dismiss that flash of red in the brown depths as a trick of the light.

Sebastian, on the other hand, was *not* easy to overlook. He was as tall as, maybe taller than, Angie's six-foot height, with wide shoulders, a lean, athletic frame, and a ridiculously handsome face. Really ridiculous. Men weren't this handsome in real life. Movie stars were this handsome. Soap stars were this handsome. But not men you met through an old acquaintance.

His dark brown hair was cut short and tight to his head,

his dark brown skin was smooth and ageless, his jaw clean shaven. He was dressed simply enough in a black t-shirt and dark colored jeans, but he filled out the jeans and t-shirt in ways that was impossible to ignore and that did funny, fluttery things to her stomach. He moved with an easy, lethal grace that reminded her of a predator. One of the big lazy ones. One of the cats—a lion or a jaguar. The ones you could fool yourself into thinking were just soft, snuggly animals. Right before they ripped your throat out.

She'd have thought that edge of danger would have her thoroughly on guard with him, not in any way distracted by the subtle spice of his scent. And she would have been wrong.

The red flash in the depths of his dark brown eyes was a little fainter than Aidan's. Easier to dismiss. Easier to pretend it wasn't there. But unlike Aidan, he didn't blend in to his surroundings. He stood out. A beacon call of handsomeness that demanded she look and appreciate and dwell on.

It was infuriating.

She tried not to study him. Tried to keep her attention on the situation at hand—demon had broken loose, they needed her to ensure it went back to a demon realm, lots of dangerous stuff about to happen. But she kept…staring at Sebastian. Getting caught in the way his mouth quirked when he was amused. The way he let his gaze linger on her. The way he moved.

She jerked her gaze away from him. Again.

He was almost as dangerous to look at as the surrounding trees.

"Something funny?" she asked, her tone as brittle as she could make it while her heart was pounding so hard.

"Nothing at all," he said, his voice low.

To add insult to injury, the man had a deep, smoky voice and an English accent that danced like little sparks of fire down her spine. Just…unfair!

"This is a serious situation," she said, her tone harsh because she was embarrassed and disoriented. "One I shouldn't be involved in." This last she directed to Aidan.

"You'll be fine," Aidan said. "You've been working with Esmerelda."

"On my magic," she said. "Not…this."

Well, not *this* in a while. Esmerelda was her first magical mentor, and still one of her most influential. She'd known Esmerelda since she was five years old. After her mother— the only moderately magical person in her immediate family —had approved the pairing. Aidan had brought Esmerelda into her life, something Angie would be forever grateful for.

And so, yes, she did feel like she owed Aidan. Help at least. Since Aidan had helped her. But this wasn't…

She'd have preferred using her ordinary witch magic. The magic she was called to. Spells, harnessing the elements, even her touch psychic skills… Anything but *this*.

"I have midterms next week. I should be studying for those." She was in her senior year at University of New Mexico. She was due to graduate this spring with her Bachelors in Psychology—if she didn't fail her fall classes because she got sucked into helping Aidan with demons.

"What classes? Maybe I can help," Sebastian said.

She tried to ignore the way her toes curled at the sound of his voice. "No." She couldn't imagine trying to study with him around. She couldn't imagine trying to *think* with him too close.

And why was he letting her see him like this? Hmm? He was a *demon hunter*. He could ensure she saw him in any way he wanted, with just his will. It was one of their best tricks, blending in, fading into the background, looking harmless and ordinary. She had no idea if Aidan *really* looked so ordinary. But she knew Sebastian *could* make himself look ordinary and harmless or he wouldn't have been able to do this job for very long. Didn't do to stand out to the humans who summoned demons. They might remember you later. Demon hunters didn't want to be remembered. If someone remembered them, they might think to call a demon and target them. Demon hunters had to be forgettable.

Angie could never easily forget Sebastian.

He had to be doing this on purpose. He had to be. And that was what pissed her off so much.

They moved as quietly through the woods as the crunchy fall undergrowth allowed, which, given they were hunters and she was a witch with ties to the elements, meant they managed it better than the humans in the distance. The men were making enough noise to cover any approach anyway, but demons had better hearing than humans so it was safer to be cautious.

When she finally got a look at the spot in the woods the humans had staked out—so to speak—for their demon summoning, Angie frowned. They'd cleared a space in an open patch of ground, pushing away all the leaf and twig detritus until there was only smooth, dark dirt. And then they'd formed a circle using rocks. A good, sturdy base. As good as chalk and more stable in the dirt than chalk might have been. Obviously, they hadn't planned to let their demon out.

There were candles dotted around the circle, just outside the rocks, illuminated the scene in wobbly orange light and filling the clearing with the waxy scent of candle fire. Angie looked at the dried leaves at the outer edge of the clearing and shook her head. Fire hazard this time of year, having unguarded candles. Even if they'd cleared space for it. Sparks flew off candles, especially during ceremonies when elements like wind could kick up more.

The little flickering flames danced in a gentle breeze, as if in answer to her thought. But so far, no sparks had jumped. One less thing to worry about immediately.

Despite Aidan's warning, though, it was obvious the demon hadn't escaped the circle yet. It was still firmly inside the stones as the three human men who'd summoned it danced around the circle, making whooping noises and chanting something Angie couldn't make out. Most of her focus was on the demon.

She hadn't seen one like this in… Maybe ever. Not outside their own realms. Except that one time. But never like this. Though technically, being inside the circle linked them to their realms and ensured they weren't fully in the human realm. Even then, she wasn't a hunter so she didn't run around the world stopping idiots who summoned demons, which meant she didn't see these demon summoning ceremonies.

Her history with demons was…different.

This wasn't a demon species she'd encountered before either. Was that good or bad? It was squat and wide and blue-colored, with four leg-like, short, stubby limbs tipped with wickedly long claws. There were tentacles along its back that waved around its blobbish body. Its head was another blob on a blob, though with four glowing red eyes in the center, a set of wicked looking horns curving from its blob head, and a mouth too wide for the round face, filled with an awful lot of sharp teeth.

There was a kind of fog covering the ground inside the circle. Angie couldn't tell if that meant the demon was one of the ones that issued cold rather than heat, or whether it was just part of the summoning.

She hoped it wasn't the cold kind. She couldn't look into those realms, didn't risk it. And if a cold bastard got out, they'd all freeze instantly before they could do anything to stop it.

Despite her curse-gift, she was not a demon expert. She didn't *want* to be a demon expert. That was a demon hunter's job. And she left it to them. Or at least, she'd tried.

"It hasn't escaped," she murmured to Aidan as they stood just inside the treeline, in the shadows outside the uneven candlelight. There wasn't much of a moon overhead. And they'd turned off their flashlights back a ways so the humans didn't notice them approaching. The deep shadows would keep them hidden from the three men dancing around the circle. But even if the darkness hadn't helped, Aidan could *will* the humans not to see them.

"Actually," Aidan said, her voice trailing off as she stared at the circle.

Angie glanced between the hunter and Sebastian. "Well?" she mouthed to him.

He was frowning, his gaze moving between Aidan and the dancing humans. He ignored her question.

She tried really hard not to huff out her irritation. She must not have succeeded though, because his gaze flashed to her and he smiled, very faintly and lethally.

She forgot what she'd asked.

Damn it. This was no time to be distracted. There was a demon *right there*. And she didn't know what it could do. Aidan looked…intent, which probably wasn't a good sign. The dancing men seemed to be chanting louder. The fog inside the containment circle was swirling. And if this was a cold beast instead of a hot one, they might all freeze if it escaped.

But one smile from the absurdly handsome Sebastian and her brain frizzled.

Because she needed the comfort, she rubbed the little pentagram hanging from the beaded bracelet around her wrist. It was a ward, an…aide that helped bring her back from the brink if she accidentally looked into the naturally formed V of a tree. The bracelet was a gift, from Esmerelda, and it helped a lot to keep her focused and harness her reserves when she got sucked into her *other* gift-curse.

Reminded her she was a witch, not a hunter. Reminder her she was in control.

She didn't feel in control right now. She felt wildly out of her depth. She hated that feeling with a deep and abiding passion.

Control was extremely important for her—controlling her magic, controlling her touch psychic skill so she didn't accidentally read every little thing she touched—and feeling out of balance was dangerous.

She pressed the little silver pentagram between her fingers, hard, letting the metal dig into her skin, reminding her who she was. What she was.

Then she started to murmur a little spell. Nothing that would interfere with Aidan and Sebastian's efforts to banish the demon. Just a little something to…help.

She released the pentagram to form the finger gestures necessary to setting the spell, keeping her gaze on the containment circle, the dancing men, the demon, but her mental focus wasn't on her surroundings. It was on calling forth her real power. Her magic tingled in her blood and rose through her feet as she grounded in the earth. Elements were her domain. Not the demon realms.

Not the demon realms.

A snap from the clearing made her heart beat harder. She got her spell to the trigger point then held it in a waiting pattern. One last word and hand gesture would set it into motion. But she wasn't quite ready for it yet.

Neither Aidan nor Sebastian had moved. They stood as still as the surrounding trees. Still enough that if she wasn't hyper aware of Sebastian next to her, she might be under the illusion they'd left.

That was a demon hunter's power. That was their will.

She searched the clearing for the source of the sound that had almost brought her out of her conjuring. The dark woods beyond the clearing were deeply shadowed. She couldn't afford to look too closely, so she kept her gaze angled toward the ground at the base of the trees, looking for movement in the darkness.

There could be more humans out there. Aidan hadn't told her how many were involved in this. Aidan might not even know. Though Angie had a feeling she did. The hunter always seemed to know more than she said.

What she *had* said to Angie was that a demon had escaped and they wanted her help returning it to a demon realm.

They didn't *need* her help, strictly speaking. Since people with her skill were…well, generationally rare. One every four hundred years, if that. Or so Aidan had told her. The demon hunters couldn't rely on someone like Angie to send back escaped demons. They used their skills, knowledge, and most of all their will to do that. Most of the time.

But a freed demon was always more dangerous. They were fully in this realm at that stage. Not linked to their own. And while they sacrificed power to get here, even a weak demon was a deadly demon.

But that was as much about the situation as she knew.

"You said it was free," Angie murmured very quietly to Aidan. "Is there more than one?"

The words left her mouth as the thought occurred to her. The rightness of the question appalled her.

"There is, isn't there?" she asked.

There was more than one. There had to be. That was why Sebastian was here. That was why they'd called her for help. Aidan could handle a demon on her own or she wouldn't still be alive. Aidan could handle more than one demon on her own or she wouldn't still be alive.

Terror caught Angie's throat.

What had to be happening that Aidan brought backup?

"How many are there?" she whispered, swallowing hard. Her heartbeat pounded like a drum, loud enough she was sure the demon in the circle would hear it. She searched the shadowed ground beyond the containment circle again even as the hairs on the back of her neck prickled.

Neither of the demon hunters answered her question. But they didn't need to. The truth hung in the autumn crisp air.

There were more demons in these woods than two demon hunters alone could handle. Demons that were already free.

She was going to need a bigger spell.

Don't miss
Howling Dreadful, A Demon Witch Story
Out Now!

BOOKS BY KAT SIMONS

Demon Witch Series

Howling Dreadful

Moonlit Strange

1-Bone Lantern Witch

2-Spiderweb Witch

3-Storm Shadow Witch

4-Darkling Mist Witch

5-Apocalypse Witch

Urban Fantasy

The Cary Redmond Series

Cary Redmond Short Stories and Collections

Joan of Kerry Series

Friday's Curious Shop Series

Paranormal Romance

Dragon Thief Series

Seven Families: Wolf Series

Tiger Shifters Series

Destiny Cats Series

Romancing the Leopard: A Tiger Shifters-Cary Redmond Crossover Novel

ALSO BY KAT SIMONS

Contemporary Fantasy

Haunts and Howls Collections

**Tombstone Wizard * The Unshattered Sword * Going Out of Business: Everything's for Sale * Anger Management * Demonic Dates * The Museum of Small Art's Everyman * Burning Inside a Stone Circle * Bored Questless * I Just Ate a Bug * Ting Ling * Sophie Saves the World * Black Water Hawthorns * To Dance in Fallow Fields at Midnight * The Troll and the Dressmaker*

Stories from the Café

The Café Collections

Stories from the Café: Volume One

Pick Your Genre Collections

Who Steals a Dragon

Contemporary Romances

Designed for You

Poinsettias and Possibilities

Mystery and Thriller

ROSS AND O'NEILL ADVENTURES

Galileo's Pendulum

ABOUT THE AUTHOR

Kat Simons earned her Ph.D. in animal behavior, working with animals as diverse as dolphins and deer. She brought her experience and knowledge of biology to her paranormal romance and urban fantasy fiction, where she delights in taking nature and turning it on its ear. She writes urban fantasy, contemporary fantasy, and paranormal romance in series which combine action adventure, the otherworldly, and a frequent dose of sexy romance.

The newest book in her bestselling romantic urban fantasy series about Protector Cary Redmond, The Trouble with Shifters and Fae Courts, sees a new direction for the intrepid Protector, her sexy leopard shifter mate, and the entire crew. Kat also launched a new novella length Urban Fantasy Romance series that follows the adventures of a magical thief and the dragon shifter prince she just can't seem to shake—and really doesn't want to. The first season of the Dragon Thief series released throughout 2024. Season Two begins in 2025 with The Crown of Kingship Job.

For something a little different, Kat also publishes fantasy, science fiction, and the occasional hockey romance under the name Isabo Kelly (https://www.isabokelly.com).

After traveling the world, living in places like Hawaii, Germany, and Ireland, Kat now lives in New York City with her family and a library's worth of books.

Join Kat's Newsletter

Stay Up-to-Date

On all Kat's News, Updates, and fun extras

New Subscriber Get Two Exclusive Stories Just for Signing up!

bit.ly/KatSimonsNewsletter

KATSIMONSBOOKS

Mystery

Urban
Fantasy

Romance

And More!

KatSimonsBooks.Com